What peop

Dungeon Party

Every aficionado of D&D or other fantasy RPGs will enjoy Gastil's inspired take on the genre. This big-hearted, imaginative satire brings all the thrills, chills, and feels of the best campaign you have ever neglected the obligations of life and work to play. Once you start reading *Dungeon Party*, you will not want to make your saving throw!

Paul Witcover, author of *The Watchman of Eternity*

In *Dungeon Party*, Gastil has woven a delightful, decadent, and often dark tale of loyalty, bravery, and friendship among some of society's most socially dispossessed—fantasy role-playing gamers. It offers a celebration and critique of gaming culture, pointing to the power of games to both hurt and heal. *Dungeon Party* is about the stories we tell—to ourselves, to others, and to the communities we call home. With subtle nods to Tolkein, McCarthy, and Le Guin, Gastil moves us to consider what might happen when we stay in a game long enough with others. I recommend it to role-playing enthusiasts, pop culture fanatics, game scholars, or anyone who believes in the transformative power of play.

Katie Salen, co-author of *Rules of Play*

Nerdliness is finally having its moment, but *Dungeon Party* speaks to the timeless themes of friendship and bravery that transcend popular culture.

Bruce Worden, author and illustrator of *Woodstalk: 3 Days of Peace, Music, and Zombies*

Gastil toys with readers who can't be sure what is and isn't real until the last page. Dispensing with gamer stereotypes, *Dungeon Party* is intelligent, sly, but most of all fun.
Jonathan Amsbary, Dungeons & Dragons veteran and author of Cyberblood

Dungeon Party

A Novel

Dungeon Party

A Novel

John Webster Gastil

COSMIC EGG
BOOKS

Winchester, UK
Washington, USA

JOHN HUNT PUBLISHING

First published by Cosmic Egg Books, 2020
Cosmic Egg Books is an imprint of John Hunt Publishing Ltd., 3 East St., Alresford,
Hampshire SO24 9EE, UK
office@jhpbooks.net
www.johnhuntpublishing.com
www.cosmicegg-books.com

For distributor details and how to order please visit the 'Ordering' section on our website.

Text copyright: John Webster Gastil 2019

ISBN: 978 1 78904 500 0
978 1 78904 501 7 (ebook)
Library of Congress Control Number: 2019950742

A CIP catalogue record for this book is available from the British Library.

Design: Stuart Davies

UK: Printed and bound by CPI Group (UK) Ltd, Croydon, CR0 4YY
US: Printed and bound by Thomson-Shore, 7300 West Joy Road, Dexter, MI 48130

We operate a distinctive and ethical publishing philosophy in
all areas of our business, from our global network of authors to
production and worldwide distribution.

Dedicated to all those avatars
who have fought and fallen
in fantasy realms.
You are (sort of) gone
but (mostly) not forgotten.

Prologue

Two minutes before the accident, Karen leaned forward in the front passenger seat. She pulled bobby pins from her hair and clipped them to the collar of her nurse's blouse. One fell from her hand and dropped beside the emergency brake. She flicked on the dome light and reached for it.

"Your father and I have an idea," Karen said. "This fall, maybe you and Randall could share an apartment near the university."

Alan winced at his mother's awkward timing. This prospective roommate sat just inches away on the left side of the backseat. Alan already spent every weekend with Randall. Their shared passion for a role-playing game was the gravity that made them a binary star, but Alan felt the need to break free. Pursuing an adult life would require escaping their linked orbit.

In the rear view mirror, Alan's father smiled. "Whaddaya think? We'd help with rent."

"Sounds great," Randall said and punched his seatmate. "That's a generous offer."

Alan rubbed his shoulder and muttered, "I don't know."

"What's that, honey?" Karen turned around. Graying curls in her perm bounced gently, then settled into place.

One minute before the accident, Alan cleared his throat. What he chose to say next would put the rest of his life in motion. He closed his eyes and replayed a scene from the afternoon. Randall shouted—"Just a game?"—and hurled a twelve-sided brass die at a sliding glass door. The impact left a chip Alan would have to buff out before his parents noticed.

He knew what he had to do.

"Before you say anything," Alan began, "let me explain—"

Alan braced himself for another punch.

Instead, he heard a loud pop beneath his father's Pontiac Sunfire.

"Hold on!" Dad shouted.

The car swung toward the median and climbed the concrete barrier separating the northbound and southbound lanes. A rear wheel came down before the front, and the Sunfire gave its passengers a tilt-a-whirl ride across Interstate 5.

Headlights shone through the windshield. A brown station wagon barely missed head-on collision but brushed doors hard enough to reverse the Pontiac's rotation. Somehow, Dad had left the driver's seat.

Karen screamed as the coupe spun off the freeway, up a grass embankment. When the Sunfire came to a stop, the station wagon that had hit them raced up the same steep incline, over a guardrail, and out of view.

Karen pushed open the passenger door and ran back toward traffic.

A moment ago, Randall roared obscenities. When they hit the wagon, his head whipped into the window frame. He'd fallen silent.

Alan's mouth hung open. He closed his lips to swallow. The metallic taste of blood crossed his tongue. He breathed in through his nostrils hot air scented by sweat and oil.

To dispel a swirl of confusing images, Alan closed his eyes. Within the stillness of his mind, he saw the Sunfire's sparkling finish. The week before, he'd helped Dad strip, sand, and paint it burnt orange. Red flames accented the hood and side panels. How cool it would have been to pull up to the 2001 Middle Mirth convention in this glowing fireball of a car. He and Randall would have emerged from it like rock stars, flipping crisp five dollar bills to his parents as tips.

"Look at me!" Karen shouted.

Alan found himself twisted in a seatbelt, his back pressed against Randall's chest. He looked up through an open car door at his mother, her wet face framed by a darkening sky.

Karen folded the front seat forward and ran her hands across

Alan's face, neck, and shoulders. As she worked, she repeated three times, "You're gonna be all right."

Alan croaked, "It's a trap!"

His mouth felt dry. He wanted to explain why he couldn't move into a shared apartment. Randall spent their first two years at San Diego State obsessed about role playing more than anything else. Now Randall wanted to recruit dedicated players who could turn their weekly game into a nightly one.

Though his elbow stung, Alan lifted his arm to point toward the trunk, where investigators could find evidence of this plan. A pair of sleeping bags. Overnight duffels. Backpacks stuffed with snacks and rule books for an epic gaming binge. Hotel staff awaited their arrival in a basement ballroom that suited their community's nocturnal habits and its limited means.

"I'm reaching below you," Karen said, "to check on Randall."

"He's breathing," Alan said.

Karen stretched an arm past Alan and pressed two fingers into the folds of Randall's neck. "Brachial pulse strong."

Alan squirmed to face Randall.

"Don't move!" Karen said.

Alan half expected to see Randall shooting him the bird. Instead, he found his friend in repose. A bloodied cheek rested against a broken window. The sleeping giant's girth might have prevented internal injuries, but this was no zombie makeup kit coloring his face.

Karen lifted herself out of the car, then shut its windowless door. She put a hand on Alan's shoulder but looked away.

"There's another car," she said. "I've got to—"

"Where's Dad?"

Karen remained impassive.

"I'll check the other car. Three passengers, maybe."

"But where's—"

"Keep an eye on Randall until paramedics arrive."

Alan reached to unfasten his seatbelt, but he stopped when

Karen squeezed his shoulder.

"Hold still!"

Karen released her grip, bounded up the incline, and vanished over the guardrail.

Mom didn't understand. Holding still was what Alan feared most. Every hour of gameplay required three hours of preparation. Orchestrating a game world left little time for anything else.

Alan stared at Randall and repeated—or maybe just remembered—the words that caused prized dice to fly across the living room. "What if we finished our degrees, then planned our next moves? What if we treated this convention like it was our last? After all, it's just—"

Reds and blues danced on the Sunfire's windshield in synch with the wail of a siren. Alan wondered if the sound could wake the dead.

On cue, Randall's eyelids lifted.

"We're okay," Alan said. "Gotta hold still. Help's on the way."

Two paramedics hopped out of an ambulance. Within seconds they were inside the Sunfire and repeating Karen's inspection. Their hands flew about the back seat until one of them cast a levitation spell that lifted Alan and Randall out of the car. Both lay on the grass, strapped onto matching plastic backboards.

Alan felt unaccountably calm.

"Look at the car," he said. "It's probably totaled, but the paint still looks amazing."

In reply came sobs. These soon became wails, unlike anything Alan had heard. A grizzly caught in a trap might howl like this if it knew its wounds were mortal. The sound was contagious. Alan commenced weeping.

Minutes later, when Karen returned to his side, Alan beheld a changed woman. Blood encircling her lips made her look like Heath Ledger's Joker. Karen wiped her arms on a blouse that had turned crimson. She glanced toward the ambulance and started to shake.

"You'll both be taking rides to Mercy," she said.

"Where's Dad?"

"His condition is—stable."

"Everybody's okay?"

"Not okay," Randall said through coughs. "That wagon almost killed us!"

"Yeah, what about them?" Alan said.

"The boy's critical," Karen said. "He's breathing again, but—
"

"He'll be all right?" Alan said.

"Nobody's gonna be all right," Randall said.

"He's about your age," Karen said. "Got real strength, like your friend here."

Karen lay her head on Alan's chest and resumed shaking.

Alan wanted to hug her, but canvas straps held him fast.

Ten Years Later:
The First Weekend in June

RANDALL

"C'mon," Randall said, "you've gotta get up."

Alan tried to stand but couldn't put weight on his left foot.

"I think I twisted my ankle," Alan said.

"They're still coming. We've gotta move."

Alan pushed a wooden spear into the grass like a crutch. He managed to hop at a respectable clip. "What hit me?"

"The ground."

They'd been ambushed amidst the park's eucalyptus trees. Alan had fallen while dodging dozens of colored beanbags hurled by a clutch of enemy wizards. Randall resented the conceit of flying bags of rice. Nothing could represent the majesty of magic, but even for a live action role play, this was undignified. Mixed with the scent of anachronistic hotdogs on a nearby grill, the scene evoked a picnic more than a medieval melee.

The seven teenagers dressed in matching green cloaks showed no such misgivings. Moving in a triangular formation, they closed quickly on Randall and his hobbled companion. The wizards seemed to have run out of spells because they now held short swords forged from plywood and silver duct tape. In spite of such motley origins, the weapons sparkled in the unrelenting sunshine.

"Death to the invaders!" one shouted.

Whether it meant victory or defeat, Randall welcomed the battle's end. He'd only agreed to attend the Friday Festival because Alan's too-helpful mom had bought them tickets and made their outfits as a surprise for her son's thirty-second birthday. For Alan, she'd fashioned a leather jerkin and pants that made him look like a Burning Man initiate. She bestowed on

Randall plate armor crafted from cardboard and aluminum foil.

Credit Karen for getting at least one detail right. She'd used glossy black urethane paint on Randall's enormous two-handed sword. This was the signature weapon of Boldheart, the character Randall had played for more than a decade in Dungeon Lords. That game relied on dice and statistics, which better suited Randall than actual swordplay.

Alan hopped on one foot and pointed his spear at the encircling attackers.

A wizard half Alan's age covered her face. "What are you supposed to be? Is the Karate Kid's older brother still living at home?"

It was a fair burn on many levels. She had Alan's current residence right. And he was not an imposing figure, with a thin moustache that refused to grow out and a stature well below the six-foot spear that wobbled in his grasp.

Alan needed saving. Again.

To focus his disdain into a berserker's rage, Randall reviewed the day's most ridiculous events: incompetent jugglers, ad-libbed clerical blessings, a shameful vegan barbeque. Beating down these kids might salvage a wasted afternoon.

"That does it."

Randall gripped his sword in both hands.

"Who'll be the first to taste my blade?"

At six-two and three hundred fifty pounds, Randall made an impression. His shoulder-length brown hair flowed out the bottom of a helmet, which gave the unwashed mane some flair. Foil armor covered all but his neck and face, where he bore acne scars as rough as redwood.

"Ye, gods," said an elfin girl half Randall's age. "This one's as big as the Mountain. We needs enlist Brienne of Tarth to topple such a foe."

Randall resented the offhand Game of Thrones reference. He heard enough cheeky banter from Carlos, their regular role-playing companion. Carlos' absence made this outing tolerable, but just thinking about him induced a properly foul mood. Randall swung his wooden sword and shattered the tallest wizard's weapon. The boy yelped in pain and tried to shake off the sting of the blow.

A tap on Randall's shoulder made him wheel around so fast he almost hit his comrade.

"Careful," Alan said. "You might hurt someone. Let's just surrender."

The wizards nodded in unison.

Randall spat into the grass.

"None of you have a taste for battle. If you can't stand the gore, get out of the genre."

Alan cringed.

"What?" Randall demanded. "Death comes for us all! Am I right, or am I right?"

"You're right," Alan said. "Righter than you know."

ALAN

Every weekend, Alan orchestrated dozens of deaths. But how long had it been since he'd killed someone important? The deceased rarely would be mourned, or even missed. Murder was commonplace at the living room table because the unforgiving rules of Dungeon Lords made survival itself a triumph. It felt different, though, when the victim was a friend. Whatever else Randall might be, he was certainly that.

Worry manifested as an itch on top of Alan's bald spot. He resisted the urge to scratch and instead rubbed the ankle he'd sprained during the previous day's ill-fated frolic. Unfortunately, a quick foot rub couldn't relieve the tension built up over four hours of nonstop role playing.

To Alan's left sat the source of his anxiety. Randall's elbows rested on the vinyl surface of a rectangular folding table strewn with dice, graph paper, and medieval miniatures. Randall gripped a clipboard that held the official record sheet for his character. Its boxes and columns were filled with penciled text and pink eraser marks. This sacred piece of paper featured a hand-inked portrait of an armored knight holding an obsidian sword over one shoulder. A silver-tipped pen traced the outline of the warrior's plate mail, which accommodated overdeveloped shoulders and thighs. Above the picture, Randall had written in calligraphy, "Boldheart."

"Your character's in deep trouble," Alan said. "I can't even promise they'll find him."

Randall pointed at Alan.

"You're doing this because of that fiasco in Balboa Park."

Alan waved off the accusation.

"Of course not. You didn't mean to break that kid's hand. What's happening to Boldheart right now is just bad luck."

"I'll make my saving throw if I get another try. Just let me re-roll."

Ah, the infamous re-roll. When they were kids, taking a mulligan was standard. Alan had banned the practice during his freshman year of college on the same day he swore off video games. If console play taught one thing, it was that repeated do-overs drain dramatic tension.

Even so, Randall expected special favors. This re-roll request was only the latest in a lifetime of unhelpful suggestions. When they'd first learned the game as kids, they made up rules to fill gaps in their knowledge. Once Alan mastered the game, he came to recognize Randall's tweaks as transparently self-serving. Boldheart's exceptional height should let him jump even farther. Two-handed swords should have the same defense modifier as shields. Law-abiding paladins should get extra spells. It never stopped.

A line had to be drawn.

"You know the rules," Alan said. "When I call the others back in, you can't say a word about what just happened. Their characters weren't there, so they shouldn't know."

"Don't condescend. All I'm saying is, you'd better not kill Boldheart."

Alan exhaled. Randall and Boldheart had scaled mountains and trudged through swamps together in the Mythos. They'd stormed castles and cleared out catacombs. Losing Boldheart would be like losing a brother.

"Look," Alan said, "I can't promise—"

Randall stood and brandished his clipboard.

Alan raised himself up, as if rising to Randall's challenge. They pushed their chairs backward in the same moment. The gesture caught Alan off guard. His pulse quickened. With a high-stakes Dungeon Lords tournament just weeks away, he had to prevent any further escalation. Now more than ever, it was his job to cool Randall's temper, not to stoke it.

"Check out the divots in the carpet," Alan said with a chuckle.

Randall cast his eyes down at worn Berber. What Karen had once dubbed "eggplant" was now a mix of sun-bleached pinks and noncommittal browns.

"We've worn permanent holes in there."

"Yeah," Randall said. "I'd noticed. Figured it just needed a shampoo or something."

Randall set down his clipboard and touched the marks on the carpet with what looked like reverence. He slid his chair forward, and it almost clicked in place. Randall settled back into his chair and folded his hands in his lap, the lion tamed once more.

Alan limped to the sliding glass doors that framed the backyard of the ranch-style house. A small chip in the glass lay between the faces of two men standing on the patio's flagstones.

It was always boys, then men who visited the house Alan shared with his mother. Few female gamers had crossed Alan's path. Randall deemed unacceptable each of those who had accepted Alan's invitation. The latest was a fellow college student who overheard Alan explaining the August tournament rules to Randall as they waited in line at a taco truck. Alan couldn't recall the details of the encounter, except that the woman wore a t-shirt showing werewolves in business suits riding the Tube. It wasn't romantic possibility that piqued Alan's interest in her joining their group. He relished the prospect of the fresh storylines a female adventurer might inspire. Randall scuttled that opportunity with the rude dismissal, "Girls can't handle the violence." The more likely explanation was that Randall worried he'd feel self-conscious sweating through all-night gaming with female company.

Whatever was lost that day, Alan had no right to complain. The two men standing on the back porch were the best players he'd ever known. When they'd first met, Carlos Morales was the one who needed Alan and Randall to get back on his feet. Since then, he'd run laps around Alan—a truth made literal the one time he dragged Alan to the track. Carlos was only a year younger than Alan but retained the build of a collegiate athlete. The best groomed of the bunch, Carlos' black ponytail hung over a burgundy dress shirt.

Carlos listened intently to the newest member of the group, Lance Langdon. At the tender age of twenty-five, Lance ranked as their junior member. Blond hair flopped above Lance's sunglasses as he gestured wildly in the midst of some tale. Functionally blind since birth, Lance gained some swagger from his signature accessory, a pair of black Ray-Ban Wayfarers with mirrored lenses. Alan admired the ease with which Lance navigated a social world he couldn't see. If the tales were to be believed, Lance kept busy with a rotation of suitors, though he'd never had a steady girlfriend in the two years they'd known him.

The sunlight reflecting off Lance's shades forced Alan to close his eyes. For a moment, Lance's body was replaced by his Mythos counterpart, the Norse priest Lancelot, who shared his creator's yellow mane but had a more stoic demeanor. Beside him, Carlos morphed into the rakish Santana, the bronzed sorcerer who smiled even in battle.

Every weekend, those two characters and Boldheart would work together to overcome whatever challenge Alan threw at them in the Mythos. Alan spent so much time each week prepping for the next gaming session that these avatars occupied his mind as much as the real people who played them. The juxtaposition of real and imagined worlds could disorient Alan, but he'd become accustomed to his mind wandering between them.

Alan slid open the patio door. "You're on, gentlemen."

"Time to crack some heads," Carlos said as he strode into the living room. He re-tied his ponytail and ran a fingertip over the water moccasin of scar tissue that ran from the top of his head to the bottom of his neck. Once the ritual was complete, Carlos spun his chair around and took a seat opposite Randall.

Lance closed the glass door behind him as he entered. He

tapped the floor with his cane until he found the back of a wooden chair beside Carlos.

Alan sat down last, glad to get the weight off his ankle. He readjusted his cardboard game director's screen, which served the dual purpose of concealing notes and providing reference tables on its inside panels.

"*Qué pasa?*" Carlos asked. "I've seen brighter faces on burn patients. What'd Boldheart do this time?"

"Surely," Lance said, "'tis nothing Lancelot's holy might can't set right."

"And no enemy," Carlos said, "can defend itself against Santana's arcane magic."

Across the back of Alan's cardboard screen, a dragon still flew toward its mountain lair, years after Randall had inked it. Alan wished he could make a similar retreat. He'd become an insurance actuary because the job taught one how to hedge against death, if only in the aggregate. Perhaps he miscalculated the fate awaiting his friends' beloved characters, but the estimated mortality probabilities looked grim.

"What does Santana see?" Carlos said.

"The same cavern walls where we left off," Alan said. "Black as coal and sharp to the touch, they extend—"

"What do we hear?" Lance said. "Or smell?"

"Make a Perception check," Alan said. "Both of you."

Carlos and Lance each picked up twenty-sided dice and rolled them. Carlos' die clacked on the table until it settled with the top side showing a sixteen. Lance rolled a more wobbly die that featured deep braille insets and a microchip in its core. When his so-called "Precious" came to rest, it announced a three.

"Lancelot doesn't notice anything odd," Alan said, "but Santana does."

Alan considered his next words carefully. He prepared for moments like this by reading the scenario guide and rehearsing the most likely encounters that would ensue. Describing scenes required improvisational skill and a kind of empathy. Alan never played a character of his own in the Mythos. Instead, he had to imagine what each of his friends' avatars could see and feel.

He had years of experience exercising his mind in precisely this way, but the stakes were now higher than ever. Alan had entered his gaming group into a Middle Mirth tournament unlike any ever held before. In eight weeks, they'd compete against three dozen rival teams for a chance to visit a genuine European castle.

The destination held more meaning for Alan than any of his players, including Randall. The last decade that Alan had invested in their game represented a significant chunk of an adult life. Middle Mirth would be a referendum on this unpaid career. Alan knew his friends respected him as a gifted storyteller, but they owed him too much to serve as neutral arbiters.

It remained a mystery who would judge the contest, but Alan expected one of the game's creators would decide who "told the best story". The rules were cryptic about the meaning of that phrase, but Alan suspected a Willie Wonka situation. A worthy game director might win more than an all-expenses-paid trip to Slovenia.

If he wanted to touch the Golden Ticket, he needed to avoid the pitfalls of mediocre gaming. No dull descriptions for crucial settings. No predictable encounters with lifeless non-player characters.

Alan's principal worry was plotline discontinuity. His version of the Mythos was uniquely his own. The conventional Dungeon Lords playbook dropped players into a land resembling Lord of the Rings. The only differences were disjointed deviations from Tolkien that one could trace back to the mythology texts and genre novels the game's creators had devoured in their youth. Alan's vision of the Mythos included those same quirky conventions, but he subverted them in precise ways to startle his players with novel twists.

In preparing today's game, however, Alan hadn't taken any precautions to protect his gaming group from itself. While tidying up the details of the Mythos, he noticed how disordered his trio of players had become. What should have been an exciting battle with this afternoon's "boss monster" was becoming a more deadly encounter.

Alan's pulse quickened. Goosebumps dotted his forearms.

"Lay it out for us," Carlos said. "What does Santana see?"

* * *

Santana crouched against the rock wall. There was a faint light ahead, enough to see by. He set his torch in the dirt, extinguished it with his boot, and with both hands gripped the four-foot ironwood staff that fairies had carved centuries before his birth. Luminous engravings danced slowly around the staff in a spiral, seeming to float above its surface.

Around a bend in the cavern, perhaps forty yards ahead, came indistinct words, followed by raspy breaths. And something else—the stink of rotting meat. More than merely foul, the stench was something Santana had never encountered. For one such as he, who lived for adventure, novelty was auspicious.

The half-elven warrior priest kneeling beside Santana was more crusader than explorer. His quests were pious but also perilous, and they required him to wear a coat of chain-mail armor and hoist a teardrop shield. In loops on his belt hung the tools he used for smiting evil—the silver unicorn representing his god, Elahna, and a two-foot mace with a flanged iron head that could crush foes in a single swing. To hedge his odds before hand-to-hand combat, he also slung over his shoulders a light crossbow and a quiver of bolts. Beneath that, he sported medical supplies for those wounds he failed to heal through the divine power Elahna granted him.

Lancelot opened the grated visor on his helmet and sniffed

at the air.

Santana nodded. "That malodorous scent may signal the host of these dank tunnels. I fear he found Boldheart before we could."

"Curse his haste," Lancelot said. "He took leave of all good sense by rushing ahead."

Santana's crimson cape fluttered as he moved forward in a defensive crouch. His bent spine began to throb, having never recovered from wounds earned years ago. How many times had Boldheart danced on the edge of his own grave? The thrill of each escape escalated as Santana's sorcery grew stronger and their foes more formidable.

"If we can forever banish Lord Cynoc's accursed soul," Lancelot said, "we will have achieved something none believed possible."

That was a familiar refrain. Lancelot had promised quests serving a greater purpose than adventure for its own sake. They had nothing more than treasure and tales to show for their most recent brushes with death, but something did feel different this time.

"We shall see," Santana said. He pulled a cinched wool pouch from the right sleeve of his tunic. "Prepare yourself."

"My abiding faith is all we require."

Lancelot fingered the unicorn on his belt, then eased out his mace instead.

Santana motioned for Lancelot to follow. Their steps traced the edge of the cavern wall as it curved right. Soon they came upon a glowing lantern lying on its side.

"That's Boldheart's," Lancelot said.

Santana pinched out the lantern's wick and discerned another glow farther down the corridor. After creeping thirty meters toward the light, the dirt under their boots gave way to marble tiles. Two dozen rows of these led to a high-ceilinged chamber encircled by wall sconces, each holding a clutch of glowing embers.

In the center of the room, motionless as a statue, stood a massive man with a two-handed sword raised to strike. Beside him floated something less substantial, a gray human shadow. The shadow unfastened the man's armor, then pawed at his muscles like a breeder inspecting a horse.

"Why does Boldheart not attack?" Lancelot said.

"Frozen by a spell."

Lancelot braced the heels of his boots in the grout between the tiles. Santana raised his staff, which sharpened into a blade as he shook it.

The shadow looked up from its work, as if sensing the presence of magic. Its cloudy shape coalesced into a walking corpse, which turned to face Santana. The creature pulled cavern air into its chest, then blew out a jet of ash that struck both sorcerer and priest.

Lancelot leapt to attack but lost control of his limbs. The mace fell from his hand, and he dropped to the floor. Santana felt his own body numbing. With only an instant of volition remaining as he collapsed on top of Lancelot, Santana mouthed *no entrar* and squeezed his pouch. A puff of dust spread out from his hand to form a pink dome that surrounded their bodies.

Their enemy approached. As it reached toward Santana, fire flared and singed its flesh. It withdrew and regarded Santana with lidless eyes.

"Very well," hissed the specter. "I may not extinguish your lives today, but I will have the pleasure soon enough. Look well upon me and remember this face. When the time comes, it shall be the last you ever see."

The corpse turned back toward the frozen swordsman. It embraced the figure, and the two became a single cloud, which drifted back the way Santana and Lancelot had come.

* * *

"I'll watch the specter," Carlos said. "Let's see where he goes."

"Santana tries to crane his neck," Alan said, "but he cannot move. Soon, he loses sight of the apparition. Nothing more comes into view until the paralysis wears off an hour later."

"What the frock?" Randall roared. "This is bullship!"

Seventh Day Adventist parents had raised Randall on the God-fearing plains of Abilene, Texas. Among the many things they forbade was swearing, but their inventive son fashioned a compromise. By the time he arrived in San Diego, Alan met a boy who spewed coded curses that left unprepared listeners stupefied.

Randall jerked himself out of his chair, and his belly caught on the edge of the maple table before him. The heavy tabletop lifted and tilted sideways. Pencils, dice, and potato chips slid to the floor. Carlos reached out to secure his papers, while Alan held down books and steadied his cardboard screen. Lance laughed and shouted, "Earthquake!" He covered his head and pretended to dive under the table.

"False alarm," Carlos said. "Just a low-grade tremor."

Randall glared at Carlos.

"Boldheart is dying, and all you can do is make jokes?"

"I thought it was a pretty good one," Lance said.

"That monster just made off with my body while you two were cuddling under Mary Kay's pink fire beetle shell."

"You mean Santana's No Vacancy Roach Motel?" Lance said. "Nothing gets in, nothing gets out."

"Only sound, light, and air can pass through it," Carlos said. "That spell was all I could manage before Santana went limp."

Alan averted his gaze toward the floor and saw Lance check the Velcro fasteners on his shoes. As if readying for a quick exit, Lance extended his hand to touch his cane, which lay at his feet like a baton.

Carlos glowered at Randall. They locked eyes and both stood up.

Alan rubbed three fingers over his moustache hard enough to feel his front teeth. He sensed Carlos' impatience—not just with Randall, but with everything. This standoff wasn't helping. As a pediatric nurse, Carlos had real patients to mend and no patience for arguing over fictional deaths.

"We were goners, just like you," Carlos said.

Randall sneered. "What we needed was a decent *wizard* in the battle."

"Doubtful," Lance said. "Wizards can only read from spell books. A sorcerer doesn't need a library card. I'd rather be like Carlos' character and draw forth magical power with a simple gesture. Awfully handy, unless one's frozen like a fish stick."

Randall raised himself to full height. "Frock this! I'm out."

"Hold on—" Alan raised a hand in protest.

"I'm walking home, or something." Randall gathered his clipboard and papers. He slid them into a fabric sleeve screen-printed with Gaelic script that read, "Boldheart". This he stuffed into his backpack, which he hefted over a shoulder. After storming out of the living room and through the kitchen, he pushed open the screen door that led to the front steps. The door whacked shut on its metal frame, and Randall disappeared.

No one moved, until Lance's hands felt across the table in search of something. He tipped over an empty mug, which knocked his Precious to the floor. The die bounced off Carlos' shoe, then settled onto one of its triangular sides. A robotic female voice said, "One."

The Second Weekend in June

CARLOS

Carlos took his customary chair beside Lance at the maple living room table. Its mottled surface bore water rings and deep scratches around its edges. Like every piece of furniture in the house Alan shared with his mother, the table's best years were in the past. If they ever sold the residence, stagers would have to remove everything in sight, repaint the walls, and recarpet the floors. Aside from that, Alan and his mom kept their three-bedroom house cleaner than Carlos' tiny apartment. Dirty plates never lay in the sink overnight, even if the dish drainer itself needed to be replaced.

Alan's cardboard screen clapped the table as he set it down in front of his notes. He folded back its sides to block the view from Carlos' seat, as well as the spot opposite him, where Randall's chair sat unoccupied.

The empty seat gave Carlos a shiver of excitement. Not once had he played this game without Randall present. Dungeon Lords meant sitting down with Alan and Randall—first for two months in his hospital room, then in this house for the past nine years. However much Randall got on his nerves, he served as a perpetual motion machine of passion. When Carlos' attention flagged, he could count on Randall to pull him back in. Monsters had to be killed. Spirits dispelled. Treasures won.

Only when Alan's fidgeting caught his eye did Carlos see the other implication of Randall's apparent boycott. The loss of Boldheart would throw Alan's plans for Middle Mirth into the wind. Nobody had a gaming group with just two players. More than that, no one could replace the charisma—and mania—of Randall. The way he and Alan played off each other was electric. Randall strained everyone's patience, at times, but drama was part of the attraction.

Alan tapped the table—an unmistakable signal. "As you exit the catacombs," Alan said, "you emerge into a twilight mist. You recognize the charred logs of your campsite, and there sits the same peasant who'd first guided you down. He approaches and hands you a scrap of cloth."

Carlos accepted the typed plot note Alan handed to him.

"What's it say?" Lance asked.

"It's a map of the tomb," Carlos said. "This would have been helpful *before* we went down there. Santana slaps the peasant on the head. Hard."

Lance laughed. "Bit late, now that we're good and screwed."

"Forgive me," Alan said in a raspy voice. "When ye didn't return, I feared the worst. I peeked in the entrance and saw this wedged in beside the trapdoor. Perhaps ye missed it?"

"Way to rub it in," Lance said. "That must have been the Perception roll I failed."

"Alan, I'm sorry to step out of the game," Carlos said, "but if you couldn't get Randall to answer your emails all week, how do you know he's coming today?"

"When has Randall ever missed a game?" Alan said.

"But it's already past noon, so—" Carlos turned to Lance. "Did the big fella say anything at work yesterday?"

"Dang if I know," Lance said. "Never heard his voice, anyway."

"If Randall's bailing," Carlos said, "then it's down to just Lancelot and Santana." He couldn't believe the words when he said them. "All we can do is head back to Mythopolis and score this quest a failure."

"Did Boldheart really die?" Lance said. "I mean, he was a level nineteen badass."

"You know I can't divulge," Alan said. "It's no fun if you know in-game facts that your characters wouldn't."

"I can tell you this much," Carlos said. "I always hated that *pinche* name, 'Boldheart'."

As if sensing his namesake taken in vain, Randall opened the front door, stepped through the entryway, and dropped himself into the oak chair awaiting him.

"Greetings, j-holes. Let the game resume."

Carlos exchanged nudges with Lance, then squeezed Alan's arm. Though this day was as hot as any other, Alan's skin felt icy. The chill sent Carlos back to the first time he'd seen a kid brought into ER—an eighteen year old who'd already lost her leg from the knee down. When Carlos moved her from the gurney to a bed, her arms felt just as cold as Alan's.

"Hold on," Alan said, "We can't just—"

Randall reached across the table and snatched the note in Carlos' hand. "Who gave this to us? Was it that stupid peasant outside the tomb?"

Lance nodded.

Randall flicked a finger against the paper. "This shows a way into the lower chambers. That's probably where we can rescue Boldheart."

Alan shuffled and stacked his pages. He slid them into a manila folder labeled "The Cursed Tomb".

The label's 18-point Old English font took Carlos back two years, to the day he'd given Alan this Dungeon Lords module. It was a classic, first published in the mid-1970s. Carlos had bought a "heavily used" copy in an online auction. It arrived as advertised—a magazine-sized booklet with a torn cover and marked-up pages. Alan didn't care because he always cut the binding off his gaming modules. That allowed him to spread in front of him the maps, room descriptions, and monster statistics. At a glance, he could find whatever rare items or beasts his friends might encounter.

The same week the module had arrived in Carlos' mailbox, Randall met Lance. He was the newest employee at ProTechTed, the computer security firm where Randall toiled joylessly. Alan's gaming group had just lost two brothers who'd finished college and moved away. Randall had insisted they shelve The Cursed Tomb until Lance advanced his fifth-level cleric naturally, by gaining experience points.

"Well?" Randall said. "Let's get to it."

Alan bit his lip. "I hate to say this out loud, Randall, but it should be obvious by now. Boldheart's dead."

"Yup." Lance folded his arms across his chest and leaned back in his chair. "Knew it."

Randall pulled Boldheart's character sheet out of his backpack and snapped it into his clipboard. "Nonsense," he said softly. "Santana and Lancelot will search the catacombs until they find my—find Boldheart's body. Then they can resurrect him."

"You need to roll a new character," Alan said. "Might be nice to play something else. Maybe a monk? You once said you'd like to try a monk."

Randall spoke in a low register. "Let's go find Boldheart. *Right now.*"

"Again," Alan said, "I shouldn't be spelling things out like this, but Boldheart's beyond saving. Before you went on the quest, you heard the legends. Entrance to this tomb was forbidden by decree of the provincial parliament."

Carlos felt a sympathy pain in his heart, but Randall was the one whose chest heaved. Spreading pit stains darkened the letters on Randall's "Middle Mirth 2010" t-shirt.

"You planned this all out," Randall said. "Admit it, Alan. You split us up to get Boldheart alone."

"We'd agreed on a combat protocol," Lance said, "as a *group.*"

Carlos heard the irritation in Lance's voice. The meticulous engineer became annoyed when they'd set in motion a careful plan, only to watch Randall scuttle it. One minute Randall would fight Alan for every advantage, then the next he would imperil himself and his comrades. Whatever drove his reckless play, it made for a hell of a ride.

Now that Carlos knew the game better, he recognized how Alan would bend the rules to spare their characters a pointless demise. After the hospital released Carlos, Alan's mom invited him to stay in their spare room. Until Carlos' sister, Adelita, cleared enough space for him in her apartment, Carlos spent two weeks in the Crandall home. Propped up in a plastic lounge chair to accommodate his back brace, Carlos played Dungeon Lords with Alan and Randall for hours on end. Two days in, Santana and Boldheart fell into the lair of some chittering insect twice their height. Only a fortuitous cave-in spared them a certain death.

That was just one of many bits of good fortune, but something had changed in the past two years. Alan seemed more attuned to the harsher realities of the Mythos. The game felt grittier, more dangerous. Neither Randall nor Boldheart could count on Alan's unconditional affection. Alan and the game world itself were coming into sharper focus. Lance had never known any different. Lancelot's next encounter could be his last. Randall, though, seemed oblivious. Alan had revised the rules they lived by, but Randall hadn't bothered to read the proverbial update.

"We said we'd stick together," Lance continued. "Slow and steady. Then you barreled off and lost us when you thought you heard a ghost. Not our fault you found one."

Randall shook his index finger at Alan. "If you could get Boldheart by himself, you could frock him with some kind of— whatever that creature was."

"That," Lance said, "had to be Lord Cynoc in the flesh, sort of. He's probably a lich and uses death magic to extend his life, right?"

"Maybe," Alan said. "You don't know that."

"You act like this is a murder mystery," Randall said. "That's bullship. You lured us into that underground maze to set up a back-alley hit job."

Randall grabbed his clipboard and pulled off his character

sheet. He held the paper in shaking hands, its colorful portrait staring Carlos in the face.

"Tell me the truth, Alan. Do you hate Boldheart, or *me*?"

Randall ripped the sheet in half. He tore it again. And again. Rough-edged flakes fell to the table. When the last piece settled, Randall reared back and punched Alan's screen, crumpling one of its walls.

Alan's mouth opened wide. He looked to the others, pleading for help. Lance just cocked his head, still processing the rips and the thump.

Carlos offered a sympathetic frown but found no words. The attack on Alan's screen was more than aggression. It was a violation. The cardboard wall afforded Carlos' friend a safety and power he lacked in all other aspects of his life. It signified Alan's status as game director, the invisible deity whose presence was everywhere and nowhere in the Mythos.

"That's it." Randall pursed his lips and inhaled sharply. "I can't even look at you, Alan, you backstabbing piece of crepe. You used to mean something to me. Now, you're just a j-hole—a flat-out j-hole."

"Honestly," Carlos said, "I never have understood what the 'J' stands for."

"Oh, frock you, Carlos Felipe Morales."

Randall was the only one who ever called Carlos by his full name. Meant to sound like a scold from one's mother, it stung Carlos every time he heard it. Only Randall could find a way to echo the voice of a dead parent and get away with it. On top of that, when Randall spoke Spanish, it always sounded a tinge racist. Anyone who lived this long in San Diego without picking up even the trace of a Spanish accent was fighting against the inevitable.

"You," Randall said to Carlos, "you left Boldheart to die. After all those times my sword cut our way out of trouble. Remember the Citadel of Saint Cuthbert? Boldheart had to dispatch legions of bloodthirsty priests after you two used up all your spells. You almost got us killed trying to pluck that diamond from a statue's eye."

"Blinding a deity," Carlos said, "is what *Santana* did, not me. Santana's a rebel sorcerer without a cause. That's how I play him. You've never understood that, have you? It's just pen and paper, *hombre*."

"You were in on this, too, weren't you?" Randall said. "You always wanted to get rid of me, so you left Boldheart in that demon's arms. I can't ever forgive that."

"Relax," Carlos said, "I—"

"You act like you're better than us," Randall said. "You think you're some big shot doctor. But you're just a nurse—hardly more than a janitor. No better than the rest of your people."

"*My people?*" Carlos looked around the table. "Was that some kind of slur?"

Lance chuckled. "You are Chicano, aren't you, Carlos? I mean, you *sound* Chicano."

Carlos punched Lance playfully. "You better believe it." In a sharper tone, he snapped at Randall. "As for you, *chinga tu madre!*"

Randall squeezed his hands into fists. "This was *our* game, Alan. It wasn't my idea to bring this bilingual bullship into our game."

"I speak German," Lance said helpfully. "Does that count?"

Randall turned toward Lance. "No free pass for you, either—the atheist playing the priest."

Lance ran a finger across his character sheet. "Fortified with irony, it says here."

"I thought I was doing you a favor, bringing you in," Randall said. He opened one fist to point at Lance. "Now look at you. If you hang out with losers, you become a loser. Even a blind dude should see that."

Lance lifted his sunglasses to reveal soft blue eyes.

"I can see! What's this? A j-hole?"

"I'm done with all of you—and this game."

Randall kicked out his chair and grabbed his gray backpack.

"Want to get rid of me? I'm getting rid of *you*."

On his way toward the kitchen door, Randall grabbed an open Big Mix bag off a bookshelf and hurled it at the group. A variety of crunchy snacks flew through the air and skittered across the floor.

Alan jumped in his chair when the front door slammed shut on Randall's exit.

"What did he mean by that?" Lance asked. "He'll be back, right?"

"Not sure I know the answer to either of those," Alan said.

"Don't sweat it," Carlos said.

He pushed Alan's shoulder playfully and felt how rigid his friend's body had become. Alan's cheeks flushed. His breathing sounded shallow. It all signaled adrenal glands shooting hormones through the body. In someone like Alan, that chemical signal would likely induce more of a flight than a fight response in his muscles.

Carlos slid out of his chair and under the table to pick up the mess on the floor. A grotto shrine mosaic had formed from the dice and pencils, chips and pretzels, crumbs and dandruff. Seeing the futility of his efforts, Carlos went to a living room closet and removed an upright vacuum. He plugged it into the nearest outlet and unspooled its cord.

"Let's get on this now," Carlos said, "or your *mamá* will be pissed."

"Leave it for me," Alan said. He didn't stand up, or even raise his eyes.

It was time to go. There was a serious conversation to be had, but Alan wouldn't want to have it—not yet, anyway.

* * *

As Carlos drove Lance home along the freeway, he glanced at the wooden Superbarrio figurine that hung from his car key. Alan's mom had given him the hand-painted ornament seven years ago to celebrate Carlos' admission to nursing school. The red hood on the superhero's cape had worn down to its original pine finish. Though he believed himself free from superstition, Carlos would rub the head of his little friend to fetch good fortune. Every so often, he called on the gods of *Lucha Libre* before making a critical die roll, but he tried to reserve the wrestler's strength for more serious interventions.

"So," Carlos said, "do you think Alan wanted Randall's character to die? Was it fate, or did he tip the scales?"

"Just a statistical calamity," Lance said. "A black swan, like a market crash. I'm guessing Alan rolled two natural twenties behind his screen for Cynoc's opening attacks on Boldheart."

Even over the traffic noise, Carlos heard Lance cracking his knuckles. It was a sure tell that Lance was anxious. He'd once confessed to Carols that being in Alan's group the past two years had been a "privilege"—that was the word. It was the only consistent social connection Lance maintained outside of family. Today must have been like hearing the parents fight. Carlos felt a sting of remorse for whatever part he might have played.

"Maybe..." Lance paused. "Maybe Alan and Randall just need a break from each other for a couple weeks. Randall's a thoroughbred jackass, but it'll pass."

"I've heard Randall make dramatic threats before," Carlos said. "Then the next time we meet, he acts like nothing happened. This was different. He shredded Boldheart's character sheet. Know how many years he's had that thing? We just witnessed the end—*el fin*."

An approaching siren caught Lance's ear, and he rolled down the passenger window. "That a cop car?" Lance said. "One state trooper and one ambulance, right?"

Carlos looked in his rear-view mirror, then turned into the

right-hand lane. "Spot on, as always."

"And they're stopping ahead of us, maybe just past our off-ramp?"

"Right again."

Carlos led his black Honda Civic toward the shoulder of the freeway, with several other cars falling in behind him as three more emergency vehicles raced to the scene.

"Holy crap," Lance said. "Gotta be a nasty accident."

A pickup with lifted wheels had crushed a Mini Cooper. Around the wreck, five more cars and a moving truck had crashed into each other.

"Don't spare the details. What do you see? Red asphalt, right?"

Carlos considered bringing his car to a complete stop and punching Lance in the face. Life's relentless cruelties were a joke to Lance, who took his own disability in stride but never considered what images his friends might wish they'd never seen. Somebody should have told him that the three buddies he gamed with each bore deep wounds from the day their lives collided.

What good would it have done to tell Lance that story? The basic facts were clear enough, but the details were disjointed. Carlos lost consciousness two seconds after losing the parents who'd loved him with a force equal to the impact that killed them. When their station wagon dived over the freeway and down to the asphalt, their broken bodies cushioned his. He also owed his survival to Alan's mother, who kept him alive until the medics spirited him away. He tried to repay that kindness as a nurse, but he left the ER for other duties, unable to stomach the carnage from scenes like the one before him now.

"Right again," Carlos said to Lance. "It's a bad wreck."

Lance whispered, "Fuckin' A."

Carlos shook his head and descended the freeway off-ramp. The roadside ice plant in Lance's neighborhood was as lush and well-groomed as the drought-denying lawns that skirted its houses. There were a lot of ways to live in San Diego, and Lance's people lived well. Faithful Dungeon Lords companions weren't the only privilege that boy enjoyed. He needed truth more than sympathy.

"You know what?" Carlos said. "When Randall stormed out last weekend, I was relieved. When he slammed the door, I was glad our game was ending. I've outgrown it."

Lance's face turned as red as his freckles.

Carlos' gut clenched with guilt, teetering on the edge of regret. It reminded him of when he'd broken up, too abruptly, with his first college girlfriend.

"I turned thirty-one this year," Carlos said. "When do we move on from this scene? When do we go start real families?"

Lance put his head out the window, perhaps to cool his cheeks in the night air.

"I should've seen this coming. They were always fighting. Randall would get furious with Alan, though you were usually the one provoking him."

Carlos smirked.

"If he really is gone," Lance said, "we'll have to reboot the group quickly to get ready for Middle Mirth."

"Or, maybe—" Carlos began, but cut himself short.

Dungeon Lords felt played out, but Alan deserved every chance to shine. From the day Alan first announced he'd entered the contest, Carlos sensed that it meant more to his friend than it should. His craziest guess was that this was a kind of quest for Alan—to conquer a convention that, in its own way, had precipitated his own father's death. That was twisted Shakespearean shit, but Alan was capable of no less.

"Assuming we do find a suitable replacement," Lance continued, "there's no denying the upside. I mean, I've got mad respect for Randall's genre knowledge and all, but I won't miss his odor. I've never felt his face or anything, but he smells and sounds like a Hutt of a man. His footsteps thunder when he stomps around the carrels at work."

"That's pretty harsh. How detailed is your mental sketch of the dude?"

"In my estimation, he's a stereotype-reinforcing insult to more modestly overweight gamers. But I wonder, what sort of shirts does he wear? At work, I once brushed up against what felt like professional attire, maybe a poly-blend dress shirt. But his weekend wardrobe has the leathery smell of sweat suspended in full-cotton tees."

"Again, too harsh."

"But?"

"Yeah," Carlos conceded in a laugh. "Pretty much nailed it."

The pair drove the next two blocks in silence. The closer they got to Lance's house, the finer the architecture. Each home had its own signature mix of Spanish tile, stucco, wood, or adobe. Some curved like cylinders, while others jutted out at sharp angles. Palette-cleansing shrubbery and mature trees separated each lot from the next. Outside Carlos' three-story apartment building, nothing green grew excepting the ferocious weeds nobody had planted.

Lance cocked his head and turned toward Carlos.

"I don't get how Alan chooses his friends. You're so nice to him, but Randall's so mean. Why does Alan even let him in the house?"

"Their history's more complex than you'd guess," Carlos said. "I used to think Alan was afraid of Randall. But Alan surprised me today. Did you notice he talked about Randall in the past tense? Maybe Alan's ready to move on too."

"What don't I know?"

"Nothing imperative, just history."

"Are you holding back on me? I think you are. When I was telling Mom about the game once, she asked about you guys. I tried to connect the dots but realized I know jack all."

"We're not that mysterious. Just dudes too old to be playing a game every weekend."

"I've figured out a bit here and there. Like, since Alan's mom is a nurse, she's a role model for you, right?"

Carlos exhaled a breath he hadn't realized he was holding.

"Sure, kind of. I was already studying biology at UCSD when I—met her and Alan. And Randall."

Carlos pulled up to a stop sign. He looked left and right for oncoming traffic before turning onto Lance's street.

"After I got out of school, Karen said there were jobs in nursing, so I hopped into an RN program."

That was half the truth. Half was enough for Lance.

"The job at Children's, is that a good gig?"

"It pays the bills, but I want to do research. That's why I'm doing the part-time Masters."

"Scary bug shit, right?" Lance said.

"Infectious diseases," Carlos said with a nod. "Mutations of old-school plagues pop up all the time, even in yuppie neighborhoods like yours. A little viral reactivation, and they can go from dormant to virulent just like that." Carlos snapped his fingers. "Every day's a die roll."

"Every fuckin' day." Lance clapped his hands together with a bang. "But on this guy's die? Every side's a twenty."

"True that, *pendejo*."

Carlos rolled his Civic into the Langdons' half-circle driveway.

Instead of getting out of his seat, Lance reached out with his right hand and traced his index finger from the doorframe to the glove box, then to the dashboard shelf that held dried-out Post-Its, a ballpoint pen, a binder clip, and a three-inch wide oblong object with two hollowed indentations on its front. Lance had inspected that papier-mâché skull dozens of times. He always gave it a glancing touch, never a full inspection. Perhaps it was a tactile puzzle Lance wanted to figure out for himself.

"How come we don't play more often at my place?" Lance

said.

"You mean your *parents'* house?"

"Same thing."

"Your mom's probably afraid we're a bad influence on your kid sister."

"My sister?" Lance laughed. "You don't even—do you even know her name?"

Carlos looked through the windshield at the Langdon residence, a gracious two-story craftsman with yellow brick walls and broad windows. Inside sat a girl with a reddish bun of hair. Curled up in a big chair, she read a book, or maybe a tablet.

"Fair enough," Carlos said. "But you don't know my sister's name either."

"I haven't even *met* her, or your parents." Lance unbuckled his seatbelt. "Is your family part of the Mexican mafia?"

Carlos breathed in fresh air. Held it. Exhaled.

"Face it," Lance said. "We're *gaming* friends, not amigos." Lance opened his door, stepped out, and turned back to Carlos. "I know Santana the sorcerer—and you know Lancelot the cleric—better than we know each other. That's kinda messed up, right? But also kinda cool. You and me, we just play this game each weekend. Then you drive me home."

Carlos considered the countless hours he'd spent with Alan. Randall. The weight of it.

Lance pointed at Carlos.

"We're *gaming* buds. Kinda cool, right?"

"Maybe," Carlos said. "Maybe not."

RANDALL

"Frock Alan," Randall said to himself.

With deliberate steps, he continued the impossible five-mile walk from Alan's house to his own apartment.

"Frock Carlos," he muttered.

Then, to complete the trinity, "Frock Lance."

Under the heat of the afternoon sun, this self-righteous rage felt stifling. It gave way to a cooler introspection. He hadn't planned to storm out of the game for a second week in a row. Nor did reason guide this choice to walk home by foot, with a heavy backpack biting into both shoulders.

No, today's exit had been an act of faith. Randall was not the church-going sort, but his parents had steeped him in the Adventist vision. He knew well the mantra that God "inhabits, transforms, and triumphs" through a delicate balance of divine guidance and free will.

Randall daily exercised his will. No problems there. But he hadn't let go of the hope that some supernatural force had his back. When he left Alan's house the week before, providence had placed in his path a taxi—one of the rarest of beasts in the wilds of suburban La Mesa. Today, no such luck.

For personal reasons on which he dared not dwell, Randall had no car. He hadn't sat behind a wheel, nor taken a freeway since spinning off of one and nearly dying. Instead, he'd been ferried to and from every gaming weekend for years. Even on weekdays he rode city bus routes that transported him from apartment to office building with less than a hundred yards on foot. Again, providence.

As Randall kept walking, his vigor melted away. His pace slowed. He recalled a tale told at last year's Middle Mirth by an unlucky teenager who'd encountered the worst sort of wandering monsters just blocks from her home. For no reason, a pack of teenage trolls had pelted her with paintballs in a drive-by assault. That confession spurred another to admit suffering the same fate. Randall had recounted how in grade school, he'd rescued Alan from a score of unprovoked assaults. The most satisfying incident had ended with Randall forcing a lactose-intolerant bully to drink the four milk boxes his posse had hurled at Alan.

Randall felt a disquieting self-pity. Who would protect the protector now that he was culled from the herd? What if his bravado had just been a role he'd played, both in the game and at Alan's side? Randall tried to remember who he was before he'd met Alan—before he'd mastered Dungeon Lords. He'd been a quiet and sickly child, more alone than aloof. With Alan, he'd grown into a proud giant. Having forsaken that role, he risked being merely a freak.

Randall blinked and wiped away sweat, or worse. Stomping off alone was an act of defiance. Blubbering all the way home would be unthinkable cowardice. He refocused on the walk itself, which he took along a gravel shoulder facing oncoming traffic. When he and Alan were children, they'd often traveled great distances that way, whether to see a movie at Parkway Plaza or on a grocery quest at the behest of a parent.

Such distances were beyond the limits of Randall's asthmatic lungs. Shallow breaths had him jonesing for an inhaler. He pulled an Albuterol puffer out of his backpack. It blasted into his mouth nothing but propellant. No surprise. He hadn't refilled his prescription in months.

His knees were the next betrayal. Each step brought hundreds of pounds down on them, like sledgehammers driving railroad ties. Randall couldn't recall which term the condescending orthopedist had used to describe the condition of his joints. Its alleged cause was his own bodily mismanagement, rather than a bad roll of the genetic dice.

Such infirmities could be overcome. They hadn't stopped him

from taking part in the ill-fated birthday adventure in Balboa Park. They would not stop him today.

The more serious challenge was the road itself. He'd chosen one of the not-so-whimsical roads where the sidewalk literally ended. The next leg of his trip would require walking a quarter-mile down a street just wide enough for two cars, with little room for extraneous foot traffic. The six-inch shoulder abutted high stone walls and the occasional driveway. If he could make it through this stretch, he'd be able to rest at an Exxon and recharge himself with a 64-ounce cup of something cold and caffeinated.

Imagining the sound of ice falling into a plastic cup only magnified the afternoon heat. The air was dry, at least, but the sun cooked him at a temperature in the low nineties. Sweat drenched his shirt and shorts. His thighs rubbed together with every step.

Then again, the treacherous path made this trek all the more epic. Traveling this way gave Randall the chance to leave not just Alan's house, but to depart the very world they'd created together. Randall had a job that paid him well enough and an apartment of his own, but he hadn't proclaimed his true independence. He imbued Boldheart with courage and convictions, but he hadn't claimed those traits for himself.

Randall's pace quickened. The pain in his joints faded. His lungs filled with the kind of second wind Carlos would brag about after running a marathon. He reminded himself that the unwelcome weight he carried was nothing more than what Boldheart endured when dressed in full plate armor. Not quite reaching a jog, Randall found a steady gait that made the oaks and willows fly past as he ascended the steepest stretch of road. He'd soon catch a glimpse of the fountain drink oasis that awaited him.

Just beyond the crest of the hill, an approaching engine roared. Randall kept moving forward but prepared to step aside to let the speeding car pass. At that moment, however, there was no shoulder at all. In its place stood a seven-foot wall of cut granite, mortared with as much care as a castle. A cautious impulse brought Randall to a full stop. He stretched himself as thin as he could against the stones.

A bright-green muscle car burst into view. It passed without incident, but something about its passengers seemed odd. The two boys in the backseat appeared to be kneeling. Both of their heads were at the side window, with something like a pipe in their hands. They wore striped rugby shirts and red bandanas over their faces. Before Randall could parse the image, brakes squealed. The car shifted into reverse.

The adrenaline surging through Randall offered him two choices. Were he facing a single foe on foot, he might have chosen to fight. Were he given a viable route of escape, he would have fled, for even Boldheart would elude an enemy when overmatched.

On this day, on this road, Randall discovered a third option, fright. He stood still as a deer.

Randall soon learned that the pipes the boys held were, in fact, paint guns. They disgorged what felt like a dozen angry hornets. The taunts and insults accompanying the assault were indecipherable, but he heard the ones that came after the ammunition was exhausted.

Yes, it was accurate to state that he was overweight—obese, technically. And yes, he was homely. No, he was not a homosexual, though what if he was? Such invective was cliché. Before his assailants' car shifted back into Drive and sped away, one final epithet caught him off guard.

"Go back to your mama's basement, dragon fucker."

Randall collapsed against the wall. His head sunk into his chest. He regarded the prismatic dragon, still coiled peacefully on the shirt he'd bought at Middle Mirth. The convention played out in a hotel's lone subterranean level—a fact these thugs couldn't possibly have known. Other particulars aside, they had a point.

After a brief struggle to lift the paint-soaked shirt over his head, Randall threw it into the center of the road. Welts covered his chest. He felt the sting of each injury, and that fact disgusted him. As Alan's bodyguard, he'd never flinched when struck by a foe.

The first time Randall saved his friend was the day they met. Alan had been reading a comic book on a kiddie-sized merry-go-round. Three punks surrounded him and spun him in violent circles. The boys' laughter attracted Randall's attention, but he approached more quickly when he heard Alan's cries. When they wouldn't stop torturing the kid, Randall punched the shortest boy in the back. That got their attention, but before they could organize a counter-attack, Randall had two of them squirming away in the woodchips. Alan tried to disembark but lost his balance and kicked Randall squarely in the nuts. From that awkward beginning, an unlikely friendship ensued.

As they moved from junior high to high school, Randall had to re-establish his reputation each year as Alan's protector. He enjoyed the status it gave him on the playground and in the hallways. He made his main character a paladin and named him as a tribute to himself. Unlike his Mythos avatar, Randall was selective in whose safety he guaranteed. Once Alan assumed the job of game director, Randall recognized a professional obligation to protect not only Alan but also their fellow players. The director built their adventures, but his fellow players were necessary comrades-in-arms for any of the serious quests the game offered.

The life of a solo adventurer was a rough one. If Randall were to embark on that journey now, he'd require an even thicker hide. He closed his eyes to summon Boldheart. All he saw was the once-proud paladin's charred body. Boldheart stood perfectly still, under the spell of Lord Cynoc, just as Randall had frozen before his own assault.

Randall's imagination shifted back to the muscle car, which had sped out of view. Whatever plane of hell had spawned these furies, he'd received their message. In spite of all that he had done for Alan, Carlos, and all the other hangers-on who had come and gone over the years, Randall had become expendable. They no longer needed him. They were content to cast him out.

He could never again sit at a table with them. He could no longer live in the Mythos. On his own, he would have to find— or build—a new world.

Bare-chested and bruised, but with no tears on his war-painted face, Randall raised himself to full height. He resumed his march to Exxon, and beyond.

ALAN

The front door opened. Keys dropped onto the kitchen counter. Mom was home.

"Honey? Are you here? I—"

Alan lay atop the same lumpy mattress he'd slept on since junior high. The bed's tan blanket carried a faint mustiness, even after re-washing. Alan resisted replacing it because the familiar scent helped him fall asleep. Once Carlos and Lance had gone home, he'd meant to lay down atop that blanket for a quick nap, but he'd conked out completely.

The proper thing to do was to answer his mother and get out of bed, but Alan barely flinched when she called a second time. She didn't ask much of him, but she insisted he keep the house tidy. After Randall's meltdown, Alan didn't have the strength to fulfill even that obligation.

When Karen repeated Alan's name a third time, he felt a burst of energy to clean up the living room. The impulse did not precipitate action.

"I know you're home. Promise I won't bite your head off. Not all the way."

Footsteps came toward his room.

"Honey?"

Why did she still use that word? She knew he detested it. He used to fear that each of Mom's endearments were enchantments, a kind of life-changing magic that one day would seize him. He'd since come to doubt the potency of whatever spells she cast.

Karen rapped lightly on the bedroom door.

"Honey?"

"It's open."

The door knob made a quarter turn, then snapped back. A soft yelp startled Alan, and he recognized the sound. It was one he'd been hearing from Karen more often. Her arthritis was flaring up, usually in the right arm. His mind glimpsed a blade striking out from a warded dungeon door to wound a grasping hand.

When the knob turned again, the door opened. Alan felt the distinct pleasure of seeing a deduction proved correct. This time, she'd used her left hand.

Into the bedroom stepped Karen, worried wrinkles above fatigued eyes.

"You okay?"

"Just been sleeping."

Alan sat up and swung his legs over the edge of the bed.

"What's with the mess out there?"

"I was gonna clean up."

Alan pinched his nose. He wiped away the moisture he found there.

"Honey, have you been crying?"

"It's nothing. It's just...Randall." Alan rubbed his eyes. "Such an a-hole."

"Wouldn't he be a *j*-hole?" Karen said with a wry smile. "Did you have another quarrel?"

Directly behind Karen hung a blue ribbon awarded to "Randall and Crandall." They'd won it at a Dungeon Lords trivia contest thirteen years ago, using a nickname coined by their ill-tempered science teacher at Grossmont High School.

"I told you what happened last weekend," Alan said. "Today, I might've kicked him out of the group."

"Oh dear."

The indifference in Karen's voice stung, but he shouldn't have been surprised. Not a month ago, Mom had called Alan's friend "ballast." The label offended Alan, even if she only meant it figuratively.

"Maybe time apart will be a blessing," Karen said. "You've got other buddies."

"Hardly."

"Carlos is a true friend."

That, he couldn't refute. Alan remembered the afternoon he helped Carlos create his first Dungeon Lords character. Carlos had regained the use of his left arm from the elbow down, and he could roll for his hero's traits using the rectangular food tray that extended over his hospital bed. Into the Mythos had stepped Cuauhtémoc, a druid named for the Aztec ruler who fell to Cortez. Alan had never seen a Latino surname in the Mythos, but the fresh idea breathed life into that world.

From the outset, Carlos showed a genuine appreciation for Alan's deft direction of their adventures. In return, Carlos tried to match the energy his new friends put into the game. When Randall bought him a book on Mesoamerican mythology, Carlos devoured it and wove intricate cultural details into his character's story.

The power of Carlos' Mythos character grew as he got back on his own feet. Soon, he moved into his sister's apartment and started a regimen of daily physical therapy. Within a year, he'd returned to school and took up residence in a dorm. As Carlos' strength returned, his presence in their group grew stronger. Alan took pride in the small role he and his mother played in helping this "true friend" reclaim his life.

Randall's status might have changed in tandem with Carlos' ascendance. Alan hadn't seen it happen, but on considering this possibility, heat spread out from his chest to his arms. Too many emotions, of too many kinds, flowed through him.

Alan rubbed a hand across his face and looked at his mother. She hovered in the doorway, unsure of whether to sit down on the bed beside him or give him space.

"With just Carlos and Lance, we don't have a decent-sized group." Less to pout than to punish himself, Alan said aloud what he'd already concluded. "There's no point even *going* to Middle Mirth."

Karen smiled brightly. "Does that mean we'll be eating dinner together on weekends? I can move my shifts around. I've got seniority."

"Um..."

Alan scrutinized his mother but found no deeper meaning in her words.

"Sure, I guess so."

Alan's unenthusiastic agreement received a sigh in reply.

"Tell you what," Karen said. "If you want to find some new friends for your game, I've got good news. Pick up that mess, which is a Category 4 by the way, and I'll tell you what I saw on the drive home tonight."

"You don't have to bargain with me. I'm not a child."

Karen closed her eyes.

"Just clean it up."

* * *

Once the living room was back in order, Alan grabbed his keys, dashed to the garage, and hopped into his Kia Rio. The previous owner had painted it dark bronze. Naturally, its maiden voyage with Alan had been to pick up Randall. Alan had boasted that its color reminded him of King Tut's sarcophagus. Randall scoffed and christened it "King Turd." The nickname felt cruel, particularly since Randall was an unrepentant car moocher. Still, it was a solid slam, so it stuck.

With the last streaks of a red sunset in the rear-view mirror, Alan rounded onto the stretch of La Mesa Boulevard known as the Village. In his childhood, it had been a nondescript commercial district, but town elders used zoning laws and urban development grants to give it a personality. Unfortunately, the one it ended up with was schizophrenic. Storefronts alternately referenced an Austrian hamlet, a Spanish mission, or a Wild West outpost. None of these styles, nor the generous sidewalks adorned by birch trees and unused iron benches, could overcome the strip-mall aesthetic of the slant-in parking that local business owners demanded.

Alan dropped King Turd into one such slot. He got out to look for the address his mother had written on an oil change coupon. Up and to his left, against the darkening sky, stood a neon sign whose calligraphic letters announced, "Players." In red lights, the name sounded vaguely porno, like Alan was about to enter the Village's first gentlemen's club.

The store display featured an elaborate collage, a posthumous birthday celebration of famed Dungeon Lords creator Ernest Carpenter. Alongside a photo essay of his life lay original hand-written manuscripts by Carpenter and his longtime collaborator, Jeff Jacobson. The collection's auction value likely exceeded what Alan made in a year. It begged the question, what kind of person has the cash to buy such things, let alone open a game store?

Similar businesses had risen and fallen over the years. Few remained. Sometimes it felt as though the entire world had migrated to massively multiplayer online gaming, particularly the infamous World of Karnage franchise. Meanwhile, with the swiftness of the Black Death, Amazon.com took to the grave every one of the card, comic, and hobby shops of Alan's youth.

Yet here stood this aberration, which the front door proclaimed to be "open 'till the witching hour." That same door featured a stained glass inlay of a caped hero, perhaps Storm from the X-Men. When Alan squeezed its metal handle and pulled it open, an iron bell clanged. Without as much as a glance, a dozen or more customers inside shouted, "More cowbell!"

Alan blushed and stepped onto a polished pine floor. The store was narrow but extended back fifty feet. This location had been a coffee shop for several years. A bakery before that. To Alan's delight, the new owners left up the mural that made the ceiling resemble a cloudy sky.

"A feast for the eyes," said a voice to Alan's left.

Beside a desk and cash register in the front corner of the store stood a short African-American man in his mid-fifties. He wore a tailored suit, wide smile, and cropped hair. Even in dress shoes with one-inch heels, the top of the man's head wouldn't reach Alan's chin.

Alan meditated on the most suitable Mythos avatar for this fellow. He was too small for an elf. Too well dressed for a dwarf. Perhaps a gnome? One way or another, he'd prove useful. For Alan, even the precise Dungeon Lords modules provided nothing more than templates into which he'd insert people, experiences, and emotions from everyday life. He believed this gave his adventures a real-world texture too many fantasies lacked.

A hand approached in greeting. "Devon Washington, proud owner. Welcome to Players. What's your pleasure?"

Alan blushed. He again considered the possibility that this establishment was not what it seemed.

"The store name?" Devon said. "Yes, that's just me having a bit of fun with passersby. Here, have a look."

Devon steered Alan toward the center of the room. The shelves on the right-hand wall rose twelve feet, stacked to the top with books and boxed games. Bottom rows held sixteen copies of the best-selling Castaways of Catalan, along with dozens of mutually incompatible expansion sets. The higher shelves featured titles from the main publishing houses, including tedious EU Games, probably themed on the debt crisis or the complexities of immigration law. At eye level were books and equipment for popular role-playing adventures, from the pre-teen Ghostbusters to the more gruesome Apocalypse.

"The library-ladders straddling each wall are genuine antiques. They cost more than you would believe, but they are handsome and necessary."

Alan's eyes shifted toward the two oak tables in the middle of the store.

"Newly refinished," Devon said. "Gleaming from four polyurethane coats. As you can see, this first table offers a banquet of statuettes, toys, and so on."

"But the back one's empty."

"Reserved for true gamers who need the space and appreciate the atmosphere."

Alan felt an irresistible compulsion. He walked to the back table and arranged more evenly its mismatched wooden chairs, one of which had the high back and delicate carvings of a throne. A broad oilskin covered the entire surface. It had the distinctive hexagonal pattern used to diagram dungeons and arrange elaborate battlefields. Alan tried to straighten it.

"Yes," Devon said with a friendly laugh. "I believe the cloth was cut uneven. But excuse me, I have yet to ask your name. More to the point, what's your game?"

"Alan. And Dungeon Lords."

Regret tightened Alan's chest, as if he were speaking for the first time at Alcoholics Anonymous. Dungeon Lords had become the Mark of the Dork, even among many in the otherwise ecumenical game-playing community. A holdover from the pre-digital age, Dungeon Lords and its players were as cutting-edge as vinyl records.

"Dungeon Lords?"

Devon tilted his head and gave a dramatic wink.

"Sir, behold your new home away from home. The left wall, you will see, has both the latest modules and my personal favorites from among the classics."

Alan stood still and quiet, mouth agape.

"Have you tried The Cursed Tomb?" Devon said.

"Spooky. We just finished it this afternoon."

"Marvelous. Did you push a sword through the cold, dead body of Lord Cynoc?"

"Other way around."

"Try, try again! Or, maybe you should invent a new scenario for this summer's Middle Mirth. First weekend in August. Not far away."

"Oh, I'll be there. My group—"

Alan found himself unable to gather words.

"You simply have to go."

"Of course—"

Alan suspected that this annual gathering meant more to him than to anyone. He'd not missed a single day of the convention for close to twenty years, except for the one he tried not to remember.

Devon waved his hands like a children's magician.

"So, who do you think is the *mysterious* sponsor behind this year's high-stakes DL tournament?"

Alan was stunned to hear the Dungeon Lords abbreviation used favorably. Trendy gamers often dismissed his ilk as being "on the DL."

"I don't follow the Twitter," Alan said. "I don't know what others are saying. I have a theory, but I'm keeping it to myself."

Devon winked.

"Let's see...Who would want to bring back the spirit of role playing? Who would seek to rejuvenate face-to-face gaming in the age of the almighty computer? Who would endeavor to make it less about statistics and more about, as my daughter would say, who 'tells the best story'?"

"Your daughter plays?"

Devon nodded.

"Who would bankroll a two-week vacation at Bled Castle? Who would profit from recording a gifted DL group playing in an honest-to-goodness medieval fortress?"

Alan stared at Devon for a second too long.

"Bled Castle is in Europe," Devon said. "Remember the former Yugoslavia?"

"Oh, I know both where and what it is," Alan blurted.

He'd incorporated the floor plan for that fortress into older gaming modules. Touching the bricks of that landmark was a dream he and Randall shared. Travel guides from the public library shaped their half-formed plan for an overseas castle-quest, a rite-of-passage into adulthood they'd never taken.

Devon tapped his thumb on his fingers, as if counting.

"A twenty-five thousand dollar prize. From whose account might that be drawn?"

Alan couldn't help himself. "Jeff Jacobson."

"I suspect the same."

"How do you think he'll judge it? Who's to say which group, um—"

"Tells the best story? Good question. Fifty percent of each group score comes from its written submission, which must be an original or adapted module that includes everything from monster minutiae to narrative arc."

"Yeah, that's my first problem," Alan said. "I've got my own take on the Mythos, but for the actual quests, I still work from pre-built modules."

"If you amend one sufficiently, that should do. You just took your players through The Cursed Tomb, yes?"

Alan nodded.

"When I read it, years ago, I sensed that particular tale was an unfinished symphony. Surely old creepy-bones aspires to more than hoarding rusty coins?"

"Agreed."

"There you go. Now, the other half of your group score will come from player performance—the artistry of role playing."

When Alan submitted his entry online, his heart had raced at the prospect of judges watching his group in action. Lance was a charmer, and Carlos could hold his own. At Middle Mirth, however, Randall stood apart from all pretenders. When he spoke in the commanding voice of Boldheart, even the hum of the hotel basement's ceiling lights would fall silent.

"That's my more serious problem." Alan looked down. "I don't have a full group just now."

Devon scoffed.

"Membership springs eternal, I say."

This was not the kind of proprietor one expected to find in downtown La Mesa, or anywhere. There was something genuine in this man's enthusiasm, as though Alan, or maybe anyone like him, meant more than just another customer.

Devon reached up to Alan's shoulders, then steered him toward the front of the store. "Have a look at my corkboard."

"A *corkboard*? Really?"

"Luddite by choice, not for want of ability. Look here—a few puppies are hoping to find good homes. One or two of those I can vouch for personally." Devon's eyes sparkled. "Surely you recall the admonition from the television ad that aired during our game's zenith."

"Before my time."

"Well then..."

Devon struck a classic disco pose, feet wide apart and index finger raised skyward.

"The adventure..."

Alan knew where this was going. He tried to resist, but his feet moved apart. A hand shot up from his side.

"The adventure..." Devon repeated.

Alan couldn't help himself. He pointed toward the sky painted on the ceiling and shouted, "The adventure *begins today!*"

RANDALL

Unaccustomed to being alone on a Sunday, Randall stepped out of his apartment building and into the afternoon sun. Since returning home after yesterday's drive-by indignity, he'd done nothing but lick wounds. That meant binge-viewing every episode of *The Guild*, a web comedy about online gaming his boss had recommended months ago. Watching it made Randall realize Alan was the one who'd effectively prohibited all other forms of gaming. There were worlds yet to be explored.

That impulse pushed Randall onto the sidewalk, but in no particular direction. When a city bus approached a minute later, Randall hopped on board without even checking the number.

The route soon passed by the La Mesa American Legion building. Randall's gaze fell on the decommissioned cannon out front. That took him right back to senior year at Grossmont. Their social studies teacher had selected Alan to give a speech on rites of passage, with a modest Legion scholarship on the line. Randall urged Alan to decline, afraid he'd make a fool of himself, but Alan insisted. The evening of the competition, Alan spoke last, after four other boys had given homilies on the journey into manhood via military service. The lone female entrant also pandered to the aging audience. She alleged that welcoming her older sister's first child into the world had stirred her own nascent maternal instincts.

But Alan? Randall laughed at the memory while his bus idled at a stoplight. Alan had given a passionate speech—five full minutes over the allotted time—on the mysteries of the Middle Ages and the journey he would take to Europe with his father and best friend. It was a dreadful bit of speechwriting. Randall recalled one particular line he'd urged Alan to cut: "Whereas the Knights of Old tested themselves in joust and battle, we will test our knowledge of antiquity by touching their armor, their swords, their stories."

At the time, Randall had felt sorry for his friend's last-place finish. In the heat of today's afternoon bus ride, the recollection felt like an icy drink of *schadenfreude*. Replaying the details again, the memory soothed Randall until he arrived at the Lemon Grove trolley station.

Randall disembarked, then wandered toward a McDonald's. This was a place where Carlos categorically refused to eat, presumably for some stupid dietary reason. It felt like an act of defiance to pass under those golden arches. Another step toward independence.

To celebrate his good judgment, Randall ordered two Happy Meals. The athletic fry cook behind the counter who assembled his order made him think of a certain knight. Though Alan had murdered Boldheart, Randall let himself believe that the knight might return, somehow. Could Randall reprise him in a new Dungeon Lords group? The very thought of returning to the Mythos caused indigestion.

Randall picked up his food and carried it to an open table.

But what other game to choose? Randall had enjoyed smacking teenagers in Balboa Park with a wooden sword. No, that was too juvenile and too physically demanding. He needed a stationary activity. Earlier that morning while browsing online, he'd studied one alternative, the *Unspeakable Horrors* role-playing adventure adapted from the writings of H. P. Lovecraft.

He'd texted the mobile number posted by the host of this game. When Randall felt a buzzing in his pocket and retrieved his phone, he found that the goddess Fortuna smiled back at him. His message had received an affirmative reply. He could join a session this evening.

If he boarded the next trolley, it would take him to a station with a direct bus to Coronado, the odd little protrusion on the Pacific Ocean where he could find new friends and reboot his gaming career. After inhaling his child-sized meals, Randall threw their boxes and unopened toys in the trash.

Randall soon arrived at the low-rent apartment of US Marine Lance Corporal Oliver Easton. The only information Randall had about tonight's host was his job title and that he'd titled his Meetup listing, "Hate the player, not the game."

Oliver greeted Randall at the door and ushered him into the main room. In a circle sat an encampment of five men in their twenties, each with a raised TV tray and a different style of chair.

"Everyone, this is Randall. He's a last-minute replacement for Gonzales, who got another desert tour."

Oliver offered Randall a marked-up character sheet that read "Winston Witherspoon" across the top.

"You'll be playing the museum curator. His stats are already set, so we can hit the ground running. Like I said before, this is an all-night ride. Buckle up."

Randall lowered himself into the one free chair, a torn gray recliner that even a college fraternity would have tossed to the curb. It creaked ominously. The noise drew sideward stares from the other players, each of whom was as muscular as Oliver. Randall studied Witherspoon's profile. The dude had high ratings as a historian, botanist, linguist, map maker, and—what? Randall read the sheet again.

"What's 'library use', and why would we want to go to the library?"

"Dude, it's Winston's forte," said the player to his left. "Look at the picture. He's holding a book. It's his *thing*, man."

"May I see the Investigators' Guide?" The player to his right handed it over. Randall looked up "library" in the index, turned to the relevant section, and scratched his leg as he read.

The game proceeded for several hours. Randall helped his fellow adventurers find a rare folio on New England property exchanges from the early 1700s. Somehow, that led them to the Vermont dairy where a murder had occurred ninety-eight years ago. They found nothing at the site save a pregnant farmer, who showed them an arrowhead her neighbor unearthed while drilling a well. The archaeologist in their group hypothesized that the artifact originated from the Southwest. It bore markings found only in Chaco Canyon. What that meant, none could say.

Well past midnight, Oliver said to no one in particular, "Yesterday, I finished the complete podcast of The Exquisite Corpse."

"Dang, you've been listening to that since you enlisted," one player said.

Everyone laughed, except Randall, who looked up from his book.

"It's righteous," Oliver said. "They recorded every single hour of gameplay. Took 'em twenty sessions to finish one module. The audio's terrible, and their Australian accents are impossible. But the chick who played Fiona Grace?" Oliver rolled his neck across his shoulders. "Man, that voice launched a thousand."

Again, the group laughed.

Randall was incredulous. "Hold on. Am I to believe you listened to another group play this game for twenty hours?"

"Twenty *sessions*. Eighty-seven hours. But the real thing's better, eh?"

Randall realized he hadn't gone to the bathroom since arriving. Far from experiencing edge-of-the-seat excitement, he suspected he'd fallen asleep at some point. He tilted to one side and lifted himself out of his chair.

Oliver set down his papers. "Where you goin'?"

"Toilet."

Ignoring complaints that he was interrupting the game's flow, Randall trudged off to a cramped half-bathroom. While honoring his necessary bodily functions, Randall resolved to eliminate this new game as thoroughly as everything else he'd digested that evening.

When he returned, Oliver barked at him. "Fall in, soldier.

Gettin' to the good part."

Randall remained standing. Like a disdainful wine critic, he raised his nose, narrowed his eyes, and over-enunciated. "The good part's already here? I failed to recognize its arrival."

A player turned toward Randall. "There's got to be a portal to the Deep Ones under that farm house. The dairy farmer's probably carrying a Spawn Child. Explains the anomalies."

"Hey, everyone," Oliver said, "would you mind keeping in character?"

Randall hated it when Alan would ask him to stay "in game", then let Carlos get away with clowning during dramatic scenes. Special favors for the special friend. Thinking about the two of them, what they'd done to Boldheart, his face and neck grew hot. If he was done with Dungeon Lords, maybe he was done with *all* role-playing games. He already felt enough pressure at work for bearing the unofficial title, "Hard-Working Employee #1."

"Oh, I'd play my part if I had one," Randall said. "Would you like my bullship curator to shush the room using his awesome librarian powers?" Randall put a finger to his lips. "Winston says, 'Please don't disturb the cows.' And what if we *do* find these ancient monsters? They're thousands of years old. More powerful than Zeus. One of two things will happen. Either they'll devour us, or we'll go insane on the spot."

One of the other players turned to Oliver.

"Fat dude's kinda right."

Randall rolled his eyes, for many reasons.

"Look," he said, "our characters are humans with frail psyches and pistols for weapons, if anything."

Randall lifted his gray backpack, slung it over his shoulder, and stepped toward the door.

"My guy Winston, know what that j-hole carries? A letter opener."

The player to Randall's right looked at his own character sheet.

"Mine's got a walking cane. He had a pistol, but he left it somewhere."

Oliver clenched his fists.

"Don't be a dick. Sit back down."

Randall raised his hands in mock fright.

"Without a reference librarian at their side, what will happen to these brave men? Will they find the mis-shelved periodicals that hold the key?"

No reply, even from Oliver. Randall turned and exited the apartment.

Stepping into the cool night air, he picked up the scent of the beach, a brackish mix of ocean water, kelp, and fish carcass. He held his nose and walked toward his bus stop.

Randall imagined what would happen after his departure. An argument would begin. Three players would tell Oliver they didn't want their characters to die or go crazy. Shortly thereafter, two would leave the apartment, never to return. Those who remained would turn in their record sheets. Whoever's beer-heavy bladder yielded first would discover the unflushed Deep Ones he'd left for their inspection.

The evening hadn't gone as planned. He hadn't intended to insult Oliver, his troops, and their game, but they'd presented him with the opportunity to pay forward the cruelties he'd suffered at the hands of Alan, Carlos, Lance, and so many before them.

One had to welcome the gifts that providence bestowed. Randall had been offered precious few in his life, or perhaps he'd left too many unopened. Either way, he'd never miss another chance for payback like the one he'd found tonight. He looked forward to revisiting Oliver's distress on the bus ride home.

Even before reaching into his backpack, Randall realized he'd left his wallet on a TV tray. The Lance Corporal seemed an honest man and would return it soon enough, but retrieving it under the present circumstances felt—hazardous.

He dug deeper and found an old single-use bus pass. A quick check of the transit schedule on his phone showed an arrival coming soon. In the same instant, that very bus approached. He waved, but the driver looked straight ahead at a yellow traffic signal. When the light turned red, the bus accelerated through the intersection.

With no loose cash in his backpack and the massive Coronado Bridge looming ahead of him, Randall had few options. He refused to ride in cars driven by strangers, so even a taxi was out of the question.

He pulled out his cell phone.

"Frock."

* * *

As Randall fastened the passenger seatbelt in King Turd, he tried to relax. He'd forced his clumsy fingers to punch out the text, "Emerffency." Even the smartest app couldn't guess the intended word, but the typo was right. This wasn't a real emergency, just a supreme inconvenience.

He'd already thanked Alan for picking him up in the middle of the night. One thank you would suffice, since Alan confessed to having been awake. Hopefully his chauffeur had nothing further to say about the matter, or anything else.

When they reached the Coronado Bridge, Randall couldn't believe the density of its traffic. Flying past them came every kind of vehicle, from limos to airbrushed vans to hulking trucks from the naval base.

Alan sighed. "It's killing me to go the speed limit at this hour."

"You know my rules. Drive slow. Stay off the freeway."

Randall said nothing more until they neared the end of the bridge.

"What are you doing?" Randall said. "Don't get on I-5."

Their lane split into two distinct exits. Alan steered toward the onramp.

"No, take National Avenue."

This obstinate driver knew the rules to the game Randall had invented for himself, as well as the reason he played it. Winning required living in San Diego without ever traversing a freeway again.

"Look," Alan said, "I'm doing you a solid tonight. But if we're gonna stay friends, I'm done tolerating your crap. I'm taking the shortest route. We'll go down I-5, then take the Escondido to MLK."

"Not okay!"

Randall tensed his legs and pushed his feet forward.

Alan ignored the display and plunged into the traffic.

"See? Not so bad."

Randall's whole torso felt cold, drained of blood. He shivered and braced his arms against the dashboard. This freeway had a chaotic power that could rip people apart.

Alan merged with the faster cars. A tan sedan sped past, then swerved in front of King Turd to cross three lanes in two seconds.

Randall grabbed the steering wheel and shouted, "Look out!"

"What are you doing?"

Alan tried to pry loose Randall's hands.

"Let go, you idiot!"

Randall yanked the wheel to the right. They swung into the breakdown lane then slid up an embankment. With Alan braking hard, they skidded to a stop atop thick layers of ice plant.

Alan opened his door and jumped out, but Randall remained seated. His mind was a haze. He could see Alan's parents in the front seats, him and Alan in the back.

"You all right, Randall?"

Alan got back inside and shut his door. He reached for his key, still in the ignition, then hesitated.

"We don't have to talk about this."

Dead air.

"If I drive us back on surface roads, promise you won't kill us?"

Nothing.

"Okay, you crazy fuck. Here we go."

Randall turned away and shut his eyes. Alan had proven just how cruel he could be. Alan had forced this trauma on him, and for what—amusement?

Instead of boiling into a rage, Randall's anger dissolved his wild thoughts. Only clarity remained. Though his faux freeway game was ridiculous in itself, there was genius in how it imposed fresh rules and objectives on an otherwise dull world. If fueled not by phobias but by a more divine spark, that approach might offer greater possibilities.

Randall opened his eyes. At least for the moment, the lights of the passing cars looked more hypnotic than frightening. More like a surging river than onrushing traffic.

ALAN

After dropping Randall at his apartment, Alan returned home and parked in the garage beside his mother's car. Only once he turned off the engine did he feel his body trembling with fear and excitement. He tried to dispel the haunting image of Randall, frozen in his seat. He focused instead on the game store owner he'd met, and that sparked a different memory.

Stepping out of King Turd, Alan scanned the high metal shelves along the garage wall. When he got down on his knees, he found the object of his search, a green plastic storage tub. Something had gotten into it—water, maybe grease. The papers inside were filthy. Alan thumbed through them until he found a watercolor made by his sixteen-year-old self. He lifted up a stained but radiant portrait of Bled Castle.

It stood atop a cliff overlooking a blue lake. The bleached stone sentry had watched over the valley for a millennium, with generations of nobles reinforcing its fortifications and adding towers. Modern restoration with plaster walls and a red shingled roof made it look more Euro Disney than medieval. Alan had imagined its courtyards held a livery and forge, though he knew a restaurant and gift shop were more likely. Either way, it evoked grandeur.

When Randall hatched a plan to visit Europe, Alan was inspired to paint the castle. Alan's father had promised to fund the expedition, provided they finished college first.

Tucking the picture under his arm, Alan slid the plastic tub back in place. He walked along an ancient grease trail that led to the utility sink, then stared into the metal shop mirror above it. Reaching to his left, Alan picked up a pale green bar of Lava soap off its shelf. He held it in his hand, as he'd done so many times.

Alan's father had used a flat-headed screwdriver to carve into the soap an elaborate spider web. In the middle he'd etched a black widow, with the hourglass on its thorax precisely where a darker patch of red appeared in the soap. Alan never mentioned the soap to Mom, lest she toss it out like everything else his father had touched. Yet he also couldn't bring himself to remove it from its metal holder and hide it somewhere safe.

Alan ran his hands under the faucet and toweled off. He made a note to put on the shelf a bar of soap he'd actually use.

Back in his bedroom, Alan used two-sided tape to mount his musty watercolor. He regarded it for a few seconds, then undressed and slid under the top sheet. When he flicked off the reading light by his bed, the painting glowed for a second. Alan laughed, remembering he'd used luminescent paint to accent the clouds and castle. It had delighted him then, but now it seemed garish.

The same could be said of the Mythos. The original DL rulebooks laid out a gaming world well suited to the mind of a middle schooler. Alan had accepted its crude conceptions of race, religion, gender, and commerce. To stand out at Middle Mirth, Alan's world needed a bold revision. He couldn't just dump the old Mythos, but he could introduce a dynamic that complicated things. He could target its weaknesses, remake its reality.

His phone made the soft coo of a baby dragon. Carlos had texted, "Got 2 talk."

Yes, they'd have to talk, but Alan had to think things through first. Alan put his hands beneath his head and closed his eyes. He could feel Carlos' wavering commitment to the game. Alan needed to convince him to stick with it through the summer. Lance would be no problem and might even help recruit a new member or two.

A stir in his stomach signaled what those thoughts implied. Randall was out of the equation. Alan had cut loose the social anchor that steadied him on a sea he'd never navigated alone.

Lost in the nautical image, Alan's pupils rocked back and forth. He fell asleep.

During his slumber, Alan dreamed of illogical ledgers. Then his father chided him for a forgotten prom date. He reimagined a painful fight with Mom after dropping out of college. She made him move out and get a full-time job. Then she begged him to come home.

He heard his father's voice. John was knocking about in the living room and singing a song about "wildfire" in an alcoholic baritone. Alan found his mother, Randall, and Carlos holding hands around a card table. John stumbled toward them, tripped on a gray backpack, and struck his head on one of the table's legs. It collapsed and buried him in books, binders, and dice. Now dressed in a hospital gown, Randall said, "The game is dead. Long live the game." Randall hefted the corpse of Alan's father over his shoulder and walked out of the living room with an unsettling laugh.

Alan awoke. He opened his eyes and pushed himself upright. Drenched in sweat, heart pounding, he tried to remember the dream. Images and ideas percolated. From his bedside table, he grabbed a legal pad and ballpoint pen. Alan wrote freely, before even he understood what was developing on the page. A formidable foe emerged from a bed of ashes—a familiar face with unfamiliar powers. This crusader would bring to the Mythos a new way of life. Those who joined the cause would help cleanse the land of those who would stand in His way.

* * *

Lord Cynoc felt the tremendous strength of his new body as he pushed open the heavy stone doors that had sealed his tomb for a dozen lifetimes. Unaccustomed to heavy plate armor, he staggered through the high grass and gravestones until he used his giant obsidian sword as a walking cane.

The full moon's light seared his once-dead eyes, but his vision slowly adjusted. He inhaled and savored the cool night air. When he exhaled, ashes escaped his lungs. He blew into his palm and licked at it. The taste was bitter but soothing, like a licorice liqueur.

He reveled in the power of solid footsteps as he set out toward a fire burning in the distance. In his previous state, he had the power to float above the ground, and he tried to remember how he had done so. Long before that, he had worn fine silk robes fringed with ocelot fur. He had been a prince—no, a *lord*. He approached the fire up ahead and cried out, "I am Lord Cynoc!"

"Nonsense," said a man dressed in the loose leathers and sack cloth of a peasant. He sat cross-legged beside a ring of stones that held flames better suited for warmth than cooking. "Cynoc is dead. You're Boldheart, the greatest living fighter in the Mythos."

"Boldheart..."

"Don't you recognize me? I'm Nonplair, the guide who led you here. Your friends came by yesterday. They feared you had perished. I gave them a map that I found while messing about in the graveyard."

Cynoc regarded the peasant, then the campfire. He had the sensation that he inhabited a counterfeit reality, wherein things had no real consequence. Acting on that intuition, he stepped directly into the flames, which blackened his armor but licked up his body without raising a blister.

"You offer that I am Boldheart. Perhaps, but I am also Lord Cynoc. I have returned with a greater purpose than either of those individuals might have pursued in their brief lifetimes. I am something new. I am *Cynoc Coldheart*."

Nonplair scrambled to his feet and drew out a dagger. "Get back, demon! You may have Boldheart's bearing, but you cannot be the selfsame man. Perhaps you are the dead Lord Cynoc, but if so, I beg you to reenter your grave. The Lord was—*you* were—a cruel and vengeful man, whom our ancestors entombed with powerful magics."

"I thank you for speaking plainly, but you have no reason for fear. I propose not to ensnare you and your kind, but to set you free."

Looking to his left and right, Nonplair danced about nervously. "I beseech you, Lord, go back from whence you came. At least permit me a chance to flee."

Ideas and impulses fused together. "I can hear the voice of a supreme god, whose name we have never known. This god and I are in dialogue. I will share that which I come to know."

Nonplair turned to run. Before he had taken five steps, Cynoc blew a stream of gray air onto his back. Nonplair fell to his knees.

"If you accept the truth, it unburdens you. Those who resist? I cannot discern their fate, though I expect it to be grim."

Nonplair lowered his dagger. "What is this spell? It feels as if…"

"As if all you have held so closely—this life, this existence, even that weapon—were naught but illusions?"

Nonplair nodded.

"You say you are a guide. I need to find a people who know but one truth and who have refused to hear any other. They shall be the first pups to open their eyes and unsuckle the dry teats of their dead mother world."

Nonplair pointed to the north.

"The Pale Elves have sequestered themselves as far back as history knows. Yet they are far away. The Fairie Realm lies closer, if rumors be true."

"The rumors are true," Cynoc said. "I came upon them once, in my youth. I still remember their tiresome prattling about magic and enchantments. I shall pay them a sobering visit. But first, the Elven kingdom. Now, let us rise." Cynoc's body floated inches above the ground. He extended a palm to Nonplair, who reached out to accept the invitation.

With a last surge of will, the peasant's other hand drove his dagger into his own heart. A pool of blood spread across his leathers. Cynoc frowned. His powers remained unpolished, yet his heart felt light. He ascended, a bright spark leaping up from the fire and into the night.

LANCELOT

A pair of loud knocks brought Lancelot out of bed and onto his feet. He opened his door to discover that his slumber at the Miramar Inn was cut short by parliamentary guards. One thrust into his face a Writ of Summons from the prime minister. She presided over the Non-Aligned Provinces, which encompassed a thousand-mile radius around the capital city.

"We ask that you come peacefully," said the guard. "It is rare that one in your position has an audience with Prime Minister Lesilla. Consider this a blessing you cannot decline."

Once the guards had Lancelot shackled, they escorted him to Santana's quarters, where they met the sorcerer and his new companion, a juvenile dire wolf. The beast made a deep-throated growl until Santana soothed her. An adult of her species stood taller than any human, but the young wolf was just three feet high at the shoulder. Even so, under thick gray fur stirred a hundred pounds of muscle and bone.

Linked by a magical bond, "Lupita" was Santana's new familiar, an animal extension of his mind and body. The previous day, Santana paid a small fortune for the cub. The purchase drained what little had been left in the sorcerer's savings since commissioning the velour cloak he wore. Santana probably thanked his fire beetle spell for sparing not only their lives but also that same scarlet cloak, which a jeweler had embroidered with a ruby mosaic of dragon's breath.

Lancelot envied Santana's flourishing prowess as a sorcerer. Success came too easily to Santana, who sought adventure for its own sake. Lancelot had worn sackcloth for years as a disciple of Elahna, who demanded humble submission to the rhythms of the natural world. The priest owed all glory to his god and daily prayed for Elahna to share another dram of her power, that he might use it to advance her name. Hers was the truth and the way, and he was pledged to follow.

He felt his god's hands resting on his shoulders even while guards led the trio out of the inn and through the heart of the city's business district. As they passed through the morning market, shoppers and vendors waved their hands wildly at one another, without words. Such was the "common hand" language used to bridge the many peoples and creatures that visited the city or called it home. Outside the crowded stalls, gourds, hard fruit, and wrapped fish flew through the air to eager customers, who seemed as engrossed in the sport of the sale as the goods they received.

Lancelot took a deep breath of spring air and felt warm suns on his face. If this was a final day of freedom, Elhonna had at least graced his memory with a good one.

Soon they were out of the streets and climbing broad stone stairs to the top of the four-story capitol known as the Roundhouse. Passersby avoided eye contact with the captives, except the few who muttered curses. Whatever their crime, word spread fast.

When they reached the top, the guards pushed Lancelot and Santana into a rectangular room with eight windows overlooking the city. At the end of a long oak table stood Prime Minister Lesilla, a radiant gray-haired elder with a warm smile and light-brown skin. Like the other Mythopoles who studied the maps and papers spread out before them, she wore a blue-and-white dress, though hers bore a purple sash.

Lesilla motioned for the prisoners to approach. Following a Non-Aligned custom that held even for their lot, she lifted the back of her hand in greeting. Lancelot and Santana touched it with their own and intoned, "Swift battle." Lesilla knelt before Santana's wolf and uttered the same words. Reply came by way of a lick.

"I regret that you must come before me in irons, but I have no time for delicacy. We face a fresh adversary of uncertain motive and means. In a matter of days, he has burned a deadly path across the Mythos. The bleakest accounts say that an invincible demon, whom some call the Lifeless Knight, leads an army of hollow souls."

Santana shrugged at Lancelot, who replied in kind. No such story had reached them as they journeyed to and from the tomb.

"Our scouts alerted us to this savagery, but none have firsthand accounts. The few babbling survivors proved such dangers to themselves that they lie in chains below us. Every province will soon hear the terrible news, and I hope to have a counterattack in motion before despair takes hold. Word of *your* actions also has spread quickly. More than one minister's aide heard your drunken boasts last night at the inn."

Lancelot exchanged a glance with Santana.

"You claimed to have entered Lord Cynoc's resting place and returned alive. I would have doubted the tale had you not already used in trade artifacts from his tomb. Under normal circumstances, I would imprison you without reprieve for such a trespass. Our city's founders kept Cynoc's whereabouts secret for good reason. One should not awaken even the ghost of a tyrant who would bewitch his enemies and torture his subjects."

Lesilla grimaced and shook her head. "That said, the talent required to enter and escape that chamber marks you as exceptional. In lieu of incarceration, I command you to provide the Provinces a service."

"With all the profound respect due to you," Santana said, "I must ask what are the charges against us, precisely? If tomb raiding were a crime—"

"Which it is," one of the older Mythopoles interjected.

"—might it be more of a *civil* offense? One we can atone for with coin?"

Lancelot raised an eyebrow and wondered whether his

companion had shared fully the gems and gold from their previous adventures. Only a fool could trust a sorcerer unconditionally.

Lesilla pounded a fist on the table. "You may have brought forth a profound evil, the cost of which cannot be balanced in a ledger! I shall not ask again. Will chains or duty bind you from this day forward?"

Lancelot felt the urge to bow, but he knew that the Mythopoles disfavored regal gestures. When the Non-Aligned Provinces brought together scattered peoples under a single elected parliament two centuries ago, they discarded the dynastic systems and symbols still favored by others. Lancelot gave a polite nod in reply. Fortunately, Santana did the same.

"For our penance," Lancelot said, "we shall do what you require."

"It gladdens me to see wisdom in you both." Lesilla raised a hand and uncrossed two fingers. The guards unshackled their prisoners and handed Lupita's leash to Santana.

"In return for that gesture of good faith," Lesilla said, "I would ask you to speak honestly about your companion, the famed paladin Boldheart."

"It is as we told the guards," Lancelot said. "He is deceased."

Santana lowered his gaze. "We shall miss his strength and courage."

"So it is true? You saw him die with your own eyes?"

"His body turned to ash," Santana said. "Death magic."

"Incredible. Boldheart possessed a holiness that rendered him all but immortal. For that power, he had sacrificed even those who found and raised him."

Lancelot looked to Santana, who shook his head.

"With respect," Santana said, "you are confused. The day the earth quaked in his hometown, we found his parents crushed under rubble."

"And so you did," Lesilla said. "But he concealed from you

the truth. Your companion was so righteous that he pledged to smite all evil, and that unconditional imperative led him home. The family that adopted him had arranged to exchange its wealth for political favor. My predecessor excused them from their required tribute, while accepting lesser coin for himself."

Santana scoffed.

"What does tax collection have to do with falling houses?"

"Boldheart's parents took tremendous pride in their adopted son. They paid minstrels to sing praises for his holiest deeds. But they were never a godly family. When the preceding prime minister felt their influence growing too strong, he bid an elder priest to confront Boldheart with their crimes. The priest gave him a lesser scroll of destruction and commanded that he use it to crush his own parents. When the deed was done, Boldheart's god repaid his piety with protection against most known magics in the Mythos. So said the priest, according to divine revelation."

"I must confess," Santana said, "during the many years we traveled since that day, Boldheart's fortune seemed more than fair."

Lancelot looked through a window out toward the cloudless sky.

"I know of no god who could bestow such a powerful blessing."

"His was a mysterious faith," Santana said. "The Adventium order never named the one they worshipped."

"If this tale is true," Lancelot said, "let us hope Lord Cynoc has not acquired these powers. If he has—"

Lancelot reached down to touch his holy symbol but found none at his side.

"May the gods help us."

"Such humility is well-advised," Lesilla said. "You will not have Boldheart's sword any longer. I can offer only a humble replacement who will help you travel safely to your destination.

Once there, I pray you might take possession of a power that acts on our world in ways as mysterious as this Lifeless Knight. Do you know of the Magic Circle?"

Lancelot had never heard the words before. Many of the assembled Mythopoles exchanged whispers. Lancelot tried to swallow his doubts but found his throat too dry.

"Is it a ring you seek?" Santana asked. "We have completed innumerable quests for such objects. We are sworn to decline all such opportunities in the future."

"I cannot say for certain. The Magic Circle appears only in children's verses, but our sages believe that those songs are a cryptic oral history of potent magic. The Circle manifests only when unseen. It can be willed into being only by those who would harness it."

"Such are the riddles of sages," said one of the Mythopoles, to nods around the room.

"We believe," Lesilla said, "this power resides within a vault in the Fairie Realm."

Lancelot rubbed his wrists.

"Why would they open it for us now?"

"Our enemy appears indiscriminate in his destruction. Even the fairies will be drawn into this conflict soon enough."

"What makes you confident," Lancelot said, "that this Circle sits in their coffers?"

The prime minister sighed. Another Mythopole spoke, as if sparing her embarrassment. "Such is our desperation that we would have you look for spilled coins under the nearest lantern, for at least some light glimmers there. The rest is darkness."

Lancelot covered his mouth, lest he speak his mind too soon. He coughed lightly.

"Again, with respect, none have seen the Fairie Realm, let alone an actual fairie."

"That is not quite so," Lesilla said. "We know of one who has met their kind. Many years ago, a gnome illusionist sought to rid the world of cursed artifacts. Only the fairies have the power to bestow magical properties on physical objects, so he searched them out and entreated them to dispel the cruel magics that held hapless souls. The Fairie Queen Tinkana herself rejected his appeal. More he would not say, out of respect for their privacy. He has since lived as a hermit in the Rolling Hills, where you will travel to enlist his aid."

Lancelot sighed and heard Santana do the same. The journey was not impossible, in theory. Mythopolis stood at the center of all things in the world. Reaching Cynoc's Tomb had required a blistering march through the southern deserts, but the so-called Fairie Realm lay several days north. The Rolling Hills were on the way, with hamlets and monasteries along the road to keep them fed. Elahna would see to their safety.

"I see," Santana said. "You would have us seek the aid of gnomes and fairies..."

"We have gotten ahead of ourselves," Lesilla said. "I promised you the services of a warrior. Just this week, we have been visited by barbarian mercenaries. The one to ask for is—"

"Prime Minister," said a guard. He had walked tall when delivering the prisoners but now spoke in a soft voice, his face ashen. "They left this morning, hired by a merchant guild to break up a hive of trolls."

"The ones that devoured twenty-two of our soldiers just days ago?"

"The same."

* * *

Lancelot waved his mace at the two-headed beast that rushed toward him, a mess of rags over moist green skin and ribbons of warts. Though this was a fresh-water troll, when exposed to the sunlight its odor came closer to that of a sewer. It climbed up the bank to engage the newcomers, who arrived to find four barbarians in a pitched battle with countless number of these beasts. Each warrior towered to a height of seven feet or more, but they struggled to keep their footing in the muddy river, which rose to their knees.

"Lupita," Santana shouted, "attack its neck, ah, necks—either one!"

The wolf bared bright fangs as she sprang into the air. She landed on her prey and ripped its throat open with a snap of her jaws.

Lancelot pointed his mace toward the troll's other head, which bit at Lupita. A burst of electricity crackled through the air and left only a charred stump where the head had been.

Santana jabbed at the collapsing troll with his staff. "Your lightning is stronger than ever, friend. You may yet find yourself a leader in the Temple of Elahna."

"I wish only to serve my god, as your new pet serves you."

"I should have thought Elahna more in need of a shepherd than a wolf."

"One lovely day, I shall lay down my mace, but not while such as these terrorize us."

Lancelot stood over the fallen troll. To be certain of its state, he hammered its body with his mace and caved in its chest. He stepped back and said, "Burn it."

Hearing no reply, Lancelot prodded Santana, who had turned away to inspect Lupita. The wolf shook her body with the gusto of a dog returning from a swim. A fine spray of blood flew in all directions. Lupita stretched front and back legs, then stood erect, panting with pride.

"Surely," Lancelot said, "you slept enough to regain strength for a spell or two?"

"Of course," Santana said. He rubbed his hands together. "*Manos del fuego*," he intoned. His fingers burst into flames. He pressed them onto the troll, which burned iridescent green.

Down in the river, dozens of two-headed monsters swarmed

the last pair of barbarians. Bent forward like hunchbacks, the trolls flailed with clawed hands and feet. Even their severed limbs, as alive as ever, fought blindly beside their erstwhile bodies.

Lancelot's heart beat louder than even the cries below him. No longer in the shadow of Boldheart, he considered leading a desperate charge into battle.

A hand on his shoulder held him back. "Remember our mission," Santana said. "The trolls are not our concern." He motioned to Lupita, who ran toward the largest barbarian. Caked in mud, the warrior stood taller than anyone Lancelot had seen, and she jabbed a trident of equal length to devastating effect. The wolf barked insistently at her. Across the barbarian's face swung twisted locks of sable hair as she turned to look at Lupita.

The other barbarian fell into the water, dead.

Lancelot edged closer.

"This way! Retreat!"

As he slid forward, Lancelot's mailed foot caught on a protruding root, and he tumbled into the melee. Claws clasped and pulled him. Unable to pierce his armor, the trolls tried to snap him in half. He felt one, then another rib pop. He could feel the vertebrae in his back separating when something even stronger wrenched him free.

The barbarian swung him over her shoulder like a child and hauled him out of the water. In a flash, the air congealed into fog, a trick Santana often used for quick escape. The barbarian ran after the fleet-footed Santana until they could no longer hear the chattering monsters behind them.

The conjured fog lifted, and Lancelot's feet found the ground. He called on the healing power of Elahna, and reached back with warm hands to touch his spine. When he saw the open wounds on his rescuer, he reached toward her instead. She welcomed his touch on her obsidian calves and forearms. As he worked, he noted the delicate yellow-inked burns that spiraled around her limbs, visible through rips in the hides that covered her body. Not quite tattoos and not quite scarification, Lancelot reckoned the marks were an enfleshed clan sigil.

The barbarian sighed, then straightened herself. She spoke in the melodic low plains dialect of the common tongue.

"I trained them fer battle, and they perished in it. Had they been from my clan, we would have prevailed. Still, they were someone's kin. If I had saved even one—"

"You rescued my friend," Santana said. "Now, we need your help to spare many more. Might you be the one called Angelou?"

Angelou nodded and cracked the bones in her neck.

"The Mythopoles spoke of a second commission, should we survive the first. This next errand, what does it pay?"

* * *

At the Mythopolis city gates, the guards recognized Lancelot and Santana as the prime minister's prisoners. They permitted entry, but reminded the men that their freedom remained provisional.

Lupita brushed up against Angelou's legs and pawed her hides in a bid for attention. The wolf had already forgotten the battle. Its relentless focus on the present helped Lancelot do the same.

As they entered the city, Angelou eyed the rubble that had once been a circle of high walls. Before becoming the capital of the Non-Aligned Provinces, Mythopolis stood alone and apart from the rest of the Mythos, closed off from Angelou's barbarian clans and every kind of elf in Lancelot's mixed ancestry.

"As you surely know," Lancelot said, "the last conqueror who stormed those walls chose to let them crumble. The stone arch above the gates still carries the words he inscribed, 'The city most solid lets any pass through.'"

Santana nodded.

"By all lights, that gambit transformed Mythopolis from a

strategic fort into a commercial hub. Town elders still greet the most alien visitor as a guest."

"Unless he wakes their dead," Lancelot added.

Angelou raised an eyebrow but did not request elaboration.

The three walked together down a long market corridor. The few customers milling about appeared distracted. Soon many of the stalls stood unattended. Lupita seized the opportunity to stand on hind legs and bite at a spit that held a glistening shank of lamb.

Lancelot tugged the wolf down, then noticed townspeople gathering near the city gates. Pulled with the tide, Lancelot and his companions joined the crowd. On a stone dais that rose eight feet off the ground stood a slight elf with gold filaments draped over her elongated ears. Wearing a loose gown the same color as her bun of emerald hair, she spoke in a lyrical voice and brandished a lute above her head as if it were a weapon.

"Woe betide!" she cried. "The Pale Elves have fallen! We have lost those of the Elvenmists, those who recorded history from the first written word. We have lost those who carried our candle, even when it guttered in times of war. Woe betide!"

High-pitched wails came from the elvenkind in the crowd. Louder voices shouted, "Impossible! Lies!"

Lancelot sided with the hecklers. The Pale Elves brought the world many gifts but, by living apart from it, had escaped all its horrors. They practiced Worshipful Isolation to sustain their own kingdom in peace. Rare diplomatic visits spread knowledge of their achievements, but those emissaries who stepped out of the Elvenmists had to pledge they would never return.

The elf atop the dais raked one hand across the strings of her lute. This released from the instrument the pained screech of a wyvern, returned to find only broken eggs in her nest.

The crowd hushed as she began to sing a novel version of "The Troubles," an elven funerary hymn that prophesied the end of days. She gave a half-tempo rendition, her voice reverberating off a nearby temple wall. The effect transformed a traditional dirge into a call to arms.

Listen, friends, you've shut your ears
To a coming calamity you cannot hear
Do you not care, or are you unaware
Of poison seeping into our community?
We've got trouble, my friends
Coming to Mythopolis City!

One dark night, children leave the keep
Heading for lessons at the armory
Then a rag-tag, shambling army
Will grab your son and daughter
With the arms of a full-grown bugbear
An idle Mythos is a demon's playground!

When she finished the song, the shoppers dropped their parcels and wept. Merchants threw handfuls of coin at the sky, a gesture of defiance against cruel gods. Even Angelou wiped away tears, perhaps feeling the grief she had not shown after her charges died in the river. Santana waved his arms in anger. Lupita threw back her throat and howled for her master's pain.

Lancelot's curiosity trumped his sorrow. He squinted at the singer upon the dais, then clucked to himself.

"This elven bard is no stranger. She is a distant cousin of mine, of whom I heard tales. She was foremost among all Pale Elven minstrels."

Angelou sniffled.

"You know this messenger?"

"I have not met her, but we all know her name. Did I not hear you, Santana, whistle one of her songs only yesterday?"

The sorcerer's eyes widened.

"Do you mean—"

"None other than the fabled songstress herself. She the world calls, *Hermione*."

LANCE

On principle, Lance stood by his little sister's decision to name the elven bard after her favorite fictional heroine, a choice that heralded the arrival of a seventeen-year-old girl to his gaming world. Brianna had learned most of what she knew about Dungeon Lords through osmosis by watching the occasional game at their house. New members were needed, so Lance volunteered her. Once Alan agreed to bring Brianna on board, Lance gave her a crash course to prepare for today's gathering at the back table in Players.

"Hermione?" Carlos hacked as though trying to cough up poison.

"Her character," Alan said. "Her call."

"No, you have got to be kidding me! *De veras?*"

Carlos' ponytail brushed Lance's cheek, probably from swiveling his head to check the customers' reaction. Lance could hear the shuffling feet of a half-dozen onlookers. When they learned the name his sister had chosen, they snickered and whispered about the faux pas. Thus broke a second wave of laugher, louder than the first.

"Leave it alone," Lance said. "Don't encourage the jackasses, Carlos."

Lance reached down for his cane and held it tight. He'd have it at the ready should he need to thwack anyone who hurled further insults at his little sister. When he caught a whiff of adolescent sweat wafting through the room, he relaxed his grip. The store's patrons were socially inept teenagers, not bullies. Their behavior was simply the transmutation of sexual attraction into nervous mockery.

Though Lance's eyes would never behold his sister, he knew her to be a cutie. She shared his build, slim but never gaunt. Her movements had the grace of their mother, who was a dancer in her youth. Their parents often commented on how brother and sister shared the same disarming smile, though Lance's had a Cheshire curl. Brianna had no such artifice. She barely brushed her flowing blonde mane, which had natural strawberry accents. When Brianna chattered with the hope and anxiety of an unsettled child, Lance would picture her blue-green eyes flashing this way and that, never hidden behind shades.

On this particular day, Lance knew his sister wore rough textured jeans and a soft cotton top—probably the one with daisies sewn along its sides. This much he'd learned as they navigated their way to the back table in Players.

Lance took for granted passing touches, which had none of the spark he imagined he'd feel when he brushed into the group's newest member. Brianna had squeezed Lance's hand with delight when they met Maya Washington, the daughter of the store owner. Brianna described Maya as wearing gray ankle pants and a matching Evergreen College sweatshirt. She had five yellow wristbands complementing dark-brown skin. Brass studs adorned her ears, and she wore a bumble-bee hairpin in glossy black hair. Such physical details remained frustratingly theoretical. Lance considered whether it had been Maya, more than Brianna, who held the attention of the store's giggling clientele.

One of the die cast figurines on the table made a scratch as someone lifted it.

"This little bard I'm holding," Maya said, "received the name Brianna chose for her."

Lance used a trick Alan had taught him. He tried to imagine Maya and Brianna morphing in and out of their alter egos in the Mythos. Brianna fit neatly into the slight frame of Hermione, but she lacked the bard's confidence. The difference made Brianna seem small by comparison, though at five-five, she was as tall as her elf. Maya probably could match the temperament of her barbarian counterpart, but nothing more. Angelou was a muscled Amazonian. Until last month, Maya was a cafeteria-fed college student.

"We all choose names that mean something special for us," Maya said.

"Yeah, but *Hermione*?"

Carlos quivered as though an evil spirit passed through him.

"I guarantee you, no one who walks through these doors celebrates the birthday of that author. Our game existed long before Harry Potter started fiddling with his wand. That boy and his mates robbed us of our monsters, plots, and self-respect. Damned if I'm casting a single spell with some 'Hermione' by my side."

"I'm so pleased to hear you come to our game's defense," Alan said. "So gallant."

"How is the name any worse than *Lancelot*?" Maya asked.

Lance ignored the cue and flipped through his braille edition of the *Players' Handbook*. He laid the book open on the table and ran his right index finger over a page.

"The name Lancelot is just as derivative," Maya continued. "It's simply from an older work of fiction. And let's face it— we're all tossing a Tolkien salad, topped with croutons from Martin and the rest of the imitators."

Without looking up, Lance threw another log on the fire.

"Don't spare Santana from ridicule."

"Right!" Maya said. "What about *Santana*? That reaches outside the genre, which I respect, but it's derivative just the same."

Lance felt Carlos' foot kick his own. He'd taken his customary seat beside his friend instead of placing himself by his sister, who sat across the table and next to Maya. He worried for a moment that Brianna might feel slighted. Then he remembered how she'd sounded yesterday when they rolled for her character with Alan. She was breathless. With wide-eyed wonderment, she gazed through the keyhole into the secret garden that is the

Mythos. His sister now sat alongside not only Maya but all their make-believe friends.

A satisfied smile crossed Lance's face. Hermione had already become real to his sister. That was the magic of this game. It's what had attracted him to it in the first place and kept him going. This was something non-players would never understand.

For Lance, the game wasn't just an escape into fantasy. It could also bring the fantastic into everyday life. Lancelot had an abiding faith, a divine purpose, and membership in a society unlike anything Lance could access. The priest's devotion infused purpose into a life Lance led one day at a time.

It was almost creepy how Alan picked up on that. Lance had chosen to play a cleric because Randall said the group needed a healer. It was Alan who had worked with Lance's initial ideas to flesh out Lancelot's backstory.

Intolerance of half-elven offspring in the Mythos shoved a young Lancelot and his mother into a life of poverty. Once he grew old enough, he helped his mother work at a clinic where they tended to lepers and crippled outcasts like themselves. A priestess of Elhonna saw promise in the lad and paid his entry into a private school. On graduation day, the priestess returned to share a prophecy. If he joined her order, Lancelot's power as both fighter and healer would grow to the point that he would impress even the gods. He would one day come to see a Truth greater than any known in the Mythos.

Lance had no idea what that meant. He figured it was probably something Alan made up to give the cleric gravitas. The crazy thing was that the story drove Lance forward more than it did his half-elven priest. Each week, he fed off the idea that his life was heading somewhere. He put in his hours at work, but, at least for now, his greatest accomplishments might turn out to lie in the Mythos. If Middle Mirth was a proving ground for Alan's game direction, it was also a chance for Lance to stand out — not as a blind-guy with talking dice but as a truly gifted role player.

Perhaps if Brianna stuck with the game through her senior year—and her bard outlived that unfortunate name—she might come to appreciate how the game could change a person. She might absorb her elf's best qualities, though he couldn't yet glean what those might be.

The copper cowbell on the front door clanged, signaling a new arrival. On cue, Lance joined the other customers in shouting, "Ding dong, the witch is dead!"

Lance smiled in the direction of the store's register, where its owner likely stood. Devon had sworn to have no role in the verbal flash mobbing his customers performed. Every so often, they probably texted each other a new catchphrase.

Seizing a lull in the conversation, Lance looked up from his book and pointed his shades toward Alan. "On a more serious note, Alan, I have to raise two game world issues."

"Oh, Jesus," said Maya. "Tell me this isn't one of these groups that argues over rules all day and night. I'm not up for that shit."

"First," Lance continued, "what was that nonsense the prime minister said about 'special protection against all known magics.' How could—"

A loud knocking on the table interrupted Lance's inquiry.

"Now, now," said Devon. "The game master reigns supreme. Alan shall tell you what he wishes, and you must trust he has your world well in hand."

Across the table, a dramatic sigh was followed by Maya's voice. "Da–ad, please. It's your store, but not your game. And isn't that a customer waiting for you at the register?"

What sounded like leather soles shifted on the floor.

"So it is," Devon said. "Excuse me. My daughter fancies herself my manager. I contend that shop-keeping is well beneath a future Yalie."

Brianna made an involuntary squeak Lance recognized as confusion. He found it endearing, but today it made him bite his lip.

"I thought you already graduated," Brianna said.

"Dad, don't—" Maya protested.

Devon lowered his voice to a dramatic whisper. "After toiling in the store this summer, she will take wing on the great steel dragon, which will fly her to Connecticut. There, she will embark on doctoral research in literature. Has she not spoken yet of her ideas? Genius! A father is proud."

Lance wasn't sure which was more exciting—that their new gaming companion had real ambition or that she was a scarce social commodity, destined to leave in a few weeks. Whatever the cause, a familiar tingling sensation prompted Lance to scoot his chair forward to obscure any view of his lap.

"Please," Maya protested, "you know I haven't decided anything yet."

"The prodigal daughter speaks," Devon said. "She would throw away a golden ticket to stay eternally with us here, in this pleasure dome."

"Wait, what?" Brianna said.

"He's just being a jackass," Maya said. "Dad's the one who ran away from the silicon circus to be a game store hermit."

"A lifetime ago, dear."

"Was it? And you're the one saying I'm squandering my talent?"

Devon cleared his throat.

"Perhaps I have overstayed my welcome at this table. My presence is required at the register. Adieu."

Fading footfalls merged with the chatter of the store.

"That father of yours is cool," Alan said, "but he's an odd duck."

"Agreed," Carlos said. "What did he do before starting this joint?"

"He wouldn't want me to get into any details," Maya said. "Suffice to say he's always been in the gaming industry, but notice there's nothing digital in this store."

"Pops was a code jockey?" Lance said. "For video games, or what?"

"Dad's business," Maya said, "is being into everybody else's business, especially mine."

Lance felt a poke in his shoulder and hoped it was Maya's hand.

"Before he butted in," Maya said, "Lance was wasting our time bullshitting about rules."

"It's not bullshit," Lance said. "What was this 'special protection' Boldheart got?"

"Since Randall's no longer in our group," Alan said, "it can't hurt to tell you. His character's covert childhood mission earned him a plus three on all saves against spells and magic."

"Damn," Maya said, "are you running a candy store? Even on twenty sided dice, that's a huge modifier."

"If I may," Carlos said, "I've played the longest with Alan. He's far from generous when it comes to life and death. He killed off my original character without mercy in my first year. And he's tweaked a few Dungeon Lords rules to make things tougher on us."

"So explain the plus three," Lance said. "And why didn't Randall tell us about that?"

"Because he didn't want to," Alan said. "It was on his character sheet—"

"Which he never let us look at," Carlos said.

"I'll admit to this much," Alan said. "What he did to earn that crazy bonus was meant to be a test even Boldheart couldn't pass. Randall wanted me to play up the Adventium Mythology in the game to make his paladin's religious dimension more prominent. So, I riffed on the idea that the righteous should fear sin, not death. Boldheart's god promised eternal glory for those who stood up against evil in the Mythos. Looking away from sin could doom one's immortal soul."

"Wait," Brianna said. "Randall was the big guy who always

played with you, and Boldheart was his character?"

"Correct," said Lance.

"So how come you don't already know this stuff?"

"Because some scenes are private," Alan said. "Boldheart's meeting with the priest happened during a morning session I held with Randall before Carlos and Lance came to the house that afternoon."

"So the story about his parents was true." Maya exhaled. "I hope I never meet this friend of yours. Who's capable of such dark shit?"

"What Randall was capable of," Lance said, "was bad-ass role playing."

"*Así es*," Carlos said. "I'll bet our game director here, who knew Randall better than any of us, underestimated that *pendejo*. What was the penalty if Boldheart hadn't followed this holy commandment?"

"That's just it," Alan said. "I never told him the stakes in precise terms. When told that their sin had been proven, he didn't hesitate. He took the scroll and put things in motion."

Carlos persisted. "But if he'd refused?"

"Boldheart would have lost a full level."

"I don't know which is more fucked up," Maya said. "Kneecapping a high-level character or forcing a player to assassinate his avatar's parents."

"Trust me," Carlos said. "Both speak volumes. When we killed a red dragon once, Alan made what should have been an epic victory into an unnerving flashback. After Santana's staff dealt the fatal blow, smoke trails came out of the dragon's nostrils in the form of ghosts. We got to see the hundreds of souls it had taken in its lifetime. Top billing went to Santana's dead *mamá y papá*. You have no idea how fucked up that is."

"Damn!" Maya exclaimed. "You *are* a mean ol' game director."

The ensuing laughter came from more than just Lance's tablemates. The attention of the store patrons had returned, and

Lance seized the chance for an audience.

"As for my second issue," Lance said, "Lupita can't be a familiar. Not for Santana, not for anyone."

"But I like Lupita," Brianna whined. "She's a nice wolfy."

Lance squirmed in his cushioned folding chair and felt the raised lettering that spelled "Players" on its back. His sister sounded too much like a child. Perhaps the crowd's snarky reaction would help set her right. With forceful taps on his book, Lance argued his case. "Not legal. Neither dogs nor wolves allowed. I double checked."

"I also thought so," Alan said, "but Carlos pointed out that Second Edition rules allowed familiars of any type, and—"

"Hold on," Maya said. "You promised we'd play Third Edition rules. The Second Edition was offensively stupid. And if you jump around from one rule set to another, we'll waste all day arguing over—"

"She's right." Lance nodded in Maya's direction. "Third Edition is what the Middle Mirth tournament requires. Besides, remember what happened when every wizard recruited a fire giant as a familiar? The system broke."

Lance perked his ears and listened for Alan rubbing his moustache. Carlos swore that Alan performed the gesture constantly. If he did so now, it was too quiet to register.

"Are we really gonna do this?" Carlos said.

"We don't have a game if we don't have rules."

Lance turned to Alan and spoke in the faux-German accent Alan had begged him to never use again.

"Iz zat not right, Herr Director?"

"That much is true," Maya said. "We've gotta all be playing the same game."

Lance's cheeks flushed. He was accustomed to Randall's put-downs and Carlos' smart-aleck commentary. This new voice, a little sweet and a little husky, offered praise. More than that, Maya spoke as one who understood the nuances of their craft.

Lance squeezed his legs together, excited at the prospect of a new playmate.

"Okay," Alan said, "slow down. We are Third Edition, but as it happens, Dungeon Lords HQ released a Game of Thrones expansion that's tournament-legal. Hence, Lupita is kosher."

"Hooray for wolfy!" Brianna cried.

"Look at it this way," Carlos said. "Alan says our job this summer is to become better storytellers—better actors. That's the point of this contest, sí?"

"Truth," Maya said.

"Knowing the damage my fireball causes requires rules and rolls," Carlos said. "But Lupita's more than hit points and attack modifiers. She adds canine color. She's like Vincent, the yellow lab in that TV show, Lost. There's a reason that dog shows up in the final scene."

"Omigawd," Brianna said, "that made me cry so hard."

"Can you give a girl a spoiler alert?" Maya pleaded. "I just started watching it."

"Maybe I can't make anyone care whether Santana dies," Carlos said, "but I can make them root for his dog."

"It's also true," Alan said in a quieter voice, "that Carlos blackmailed me into this. No wolf, no play."

"Really?" Brianna asked. "Why would you do that?"

Carlos made the same weary sigh Lance remembered from their last drive home together. This conversation needed redirection, but Lance had to swallow the saliva pooling in his mouth before he could speak.

"Are we being honest here?" Carlos said. "Truth is that I wanted to take a break from all this. If Alan would gift me a wolf, I agreed to stay on through the summer because Alan's hot-as-Hades to win the DL tournament."

"Are we all saying 'DL' now?" Alan asked.

Lance congratulated himself on correctly reading Carlos, who had almost admitted to wanting out. Alan had bought them some time, but the end of the summer would come soon. Then what? Brianna would be busy with school. Maya equivocated, but he'd heard something about graduate school. Even if Lance could win a few dates with her, he and Alan were no match for the siren call of the ivory towers. That would leave him and Alan, without a group.

The prospect of centering his life on his code jockey job gave Lance a shiver. That was an occupation that required his full attention, but it awoke in him no passion. He took pride at working as efficiently as anyone else at ProTechTed, and he knew it freaked them to see him speaking with his computer through a headset, his flat-screen monitor tilted at a random angle or unplugged altogether.

In Dungeon Lords, though, he felt he had an edge. The whole point was to use your imagination—to see the game as Lancelot might see it. Undistracted by maps, miniatures, and dice on the table, the Mythos was his primary visual reference point, not something he had to conjure.

When Santana showed up with an oversized familiar, Lance saw a vivid image of the beast, uncorrupted by whatever dire wolves might look like in contemporary illustrations, movies, or video games. He had medieval reference points from before he lost his functional vision, but those were distant memories. He'd created the world anew in his own mind. What would become of that tapestry after Middle Mirth?

Brianna's voice shook Lance out of his self-pitying reverie. "Okay, but why did you want Santana to have a wolf cub?"

"My sister," Carlos said. "Last week, she got herself a chidoodle."

"A cheese doodle?" Brianna said doubtfully.

"No, *chidoodle*." Carlos laughed. "Half toy poodle, half Chihuahua. Name is Gigi."

"After siring this abomination," Alan said brightly, "did the poodle father fashion his leash into a noose and take his own doggie life?"

Brianna tried on the neologism. "*Chi*-doodle?"

"Chi-*doodle*," Carlos corrected.

"Wait," Maya said. "Why stop there? We should find a cross-bred friend for Lupita in the Mythos. Perhaps—"

A sweaty customer hovered near their gaming table and said, "Perhaps a wererat terrier?"

"Or a gnoll-pug," Lance said.

Another customer offered a scenario. "Maybe at the dog park, you'd meet a gibberling retriever."

"Absolutely not," Alan said. "I will allow no such creatures in the off-leash areas of the Mythos. Except, perhaps, a deepspawn beagle. Pack extra kibble."

"Seriously," Lance said, "we really need to pick up provisions before we head out to find this gnome illusionist. Brianna, your character sheet should list every item Hermione can hoist onto her back. Dried food, rope, clothes, whatever."

Brianna squealed. "I love buying clothes!"

"No shopping for me," Maya said. "Alan agreed I could import Angelou from my last gaming group at Evergreen. She's already got a very solid look. Burned lines into her skin with a chemical dye made from the bile of a displacer beast's liver. Makes her harder to hit and adds a pinch of magic-resistance. Plus, she wears troll hides—skinned, tanned, and sewed 'em herself. They're tougher than leather armor, without any restriction of movement."

"Cleans her own kills?" Lance laughed. "Maybe she'll run for prime minister on the Republican ticket."

"The thing is," Maya said, "I hate, hate, hate all the sexy-swords-lady crap. If I'm playing this game, it won't be as some maiden swaddled in negligee-armor swinging a scythe. No, I'm a badass barbarian mercenary who wears dead monster flesh over her Brandi Chastain sports bra."

"I dig it," Carlos said with a chuckle. "And her trident's

nasty."

"So I can get all Poseidon on their ass."

"What's Angelou's story?" Brianna asked.

Alan coughed. "That's in-game knowledge, not for her to tell."

"Come on," Maya said. "We've got to get each other up to speed."

"Of course," Alan said, "but—"

"For her, it's all about clan. Everything she does, it's to preserve her people's way of life."

"I thought she was a merchant?" Brianna said.

"Mercenary," Lance corrected. "She's a trident for hire."

"What?" Carlos said. "Is she like a *bracero*, sending gold coins back home by Westeros Union?"

Maya laughed. "Yeah, something like that, actually."

Lance felt his character sheet slide out from under his book. He used a braille embosser between gaming sessions to update Lancelot's statistics whenever he gained a level or acquired an item. He could guess whose finger it was that made a whispering sound as it ran over the raised ink portrait of Lancelot.

"So, your guy wears pantaloons and a blouse?" Brianna said. "Not exactly your style, Lance, but they look good on our healer."

"Okay," Carlos said, "this just got interesting."

"If we're talking clothes," Maya said, "where'd you buy that top, Brianna?"

"It's my mom's. We're the same size."

Maya's chair legs scratched on the pine floor as she adjusted herself. "No way I could squeeze into it. Same height, different body."

"You're beautiful," Brianna said.

"Oh, I know *that*," Maya said with what sounded like sass.

"Can I ask a dumb question?" Brianna said.

"Shoot."

"How come your hair's flat, but you made Angelou's all bushy?"

"Excuse me?"

Lance sensed trouble. Had Brianna ever had a conversation with an African-American woman in person before this day?

"Shouldn't have asked," Brianna said. "Sorry."

Lance bit his lip and hoped Brianna was doing the same.

"My hair's flat because I *flatten* it," Maya said. "Angelou has dreadlocks because she doesn't rub moisturizer into her head and plug in Ye Olde Ceramic Flat Iron four times a week."

"It's just." Brianna exhaled. "I wanted to make my character kind of, I don't know, in my own image. Or maybe the other way around?"

Maya laughed. "You aren't gonna make the social scene by going all elfin and hanging out in game stores. Trust me."

"Hey!" Lance recognized an insult, even in the spirit of self-deprecation.

"Own it," Carlos said.

Brianna laughed. "Playing Dungeon Lords probably hasn't helped Lance-a-lot."

"We'll ignore that," Alan said.

"High school's dodgy," Maya said, "but trust me, you can get away with all kinds of role playing in college. Speaking of which, Alan, I dig this storytelling contest we're gonna do. Our group's too green to have any chance, but you've got a knack for direction. When you killed off Angelou's trainees, who had backstories and everything, that was ice cold. I played Angelou as kind of numb at that point because I really felt that way."

"Creepy," Brianna said. "I mean, cool."

"And I loved Hermione's sad little song," Maya said to Brianna. "Did you notice everyone in the store staring when you went all karaoke?"

Lance was glad to hear confirmation of what he'd hoped had been true. The store had gone silent when his sister took the proverbial stage.

"That was just me having a little fun," Brianna said.

"*Que hermosa*," Carlos said. "You've got a beautiful voice."

Maya shook her head. "What about that 'Woe betide' speech you gave?"

"I wrote that part," Alan said.

Lance nodded to himself. He'd recognized Alan's phrasing.

"We have lost those who carried our candle."

"That was dark," Carlos said. "What's it mean?"

Alan kept mum, but Brianna chimed in.

"It sounded kind of over-the-top when I rehearsed it. Then, when I said the words out loud, it felt like Hermione knew what they meant, even if I didn't."

"Baby," Maya said with a laugh, "don't start talking like that at school."

"The kid's already got the spirit of it," Alan said. "With you two joining us, we'll be the most diverse group at the convention. Could be our edge."

Lance scratched his head.

"Diverse because we have a singing spellcaster and a troll-armored fighter?"

"Funny stuff," Carlos said. "It's because we'll have two *ladies*. Nobody's got that."

"Not true," Alan said. "Remember the Wiccan Convent?"

"Who're they?" asked Brianna.

"Girl gamers who got a bit famous," Alan said. "Had a fanzine for a hot second before the Internet was a thing. Then a blog for a couple years. They were a smidge older than me and—and Randall. They'd dress up as their characters—thief, priestess, sword mage..."

Lance could picture each of them, cosplay style. "Sounds hot," he blurted.

"It's because of dorks like you," Alan said, "that the Convent retired."

Carlos' chair creaked as he leaned back.

"Yeah, Randall told me about them once, but we never met. Back in the day, I knew a few *chicas* who gamed in college, before I really knew what all this was about."

"I must confess," Lance said with a nod toward Maya, "you do have a, um, sultry quality to your voice when you speak as Angelou."

"That's my stab at the low plains dialect," Maya said.

Lance heard sniggering from the clutch of customers who'd seated themselves at the other large table in the store. They made little clicking sounds as they repositioned tiny samurai and siege weapons in a Japanese miniatures battle.

"Brianna's the real vocal artist," Maya said.

Lance had hoped to keep the focus on the store owner's daughter. The deft topic shift, however, beckoned him to follow. "Brianna may seem shy," Lance said, "but she and Mom go all vaudeville when Dad plays piano in the evening. They've memorized a whole catalog of god-awful show tunes, and now they're into modern Broadway crap—jukebox musicals and the like."

"Is that where Hermione's lyrics come from?" Maya asked.

"Alan suggested improvising," Brianna said. "Since show tunes are what I know—"

Carlos laughed, "Wait, does Lance sing along with the rest of the family?

"Very funny," Lance said. "But I can sing better than Randall ever could."

"Who?" Maya said.

Lance turned back toward Maya.

"That's the dude you replaced. You'd have liked him."

"Ignore my brother," Brianna said. "This Randall guy left the group after a big ol' roadhouse fight at Alan's house."

"Okay," Lance said, "now that we've opened this up, can we talk? I mean, about Randall's *smell*?"

Carlos poked Lance's shoulder, hard. "Not cool, amigo. Demonizing is bad juju. Don't speak of the dead that way."

"Actually," Lance said, "I was going to say that his scent was never as horrible as I imagined it should have been. I mean, the stuff he ate—the volume, the grease. Must have a gut bigger on the inside than on the outside, right?"

"No, seriously," Brianna said to Maya, "he looked like the Comic Book Guy on The Simpsons."

"Stop it!" Alan shouted. "Cut it out, all of you. You're better than that."

Lance wrung his hands. He remembered the Halloween night at Alan's house when he'd first joined the group, along with the twin brothers Randall had recruited from the Adventist Community Church. In spite of the twins' theological apprehensions and Lance's sophisticated pose, Randall had bewitched all three that weekend.

While Carlos made quesadillas and Alan arranged miniatures on a scenario map, Lance and the twins sat like summer campers on a log to hear Randall recount epic battles. Lance held his knees to his chest when he heard how a disarmed Boldheart clawed his way out of a pit filled with writhing corpses. Afterward, the twins huddled on the back porch, trying to calm themselves down. The next week, their pastor made them leave Alan's group after hearing how they'd talked about it during Bible study. Alan explained that they weren't the first players to have become enthralled by a power Randall possessed, which Alan called "The Effect."

"Shit," Alan said in a softer voice. "I'm sorry. It's just— sometimes Randall gets in his own way. He can't help it. He's always been a big dude." Alan moved his chair back and stood. "I've gotta take a leak."

Seconds later, Carlos spoke in a conspiratorial whisper. "Anyway, Lance had the guy all wrong. The cartoon dude on The Simpsons is short and pudgy, balding head. Randall's six-foot-plus. Full head of hair."

"I sit corrected," Lance said. "Lady Maya, you shall miss not the company of Comic Book Guy. Instead, you shall be denied the companionship of a broad-shouldered woodsman."

"As a consolation prize," Carlos said, "you will also receive the flirtatious impositions of our blond imp, Lance Lannister."

"I am *so* lucky," Maya said.

"Blessed are the geeks," Lance nodded, "for they shall inherit the mirth."

When the groans subsided, Brianna stage-whispered, "Chi-*doodle*."

Together, the group rocked with convulsive snorts and pounded their table. Every customer in the store was surely worried. And jealous.

ALAN

"What was it like today?" Karen said.

"The store's fine." Alan smelled chicken in the oven. "It's a great space."

"Without Randall, I mean."

Karen opened the refrigerator and lifted a head of iceberg lettuce out of the crisper. She set it on a cutting board and pulled a cleaver from a wooden block. The blade's handle slipped from her palm. When she grasped at it, her hand went limp.

"Mom?"

In his mind, Alan heard the professional diagnosis Carlos would have given: arthritis, again. Prescription: not clear. Probably a cream.

Karen leaned back against the counter, arms hanging at her sides. "Remember that day I told you about the game store? I'd come home early because at work, I dropped a full tray of meds and made a spectacular mess in front of the nurses' station. Every color of capsule scattered across the floor like jumping beans."

Alan stared at his mother, unsure what to say.

"When I went to pick them up, I couldn't bend my wrists. Each time I tried, it felt like reaching into scalding water."

Karen hugged herself and sobbed. Alan took a step toward her. To see her crying right in front of him, that was new. The last time he'd seen it was five months after John died. She'd wept hysterically for half an hour over some reminder of him she'd found. Then she loaded the car with their stereo, records, and nearly every physical memory of Dad. She filled the passenger seat so Alan couldn't come with her to Goodwill.

It pained Alan to remember the money they'd lost by donating all those things instead of selling them from the yard. With only a meager life insurance policy and her nurse's salary, money was tight—even after Alan found part-time work at El Cajon Life and Casualty.

What he'd really lost was the chance to say goodbye to Dad's stuff. And to Dad.

Alan stepped around his mother and picked up the cleaver she'd dropped. He started chopping the lettuce. Wanting to provide some kind of reassurance, he leaned toward Karen and gave her a gentle hip bump. He wasn't sure it was the right gesture.

"Salad's a great idea," Alan said. "I wish Randall would—"

"I know. I worry about your friend."

"I don't think we're 'friends' anymore."

"I'm serious. He's headed for diabetes, or worse. You probably haven't noticed, but he put on even more weight this summer. His body's so overstressed, he's compromised his immune system. He's an incubator for bacterial infections. That's why I'm so fussy about cleaning up after your games. I disinfect the entire kitchen and living room before I go to work each Monday."

The realization came slowly, but Alan saw how deftly his mom had shifted the topic away from whatever uncomfortable subject they weren't quite talking about a moment ago.

Karen relaxed her arms and opened the refrigerator. With great care, she lifted a bottle of raspberry dressing and set it on the counter. Alan finished chopping the greens. He pulled down a metal bowl from the cupboard and filled it with lettuce.

"What's that I smell cooking?"

"Baked a whole chicken. Wanted us to have a nice dinner together. Wasn't sure when you'd come home, so it's on low."

Karen donned a pair of oven mitts, but Alan nudged her aside, stole the mitts, and pulled out the bird. He set it on a trivet on the dining room table, then made Karen sit in one of the oak chairs while he laid out place settings.

"I miss John. Every day."

Alan looked away from his mother's eyes and noticed her

flexing her left elbow.

"I miss you, too, Alan. You're gone every weekend."

"Not *every*—"

"No, it's just about every weekend, when you don't play here. I know your game's important to you. And to Carlos. It means a lot to just keep playing, like nothing's changed."

"The new group is great, with Lance's sister and this new woman, Maya. She's just out of college. English major, I think."

Karen gave Alan a grin.

"Don't go there. I'm a decade older than these girls." Though it hadn't been a conscious intention, Alan considered the possibility that he'd recruited these two *because* they were outside his age bracket. Neither would rekindle his mother's futile hopes for him to find a mate.

No amount of reassurance could dissuade Mom from the belief that her son, like Randall, suffered from never having a girlfriend. She'd once suspected that the two boys loved only each other. Around Alan's twenty-sixth birthday, she'd tested that theory. After returning home from a Saturday morning shift, she made a loud phone call from the kitchen saying that she'd left her purse at work. Too quickly to have driven all the way from the hospital, a male nurse showed up at their house with the lost item. Feigning an interest in their game, this curious visitor got Alan's group into a lively banter with little effort. Ten minutes later, their guest bid fond farewells, and Karen followed him outside. When she returned, even Alan could recognize the guilty expression on her face.

That evening, Alan forced a confession. Her friend had agreed to assess her son and his playmates. None had set off his gaydar. Not one to mince words, he'd pronounced all three of Alan's comrades as conventionally hetero and horny. When pressed about Alan, the coworker speculated that Alan might be "inert."

Karen had scrunched her eyes when she said that word, which pained her. For Alan, though, it had been something of a revelation.

The truth was that Alan's libido had been dormant for years. Their senior year at Grossmont, Randall set him up with a pigtailed girl from church. That tryst, in the backseat of King Turd, was Alan's first and only legitimate make out session. It ended in wild petting and, after a half hour of determined effort on the part of his companion, his lone experience of release in another's arms. There were no repeat performances. The pigtailed nymph was on a voyage of discovery all her own, with no intention of visiting the same port twice. That, and she'd sprained her wrist.

Each evening for a week, Alan replayed his memory of that encounter before going to sleep. When he recounted the tale to Randall, however, he found the details had dissipated. Alan tried to find other willing partners at school, then in college, but no sparks flew.

When Carlos came on the scene, he offered grooming tips, but relented when he sensed Alan's indifference. He could see clearly enough where Alan's erstwhile libidinal energy flowed. Carlos followed suit by sexing up his Mythos exploits. When his sorcerer found himself in a tavern game of Texas Hold 'Em, using cards cribbed from the Deck of Many Things, Carlos directed his avatar to complete a winning hand with The Lover, which earned him a sizable charisma boost. Santana's open shirted strolls through cities and towns precipitated ribaldry. Having taken a vow of chastity, Boldheart could neither partake nor condone the behavior. These escapades would have frustrated Randall even more were it not for the pornographic flair of Alan's narration. He'd bring his companions to the edge of social discomfort. From that, Alan derived a higher pleasure, but none of the lower sort.

Alan walked back to the kitchen to grab the salad bowl and fill water glasses. He set all three down on the table and took a drink before seating himself. All the while, he felt Karen's eyes tracking him.

"How's Carlos doing? Must be a lot to manage coursework on top of the job at Children's."

Alan shrugged. "Now that you mention it, I should talk to him about plague vectors. Might tie into the new module I'm writing for the tournament."

Karen smiled and took a drink of water. "Is Carlos still playing that same wizard, Quata-something?"

"Cuauhtémoc? That's a weak blast from the distant past. That dude was Carlos' original character. Now he plays a direct descendant of Cuauhtémoc, who went to the grave nine years ago. Died bravely, you'll be glad to know."

"But I remember something about how players could bring each other back to life."

"Resurrection?"

Karen cringed.

"Sounds sacrilegious when you say it so casually."

"In my take on the Mythos, resurrection ain't easy. Clerics can resurrect, but only if they're high level. Lance's character just got there this year. It also requires expensive material sacrifice. Even then, no guarantee. If a bond doesn't form between healer and healed—if there isn't enough common purpose or shared history—the priest can't recover the escaping soul."

"How do you decide whether a character lives or dies?"

"The dice decide."

"That sounds awfully severe. Why kill a character someone loves? Look what it did to poor Randall, bless his big heart."

"I—I didn't," Alan stammered. "I mean, Randall just—got reckless. I didn't kill Boldheart, he just—"

"I'm sorry, honey." Karen covered her mouth. "I just wish you made happier stories with your friends. Playful fairies, that sort of thing."

Alan brightened. "As it happens, fairies are coming up soon."

"Well, good. The girls in your new group, they'd like some

cute little fairies."

"We don't really do cute."

Karen's eyes looked far away, out the sliding glass doors and toward the darkening sky. Alan sensed two conversations under way. One opened into a dialogue about Dad's death and the things that came with it—things he worked hard to forget. The other concerned the smaller details with which one filled a life. He preferred the latter.

"Carlos told us that Adelita got a dog. A chidoodle."

"His sister got a what?"

"Half Chihuahua, half poodle."

"Teacup poodle, I'd hope."

Mother and son laughed together.

Karen wiped away a tear. "Carlos once said that when he was little, he had a dog. A frisky mutt of some kind. Lupita, he called her."

Alan hadn't remembered that story. In the brief time Carlos had lived with them, he'd spoken nightly with Karen about all manner of things, especially when Adelita visited.

With Alan, though, Carlos preferred to stay rooted in the present—be it in this world or the Mythos. Even now, Carlos might riff on a college track meet or some other innocuous tidbit, but he avoided past tense verbs. When Lance asked Carlos how he first fell in with Alan and Dungeon Lords, Carlos simply stated, "We met through Middle Mirth." That half-truth settled the question.

Karen flexed her arthritic wrist, then touched Alan's shoulder with her good hand. "The way I remember it," Karen said, "Lupita ran away the summer before Carlos started college. She was very old. They drove all around San Ysidro looking for that dog. It upset the whole family. Carlos swore he'd never get another."

Karen reached for her drink but fumbled. The glass wobbled in her hand and tipped over. Water poured off the table. Before the glass itself rolled to the floor, Alan caught it.

"Your mother's getting old, honey."

"Old wizards are the best wizards," Alan said. That wasn't quite what he meant to say, but the analogy didn't seem to offend.

"Full social security benefits kick in next year, but—"

"If you're worrying about money, don't. I could put in more hours."

"I haven't retired because the hospital's the only place I see anyone I know. You've got Randall, Carlos, Lance—"

"Probably not Randall."

"Think about how much time you spend together. Each weeknight, you're in your room doing what you do to get ready. Then each weekend, you take over the living room. When I come in to say hello, Carlos is the only one who even sees me. I've watched you boys playing that game since you were kids. You sit there for hours, without even getting up to pee. You just sit and talk. Maybe I want to talk sometimes."

"We're talking now."

Karen smiled.

"I suppose we are."

"If you'd rather, we could probably start playing more at the Langdons' house, now that Lance's sister is playing."

"I want to see *more* of you, honey, not less."

"So you don't want me to get a place of my own?"

"When did I say that?"

Alan frowned. Surely, she knew the answer.

"I'd like to have you stay here. Maybe we could spend a little more time together? We could see a movie or—"

"Sure, mid-week."

Karen reached across the table and took Alan's hand.

"I'm tired after work. Maybe a weekend now and then?"

Alan swallowed. No sooner had he assembled a new group than he encountered the next obstacle. The cobblestone road to

Middle Mirth would be a treacherous one.

"Is that too much to ask?"

"I can't promise, but I'll try."

"What more can a mother ask?"

RANDALL

The San Diego Metropolitan Transit System's Number 7 bus pulled to a stop at Palm Avenue. In its back row, Randall sweated, more from internal combustion than from the hot evening air. He'd wasted a whole Saturday at the office doing paperwork that somebody else at ProTechTed should have done in his stead. He was a cybersecurity engineer, not a file clerk. The long bus ride home added diesel fuel to his resentment.

Up ahead and to his right stood the Players sign. He'd glanced at it before, but this was his first time really seeing it. The neon made him wonder if the Village had changed its zoning laws. Some of his more disgusting cubicle cousins at work frequented San Diego's adult establishments, but Randall refused to join them. He preferred complete privacy when he felt compelled to debase himself in such ways.

For the first time, Randall studied the storefront window display. A game shop! His mind flashed to the strip mall on University Avenue where, eighteen years ago, he'd purchased the *Dungeon Lords Guide to Monsters and Mayhem*. To acquire it, he and Alan had saved three months' allowance. "Go-out-and-play money," Alan's dad used to call it. When the clerk handed the book to him, Randall tore open the wrapping. They took it to Eucalyptus Park and read through page-by-page. Arachno. Beholder. Cockatrice had cracked them up. Genie. Gorgon. Orc. Sprite. Urchins seemed lame. They'd just dissected one in science class. Xorn. Yeti. It ended with a timeless classic—the flesh-biting and brain-seeking zombie.

Nothing in that compendium prepared Randall for the horror he now beheld. Out of the Players door walked Alan, Carlos, Lance, and...two girls? One was Lance's sister, whose name he'd never committed to memory. He didn't recognize the other, a black woman, maybe in her early twenties. He hunched down to avoid detection and watched as she ran back toward the store, her short hair bobbing above her sweatshirt. She said something to a man who might have been her father, then gave him a kiss.

The Number 7 bus rolled on, and Randall turned to keep his eyes on the store. His cheeks grew hot. Barely two weeks since Alan had murdered Boldheart, and already he'd started a new group—one that included females, no less. Alan had gone rogue.

"Those two-timing, gold-dame losers," Randall muttered. He lifted up his knees, braced them against the seat back in front of him, and pressed chin into chest. He and Alan had built a world together. They'd collected many hangers-on, with Lance only being the most recent.

They'd opened their world fully just once, out of pity. When Carlos got ripped to shreds in that station wagon, they'd bolstered that ungrateful soul so he might regain footing on a foundation they'd already built. At first, Randall saw Carlos as a charity project—the kind of good works his parents might have appreciated.

Once Carlos caught his stride, however, his arrogance became wearisome. Such behavior was appropriate for Santana. All sorcerers are loathsome in precisely that way. To see it in a living person, however, was repulsive. After his convalescence, Carlos bulked up to the point that he looked sharp in thrift shop clothing. When Carlos started taking nursing classes, he proved to be the most eligible of the few men in his cohort. His cell wouldn't stop ringing. More than once, Carlos tried to add into their group some woman he'd met. If it weren't for Randall's intervention, Alan would have directed a harem of noobs.

It was only a matter of time until Carlos poisoned Alan's mind. This interloper turned Alan against the person who'd been his best friend for nearly twenty years. After that, it was no challenge to make an ally out of Lance, who'd proven a most disloyal coworker.

Randall's eyes focused on the gray fabric of his backpack. He pulled out of it a thick, brown Sharpie, which he kept there at all times. Randall imagined the pen plump with poison. He pulled off its cap and jabbed it back and forth over the intricate drawing of a knight who had lodged his sword in a gargoyle's head. The tableau stretched seamlessly across the back flap and onto the sides of the pack. Randall cursed to himself as he scribbled out the labors of four hundred and fifty-two rides home from work.

* * *

Still fuming after his unpleasant discovery outside Players, Randall saddled up his transit stallion again the next morning to find a game that better fit his evolving tastes. Dungeon Lords had fed Randall's desire to be the protagonist at the center of the story. In hopes of recapturing that feeling, he approached the gravel yard of a small Santee bungalow at the exceptionally early hour of 9:40 AM.

When he rang the doorbell, he was greeted by Erik Olafson, the host of the Gorehammer Gathering and a college history teacher whom Randall had taken a course from years ago at San Diego State. Erik briefly introduced him to the five other boys and men in attendance, then offered Randall three figurines — two muscled goat-men and a haunted oak tree carrying a flag with a Celtic crest. Following Erik's lead, Randall placed his charges on one end of a grid that stretched across a ten-foot polyethylene table. At the other end of the battlefield, opponents placed rival figurines beside a bronze banner.

After an hour of troop movement, which involved intricate positioning and repositioning, the warring parties stood somewhat closer to one another. From a distance, each took cover behind the tiny pine trees and boulders that dotted the terrain on the grid.

One opponent, a bright-eyed graduate student nicknamed "Igor," stretched a tape measure from his archer toward one of

Randall's goat-men. "Close enough for me to shoot," Igor said. He rolled a die, checked a chart, and called out a hit. More dice, and the damage was assessed. Randall adjusted the delicate counter on the goat-man's stand and placed him back behind the inadequate protection of an aspen.

Each time Randall's team advanced, another volley of arrows pushed them back. A few rounds and two hours later, Randall's battered side began a retreat.

Randall turned to Erik while sliding his oak back to the far edge of the table. Loud enough for all to hear, Randall declared, "This is bullship."

"Bull *what*?" Igor said.

"We never had a chance," Randall said.

"Just bad dice," Erik said. "We'll do better next time."

"No, the rules and the armies on the map don't work. They're ad hoc and unbalanced."

"Nobody likes a whiner," Igor said. "The game works fine."

Randall laughed. "Don't tell me you can't see it. This system doesn't frocking work. We're the Satyrs, right? And we're battling the—the what again?"

"The Hogmen," Erik said.

"And let me guess. The Hogmen are a newly released army."

"Brand new," Igor said. "Look pretty cool, you have to admit."

Randall snorted. "The Gorehammer people, they just want to move product. They don't care enough to test out these new armies against the old ones. No, they're probably so greedy they deliberately make new units more powerful. Whoever buys the Hogmen gets to beat down their friends, until they rush out to counterattack with the new Frogfolk or whatever."

"No," Erik protested, a hitch in his voice.

"There's even a name for it—power creep." With a flick of his fingers, Randall knocked over his goat-men. "I call it 'buying and dying.'"

Randall saw nods and frowns across the room. Igor shook his head, but the gesture was more uncertain than defiant.

"I've met the Gorehammer folks," Erik said. "They'd never do that. They're good people."

Randall laughed. "I'm sure your buddies are grateful for this Tupperware gathering you throw each week. Quite the field rep, you are."

Even Igor now stared at Erik.

Randall picked up his backpack, pulled his bus schedule from a side pocket, and walked out the door. The intensity of the midday sun caught him off guard. He closed his eyes for several seconds to let them readjust. With lids shut tight, he experienced what felt like a psychic flash. Endorphins exploded inside him, then spread out from his chest so fast his body shook.

The image that came with this sensation was a vision of what happened next inside Erik Olafson's house. The fleeing goatmen would find no new shepherd. The plastic bag into which they fell ten minutes later would become their sarcophagus, for the following weekend, Erik wouldn't heed their muffled bleats. He would suspend his Gatherings indefinitely and pass the evening on his girlfriend's couch watching a Bruce Campbell marathon on Syfy.

Randall knew this was his private fantasy, but he was also quite sure Erik's game wouldn't resume. Like a spiteful lich, Randall had drained its magic. His persuasive powers were as potent as ever.

With sure steps he walked to, then past, his bus stop. He strode a quarter mile to an intersection that would permit him to skip the transfer he'd taken that morning. The long trek up a two percent grade made him feel athletic. His massive body was not a prison but a citadel. It hosted a new master, a wanton destroyer of the gaming world.

Randall remembered the ruse he'd used to mask his traffic phobia. After a decade of playing Freeway Dodge, today he'd stumbled upon a new challenge—the ultimate meta-game. He'd created the game to literally end them all. He would forswear all games, excepting this grand one, which he could pursue in the guise of playing others. This new mission made his heart swell. Something was still missing, but he'd found the right path.

A bus arrived and slowed to a stop. Randall climbed aboard, flashed his pass, and walked to the back row, where no passenger would bother him.

He'd have dinner at his parents' house that evening, a promise that he'd previously intended to break. Mom and Dad would be proud if they could grasp what had just happened. He couldn't tell them. They'd never understand. But the fact remained that Randall Josiah Keller, the son of fourth-generation Seventh Day Adventists, had begun to hear, and answer, a higher calling.

* * *

Randall's cheeks were still rosy from this revelation when he opened the unlocked front door to his parents' home. They lived in half of an aluminum-sided duplex, which they'd leased ever since arriving in Spring Valley, the less affluent San Diego suburb adjoining La Mesa. Before Randall could throw his backpack on the couch, his little sister bounded up to him.

"Guess what Mom and Dad gave me for my birthday."

Randall marveled at how much Tiffany tried to look like their mother, despite the fact that his parents had adopted her from South Korea sixteen years ago, when she was but an infant. Tiffany was as short and wiry as his mom and dressed herself in the same style—no makeup or jewelry, a plain white dress, leather sandals. She clutched to her chest a blue plastic binder with the Grossmont High School logo.

"Guess!"

Tiffany hopped an inch off the floor.

"Guess, guess, guess!"

Randall offered a manic smile.

"They got you a pony?"

"First week in August, we're all flying to Korea to see my hometown!"

"Hold on. Who are 'we'?"

"All of us. They got tickets and everything for the whole family."

Randall scanned his memory and found no recollection of setting aside time at work for a vacation. Family travel meant going someplace he didn't know and doing things he didn't like. If this was meant to be a surprise, it was an ugly one. Had they already cleared this by speaking directly with Ted? Conspiring with his boss wouldn't be especially odd. Like their venerated God, they worked in strange and annoying ways.

"I dunno, sis."

Randall set his backpack on the floor and walked into the kitchen.

"What's for dinner? I can only stay a little while. Got stuff to do."

Following the sound of the conversation, Randall's parents came from the hall and joined him in the kitchen. Both were nearly seventy, having been blessed with Randall just before they would have accepted the fate of being childless. His mother had lightly brushed silver hair and a wide smile that sent wrinkles up to her eyes. She wore the same clothes she'd probably put on for church that morning, a cream dress with beige flowers, accented by modest low-heeled shoes. His father was a Norman Rockwell grandfather, lanky and cheerful with wisps of white hair on his temples, matching shirt, tan slacks, brown loafers.

"She told you the news?" his mother asked.

"Right."

Randall sat down on the wooden bench in their cramped breakfast nook. When he was little, he used to crawl under the table and pretend he was hiding in a bear cave. The last time he remembered fitting into that space was the long week in junior high when Alan and the rest of their classmates got chickenpox. It spooked Randall's parents, as their son had a notoriously weak constitution. He'd alternated from bronchitis to pneumonia through much of his childhood. Even if he'd been a hearty child, Randall would have been confined at home for religious reasons. His parents' pastor preached that vaccination—or, rather, "preemptive infection"—was a violation of their son's pure body. Thus, Randall was held out of school for nine days. He spent much of that time under the breakfast nook, reading the *Dungeon Lords Spellcraft Compendium*, a book he dared not let his parents see.

By the following year, Randall had become rebellious enough to tell his parents he'd begun role playing after school. Their church made its view on the matter plain in the pamphlet, *Adolescence and the Occult*. When the time came to announce his heresy, Randall told his father that instead of becoming a private first-class in their Christian Soldier Academy, he'd instead chosen to be a first-level ranger/thief.

"Aren't you excited about Korea?" his father asked.

His mother gave Tiffany a squeeze.

"We know you love your brother very much. We made sure he could get two weeks off from work."

"We're going as a whole family," his father said.

Randall often felt double-teamed by his parents, with one elaborating on a criticism or commandment the other started. Disappointing them had become routine. It felt comfortable, like sliding one's feet into a familiar pair of slippers.

Still, he considered the amusement he might derive from steering Tiffany around a foreign country. She would follow her only sibling anywhere he led her. Perhaps he could incorporate her into his larger game. Maybe she could unwittingly break up Korean children's games. Then he remembered they'd be traveling *as a family*.

He fingered the breakfast table's salt and pepper shakers, two brown crucifixes in fine china. The pepper had Jesus on it. Randall had always suspected his parents, unlike God, were unable to forgive their son's sins. Instead, they asked for a do-over and bought an Asian daughter.

"Can't go," Randall said.

Three pained faces stared back at him.

"I'm going to Middle Mirth."

He meant it as a lie, a gesture at a reason for declining the invitation. Once he said it, though, he realized he *would* attend the convention. Where better to play his new role than at the most infantile festival of mundane games? Better still, the event might be his best chance to hit the target otherwise beyond his reach. Alan, Carlos, and Lance would surely be there with their girlie gamers. Since he was now dead to his erstwhile companions, they wouldn't even notice him. He'd wait in the shadows, then strike. It would take fewer than five minutes to point out the foolishness of their game, just as he'd done at the Unspeakable Horrors club and the Gorehammer Gathering.

"No," Randall's mother said, "you are not going to that awful thing again. You are coming with us to see your little sister's homeland, and—"

"It's very important to Tiffany that you go," his father finished. "Your friends will play their games whether you go there or not."

Randall cringed at the truth in his father's words. Alan's group might prove impervious to his magic. They knew the messenger too well. They'd ignore him. Randall exhaled all the aspiration that had built up inside. He felt empty.

Tiffany tossed her hair to the side and frowned. He'd never meant to become important to her, but it had happened. A brief sense of shame passed through him. Randall intuited that he should say something reassuring, however false.

"I'll think about it."

Tiffany set her binder on the table and squeezed into the nook beside him. She reached around her brother with spaghetti arms and tried to hook her left pinkie onto her right. Unless she hugged his neck, it was impossible, but she liked to try. From when she first learned to speak, she'd called him "Big Boy." It was the name of his favorite restaurant, and he bore no small resemblance to the smiling statue in front of it.

Randall puzzled through Tiffany's cloying sweet-girl act. For all the coolness he showed, his sister seemed determined to honor and adore him as much as she did their parents. Perhaps her performance was not for him but for a mother and father who were desperate to have raised at least one Christian child. And why shouldn't she make a show of gratitude toward her saviors? She fulfilled their wishes, even if it required practicing a religion that had never been explained convincingly. His kid sister had invented her own kind of game, which she played with conviction. It required fawning over a wayward brother.

"Will you really think about it, Randy?"

Tiffany pressed her head into Randall's shoulder.

Her school binder caught his eye. He sensed an idea forming. Alan's group could shield itself from a direct assault, but that merely forced him to raise the level of his game. To reach into their world, he'd have to think like a grand master. He'd plan a sequence of moves to lay an unseen trap, far ahead of them.

"Randy," his sister-pawn said, "please do come with us. I love you so much, Big Boy."

He fixated on the Grossmont High School logo on Tiffany's binder. It revealed his first move.

"You have a class with Lance Langdon's sister?"

"What?"

Tiffany sniffed and stood up.

"Brittany? Or Brynnen?"

"Brianna," Tiffany corrected. "We're friends."

Randall again felt a stab of guilt at the prospect of turning

Tiffany against one of her peers. But Tiffany was a popular girl. She had dozens of "super-best-friends." She could afford to sacrifice a mere "friend" on her brother's behalf. Recalling high schoolers' appetite for cruelty, the task he required would probably raise her status.

"About this Brianna," Randall said. "Stop hanging out with her. She's a total loser."

"What? Because she's doing summer-session Honor Band? Randy, *I'm* in summer Band."

"No, it's not that, though I keep telling you, band's just one floor above the subbasement in the high school hierarchy."

Their parents moved about the kitchen and ignored the conversation. They found it excruciating to speak with their son and had reached their limit.

"For realzies?" Tiffany's eye twitched. "You're not, like, teasing me, are you?"

Tiffany attended the same schools Randall had. Many of her teachers remembered him fondly. Her computer science teacher insisted Randall was something of a prodigy. When the school had upgraded its PCs, Randall taught the faculty how to use them. After school, they paid him under the table to create small applications, such as grading macros.

Myths such as these gave Randall credibility. Even as Tiffany came to rely more on her own instincts, she still trusted her Big Boy. Tiffany invariably followed Randall's admonitions, usually to greater mutual benefit than expected. Though Randall himself had never craved popularity, Boldheart had amassed an army of followers. In the real world, Randall understood social rules more than he cared to follow them.

"Tiff, band is a bad bet. But that's not the issue."

Randall remembered the awful scene he'd witnessed from the Number 7 bus. He saw Alan coming out of that game store with his entourage. The two girls beside him, rapt with fascination. Hanging on his every word.

"That Brianna chick?" Randall said. "She's a total loser, just like her brother. They're both hanging out at a game store downtown, playing Dungeon Lords."

Tiffany looked confused.

"But you play that, don't you?"

"Not anymore." Randall swallowed. "That game's gone soft. I jumped out of that scene, and you should steer clear of it. If you hang out with anyone who plays it, kids'll start making fun of you. Trust me."

Tiffany chewed the cuticle on her thumb, a giveaway Randall recognized. She was preparing to agree, out of loyalty, to something she didn't fully understand.

"Like, what should I do?"

"Don't let her drag you down."

"Got it."

"No, I mean it."

Randall grabbed his sister's hand.

"There's room enough at the bottom even for you. If you don't ditch her hard, she'll take you down with her."

"What are you suggesting, exactly?"

Randall remembered the first day of high school phys ed. Students sat on hot blacktop behind the gym. Some athletic Adonis was choosing the next player for his basketball team. Randall had no practical skill at the sport, but the boy picked him early based on size alone. Eventually, only two classmates remained unchosen. The boy who'd taken Randall pointed to Alan and said, "You." Alan leapt up and shouted, "Victory shall be ours, my Lord!"

The humiliating laughter that ensued rang anew in Randall's ears. He locked onto his sister's eyes and gave his instructions.

"Drag her down first."

The Fourth of July Weekend

SANTANA

"Look!" Angelou said with delight. "The tower lies just ahead."

Santana shaded his eyes from the afternoon suns. A high tower's smooth walls reflected almost no light. Instead, its stones mimicked the hills and sky that lay behind it, a concealment that might have succeeded had the prime minister's scouts not briefed them on this very fact. Santana smiled at seeing what was surely the Tower of Devotus, home to the gnome illusionist who could lead them to the Fairie Realm.

Wearied by their weeklong trek from Mythopolis, Lancelot and Hermione stopped to rest. Lightening the mood, Santana needled his newest—and most earnest—companion.

"As you shall learn, Hermione, brave adventurers spend most of their lives looking for people or hunting for things. It feels as though every time I leave Mythopolis, I am on the hunt for enchanted books or sacred gemstones."

Angelou and Hermione looked at each other in puzzlement, but Lancelot nodded.

"Or perhaps a holy scepter," Santana continued. "Or an amulet, which was broken into five pieces and hidden in the far corners of the Mythos. Each shard is cursed, but when combined—"

"Ahem," Angelou said, hands on hips.

Santana felt Lancelot's touch on his shoulder. "For this mission, we need a sorcerer, not a cynic."

It pained Santana to admit it, but the priest was right. He was grateful for Lancelot's companionship, which might steady him now that Boldheart was gone. Losing the brash swordsman left a hole in Santana's heart, not for the first time.

Santana's parents had sent their only child to academy that

he might retrace his mother's footsteps and become a renowned wizard. On the first day of college, the headmaster pulled him out of class and relayed terrible news. His parents had died trying to protect Mythopolis from a marauding dragon. Numb beyond reason, Santana did not shed a tear. He gathered his few belongings, abandoned wizardry, and used his inheritance to apprentice with a sorcerer who could teach him how to channel the same fires that consumed his parents.

With that wish now fulfilled, Santana found himself unsure of its purpose. Perhaps he had sought and found new family through Boldheart, who became the sibling the sorcerer never had. Likewise, the priest at his side might stand in for a younger brother. The bard and barbarian who traveled with them, however, were strangers—nothing more than useful mercenaries. Santana's heart felt empty. He tried to refocus on their quest. Its success might require more from him than he had to offer.

While the others rested, Angelou showed no signs of fatigue. She sprinted ahead, Lupita loping by her side. The pair returned just as swiftly, and Angelou reported that the tower's Ent-wood door was shut tight.

Lupita barked the same news at Santana, but with greater impatience. The wolf paced anxiously in front of the sorcerer and bobbed her head to hurry him along.

"Devotus was said to prize his solitude," Santana said as he stood up. "He welcomes no visitors, friendly or otherwise. I suspect some kind of transmutation secures that door. To open it, I'll need—"

Lupita interrupted with a nudge to his hip. In her teeth she held the end of a brass key.

"Just so we are clear, Lupita, I felt you take that from me."

Santana took the item from her mouth and walked within twenty meters of the tower. He held its round handle over his left eye and focused carefully. When he said *"Abre,"* the door shattered into fragments.

Angelou ran through the debris and into the tower's entryway. "This is it," she said. "I can feel—"

Before she could finish her announcement, a dark shape wide and tall as a nomad's yurt dropped down from inside the tower and knocked her flat. The hairy spider had a polished black body and legs the size of trees. It reared up its egg-shaped head and stuck javelin fangs into Angelou's back.

Within seconds, her companions had surrounded the creature. A flurry of metal and wood beat the eight-legged beast back against a wall. One final swing of Lancelot's mace ended the giant spider's malevolent career, which had foreshortened the journeys of countless trespassers.

Hermione crouched over Angelou, whose body lay in a fetal curl. The barbarian's skin had begun to dry and harden, but Hermione found a pulse.

"An inky death stirs in her. My spells can impede the poison's progress through her system."

Hermione pulled Angelou's dreadlocks away from her face and sang into her ear, "We don't want to see a frown. We just need to slow you down."

Angelou's body relaxed. Lupita licked her face, but Angelou did not stir. The wolf pushed her snout under Angelou's hand and whimpered when no fingers scratched a reply.

"She will live," Hermione said, "provided she gets help by nightfall."

Lancelot shook his head. "I regret I did not pray for a stronger healing spell last night. I had not anticipated—"

"Shush," Hermione said. "Regrets will not revive her." Using Angelou's trident, Lancelot's shield, and long strands of broken web, Hermione made a litter.

"The gnome we seek should have an antidote," Lancelot said and gestured toward the stairway that wound up the inside of the tower's wall. "Let us proceed."

Santana nodded. He noticed that the stone floor featured the name "Devotus" carved in Draconic, the language of dragons that carried powerful magic. Santana had studied the language and could read it, but his efforts at writing had been painful lessons. Odd that the home of one who could write out his name in that combustible script had a front door that gave way so easily. This Devotus was a man of uneven talents.

While stepping ahead of the others, Santana pulled from his sleeve a small piece of flint. He snapped his fingers across it and intoned, "*Luz del sol.*" A glowing orb appeared above his head and illuminated the entire entryway. The ball of light bobbed above Santana as he ascended the stairs, Lupita bounding after him.

What followed was confusion, then chaos.

In retrospect, Santana realized he had fallen for a parlor trick, a hall of mirrors that made him see one door when there were, in fact, two. As a result, he and Lupita went one way, his companions another. At the end of the long corridor he had chosen, he turned to find three dozen goblin spears pointing up at him. Jabs and thrusts nearly overtook him and his wolf, as they retreated at a full run. When they reached the door they had first entered, Santana slammed it shut, barred it with a spell, and marked it for good measure.

Once he saw through the illusion and found the second doorway, he entered it only to discover another calamity. In a musty chamber stood a canopied bed. A pool of blue water shifted inside its frame and spilled to the floor as a pearlescent woman drew Lancelot down beside her.

"We are—spellbound," Hermione said softly, as if lost in a dream.

Santana heard the soothing sounds that caused Hermione to waver. A hypnotic humming from the water-woman pushed his mind into the same delusion that held fast his companions. He now sat beside them in a narrow skiff, which Lancelot rowed across a sapphire lake. Wisps of clouds floated above them.

Through the ripples on the water, rainbow colored fish swam and jumped. As Lancelot pulled the oars back, a silvery eel rose up from the water and twisted itself around his arm. It spiraled gracefully toward Lancelot's neck, then raised its head and gave him a sharp peck.

When Lancelot did not cry out in pain, the dissonance gave Santana's mind an opening. He pulled himself back out of the dream.

Hermione did likewise. She unsheathed her scimitar, which shimmered while she quickly recited a couplet, "We don't die, fencing our foes! Bleed them dry, head to their toes!"

A massive blue eel had in its beak a piece of Lancelot's flesh. Hermione sliced across the eel's body, causing it to screech. It morphed back into the shape of a woman, lifted Lancelot's helmet over his head, and kissed him deeply. The priest recoiled and pushed at the creature, which became a pillar of water that fell back into the pool.

"Damn this madness!" Lancelot roared and groped about madly. "I am blinded!"

Hermione dropped her scimitar and grabbed Lancelot's leg as he tumbled into the bed of water, which now flooded onto the floor.

"Release me!" Lancelot twisted himself back out of the bed, reached for his mace, and buckled Hermione's knee with a quick swing. "You will find only wrath in these hands!"

Hermione cried out in pain and tried to back away, but Lancelot held her fast and continued to bludgeon her. She grabbed his flailing hand with her own and pleaded with him.

"You'll smash my lute."

Lancelot twisted away and gripped his mace with both hands.

"What trickery is this, water witch?"

Lancelot swung his head about the room.

"Hermione?"

Backing into a bedpost, Lancelot slipped on the floor and

crashed to the ground.

"She robbed me of my eyes!"

Santana gave Lancelot a bracing slap across the cheek.

"Quiet yourself. We can afford no more mishaps."

Hermione offered her arm, and Lancelot accepted it. Lupita worked her shoulders back-and-forth like a lumberjack preparing to lift a trunk. She clamped her jaws onto the handle of Angelou's trident, then dragged the litter toward Santana.

"Half blind, poisoned, and disorganized," Santana said, "we have little chance to make it out alive, unless our host wishes it." He looked up toward the ceiling. "You have made your point, Devotus. We are duly chastened."

Santana took the litter from his wolf and dragged it toward an exit at the other end of the bedchamber. He stepped into a hallway and motioned for the others to follow.

"Dammit," Santana said. "Not again."

The goblin spearmen had found him. All warts and wrinkles, the beasts were not three feet high from boots to ears. But there were dozens of them, all charging toward him.

A sweet strumming filled the room. Hermione sang a lullaby, breathing softly between each verse.

The sleep, it gently came
Sweet song of peace it sang
A voice now hums my name
And so I dream again

Lupita leapt toward the attackers, but they fell before she could strike. Tiny shields, armor, and spears clattered to the floor. The room was still but for the jagged snores and yips of slumber. Lupita landed on soft paws and wove deftly through the pile. As fierce as she was in battle, the wolf had no hunger for murder.

"Goblins," Hermione said with a smile. "I had to save you from goblins."

"We shall speak of this to no one," Santana said.

"No one," Lancelot agreed.

Moving more cautiously up the stairway, Santana led his companions into a circular room at the top of the tower. High shelves of books and scrolls were topped by a glass ceiling that let in the last orange light of the evening. Hermione collapsed onto one of the faded cushions that lay about the floor. Lancelot felt his way onto another. Lupita released Angelou's litter and weaved between Santana's legs. He reached out to offer a pet, but she had collapsed already onto a pillow beside Angelou's limp body.

Only Santana stood. He shook his staff with his wrist. It went bolt-straight, and he pointed it along his line of sight.

"Surely you know I can see you," Santana said.

A high, disembodied voice lilted across the room. "Oh, then what am I wearing?"

Hermione scrambled to her feet and pulled out her blade. Lancelot squirmed in the cushions and rolled over Angelou's unconscious body. He managed only to find his silver unicorn, which he held aloft.

"A predictable gown and an embarrassing pointed hat," Santana replied.

Hidden by a conventional invisibility spell, the light in the room bent around the figure. When Santana concentrated, he could see the outline of a small man. His face was as wrinkled as a raisin, his skin freckled with age spots. The illusionist's muslin robe touched the floor and nearly covered slippers small enough for a child's feet.

"You can set down your scimitar, Hermione. We found our impish host."

"An outrage!" the man said. As his cloaking spell dissipated, he scrunched his face even tighter. "I am a *gnome*. Respect, please."

"Devotus?" Hermione said.

"I know why you came. Word travels fast when one plants magic ears in the Roundhouse garden."

Santana gestured toward the room's circular walls.

"The Mythopoles believe you a great scholar with exceptional knowledge of the fairies. Your library does, indeed, hold many texts, but their crisp bindings suggest most have gone unread."

Devotus sat in the middle of the floor and folded his hands across his lap.

"I chose the wrong calling," he said, "but what I lack in intellect I make up for in lived experience. Only a pinch of this I dare share with you, lest your minds burst and bleed out through your noses."

"Tell us what you can," Santana said with a sigh. "But first, our companions have need of assistance."

"Indeed, they do," the gnome said with a grunt.

He walked to a low shelf and pulled out a sheaf of papers.

"Just look at you all. Smirking sorcerer. Self-important musician. And two fallen comrades who—in their current state—could not parry the sword thrusts of a drunken kobold."

Devotus thumbed his bound pages, then pointed at Lancelot and read aloud in a squeaky gnomish chant. The words written on the parchment disappeared.

Lancelot stood up and blinked.

"I can see!"

While walking toward Angelou, Devotus again flipped through his papers. He read quickly and raised pinched fingers above Angelou's chest. She shuddered, then scrambled to her knees. She scratched at her body in desperation, as if still stuck in a web. When her body moved freely, she slowed her frenzied movements and relaxed.

Devotus reseated himself at the center of the room, his legs folded like a yogi. "I have thought for days about the information you seek and whether I should offer it. The evil force that makes even Prime Minister Lesilla tremble? It affects me likewise. I share her fear that our enemy arose from Lord Cynoc's tomb."

"I know nothing of this tomb," Angelou said.

Santana and Lancelot exchanged grimaces, but neither chose to speak.

"It held an evil soul," Devotus said. "Cynoc had once been a talented alchemist who blended the charisma of a bard with a monk's insight and a wizard's intellect. Lacking political acumen, he rose only to the title of lord, a status he resented. Unsatisfied with ruling a mere fiefdom, he turned his talents to war. With little steel in his armory, he forged weapons that affected not the flesh but the mind. Until the day he was subdued and his spells broken, his followers had been growing exponentially."

Hermione frowned.

"Is this new malevolence—this Lifeless Knight—Cynoc himself?"

"Perhaps. Word has spread that this enemy recruits into his army from among the very people he slaughters."

"I suppose you also know," Hermione said, "that we have been sent to find a magic that can end this, one that lies in a vault within the Fairie Realm?"

"The survival of the Provinces, and the Mythos itself, requires that which you seek. But it is an elusive object. You follow a difficult path, and I am certain neither you nor Prime Minister Lesilla understand the true purpose of your movements."

Hermione huffed with impatience.

"Show us our course and we will away at once."

Devotus raised his hand, as if to beg forbearance.

"I will provide a map, of course. I ask that you permit me also to offer something less concrete but more useful."

"Does this concern the Magic Circle?" Santana said.

Devotus nodded.

"Each of us possesses a power within us that we can hone and channel into ever-stronger fists, spells, and prayers. When wielded well, this brings good fortune. A far greater power, however, lies beyond and between us. The fairies and I both know it well and would have you use it." Devotus eyed each member of the group. "I wish I could say more, but this power cannot be granted or gained directly. If you look closely, you will never find it."

Hermione's lute sang softly to itself as she turned it over in her hands.

"If the fairies possessed a magic that could stop this blight, why did not they, the creators of all the world's enchanted vessels, grant that power to the Pale Elves before they were overtaken?"

"The might of which I speak comes not from forge or alchemy. The power you must gather comes from no living being—be they human, gnome, elf, or even fairie. It has no tangible origin. Yet it can block the swiftest blows and deliver ones more terrible still. With it, you may prevail. Without it, you—no, we—are doomed."

ALAN

Devon stood up and took a graceful bow, first to Alan, then to his fellow players, then to the Players clientele. Alan began a slow clap in his honor.

Behind the cash register, Maya caught the cue to rejoin the group. A proud smile stretched her cheeks.

Brianna and Lance clapped along as the tempo quickened. The applause grew absurdly loud as Carlos joined in, along with every remaining customer in the store.

"For such a little cameo," Carlos said, "it's quite an ovation."

Devon straightened the star-spangled tie inside his navy suit jacket. "A showman never begrudges approbation." He nodded toward Maya. "And this once-more-retired gnome gives thanks to his dutiful daughter for the watching of the till."

"No worries," Maya said. "Angelou was basically girlfriend-in-a-coma thanks to my boneheaded play."

A man with a sandy mullet, who Alan estimated was mid-forties, tapped Devon's shoulder. "Dude, is this your game?"

"No," Devon replied, "I was just passing through."

"I'm lookin' for a Dungeon Lords group, and word is this one's pretty sweet." The man looked to Alan, seated behind his cardboard screen. "What module you guys runnin'?"

"It's a custom scenario. But I'm sorry, we aren't taking on anyone else."

"If I may," Devon said to mullet man. "In honor of Independence Day, I am hosting a gaming open house tonight. You should visit. I shall keep the lights on as late as the last game goes. The signup sheet stands ready, by the register."

The man nodded and turned away, his mullet waving goodbye.

Lance adjusted his brown monk's robe and turned toward Devon. "Devotus' message was kind of cryptic. What was he talking about?"

"I might have a sense of it," Devon said, "but you know I cannot say anything more."

"Ah, yes," Carlos said. "The tedious laws of the game director. Keeping us all in the dark. No offense, Lance."

"None taken," Lance said. "Even Lancelot lost his eyes for a moment when—"

"That wasn't my fault!" Alan blurted.

Even he could hear the defensiveness in his unprompted reply. He flashed back to Boldheart's death and felt a sting in his chest.

Lance nodded.

"We all heard my die say 'three.' I just failed another saving throw, like Maya did against the spider. The dice never lie."

From the cell phone lying beside Alan came the voice of Leonard Nimoy. He sang "The Ballad of Bilbo Baggins," a ringtone Alan had set up for himself and Carlos. Before Spock got to the bit about "fuzzy wooly toes," Alan flipped his phone open. He whispered to the group—"It's Mom" —and half-listened to his mother's voice.

"You played a blinded priest expertly today," Devon said to Lance. "I am always impressed when someone portrays a character as though lacking knowledge the player actually possesses. You performed Lancelot well within your conception of who he is. That merits bonus experience points under Third Edition rules. Is that not so, Alan?"

"Sure," Alan said without looking up.

"I still don't get it," Carlos said. "Who can judge whether a character is within conception?"

"The game director judges," Lance said. "Herr Director runs the game, makes the calls."

"But does anybody really fit a 'conception'? I reinvent myself all the time. Am I out of character if I'm not the same person I was five or ten years ago?"

Alan looked up at Carlos but said nothing.

"Depends on how quickly you change," Maya said. "In your case, I can't picture you as anything but a self-assured, lawless rogue."

Brianna giggled. "I thought he was a sorcerer, not a rogue." Maya ignored the joke.

"A story needs characters that the reader, or the players in our case, recognize as distinct and interesting. Santana has his own history, goals, lifestyle. In a crisis, he wouldn't make the same choices as Lancelot. Santana's conception is a stylish, cunning adventurer, whereas Lancelot's a simple priest looking to please his god."

"And our young cleric dressed the part today." Devon put his hands on Lance's shoulders. "Is that a friar's frock you have on?"

Lance fidgeted with the rope belt that tied his brown robe tight.

Brianna reached across the table to straighten Lance's hood.

"He got that last year as kind of a triple-threat. He's worn it for Dungeon Lords, obviously, plus once for Halloween, and today he's trying it out for the—"

"Dang, the Padres game." Maya glanced at her watch. "It starts in an hour!"

"Does it matter if we're late?" Brianna said. "I've never been to one. Aren't we really going for the fireworks afterward?"

Maya shook her head. "We gotta haul butt."

While the group gathered its belongings, Devon gave his daughter a quick peck, then slipped back to the front of the store.

Lance zipped up his brown backpack. He turned toward Alan's end of the table. "Hello?"

Alan said a quick, "Gotta go," into his phone and looked up. "I can't go with you tonight."

"What?" Carlos said. "You know Adelita dropped me off today. You said you'd chauffeur us in King Turd."

"Can't."

As Alan chose to remember it, he'd only agreed to drive as a goodwill gesture. He didn't care for baseball—or for sports generally. Even among fellow nerds, he had the humblest of physical gifts. The ill-conceived fighting festival in Balboa Park had reminded him of this unhappy fact. Hence, he found no joy in watching athletes run and strut.

On top of that, Alan preferred to stay out of stadiums and other poured-concrete structures. He viewed all such buildings as cleverly-disguised traps. At work, he'd read of many fatalities resulting from the interplay of earthquakes and poor engineering.

"You're chickening out, aren't you?" Carlos said. "It's just a baseball game, Alan. Nothing to be afraid of. You've got to grow some *cojones*, amigo."

"That was Mom on the phone. She needs me to come home tonight."

"For what?"

"I'm not sure, but I can't go with you."

Technically, Alan knew he wasn't needed at home, but when Karen had called, she was upset. He couldn't discern what troubled her. Then again, she didn't have his full attention. She told him not to worry and to see the ballgame with his friends. But he did worry. He would need to check in with her more often, even if in this case, it was more of an excuse.

"I think she's feeling lonely," Alan said.

"Seriously?"

"Seriously. Take the trolley."

CARLOS

The red trolley car pulled away from the La Mesa Boulevard station and headed toward downtown San Diego. With tan and white interior, vinyl seats and faux wood paneling, the trolley was equal parts functional commuter train and quaint cable-car.

Carlos sat beside Maya on the bench opposite Lance and Brianna. After passing the first mile quietly, Carlos swung his foot across the aisle to give Lance a gentle kick.

"You look *ridiculoso* in that outfit, padre. Like the mascot of some used car dealer."

Lance rapped his cane on a metal pole. "You talkin' to *me*?"

"I have to admit," Maya said, "now that we're out among the people, you do look like Saint Dorkus of Nerdia."

"Maybe so, but it's all in how you wear it." Lance pointed his cane upward until it touched the ceiling. With a sharp downward jerk of his wrist, he telescoped it into his hand. It closed with a loud snap. More than a few passengers jumped. One eyed Lance warily, then moved to the opposite end of the car.

The trolley pulled into the Lemon Grove Depot, and a dozen passengers climbed aboard. Half sported Padres caps, and a few showed their holiday spirit with American flag t-shirts. The last to get on was a Transit Authority officer, who wore a black, short-sleeved uniform resembling that of the city police.

"Hold up your tickets please." The officer moved to the far end of the cab and began a visual inspection of the passengers' paper slips.

Carlos patted his pockets and tried to think. "*Mierda.*"

"What?" Maya said.

"No ticket."

Brianna bit her lip and leaned forward.

"You sure?"

"Maybe an old one."

Carlos dug deeper into his pants. He couldn't afford the fine, which was severe. Maybe the officer would cut him a break. Sensing his companions' vicarious anxiety, he tried to shrug it off.

"Hey, sometimes you just play the odds in life. How often do they check tickets on these things? I just failed an easy saving throw—that's all."

The transit officer was just two seats away. Lance reached across the aisle. Between two fingers, he held a stiff white slip of paper. He raised his chin at Carlos.

"Who's your hero?"

Carlos snatched the ticket and held it aloft, never taking his eyes off Lance's sunglasses.

"Nice save," Maya whispered.

The officer took Carlos' ticket and handed it back to him. She did the same for Maya and Brianna. She smirked at Lance and said, more loudly than necessary, "Got a ticket in those robes, padre?"

Lance gave her a Stevie Wonder head bob.

"No, ma'am. Nothing under this at all."

"Going to the Padres game in that getup?"

"Yup."

"Not without a ticket you aren't."

The entire car erupted in laughter, as if every passenger had wanted to say something at Lance's expense. Only the transit cop had the nerve to take a shot.

Carlos cleared his throat.

"He gave me his ticket, ma'am."

Before the officer could turn around, Lance touched her arm with two plastic cards, a Monthly Senior/Disabled pass beside a Disabled ID card.

"Oh, I'm sorry, sir." Her cheeks flushed. "Enjoy the game."

Through the shifting bodies of the standing passengers, Brianna squeezed in closer to her brother. She leaned into Lance's shoulder. She spoke softly, but Carlos could hear.

"You don't need tickets, Lance. You bought one for him at the station, didn't you?"

"Nah." Lance laughed. "Bought it for Alan, as a token of appreciation, before I remembered he's not with us."

Across the crowded aisle, Carlos caught Brianna's gaze. She looked away. Lance adjusted himself and put his hand on Brianna's. She squeezed his fingers, then let go.

The car continued to roll down the tracks toward downtown San Diego. It passed a tableau of razor wire, graying industrial buildings, and vacant lots. Carlos' thoughts had gone far away — back to his childhood home in San Ysidro, which lay between their trolley route and the Mexican border. Each weekday, his parents had driven him to a private school in National City. They got part-time janitorial work together at Subaru and GM dealerships scattered along the Mile of Cars, being part of the Chicano labor wave reoccupying the territory once known by the Spanish land grant name, El Rancho de la Nación.

Their shift schedule often required Carlos to stay after school, and he found ways to occupy the hours. When he started tenth grade, he joined the Grupo de Aztlán until he realized it was a political organization, not a social club. He competed in high and long jumps, but that was just to spend more time around girls in running shorts. When the nickname "Jumping Bean" stuck, he quit track and field. He tried the chess club, but he was a late-blooming wood pusher and never rose high enough to join the tournament team.

Some days, Carlos had three hours on his hands before either parent could pick him up. He often did homework at the McDonald's because nobody would bother him in its Playland Park enclosure. He also chose the location as an act of rebellion.

His parents had forbidden him to cross under the Golden Arches since the last time they ate there together, when he was still a toddler. That day, his parents had taken him for a late lunch. His father had begun to unwrap Carlos' cheeseburger when people started shouting in English about something on KOGO news radio. In a panic, customers and employees alike ran out of the restaurant. Carlos' parents couldn't understand the commotion, but they followed the stampede when Carlos approximately translated the news.

"*Un hombre con una pistola mató a Ronald McDonald.*"

Two miles from where they sat, a recently terminated security guard had taken his time firing and reloading a semi-automatic Uzi, a 12-gauge Winchester shotgun, and a 9 millimeter Browning Hi-Power handgun. Twenty-one patrons and employees left the Earth at his hands, most of them first-and second-generation immigrants.

Carlos' parents never returned to McDonald's because his mother swore the chain bore a curse. Both of Carlos' parents were born in the Yucatán, and their spiritual convictions reflected the region's syncretism between Mayan traditions and Spanish Catholicism. Applying that belief system to their present circumstances without the aid of a priest, Carlos' mother reasoned that the Kroc family had purchased land for its restaurants on the sites of old Spanish missions and haciendas, nearly all of which treated natives like slaves under their *encomienda* labor system. Golden arches had become a gateway to the afterlife for anyone with an ounce of Spanish blood.

The trolley rattled over a loosely-coupled stretch of track. Carlos idly traced the scar on the back of his neck, which felt as hot as a fever. Wanting to touch something cooler, he pulled his Superbarrio figurine from his pocket and rubbed its balding head. He closed his eyes and remembered the fear he'd known as a child, warned by his mother of how evil spirits lingered all around us and settled in the dust. His mother stood behind him. She held his little hands in hers to show how a broom could sweep away *malignos*—the bad spirits born from untimely deaths. Carlos breathed the stale trolley air and sniffed for burnt cumin or chili powder.

The ruminations in Carlos' mind shifted to Alan's mother. He tried to remember what Alan said about her. Something like, "She needs me." Probably just an excuse to beg off on the baseball game.

What if something really was wrong with Karen? Alan probably hadn't noticed the pattern—how Karen would start to withdraw each July. She could become as melancholy as Alan was vacant. The past would creep up and tug at her like an impatient spirit. Was Alan finally beginning to sense it, after years of emotional hibernation? Maybe this would be the year Alan would accompany Karen at the cemetery and sweep those *malignos* out the door.

Carlos' ringtone fired. Before he could jam a hand into his jacket pocket, Leonard Nimoy half-sang about a brave little hobbit. Maya cocked her head. Carlos made eye contact neither with her nor the passengers who had shifted their curiosity away from the monk and toward the dork with the Middle Earthen phone.

A text message from Alan: "Whats your problem? You were an ass at DL. Making fun of questing. If u dont take the game seriously, nobody will. Help me out. OK?"

Carlos shut his phone and felt his chest grow hot. For the first time he could remember, he envied Randall, of all people. Randall had severed his ties to a time-consuming game that governed too many hours of one's life. He'd just walked away, which left him whole weekends to do who-knew-what. Thanks to Alan, present circumstances had Carlos chaperoning a field trip to the ballpark.

Careful of the standing passengers, Brianna leaned across the aisle. She spoke in a voice loud enough for Carlos to hear without waking Lance, whose hood covered his slumped head.

"Do you ever ride the trolley to Tijuana?"

"What?"

Carlos narrowed his eyes.

"Do you ever ride the Blue Line to Mexico?"

"The trolley didn't exist when I was a kid."

Brianna looked at Maya and laughed.

"I mean, do you ride the trolley to Mexico *now*?"

Carlos sat up straight.

"What? You think I live in Mexico? Jesus, *gringa*, haven't you noticed that most of the Chicanos who work in your city also live here? Got their own homes and everything."

"Carlos, no, I was just—"

Brianna's cheeks became a mottled pink.

Maya put a hand on Carlos' thigh, but she hesitated to speak.

"No," Carlos said. "I don't ride the Blue Line. I drive my own car. You can ride in it sometime, but I'd have to buy you a child's seat."

Brianna gasped. Carlos sneered with satisfaction until he saw Maya's scowl.

"Hey, there, Brianna," Carlos said more softly. "I didn't mean to, I just—I never go south of Chula Vista. Not even to San Ysidro." He tried to catch Brianna's eye, but she'd turned away.

Carlos felt ashamed twice over. He hadn't meant to snap at Lance's little sister. He felt guilty about the fact that he avoided Mexico. He tried not to look back for many reasons, but that meant leaving behind a receding memory of his parents. He never wished to visit the narco-metropolis of Tijuana, but he also felt detached from his parents' ancestral homeland.

Maya sighed.

"Where do you—"

She closed her lips and shook her head at Carlos.

The conversation had gotten away from him. He'd probably come across as a jerk. His robed sidekick could have vouched for his generosity as a driver and friend, but Lance slumbered blissfully, his body swaying with the motion of the trolley.

BRIANNA

Brianna couldn't shake the feeling that she'd been stung by a wasp. What had she said that made Carlos so angry? She thought back to the week before, when she'd asked Maya about her flat hair. Grossmont's multicultural assemblies had introduced her to jazz and Tejano music, but those lessons offered no practical guidance on forging actual friendships.

These early miscues felt costly. Carlos and Maya might give a high school kid a couple free passes, but how many had she already used up? Ever the perfectionist, Brianna tortured herself by scanning her memory for other cross-cultural gaffes. She fixated on the moment when she'd accepted—without hesitation—Alan's suggestion that Hermione hail from the "race" called *Pale* Elves. Was that unconscious racism on her part? Or was an elf simply an elf?

Hanging out with the Honor Band at Grossmont was easier than measuring up to Lance's friends. Brianna could keep her head down and follow the lead of her best friend Tiffany, who had so much natural charisma that the band had anointed her its arbiter of what was cool. Tiff never embarrassed Brianna or anyone if they asked an awkward question about her Korean heritage. She made it easy for everyone to get along and kept the band in synch.

The trolley lurched. Brianna saw no smiles on her companions' faces. She wanted so desperately to undo whatever damage she'd done. Making a connection with these complicated sorts required new skills. She'd felt a quiver of excitement when Alan promised that Hermione would "level up" quickly. Perhaps she wanted the same for herself.

When the sign for "Park & Market" came into view, Carlos, Brianna, and Maya stood and squeezed out of the car. Still lost in her thoughts, Brianna looked at the early evening sky, a baby blue canvas without a hint of clouds.

She wished Lance could see it.

Lance clicked his cane down a step, then another. As he hopped onto the sidewalk, his robes fluttered to expose white tube socks and brown sandals. Disembarking passengers had stepped aside for Lance, but it wasn't clear whether they meant to make way for a blind man or steer clear of a freak.

By the time Brianna was old enough to understand such things, her brother had lost the last of his functional sight to severe cortical blindness, a cruel neurological condition whereby his eyes operated normally but his occipital cortex could not process the visual information it received. Brianna's parents explained that Lance was completely blind, but Brianna was the first to discover that her brother could detect strong contrasts when objects were in motion. Playing together in the brightly-lit den, he could follow her running body if she wore a black jumper.

When the family spent a moonless night at Yosemite one summer, she and Lance had tested the range of his abilities by throwing a glow-in-the-dark Frisbee back and forth. Lance never showed any aptitude at sports redesigned for the blind, such as variations on ball-with-a-bell, but over the years, he and Brianna refined "night catch," which evolved into leather gloves and a luminescent baseball. If he took off his Ray-Bans in the pitch dark, they could get as far apart as twenty meters. It wasn't a very practical game, but it taught Brianna how to catch a ball better than any of the other girls in PE could manage.

Though Lance could see very little, Brianna could see so very much. Most of all, she saw how others looked at him. She knew the many reactions—from respect to pity, discomfort to disgust, furtive curiosity to open fascination.

As Lance moved through the crowd of baseball fans, Brianna let go of her anxiety about offending Carlos and Maya and stepped into the familiar role of vigilant little sister. Lance's costume elicited shouts, laughter, and high-fives as he and his entourage entered the ballpark and climbed to the bleachers, ten rows up from the right field wall. Carlos took the farthest seat, followed by Maya, Brianna, and Lance, who gathered his robes before dropping onto the molded plastic "cushion" that made cement count as seating.

Brianna felt an early evening chill and hugged herself. She wished she'd worn more than gray gym shorts and one of Lance's long-sleeved Padres shirts.

An elderly African-American woman sat directly behind Brianna. She sported a wide-brimmed beach hat and team colors—yellow shirt, brown shorts. In her lap sat a small transistor radio tuned to the Padres' AM broadcast. She tapped Brianna on the shoulder.

"Hey there, miss. Happy July Four."

"And to you," Brianna replied cheerfully.

"Is your friend supposed to be a genuine Spanish priest? A real padre?"

Before Brianna could answer, Lance turned around. "Yes, indeed, ma'am."

The woman laughed.

"Well, isn't that something. I don't come here as often as I used to, before Gerald passed on..."

Brianna grimaced at the abrupt over-share and saw sympathetic frowns on Carlos and Maya. Lance appeared unperturbed. He was listening to the woman's radio while turning down the volume on his smart phone, which had the same broadcast on a distracting two-second delay.

"...And I don't know that I've sat in this section before," the woman continued, "but today's sold-out. I got this one from a young man selling tickets on the street. As Gerald would have said, 'Weren't no bargain, neither.' I'm sorry. Don't mind me. I can get to talking."

"Don't we know it," said a large man with a loud voice one

row in front of Brianna. The man wore no shirt over his darkly tanned body. His bald head had seen so much sun that it was only two shades paler than the oversized Guinness he hoisted. Without looking back, he nodded to the man at his left, who wore a Tea Party Patriots hat. "Ain't these folks a pair? Friar fruitcake and his chatty grandma. Jesus Christ, what a pair."

"Don't mind the loud mouth," Lance said to the woman with the radio. "My friends and I ignore people like that every day. You were saying?"

The woman patted Lance on the shoulder and stood. "No, you talk with your friends. I'm getting up for a snack." She hoisted her radio, stepped into the aisle, and ascended the stairs heading to the concession stands.

Carlos and Maya leaned toward Lance and Brianna. The four huddled conspiratorially.

"We sit," Maya whispered, "between Godzilla and Charybdis."

Brianna stifled a giggle, but Lance and Carlos laughed more openly.

When the woman with the radio returned minutes later, she remained standing as the stadium announcer said, "Please rise for a very special singing of our national anthem."

Two hundred US Marines had arranged themselves in center field to resemble thirteen stripes, and where a field of fifty stars belonged gathered what the announcer declared to be the Citywide Fifth-Grade Crossing Guard Choir. Hats went over hearts for "The Star-Spangled Banner." The bleacher crowd turned around to face the Jumbotron. Brianna, Lance, Maya, and Carlos joined their fellow fans in patriotic karaoke. The result would have displeased Brianna's band teacher, for the suntanned man and many others like him were already too drunk to follow the tune.

The next seven innings of baseball provided one and a half hours of slow-moving action, with occasional bursts of excitement.

Topics included the wisdom of Abner Doubleday, recollections of epic dungeoneering, and Brianna's all-but-nonexistent high school social life.

Brianna looked up at the scoreboard behind her, which showed the Padres leading the Dodgers 1-0. The elderly woman sitting behind her offered an opinion, as she had done many times that evening.

"Quite a pitching duel, isn't it?"

Lance fielded the question.

"Like they were saying on the radio, that's the only kind of game the Padres can win. Low scoring small ball. We got that run in the seventh because we pinch hit for a pitcher who'd only let two runners on base. That's how to manage a game, right?"

Before the woman could reply, the radio announcer shouted, "Line shot back to the mound—what a grab! Holy cow, he just stuck out his glove and caught it."

The woman nudged Lance's shoulder.

"Did you see that?"

Lance gazed up at the sky.

"Sounds like quite a catch."

The woman covered her open mouth.

"Well, bless your heart."

"Blessings are *my* job. I'm the one in vestments."

It occurred to Brianna that most of the nearby fans remained oblivious to Lance's condition. They'd noticed her brother in a brother's robes, but they ignored him. He'd remained seated, followed the game on the radio, and cheered on cue. He'd even raised his hands to receive high-fives from Brianna and Maya when the Dodgers hit into an inning-ending double play back in the fifth. And those reflective sunglasses he wore? They made him look like a World Series of Poker player more than a dude with a cane, which Lance hadn't needed since he'd entered the stadium on Brianna's arm.

Without turning around, the suntanned man in front of Brianna shouted into the air, "God, will you people ever shaddup?" He accepted a fresh tub of beer from his friend. "Watch the game, will ya?"

Brianna sensed Carlos' temper rising. Maya grabbed his wrist and waved her index finger at him. He bridled until Maya pulled him into a sideways hug.

"You've been quite the downer this evening," Maya said.

Brianna tried not to eavesdrop, but she could hear every word.

"Alan pissed me off. He bailed on us tonight."

"Wasn't there some deal with his mom?"

"Yeah, maybe, but—I guess it's Alan busting on me. Says I'm being a jerk by goofing off when we play. Truth is, I'm burned out. When I get bored, I try to just have a laugh. He wants me to take DL more seriously, like it's some kind of allegorical life lesson."

"Want my honest opinion?"

Maya cocked her head and raised an eyebrow.

"I ask because I don't know what you can handle."

Carlos grinned as Maya bent over to take a quick drink from a soda cup.

"I can handle you, *chica*."

"Truth is, you were being a tool today."

Carlos narrowed his eyes.

"No, really. You portrayed Santana as ironic and post-modern, cracking jokes about genre clichés."

"You laughed. Lance laughed." Carlos snapped his fingers. "Those were good jokes. Lance's sister didn't get 'em, but it's all new to her, the little angel."

Brianna stiffened her back and looked straight ahead. Far away, the pitcher on the mound turned sideways and tossed the ball softly to first base. That sort of drama couldn't hold her attention.

"Seriously," Maya said, "I want to get lost in an adventure, not watch some Adam Sandler flick."

Carlos breathed deeply through his nose, then exhaled. He lifted his foot, which had stuck to the lemonade drying beneath him.

"Let's go walk around the stadium. Blow off some steam." Maya turned to Brianna.

"Hey, girlfriend. You guys okay if we get up for a bit?"

"What?" Brianna feigned confusion. "Oh, sure. We'll be fine."

Carlos and Maya squeezed out of their row, up the aisle, and into the concourse behind the bleachers.

Brianna joined her brother in listening to the broadcast. The Dodgers were batting with a runner on first base, two outs, top of the eighth. The Padres still had that one-run lead. Standing at home plate was Los Angeles' clean-up hitter, a hulking left-handed batter with barbarian biceps. He fouled a pitch straight back, and the play-by-play announcer said, "Strike two."

"Come on." Lance rubbed his hands together. "Get this bum out."

Brianna could feel herself catching the crowd's vibe. Her body tensed as the pitcher stood still, glanced at first base, then began a slow windup. The pitch came in fast and low. With a clap of thunder, the batter hit the ball squarely and sent it on a high arc, above the lights and into the night sky. Transfixed, Brianna watched the towering home run clear the right field wall directly in front of her. Fans scrambled over each other as the ball ricocheted off an empty bleacher seat and fell into a pair of hands that had seemingly acted of their own accord. Her hands.

"I got it!" Brianna squealed. "I totally got it! I caught the ball!"

A brown monk bobbed up beside her, startled and excited.

"Good job, sis!"

Lance shook off his hood and showed Brianna one of the proudest smiles she'd ever seen. He hugged her harder than she'd ever felt. In a tight embrace, they hopped up and down together.

Lance released Brianna, and she turned in all directions to show off her prize. Only then did she realize the crowd had begun to chant, "Throw it back! Throw it back!"

Brianna cocked her head. Unsure of the protocol for handling an opponent's homerun ball, she got the sense that the object in her hand was no longer merely a baseball. Like an enchanted Mythos artifact, it had been touched by the fairies and now held magical power. Was she supposed to throw it? If so, where? Hermione would know what to do, but Brianna had no clue.

The scoreboard video zoomed in on Brianna and her brother. Boos began to build across the stadium. Angry faces surrounded them, mixed with laughing fans who raised their cell phones to capture the moment.

Lance traced the length of Brianna's forearm and snatched the ball from her hand.

"By decree of the Mythopoles, we shall not quarter an enemy's homerunic sphere. We must return this missile to the battlefield from whence it came."

Lance turned to face the field and raised the ball above his head. The crowd roared, and Brianna covered her ears.

"Back into Amon Amarth! Back into the fires of Mount Doom, I send thee!"

After winding up with practiced ease, Lance hurtled forward and whipped the baseball out of his hand. His sandals slipped in the liquid pooling at his feet, and he mistimed his release by a tenth of a second. Instead of launching the ball back into right field, he drilled it into the skull of the suntanned man.

The man lurched forward, stunned, while the crowd responded to the throw and not its impact. Hearing cheers, Lance raised his arms in triumph and beamed at Brianna.

"I wish Alan were here to see this."

It took all of Brianna's strength to tug Lance's rope belt hard enough to pull him down into his seat. He resisted, and when she relaxed for a moment, he stood up and pumped his fists. The grin on Lance's face turned to a frown when the crowd resumed booing, now louder than ever.

The woman with the radio said, "Son, you just hit a man square in the head."

Brianna reached out to reseat her brother but found herself instead covering up against the shower of soda and popcorn that rained down from every direction. Brianna ducked and twisted to avoid the flying cups and debris, but resistance was futile. Her loose shirt was soaked. Lance's robe had turned dark brown, and peanut shells studded his blond hair.

The downpour ended and the jeers turned to laughter. She and her monk-brother must have begun to resemble clowns. A soft, elven voice seemed to whisper in her ear, *Laugh and the world laughs with you.* She tried to smile but was too nervous to pull it off.

"Come on." Brianna tugged at Lance's sleeve. "Let's get out of here."

The suntanned man, sporting a fresh bruise the shape of a baseball's stitches, regained his footing. He turned to face Lance.

"Where do you think you're going, Friar Tuck?"

Lance appeared disoriented. Or frightened. Probably both. He reached under his seat, grabbed his cane, and stood back up. He shook his cane out to full length and tried to get his bearings.

At the same moment, the suntanned man delivered a close-range missile of his own, a sixty-four ounce hard-plastic bucket of domestic lager. The would be beer-chucker stopped himself mid-launch when he saw—and recognized—Lance's red-tipped cane. His momentum knew no courtesies, however, and the booze bomb hit Lance's right cheek with the force of a dodge ball. His neck snapped to the left, and his shades flew behind him.

Brianna felt a burst of courage, mixed with indignation. Locking her elbow with Lance's, she tugged her brother through the row and into the aisle, which had cleared of other fans. As Lance's cane clicked on the cement stairs, the bleacher crowd quieted. Brianna scowled at the shocked faces that dared to meet her gaze.

With a burly stadium security guard by her side, Brianna led Lance up the stairs. Her brother's eyes swung side-to-side, as if searching the crowd. For a moment, he held still and looked up at the bright scoreboard.

"It was just an accident," Brianna said. "Let's go."

Carlos and Maya waited at the top of the stairs. They looked as worried and relieved as parents who had found a lost child.

"We *never* should've come here!" Brianna shouted. "You never should have left us alone with those beasts!"

Carlos held up pleading hands, while Maya brushed debris off Lance's robes.

Before Brianna could formulate her next grievance, she felt a wrinkled hand on her elbow. It was the woman with the radio, and she held out a pair of lightly scratched sunglasses. Brianna accepted the offering with a confused smile and a gentle, "Thank you." She felt the tug of her brother's elbow and followed him into the concourse.

Still swinging his cane about, Lance whipped the security officer in the shin, then backed into Carlos. The officer gave the monk and his companions some room. Even the crowd that had gathered around Lance backed off and melted into the flow of pedestrian traffic.

"You hit the suntan man, didn't you?" Carlos asked.

"He did," Brianna said.

"From what, two feet away?"

"Did I?" Lance said.

"The guy's gonna be okay," Brianna said. "But he's got a nasty knot on his skull." She glanced at the security guard, who conferred with three of his colleagues.

Brianna nodded toward the clutch of stadium security, and

Carlos and Maya got the signal. Moving as a foursome, they slipped out of the concourse and into an elevator. Once the doors closed, Carlos held Lance's shoulders and looked him squarely in the eyes. He gestured for Brianna to hand over the Ray-Bans. She handed them to Carlos, and he slipped them back onto Lance's face.

"Just tell me this," Carlos said through a wide smile. "Did you hit that asshole on purpose, or was fate taking you for a ride?"

"Just bad die rolls," Lance said.

Lance's forehead wrinkled. Had he winked?

"I knew it," Carlos said. "You're a badass underneath those robes."

Brianna felt her body relax. She let Maya rub her shoulders. The elevator stopped, its doors opened, and they stepped onto the ground level.

Lance shook himself like a wet dog, then straightened his posture. In spite of his undignified appearance, he carried himself with remarkable dignity.

"My brother's no vigilante," Brianna said as they walked out of the ballpark. "He's just a bad pitcher with unshakable self-esteem."

"Which is it?" Maya said to Lance. "You a stone cold killer or a Keystone Cop?"

Lance pointed his cane toward a rising moon.

"Only the game director knows."

DEVON

Devon looked at his watch. It was well past nine in the evening, and his Independence Day promotion was not the triumph he'd imagined. Only twelve people had come into the store, and three had left already. He reminded himself that this venture was not about gathering gold coins, of which he had plenty from his first career. Besides, those few customers in attendance were a lively bunch, eager to try out the new games he'd opened for them.

A boy in a Little League uniform sat in the store's oversized throne. He scrunched his legs up into the chair and tapped on the tablet in his lap.

Looking for a distraction, Devon approached. "What are you playing?"

The kid looked up. "Until a few minutes ago, I was playing that Russian mafia game."

"*Ruthless!*" Devon drew a line across his neck and made a guttural sound. "Did you find it to your liking?"

"I was cremated in a dumpster by the second round. Seemed kinda frigid."

Devon tried to parse the last word. It probably meant "bad," or maybe "unfair." That particular game—the first from a Moscow publisher—seemed more true to its name than to the spirit of play.

"Once I got greased, I figured I'd watch the ball game. We're up 1-0. You follow the Padres?"

"Still new to town," Devon said evasively. Never a spectator and always a player, Devon had pursued one passion after another, but never athletics. His talents at wooing had won him a marriage that hadn't survived, though it did bring into the world his dearest Maya, who'd come to live with him for the summer. He'd also poured what felt like a lifetime into a successful career in Silicon Valley. Though that had ended badly

147

as well, it led him to open Players, partly to defy the inexorable trends against the kinds of games he showcased.

While Devon considered how to extract himself from a conversation about baseball, the front door swung open. This triggered its signature cowbell clang, which led the customers to ask in unison, "Got milk?"

The new arrival, in a Megadeth t-shirt, stared back at the grinning faces. Devon feared their harmless greeting had wounded this enormous man, who might have thought himself to be the bovine referenced in the joke.

Devon rushed to his prospective customer with an outstretched hand held high enough for the stranger to grasp. "Devon Washington. Proud owner, official greeter. Welcome to Players. And who would you be, sir?"

"I am, uh, Jeff Carpenter."

"Curious." Devon doubted the authenticity of the proffered name. "Did you know that your name combines the first and last names of the co-creators of Dungeon Lords, the greatest role-playing game of all time? The first module is a smidge older than you are, I would wager."

"I'm familiar with that product."

Devon heard defensiveness, maybe sadness. He pitied this man giant, whom his customers had wounded inadvertently with their cowbell catchphrase. Devon would have to work hard to win over this one, but why not? He wasn't busy. He hadn't seen a credit card in over an hour.

"Have you come for my July Fourth extravaganza?"

"Looks just like a pretty quiet night." The stranger cracked his knuckles. "I might sit in on a game or two. Spread some cheer."

"My idea was to invite customers to try something new. You could say my guests are declaring their independence from whatever particular game has enslaved them too long."

"Only to find a new master?"

"Precisely. Are you ready to do so?"

"I'm one step ahead of you."

"Oh?" Devon laughed nervously, unsure what that meant.

"I'm also entering in new territory. A year ago, I severed my ties to an awful game whose name I dare not speak aloud."

"Secret's safe with me."

Devon knew better than to trust mis-wired social intuition. Still, he couldn't help sympathizing with a fellow so shy that he greeted strangers with an assumed name.

"Very well," Devon said with a laugh. "I will confess to you that I was once something other than what you see today. Look on the shelves in my establishment and you will see no trace of the electronic world. I am the rarest of modern mythical beasts, a game salesman who forswears all consoles and computers."

The stranger's eyes twinkled.

"You are far from alone, Mr. Washington. I have never had an appetite for such games. My friend used to—I mean, I used to say, 'Computers are for work, tables are for play.'"

"Amen. I don't know what I was thinking when I took my talents to the online gaming industry. I certainly hoped it would go in a different direction than it did. I worked for years on…"

Devon backed up toward the register, the point farthest from the customers in the store, and his guest followed.

"I helped build World of Karnage."

Devon frowned. His cheeks grew hot.

"I should have destroyed it when I had the chance."

"Oh?"

"But this is something I never discuss. Our little secret?"

"Lips sealed."

"Truth is, I can get a bit paranoid. See that boy with the tablet?" Devon pointed to the Little Leaguer on the throne. "Earlier this evening, I feared he was firing up the WOK right in my store. Turns out he's just watching a baseball game. Come to think of it, I should introduce you to the young man. Perhaps you could help him decipher of the two-player demos?"

The boy looked up as they approached. "Hey," he said, "you dudes gotta put your eyeballs on this YouTube bit from tonight's Padres game." He rotated his tablet, tapped a button, and turned up the volume.

Devon beheld a three-minute clip that appeared to have been recorded on a camera phone. The video was grainy, and it washed out when a bright scoreboard came into frame. The audio was mostly indistinct shouting and boos, but a few key words were clear enough. The video's protagonist shouted, "Back into the fires of Mount Doom, I send thee!" As the remaining seconds of the clip played, the tablet bounced on the laughing Little Leaguer's lap.

"Oh my heavens." Devon put his hand over his mouth.

The tall stranger beside Devon appeared transfixed. Did the misfortune of Maya and her friends disturb or delight him?

Devon cleared his throat. "What say we put that away and pull something off the shelf?"

"Yes," the stranger agreed. "I'm up for a game. And I'm full of good ideas."

RANDALL

Players didn't close its doors until long past midnight. Randall was among the last to leave. While there, he tried out three different games, each more forgettable than the last. He knew the first one would disappoint when he saw that its box wore the self-righteous label, "Cooperative Game!" He tried to be uncooperative, but the rules made no allowance for his rescue dog to relieve itself inside the burning building. Lives were saved. Huzzah.

The second one was an unwieldy mix of worker placement, deck building, and dice rolling. He understood well enough that each player was a syndicate claiming territory on a newly terraformed planet, but the motivation seemed to be nothing more than economic expansion. Strip away the laser rifles and plasma knives and it was Monopoly in space.

He stayed for the last game because of the opportunity it afforded to study the store owner more closely. The evening's finale was a fourteen-person session of Werewolf. The monsters hid their identities and devoured fellow villagers during the full-moon phase of each round. Randall drew one of the werewolf cards, so he worked with the other beasts to pick off the savviest townsfolk, one by one. When dawn broke, the other players learned who had died, then chose who to shoot through the heart with a silver bullet before the next full moon.

As the owner of the store, Devon could have led the vengeful mob, but he chose to play the role of meek villager. This was the first game Devon stepped into all evening, and he seemed eager for the opportunity. While the wolves chose their prey, he kept his eyes closed tight, hands under thighs, rocking nervously in his chair. Each time dawn was announced, Devon sighed with relief at finding himself alive. If he had suspicions about the wolves' identities, he kept them to himself. The other players prosecuted one another recklessly, while Randall's small pack of lycanthropes ate the lot. When the victors revealed themselves in the end, Devon seemed shocked.

"I would have never guessed," Devon said to Randall, "that you were one of those big, bad wolves."

"Such was the role the cards dealt me. We agreed to show courtesy by eating you last."

"Quite considerate."

Showing uncharacteristic restraint, Randall rolled his eyes only after he'd grunted a goodbye to Devon and left the store. Not until he stepped into the cool night air did it occur to him the lateness of the hour. Bus service would not resume for a few hours, but he could manage the walk to his apartment, which was less than a mile away.

Randall summoned a burst of inner strength. Were he here in Randall's place, Boldheart would not falter, with or without street lamps. Thus, one foot went in front of the other, and soon enough, five short city blocks were behind him. A half-dozen more and he was home.

Rounding the corner without caution, Randall almost tripped on a teenager kneeling on the sidewalk. The kid wore an oversized rugby shirt above blue jeans, but he had neither socks nor shoes on his feet. A sour stench told the story. He'd imbibed more liquor than his scrawny body could hold. When the boy tried to stand, he slipped and fell into his own filth.

Randall was surprised to feel no sympathy for the idiot sprawled out before him. Instead, he felt hot anger warm his chest. The emotion guided his eyes back to the teen's attire. The shirt was familiar. A red bandana protruded from jeans pocket. He knew who this was.

Two scenes from *A Clockwork Orange* came to mind. In one, a sociopath in a bowler hat carries out a savage assault on a homeless man. In the other, the tables have turned, and the

perpetrator becomes the victim. It had been years since he'd
seen the movie, but he now saw it as prophetic. This creature
on the sidewalk was one of the thugs who had covered him with
paintball welts. Fortuna had laid the lad, helpless, at Randall's
feet.

A few kicks could do at least as much damage to this punk
as those guns had done to him. Randall pressed just below his
own kidneys, where the last of the bruises remained. A dull pain
throbbed, and Randall eyed that same location on the prone boy.

"One swing of my leg," Randall said softly, "and a wound
will bloom to match my own. If I aim a little lower, I could more
than even the score. How about that?"

The teenager stirred and muttered something. Turning onto
his stomach, the boy tried to move sluggish arms and legs. This
drugged turtle was swimming in place on the sidewalk.

Impulse told Randall he had to act, lest this fiend crawl away.
As Randall pulled back his right leg, a contrary insight flashed
into his mind.

"Steady," Randall said to himself, but he couldn't quiet this
new thought.

"Please," the boy said in a hoarse voice. He turned his head
and could see Randall's foot reared back, ready to strike. "Just
fuck" —a cough— "off."

"Careful, you."

Randall drew his foot back another inch.

"Don't talk your way into the beatdown you deserve. My leg
has its own will, but the rest of me sees you are a distraction. The
only threat you pose is diverting me from my proper target."

The boy closed his eyes and braced for impact.

This pile of garbage laid out before Randall was not the
enemy, however viciously he and his kind behaved. A midnight
pummeling wouldn't give Randall half the satisfaction of simply
turning around, returning to Players, and laying waste to that
whole store, including whoever might have lingered there past

closing. The violent image caught Randall off guard. He closed his eyes and tried to sense its origin.

"I never did"—a fruity belch—"anything to you."

Randall considered the truth in that plea and lowered his foot to stand tall over the boy. "It's true. Your roadside assault leads back to Alan, who pushed me out of his house and onto the path where wandering monsters might find me."

"—the fuck?" the boy gurgled. "Back off, man."

Randall looked into the starlit sky and found Mars.

"Yes, back indeed. Much farther back. It was Carlos who poisoned the well that had once fed our imaginations. Farther still, maybe past Alpha Centauri, the world of games itself bears responsibility. Fantasies of heroism, conquest, and triumph were written into the rules of everything we played. Childish themes malnourished every one of us."

The boy relaxed his limbs and planted his face in the sidewalk. He began to cry.

Randall poked a foot into the teen's rugby shirt until he regained his audience's attention.

"Beyond bad storytelling, these games fostered phony friendships. They blinded me to the immaturity of the whole enterprise. Not anymore. Now I see past the illusion. I can become something greater. I won't delight in mayhem for its own sake, like you hooligans. No, the traps I set will be more than pranks. They will be part of a game of real consequence."

Randall stepped over the child and headed home. Soon, he found his stride. By the time his apartment building came into view, he had written a new life script.

He was neither outcast nor villain. He was the protagonist at the center of this story. Harnessing the divine power a pastor might summon to preach, he would become a true Pathfinder. As such, he would recognize and seize the opportunities that would open before him. He would deliver a message to those who needed to hear it most. He might seem, on the surface, as cruel as the troll he left gurgling on the sidewalk, but his actions would flow from a more profound love—one that required the kind of discipline his parents had failed to show their own willful child. His would be a righteous mission.

The Second Weekend in July

ANGELOU

At the knee of one of her many mothers, Angelou had heard stories aplenty of bravery and battle, but none prepared her for the path she now walked, arm in arm with strangers on a heroic quest. The Ring Bone clan had been nomadic and non-aligned. It had no quarrel with the Pale Elves, Mythopolis, nor even the kingdom of Everwinter, which sat high above the tundra where her people ultimately settled. Her clan needed little from others, so long as oxen and sheep stayed healthy, which they always had.

Strangers, after all, had introduced diseased livestock into their herd, which cost her people dearly. The Ring Bone had taken on mercenary work to shore up their coffers, and when Angelou came of age, she joined this corps of elite fighters. She relished the chance to visit other lands, and she traveled without fear. No foe had proven her equal.

The trolls outside Mythopolis had revealed her hubris. Santana had praised her brave rescue of the fallen Lancelot, but she had little doubt that their arrival saved her own life. Her foggy memory suggested she had flown into a wild frenzy mid-battle, which left her vulnerable to even the low-grade tactics of mindless monsters.

It pained her that the stereotype of "barbarian rage" had a ring of truth. She had seen it happen many times, but only when she left her home did she learn it brought more scorn than awe. Nor did she understand the word "barbaric" until her first visit to Mythopolis. After hiking a full day to reach the capital, she seated herself on a tavern barstool and slonked a bowl of brine soup. Onlookers whispered the word all around her, as though she could not hear.

It stung, but she gradually embraced the insult. She lost interest in manners and appearances. For every successful mission, she added another circular burn around a leg or arm— the signature marking of the Ring Bone. She traded her tattered tunic and leather armor for the stiffest hides, which she wrapped around her body with pride. Angelou grew disdainful of the merchants and nobles who hired her. Each needed a barbarian to settle a debt, ward off a beast, or protect a precious cargo. They needed her muscle but resented any notion that she and her kind were more than a weapon they might wield.

So it was with the Mythopolis River troll hunt. She accepted that fateful commission from the Frog Merchant Guild—an entity she had not known to exist before entering the capital. The malevolent force moving through the Mythos had been too loathsome even for trolls, who relocated their hive to what happened to be a hatchery. The coin on offer for their removal outweighed the danger of the deed, or so she thought. When she returned alone to collect her purse, the treasurer did not inquire after her charges. If the trolls were gone, so was any concern about fallen barbarians.

Was she any better? Those deaths haunted neither her thoughts nor dreams since that battle's end. Fierce indifference was the way of her clan. Ring Bone associations were brief, loose couplings. Even mother and daughter stayed together no more than three years. As such, Angelou was unaccustomed to concern for fellow travelers, so long as she survived and the mission was completed.

This latest quest to defeat an unparalleled evil, however, required working closely with strangers. Battling by their side stirred something new inside Angelou. She worried about the bard Hermione, who had strong convictions but a weak constitution. Out of her other eye, she watched carefully the cleric Lancelot. He spoke often—quite often, in fact—of a larger spiritual Truth. His search for this elusive prey left him distracted, even during combat.

As for Santana, Angelou inherited her clan's mistrust of sorcerers. Santana's magical potency made him a natural leader, but his arrogance was worse than hers had even been. Over a cooking fire one night, Hermione recounted the battles in Devotus' tower. By splitting away from the group, Santana had put them all in jeopardy. Angelou wondered whether the legendary Boldheart had died from his own recklessness, or from that of his fellow travelers. For the good of all, she decided to steer the ox cart herself.

Thus, she led her companions out of every wrong turn as they followed the route drawn by Devotus. The journey to the Fairie Realm led them through a string of hamlets, each of which offered rumors about the fallen elven kingdom. In the town of Greenwood, a barmaid related tales of a great wind storm enveloping the Pale Elves and besieging them with earth and rock. On the outskirts of Arneson, they were shown a broken elven longsword, reputed to have been snapped in half by the Lifeless Knight himself. The sheriff of Cooktown advised against venturing any farther, lest they encounter the demon's soulless followers. These so-called Naughts were a destructive force that grew ever stronger in the wake of the Knight's advance.

After staying a night in the Shire of Tweet, Angelou and the others received a firsthand account of what lay ahead. At the close of their morning meal at Skip's Grub, a human woman crashed through the door and collapsed on the wood-plank floor. She wore a hemp tunic with an embroidered visage of Helios, the twin-headed sun god.

Angelou rose from her chair and lifted the fallen worshipper. The woman's matted red hair swayed as she hung in Angelou's arms.

"All is lost," the devotee whimpered. "The candle of light gutters. The empty heart bleeds cold death."

Hermione and Lancelot closed around the woman, with

Santana and Lupita behind them. The back of her neck was red with sores. Lancelot placed his palm on her mottled skin. A warm light shone through his hand, but instead of healing, her flesh rippled and popped.

Lancelot stepped back, baffled. "Never have I seen the healing power of Elahna so utterly ineffective. It is—disquieting."

"Burn me again, cleric." The devotee pulled his palm back to her neck. "Make the wounds inside me boil, that I might die."

Hermione pulled her instrument from her back and played as she sang.

No one is able to harm you
Friends are all around
Demons are growling in your mind
We'll send them howling for their lives
Hear the lute that softly plays
And trust my healing ways

The woman regained her balance and addressed Hermione in a faraway voice.

"There was a creature. Soared down like a dragon to land before our temple. Its wings pulled dark skies behind it to eclipse the sun. Bodies fell, only to rise again, neither living nor dead. I saw the scene from the high road. I tried to run—"

"But your wounds?" Angelou asked.

"Surface scratches, those." The woman felt the back of her neck. "But flesh cannot heal without an essence within. The demon, he—"

The woman collapsed.

Lupita pawed at her apprehensively, then slunk behind Santana, her ears lowered. The wolf had seen many deaths already, but something about this one seemed different. Wrong. Eyes wide with worry, Lupita looked to her companions.

Hermione answered the plea. She reached down to help the

woman, but Angelou held her back.

"Stay clear," Lancelot said with a nod. "She is beyond even divine aid."

Santana returned to their breakfast table and lay down a thick gold coin. "For your worries," he said to the barkeep, who stood amidst a clutch of patrons.

Angelou stepped out the door and into the morning air. The others gathered behind her. A heavy haze hung like moss across the sky.

"If we move quickly," Angelou said, "we may see for ourselves these foul creatures." She held out a scrap of the woman's tunic and invited Lupita to sniff. "Lead the way, wolf."

* * *

At a measured pace, Angelou and the others followed Lupita three miles down the main road until it sloped up a short hill. From its top, Angelou saw a broad valley filled with a grid of barren fruit trees. In the midst of the orchard stood a massive temple, a two-story building with sculpted stone sides that burst upward like the flames on a torch. Thin gold leaf covered much of the exterior. Dark smoke rose from its center.

Angelou descended the hill and approached the building. She pulled the trident off her back and held it steady. Lancelot was close behind, shield forward and mace in hand. Calling Lupita to his side, Santana adjusted his staff, which he had been using as a walking stick. Hermione followed a few paces behind the rest. She plucked at the strings of her lute, hummed to herself, and nervously looked from left to right.

Together, they arrived at the building's portico. There a golden mural bore the image of Helios, an enigmatic smiling face at the center of a swirling sun. But the painting had been defaced. Charcoal and gore sketched the figure of a giant swordsman, who held up the sun god's head like a decapitated trophy.

Taking care with her steps, Angelou passed through an open door and into a dim hallway. Something was amiss.

"Would seem this is where a battle occurred," she said. "Yet I see no bodies."

"I suspect we shall see them soon enough," Lancelot replied.

"Or perhaps," Santana said, "they have walked away of their own accord." He pulled from his pouch a sultana and tossed it across the floor. It rolled for two seconds, then let loose a soft wave of light that illuminated the hall's marble floors and walls. Dried streaks of mud and cloth lined the passage, which ended at another bronze door.

Santana offered to inspect the door, which he did with a thin wire and a whispered incantation.

"Is it safe to open?" said Hermione.

Lupita put her nose to the bottom of the door and let out a low growl.

"The *door* won't hurt us," Santana said and gestured for Angelou to step forward.

Hermione thrummed her lute and raised her voice.

You can tremble, even fear it
Can't fight off an evil spirit
Welcome courage and revere it
Never doubt your heart can hear it
Hold your hopes up even higher
Into the pyre we go!

Angelou had heard many sing that ballad before, to no effect, but when Hermione performed it, she felt vigor flowing in her muscles. With surprisingly little effort, she pried open the bolted bronze door with her bare hands.

Once inside, Angelou counted twenty-one worshippers lurching about the room, each wearing pristine garments bearing the face of Helios. Their movements seemed mechanical, their eyes dull. They reminded Angelou of undead creatures. Yet they had neither the decayed bodies of a ghoul, nor the wounds of a battle, won or lost.

One priest pulled down a gold-threaded tapestry that hung on the wall. Two more tossed leather-bound books into a fire at the center of the room. Another group dragged corpses across the chamber and stacked them like cordwood.

"Looks like we found those fallen bodies," said Santana, *sotto voce*.

Angelou pointed her weapon toward an old woman who held a sheaf of parchment in her arms.

"Hold," Angelou said. "What is all this?"

"Diseeease," the woman hissed through clenched teeth.

"Yes," Lancelot said, "you need healing. An infection spreads through your bodies."

"No!" The woman raised her papers. "These *words* are the disease. They poisoned us."

As she spoke, the others in the room joined as a chorus.

"Devotion fed delusion. We are now naught, that we may see anew. So said the one true god, Aleh'en!"

"Blasphemer!" Lancelot shouted.

The woman threw her papers into the air and lunged at Lancelot. In a fluid motion, Angelou thrust out her trident to impale, lift, then toss the attacker aside.

At once, the worshippers converged. While Hermione pounded out bass power chords, Lancelot, Angelou, and Lupita dispatched one attacker after another.

Santana reached into his robe and threw a stream of darts into the melee, knocking an onrushing priest sideways. Just as Hermione's song promised, into the fire he went.

Only after spearing the last enemy did Angelou feel her heartbeat slow and her arms relax. Her resolve melted, and her eyes danced about the room. Behind their phalanx, Hermione lay prone, darkness pooling beneath her neck. Her stiffened fingers held her scimitar, still buried in the chest of an assailant.

Lupita crouched over Hermione and licked her face. Translucent eyelashes swished up and down under the wolf's rough tongue, but Hermione's pupils looked as lifeless as glass beads on a doll's head. No breath passed between her lips.

Angelou picked up a club that lay behind Hermione's head. She inspected the weapon, which still glowed a faint green.

"One of the beasts must have come from behind." Angelou whacked her own skull with the club. "Another death, my own fault."

Angelou tried to reassure herself. This was the way life unfolded. From every battle, some never return. These were warriors standing beside her, not comrades or friends.

Still, she could not deny an unfamiliar sensation. Her pulse was erratic. Her shoulders shook. The barbarian dropped the club and fell to her knees.

"She filled our hearts with song." Angelou lifted Hermione's hand and kissed her fingers.

Lancelot lay his silver unicorn behind Hermione's head and folded her arms across her chest. His fingers combed through her thin green hair to draw out a black gore that reminded Angelou of the dying devotee they had met that morning.

"She is dead," Lancelot said.

Angelou straightened to full height.

"This one will be missed."

"She *would* be missed," Santana corrected. "There is a good reason that I travel always with a high priest."

"Yes?"

Angelou felt her heart lift, but Lancelot shook his head.

"I do not know if her connection to us is strong enough. Her soul must want to return and know the way. I can channel what energy we have to call her back, but it may not—"

"Stop talking and do it," Angelou said. "Whatever afflicted these worshippers has yet to claim her."

Lancelot knelt behind Hermione's head. He turned toward Santana and held out an open palm.

"Our best hope is the Cuthbert stone."

"I have many other jewels we can use—"

Angelou shot Santana a withering look.

Santana reached into his cloak but pleaded, "That stone alone is worth more than we could ever—"

Angelou picked up her weapon.

Santana brought forth an embroidered leather pouch. Unfastening a series of ties, he pulled from it the finest cut diamond Angelou had ever seen. The stone sparkled in the light of the worshippers' parchment bonfire.

Lancelot shook his head.

"I shall never forget when you pried that loose from the statue of St. Cuthbert. Had Boldheart discovered you had done that, he would have killed you on the spot, just for the trouble it brought us."

"Our swordsman saved my life many times over. The day may yet come when I pay back that debt."

"Perhaps you are paying it now."

Lancelot set the diamond on Hermione's forehead. He placed one hand on her temple and raised the other toward the ceiling, where smoke still wafted. Leaning in close, he whispered to Hermione. Slowly, the diamond drew into itself all the light in the room. A rainbow of colors danced across its facets. When it became the only visible object, it disappeared. The glow of the bonfire returned.

Hermione sat up and gasped.

"They're coming from behind!"

Angelou embraced Hermione tightly until she got her bearings. Still in Angelou's grasp, a canine head pushed at Hermione's shoulder. When no hand came forth to pet or pat, Lupita backed up a step and let loose a shrill bark.

Hermione writhed herself free from Angelou and hugged

Lupita with something like a headlock. The wolf's groan sounded like a cat's purr. Lupita pushed her shoulders back into Hermione's chest.

Angelou stepped back and wiped at a tear.

"Try to keep your wits about you," she said to Hermione. "You are not so handy with a weapon. This is plainly true. But we may need you tomorrow as much as you needed us today."

LANCE

"Lance Michael Langdon, come to breakfast!"

From the hall bathroom just outside the kitchen, Lance sang back to his mother, "Just a minute, Mary Frances!"

Lance hadn't seen himself in a mirror since he was little, but Lance took pride in his image. After several summers at "blind camp," as he called it, he'd decided that a kid with non-voluntary dark glasses had two choices—pitiful soul or devilish rogue. His body felt like the former, so he worked hard to promote the latter.

He shut the bathroom door behind him and strode through the hall. Lance needed no cane to navigate the house and took his customary seat at the table.

"It's Friday," Mary said. "You've got work, sweetheart."

"I told you, I've got the day off from the office."

As soon as he said the word "office," Lance bit down on his lower lip. He ran his hands down his thighs once, twice, and a third time, brushing nervous energy off his slacks. Since the blowup at Alan's house, he'd heard neither Randall's baritone voice nor his distinctive footfalls at ProTechTed. But he knew Randall was there, lurking about like an Invisible Stalker. The more time that passed without encountering him, the more paranoid Lance became.

"Your sister needs to get to band practice."

"She's a grown-up, Mom. She'll get there, unless you threw her bike on the roof."

"She's just a kid, Lance. Make sure she gets moving."

"Do I smell waffles?"

Keys jingled as Mary grabbed her purse from the counter and dashed out the door. From the front porch, she shouted, "Bye!"

Lance felt across the kitchen table, not that he needed to. He appreciated the many small things his mother did to make his life easier. Plate, silverware, juice, waffles—everything was where he expected. And so it was with so much else. Even letting Brianna join his gaming group had been an indulgence, for him more than her.

Lance counted himself lucky to have such an easy relationship with his parents. Alan's mother loved him, but there was a complication there he didn't understand. Randall's parents sounded as twisted as he was, but consider the source. Carlos never spoke of his family, and Lance left well enough alone there. Maya's dad was clearly a rock star. He'd have to ask about her mom when he got himself a second date.

With a self-satisfied smile on his face, Lance lifted his fork and stabbed his waffle. He laughed to himself at the very concept of eating breakfast. His favorite author, Jasper Fforde, once observed that characters never get to eat breakfast. Fforde created an imaginary Book World in which harried actors must constantly perform novels so that their stories can transfer into the minds of human readers. Stories never include breakfast.

When playing Dungeon Lords, Alan likewise skipped over mundane Mythos details to keep the plot moving forward. Did Lancelot long for the chance to eat griffon eggs with toasted bread in the morning? After all, the recent encounter with the dying devotee at the inn had skipped over the consumption of their meal.

Lance raised a glass of what smelled like orange juice.

"Would that I were you, Sir Lancelot, that you might enjoy this refreshing drink to start your day!"

Before the glass reached his lips, Brianna rushed into the hall bathroom.

"Thanks for taking forever," she said through the door.

Lance wanted to fire back a witty retort, but he checked himself. His little sister was not at her best—not since the incident last week, which Internet hipsters had dubbed the "Petco Massacre." Mary was the one who'd tipped him off to the fact that seemingly everyone at Brianna's school had seen it. He'd listened to it himself, and the viewing statistics his computer read back confirmed it had gone viral. Not hundreds but *hundreds of thousands* had watched the most popular version, a cell phone video that incorporated a homemade synthesizer arrangement of "The Black Gate Opens" from *The Return of the King*.

Mary said the whole thing was a hoot, but mortification hid behind those encouraging words. As had happened at the stadium itself, he'd passed through stages of pride, bewilderment, and embarrassment when he re-listened to the videos on his own, perhaps four dozen times. In the end, he concluded that Mother knew best. He'd put on a brave face and accept whatever kind of fame this mishap offered.

That approach might also put him on the firmest footing with Maya. He could get pity from anyone, but her admiration would require rising above humiliation. She seemed as fearless as her barbarian and would expect no less from anyone who deemed himself worthy of her.

By the time Lance heard the bathroom door re-open, he'd managed to set out a plate of waffles for his sister. He pulled back her chair as she approached. Once she was seated, he circled back around the table and returned to his own breakfast.

"Can only eat a bite," Brianna said. "Gotta run."

"But you'll see us later at Players, right?"

She hadn't said as much, but Lance worried that she blamed him and the rest of the group for what had happened at the Padres game.

Brianna set down a glass. His sister believed that Lance could feel her smile, so he flashed a grin in what he hoped was a reply. Mary had once told him that his mere presence often cheered Brianna when she was sad.

"Of course I'll be there," she said while chewing. "Looking forward to it."

"That's good, because at this point, the story can't really advance without Hermione. You're as much a part of this quest as any of us."

"Don't know about that, but I'll be there."

Brianna opened and shut the same door Mary had used minutes earlier. When Lance didn't hear her feet hit the front steps, he suspected she was standing just outside. Maybe she forgot something.

The door squeaked back open, and he heard Brianna tease him in a sing-song voice.

"Oh, and have fun on your *da-ate!*"

MAYA

Maya steered her dad's yellow Ford Fiesta down the freeway off-ramp and came to a stop. Waiting for the light to change, she retraced the steps that had led her to this dubious errand.

When she had walked out of Petco Park the previous weekend, she'd empathized so completely with Lance's misfortune that she forgot herself. Before they'd re-boarded the trolley, Lance had asked if she was free to go out for "a meal" sometime. She'd insisted on lunch, rather than dinner, but she feared he'd construed today's meeting as a prelude to courtship.

Her only consolation was that the gesture seemed to miff Carlos, who sulked on the trolley ride home. Whether this reflected arrogance or clumsy mood management, it was hard to say. If Carlos fancied himself her suitor, he had no clue—on so many levels.

Green light.

Maya turned onto a surface street. Only the Fiesta's GPS kept her from becoming lost in the network of strip malls that lined San Diego's arterial boulevards. She wondered how Lance experienced the city. He would have enjoyed the strong scents of the forested Evergreen College campus. The asphalt that dominated his suburban environment had a whiff of its own on a hot day, but few poets reminisced about their memories of tar and dirt.

Such musings left Maya conflicted. She'd pledged not to get so close to these new gaming friends, which is all they were. Under the right circumstances, she could get intimate with boys and girls alike, but her senior year at college featured two awkward breakups. Her most recent exes had made her a grief pioneer— one of the first Evergreeners to have lesbian and straight lovers leave her to run into each other's arms. She knew that college was a time for experimentation, but that was humiliating.

The last she heard, the lovebirds were shacked up at some commune on the Oregon coast. She got an image of them walking hand-in-hand, pulling slimy geoducks out of the sand and dropping them into metal buckets. With such thoughts haunting her, restarting her erotic engine seemed unlikely.

Still, she was curious to learn how Lance approached the world and the women who inhabited it. He was certainly a more interesting prospect than Alan. That man wore the blank mask of a well-sheltered gamer, though she glimpsed a deeper person inside, nascent but potent. Carlos was anomalous, at least in her small sample of the gaming community. His clean black shoes, ironed shirt, neatly tied ponytail, and erect posture in a world of slouchers came across as professional self-confidence. Why did Carlos hew so close to Alan the man-child, let alone Dungeon Lords? Such questions felt nosy, and she had no right to pry at bonds that appeared stronger than any forged in her own life.

After all, she was becoming estranged from the woman who'd raised her. Even after Devon moved out, Maya remained Daddy's girl. Her mother wanted a serious daughter, but Maya became something between a poet and a gamer.

When Maya spoke to her mother on the phone the night before, she heard the familiar sound of grinding teeth. Mom did not approve of Maya immersing herself in Devon's world. She accused her daughter of doing so out of spite.

Either way, Alan's group and the cushy job at Players provided the perfect opportunity for trying on the life of a slacker. She could let go of parental expectations, as well as those she'd created for herself. No grades, no graduate studies. No worries.

A tangle of residential roads baffled the Fiesta's navigation system, and Maya realized she'd left the commercial zone. She now traversed streets lined with all manner of trees—walnuts and willows, eucalyptus and palms. Maya spied Essex Street, the short-lived continuation of Primrose Drive, and pulled up to Lance's house. He stood waiting outside, leaning on his cane like

Fred Astaire between dance numbers. Maya wondered how he knew the pose if he'd never seen the movie. This was becoming more than a "pity date." She was intrigued.

"Maya?"

"Lancelot?"

"Please. It's *Lance*."

"Sir Lance of Essex."

Lance bowed gracefully.

Maya got out of the Fiesta and walked to the passenger door. She took Lance's hand, and he accepted her assistance. He eased himself inside while Maya hustled back around the car and hopped into the driver's seat.

"Lead us onward, Ms. Washington."

"Where you wanna go?"

"Chinese food?"

"How about soup and salad?"

"Buffets weren't made for the blind."

Maya reached out to touch his forearm.

"Right. I'm sorry."

"In truth," Lance said, "cafeteria-style food is remarkably predictable. The overall organization varies from one venue to the next, but I've come to believe that there exists a food service certification course somewhere that teaches every hotel and restaurant employee in these United States the same sequencing of cold salads, hot dishes, condiments—"

"Probably the cheapest stuff first, yeah?"

"Perhaps. But no buffet today."

Maya squeezed Lance's arm, then withdrew her hand. Having dated both sexes unsuccessfully, Maya knew that to a woman, a friendly touch was simply a touch, but to a boy? Even an accidental brush-up could convince him that tonight was the night. Lance had a swagger that suggested he was more suave than that, but one could never be too sure.

"What cuisine would you recommend?" Lance said.

"There's a great Ethiopian place on University that Devon showed me."

"Let's do it. African's good."

Lance cleared his throat. In a barely recognizable Elton John impersonation, he sang the opening lines of "Circle of Life."

"Lion King? Really?" Maya started the car. "Ethiopian food — Eritrean, I should say — comes from *North* Africa. That stupid franchise was based on South African music and depicts the East African ecosphere..." Maya stopped herself and looked at Lance. "But you were just trying to sing a dumb song to have a laugh, weren't you?"

"Of course." Lance flashed a mischievous grin. "That, and nothing more."

They soon arrived at the Red Sea, ordered sampler plates, pinched injera bread to pick up lamb and beans and greens, then found themselves back in Maya's car. The meal had been delicious, the conversation rapid.

"Hope you're not in a rush," Lance said. "I have a little diversion for us before you take me home."

"Oh?"

Maya hesitated, unsure how to respond. Maybe it was having a gamer in the car, but she felt the Dungeon Lords ethos take hold — the adventure beginning today and all that.

"Very well," she said. "Lead us onward, Sir Lance of Essex."

Following her passenger's directions, Maya made a series of turns onto one street after another. She lost her sense of direction amidst the twisting roads, but the route seemed precise. Lance told her to reduce speed just as she passed a traffic sign onto which someone had spray painted "Me" below the speed bump advisory, "Slow Hump."

"Stop here."

Maya pulled the car onto the wide shoulder of an underpass, with the freeway just sixteen feet above them. It was hardly a romantic setting. Asphalt lay beneath them. Sloping concrete walls rose up either side of the road.

"Here?" Maya said doubtfully. "There's nothing—"

"And everything. Now, do as I do."

Lance unfastened his belt, lowered his seat three notches, pressed the button that rolled down his window, and put his hands behind his head.

With a shrug, Maya lowered her window. She heard the interstate roar above them like a back-masked recording of an angry stream. Two loud thumps sounded out.

"Semi-trailer with an unbalanced load," Lance said. "Sounds like someone pounding on the ceiling, doesn't it?"

"I guess. Maybe."

A humming approached then descended in pitch as it passed.

"Corvette, down shifting. Could be the Z6, but it's likely a newer model." Lance paused. "Belts could be loose. Probably driving it hard."

Maya laughed and reclined her seat two notches.

"You're playin' me, yeah?"

A slow chugga-chugga-chugga floated down the river of cars overhead.

"I refuse to believe that was a '76 Chevy Chevette," Lance said with a laugh. "Those things can't pass the emissions tests. More likely the '85 hatchback, both horrible cars."

If he was making this up, it was convincing. There was no point in challenging him. Maya knew next to nothing about automobiles, let alone their makes and models. The only reason she knew they sat in a Ford was that her dad's pet name for it was "Harrison."

"One, two, three vans—probably each a twelve-passenger heading to the East County. Also Chevys, but good engines."

Maya recognized how much she had in common with this misfit and his friends. There was no greater safety than dwelling among the socially dispossessed. Theirs was a story she could believe, one that included her. With their feet dipped into the Mythos, she and Lance were just another couple of kids more concerned with having fun and exchanging arcane knowledge than comparing each other's social class or physical markers.

Lance offered more vehicle IDs, but only intermittently. As he quieted, Maya discerned a strategy. He'd hoped to come across as having extraordinary auditory ability, which might imply he was exceptional in his other senses. With the spell lifted, she wondered if he had a Plan B. He did.

"Let me guess what perfume you're wearing."

"I'll help you out, chief. Today's password is, 'None'."

Lance inhaled audibly.

"Yet you do have on an antiperspirant deodorant. Not a sporty one. Not Teen Spirit. Maybe Secret—Vanilla Sparkle. Smells like slow churned Dryer's."

"Damn."

Maya shook her head in disbelief.

"I think that's right. Do you really have super senses, like some Daredevil superhero?"

"Genre mixing is forbidden in my presence."

Lance snorted out a ridiculous laugh.

Maya sensed that he'd given up the game. The poor guy couldn't take seriously his own faux sincerity.

"The awful truth is that I recognize this particular fragrance from a successful conquest—that is, from a happy liaison last summer. One of my former counselors, only five years my senior, became smitten with me at the ten-year reunion. She wore that same perfume. 'Twas all very sweet and innocent, I assure you. A dalliance."

Maya worried that this auto-seduction charm might have worked if he'd named sexier models. "Corvette" had been a good start. She imagined that she felt the warmth of a convertible's sun-baked leather seat.

No, Lance had pointed out clunkers and vans, as though

he were too honest for his own good. Or had he named those because he actually heard them? What if Lance was just showing her a good time and taking his little game seriously? Perhaps she was the one who read a more combustive purpose into his engine identifications.

"I should probably get you home," Maya said.

She started the engine and punched the Langdons' address into the GPS. Harrison's motor groaned and sputtered in its own distinct way. As they entered the freeway, the car's voice became one with the chorus of traffic.

BRIANNA

Brianna entered the Band Room to join nine students already seated. Most had arrived early to unpack and tune their instruments. Some chatted among themselves. With each passing minute, more students filed into the room.

The sound of a sophomore testing out her tuba made Brianna smile. It honked like an elephant with a head cold. Brianna wondered if anything in the Mythos made the same sound.

She set her flute case beside her chair and rummaged in her book bag. Pulling out an iPad, she brought up *Dungeon Crawling for Toddlers*, a beginner's guide she'd downloaded the day before the Padres game. She was eager to learn more about the mechanics of combat, lest her bard get caught out of position again during battle.

It scared her that Hermione had almost died. Worse still, it had been her own fault. If she'd remembered to tell Alan that Hermione was covering the door through which they'd entered, or if she'd remembered to close the door behind them, she—or rather Hermione—wouldn't have been outflanked.

This fantasy role-playing world—and the real people who put it in motion—had become the most exciting part of her life. Maya was an inspiration, with her Angelou a model of fierce courage. For the first time, Brianna understood her brother's passion for the game. Lance channeled some of himself into Lancelot, or was it the other way around? She preferred the company of Santana to that of Carlos, though she sensed that, in spite of their suave personae, both the sorcerer and his creator had generous hearts. She marveled at the hours Alan put into their game *between* each weekend. How could someone devote so much of his life to building a world for others? Or did he build it for himself?

Only then did Brianna notice writing on the dry erase board at the front of the room. Today's session would run an hour late.

Unless she left early, she'd miss the first hour at Players.

Brianna chewed her nails. The Band Room housed those closest to what she might call friends at Grossmont. These were kids her own age who went to the same school. That still counted for something. She whipped a phone out of her pocket and texted Maya.

Tiffany Keller sat down in the chair to Brianna's left. As usual, she wore a simple pastel dress with a modest silver necklace, an accessory Brianna knew her friend would never let her parents see around her neck.

Neither Tiff nor Brianna had chosen to join the woodwind section. Brianna had preferred guitar and Tiffany drums, but three years earlier, in their first weeks at Grossmont, Mr. Weiss needed neither instrument and was short on flutes. When they protested, he flattered them by explaining—correctly, it turned out—that they had exceptional musical aptitude and would adapt. Out of that shared experience, a friendship grew.

Brianna looked up from her iPad and smiled.

"Hey, Tiff."

No reply. Ignoring Brianna, Tiffany set her notebook on the floor and pulled out her instrument case. Tiffany's serious expression suggested that something else was on her mind.

A week had gone by without Brianna exchanging so much as a word with her friend. They'd avoided each other in the hall, which was awkward because they'd chosen lockers in the same building.

Then again, Brianna had avoided everyone as best she could this week. It felt like every soul in summer school—maybe the whole world—had seen the ball-tossing-fail video. Though her brother was the punch line, Brianna was implicated in the fiasco. Thus, the rain of teasing and snickers Brianna had endured at school seemed more torrential than the beer that had soaked her and Lance. As one of Brianna's few known friends, perhaps Tiffany now felt her peers' eyes watching her more warily.

Tiffany took out her flute and leaned toward Brianna. When their eyes met, Brianna's smile was snuffed out by Tiffany's menacing scowl. Suddenly, Tiffany snatched the iPad from Brianna's lap and stood up.

The room was almost full, with the last stragglers filing in through the double doors at the back. Everyone looked at Tiffany when she shouted, "Oh—my—*gawd!*"

Tiffany read aloud from Brianna's tablet.

"The chaotic neutral bard is a merry minstrel, glad for an adventure but happiest when singing to an appreciative audience."

A few kids laughed, while others cocked their heads.

Brianna couldn't understand what was happening, but instinct told her to act.

"Give me that," she said and swiped at her iPad.

Tiffany dodged Brianna and turned away from her. She read to the other side of the room.

"Handsomest of all the Mythos heroes, the young bard can be vain and foppish. If ability score improvements are devoted to raising charisma ever higher, a mature bard will have to brush away admirers and spurn many lovers."

A bearded boy sat down behind a drum kit and pointed toward Tiffany. "Oh my god, that's Dungeon Lords."

Tiffany nodded. "And guess who's playing it?"

The drummer stared at Brianna, who sat on her hands.

"No way! The monk's sister?"

"Lady Dorkus herself."

"People still do that?"

A rim shot hit the cymbal, and the summer Honor Band burst into laughter. Tiffany feigned a giggle of her own.

This time Brianna reached out more quickly and seized her tablet. She stuffed it into her bag and ducked through the aisle toward the exit. As Brianna pushed open the back door, she froze. She'd grabbed her flute but forgotten its case. Tiffany reached down to pick it up, then held it high.

"Think Mr. Weiss might trade her flute for, like, a magic sword?"

The band roared and Tiffany beamed at her admirers. Brianna felt Tiffany siphoning away all the inspiration that Brianna had felt in herself just moments ago. The exchange infused Tiffany with a glowing vitality. Tiffany stood so tall and strong that the spritely figure brought to mind a memory of Randall, Tiffany's hulk of a brother. Brianna pictured him looming over Lance and his friends at the dining room table.

The thought disquieted Brianna, and she slammed shut the Band Room door behind her. Just before it closed, she saw Tiffany tapping on her phone.

Once Brianna stormed away a safe distance, she checked her tablet. Had she received a contrite text? She had not.

MAYA

Maya was unpacking a shipment of German board games when the store's lone customer approached, hands deep in the pockets of his corduroy pants.

"Do you have the Dungeon Lords Online Companion?"

"I'm still new here," Maya said. "Is that some kind of software you use to build game scenarios? Or something to use behind the game director's screen?"

"You mean a computer screen?"

The customer scratched his head and gazed at Maya's white peasant blouse, which hung low enough to expose her left shoulder.

"Something in there you'd like instead?" Maya said.

The customer shifted his eyes toward the floor and found a direct path out the door.

From the back of the store, Devon called out, "Very smooth, dear daughter."

"He was a perv."

"Four-fifths of our customers are male. Some of them talk to very few women, except for sisters and mothers."

"Am I s'posed to feel sorry for them?"

"I sat alongside such people when I was a code jockey. Many are on the high-functioning end of the autism spectrum. Tact is as mysterious to them as differential equations are for others."

Maya saw an opening to talk about something real. Since her arrival in June, they had spoken principally of games and genre fiction, plus a bit about her life, but not his.

"Do you miss making computer games? That was your life for as long as I can remember."

"What I missed was *you*. You're the one thing your mother and I got right." Devon carried an unopened carton of books to the front of the store. "Until this summer, you and I had not

181

spent a full month together since the divorce."

"Well, I'm here now. With Mom's blessing—sort of."

Devon nodded.

"I know what she thinks of me—that your father is at once flaky and obsessive. She wants you to stay focused on your studies. Pursuing a humanities Ph.D. is not the most practical career choice, but it still counts as graduate education."

Maya sensed her father parrying the conversation away from himself. She countered with a dodge of her own.

"What was that customer asking about?"

"For a brief while, there was a version of Dungeon Lords that one could play online."

"Isn't the whole point to be playing together, face to face?"

"The company worried that nobody was spending long weekends together anymore, let alone devoting the time required to be a game director. So they wrote software to guide you and your AI-comrades down a toboggan-run plotline, just like almost every computer game ever written."

Maya smirked. "Including one we won't say by name."

"One we will *never* say by name."

Maya returned to unloading her shipping box. The next board game she pulled out had large block letters that read, "Postamt." It showed a boy in lederhosen handing a stamped envelope to a uniformed woman with a satchel full of mail. The bottom of the box provided a confusing description in English. Something about planning a postal route.

"Do people buy these German games?"

Devon took the game from Maya's hands, turned it over, and read through the shrink wrap.

"My Deutsch is dusty, but I fear this one will make itself comfortable on our shelves. To be perfectly honest, I have no clear idea of what to order. On an eBay binge last week, I bought an assortment of unopened EU games and discount novelties— mostly medieval themed doodads."

"I love this store, Dad. It's like a temple for some beautiful religion almost nobody practices."

"Like Quakerism, without the glorious past."

Devon gave his daughter a sideways hug, and the pair worked together in silence. Maya pulled one game after another out of shipping boxes and slid them into the open spaces on the wall. Every fifteen seconds, a new board game went into place until her shipping box lay empty.

Maya enjoyed the physical labor of chores like this. They stilled her mind and eased doubts about the future. She'd caused a domestic scene when she announced that after Evergreen she intended to continue her studies in comparative literature. Her mentor at the Minority Affairs office had warned that her parents would expect a more practical career path. He was right, though only about her mother. When the acceptance letter from Yale arrived, Mom did an about-face. After a brief campus visit, it was Maya who became ambivalent.

She knew it was cliché, but seeing Yale made her feel like an impostor. What right did she have to walk on stone stairs worn concave by centuries of scholarly shoes? Why should she have access to the restricted section of the library, with its ancient volumes sealed away like forbidden books at Hogwarts?

Even the turtlenecked graduate students intimidated her by using jargon she hadn't ever heard. Some of their research sounded like abstruse exercises in postmodern posturing. Still, she could sense the excitement of buzzing inside a hive, dancing with the other bees as they told of their discoveries during that day's flight.

In the end, she accepted the offer of admission, then announced that she would spend a summer relaxing with her father in sunny San Diego. Having tried on Devon's lifestyle for the past few weeks, she wasn't sure she could walk away from it. She'd found herself a clutch of gaming friends, and Dad seemed more engaging and self-assured than she'd remembered.

Maya launched a trial balloon.

"What if I wanted to stay past August?"

"That would no longer constitute a summer job, now would it?"

"What if I don't want to go to Yale? I've been in school for sixteen years without a break. I like this job. Maybe I'm needed here."

"Your Jedi mind tricks *are* needed here, Maya-wan. And everywhere. But this is my retirement hobby, not your career."

Maya folded up a shipping box. She carried the cardboard to the back of the store, where she set it atop a two-foot stack of empties.

"It's never easy to choose a path," Devon said. "You need to understand where you excel. Find your niche."

Maya spun around and startled her father.

"So you want me to fly off to the East Coast to take seminars on books I never liked? To teach English composition to brats whose daddies donated to the library?"

"No, I just—"

"This store is your passion, Dad, but how long did it take you to get here? Remember all those years you were miserable writing lines of stupid code? You worked with people you hated so much that you started hating *me*. And Mom."

"That is not fair. I—"

Devon interrupted his own thought. He turned away from his daughter and wiped at his face.

Maya suppressed a reflex to wince. She'd never punished him for leaving home, not like he deserved.

Devon rubbed both hands across his face and looked up at the clouds on the ceiling.

"Your dad used to love his job. We were rushing products to market just so we could move on to the next crazy idea. Always trying out new angles, new tricks. We cut corners and skipped the boring stuff, like packaging, marketing, server security…"

Maya felt her shoulders relaxing.

"Our games were ugly and obscure, but they were fun." Devon laughed to himself. "That is, if you could find them—and get them to work. We would stay up all night, arguing about how the online platform might subvert traditional rules of game design."

"But then—"

"Yes, but then. Then we struck gold with the game-that-must-not-be-named. We got rich, every one of us." Devon scrunched up his face and wheezed like a wizened miner. "We chained ourselves to our cubicles and became prospectors. Traded paint brushes for pick axes."

Devon cleared his throat.

"Enough about your old father. Don't you have friends coming over soon? There's lots we need to do here before then."

"Roger that."

Maya sighed. Some conversation was better than none.

She picked up slips of paper and loose packaging from the inventory she'd shelved, then cleared off the gaming table at the back of the store. When Devon walked past her, she turned to face him.

"Dad, the module Alan's creating is fascinating. I guess you know that there's this Lifeless Knight roaming the Mythos and destroying everybody, or turning them into creepos, like those acolytes we encountered. One of them killed Brianna's character, Hermione."

"But she popped right back up, yes?" Devon laughed. "Nobody ever dies in such games."

"It wasn't like that at all. Alan's strict about the rules, so death can be very real. The only reason I got a seat at his table is that he'd killed off another guy's character."

"Surely he did not intend for the poor fellow to lose his avatar?"

"No, probably not. But still, it was scary when Hermione went down. Resurrection in Alan's Mythos is, shall we say, dicey."

"Good one."

Devon winked at his daughter, who had learned from her father to never resist an easy pun, even mid-monologue. Maya responded with what she considered her signature gesture, the disquieting half-grin of a stroke victim.

"Perhaps," Devon said, "Alan shares my view that mortality makes life worth living."

"Certainly makes things more interesting. I can't even guess who'll still be alive in the final act. I think Alan knows that the well-timed death of a hero makes a story more powerful, whether it's A Tale of Two Cities, Serenity, or whatever. Look at the difference between Gandalf's death and Dumbledore's…"

"Do you not see what you are doing?"

Maya cocked her head.

"You, my dearest one, are meant to be a literary critic."

Maya tried to feign annoyance by folding arms over chest. Inside, she felt her heart expanding for this runaway father of hers.

"But Yale must wait!" Devon said. "First, there are boxes to be opened. Cardboard to be stacked. Games to be shelved. Surely, no purpose on this Earth better suits your many talents."

ALAN

Opening the door slowly to foil its bell, Alan followed Lance and Carlos into Players. Lance had become comfortable navigating the space. He used his cane to scout the floor only for loose boxes. He glided to his customary chair beside Carlos and across from Maya, who was seated at the back table already.

"Brianna texted a while ago," Maya said. "Band practice might make her late."

Alan set his papers on the table and excused himself to speak with Devon, who was marking up receipts beside the register.

Devon looked up from his work and offered a warm smile.

"Maya tells me you are directing quite expertly. This is your sequel to The Cursed Tomb, yes?"

"That's what I wanted to talk about." Alan lowered his voice. "I liked The Tomb, but it didn't really go anywhere."

"So where are you taking the story?"

"That's the thing. It feels like I'm inventing something new, a kind of stream-of-consciousness campaigning. Instead of sketching out a plot arc and filling in the details, I'm working with an open-ended narrative."

"Pure improvisation?"

"Oh, I inventory the main monsters, villains, and settings each week, but I'm also finding myself reflecting on the heroes themselves—like Maya's barbarian or Carlos' sorcerer. I even think about the motivations and personalities of the people who play them."

"Sounds more like poetry than game direction."

"It's chaotic, like the membrane between my left and right brain has been chemically burned away."

Devon raised an eyebrow. "There's good and bad cholesterol, but I don't think there's such a thing as good epilepsy."

"No? Then maybe I'm becoming a sleepwalking psychic

who has imaginary adventures he can't remember and lucid daydreams that might have actually taken place."

Alan hesitated to say more. He wanted to talk to someone about this but feared he'd over-disclosed already.

As if sensing his distress, Devon offered a serious nod. Channeling the voice of Obi-Wan Kenobi, he said, "Let go of your conscious self and act on instinct."

In his mind, Alan could see himself dressed in Luke Skywalker's off-white tunic. Wearing a helmet over his head and covering his eyes, he held his lightsaber with both hands to defend against laser blasts from a training droid. Feeling the Force pass through him, Alan darted to his left to parry one attack, then another.

"Artists routinely mine their unconscious minds, Alan. Perhaps you will be among the first to tap the *collective* unconscious. My advice is to—"

The front door flew open and its cowbell clanged wildly. Brianna stormed through, slamming the door with enough force to rattle its glass inlay. She threw down her cloth bag. Its contents slid like curling stones along the length of the floor. Her green-sleeved iPad came to rest at the heels of Carlos' loafers.

Brianna began to wail. Maya walked across the room to embrace her, and Brianna fell into her arms. Devon tiptoed across the front of the store, switched the Open sign to Closed, and latched the door. There were no Friday afternoon customers. The only souls in the store besides its owner were Alan and his group.

"What's happening?" Lance whispered.

Carlos poked Lance in the shoulder.

"Bet she's still pissed about our little stadium field trip. Probably pissed at you, *padre*."

Alan had retreated back to the table and stood beside his comrades.

"He's right, Lance. Practically everyone's seen that video."

"She was upset this morning," Lance said, "but she didn't seem committed to the mood."

Brianna downshifted into heaving sobs. She pulled mucus back up into her nose and glared at Lance. "Everyone hates us! Everyone hates this stupid game we're playing. Everyone hates *me*!"

Maya stroked Brianna's hair and held her close.

"It's just friends here, girl. Nobody hates you."

Brianna tried to push herself free, but Maya held her fast. Brianna turned red eyes on Alan and Carlos.

"I didn't have any real friends before, but now I've got real enemies. Today I was dumped by one of the only people at school I liked. I didn't even know friends dumped each other. Randall's sister, Tiffany—she *buried* me."

Alan felt a chill. Was this somehow about Randall? Tiffany idolized her big brother, but Randall had zero interest in her affairs.

"Why would Randall..."

Alan withdrew the question, half-formed. Better to leave this matter to the only other female in the room.

Maya looked to Devon, who shrugged. She pulled Brianna's wet cheek off her shoulder and led Brianna to the ornate wooden throne in the middle of the store. Placed in the chair, Brianna looked like a stuffed animal posed on an oversized piece of furniture. Brianna pulled her bony knees to her chest and held them tight.

From the back of the store, Maya dragged out two tall boxes marked "Novelties." She tipped them over and said, "Behold!"

The words caught Brianna's attention. Even Devon stopped pretending to work at the register and moved so he could see his daughter clearly. After a moment of rummaging, Maya stood up and extended her arms. From them hung an assortment of costume accessories and plastic toys.

"Here sits our Blessed Lady of the Scorned." Maya spun

around to connect with every set of eyes in the room. "You, her loyal subjects, may each make an offering."

Brianna squirmed in her chair but held her legs fast. Maya jerked her head toward Alan. He stepped forward and pulled a red feather boa from Maya's right arm. When he draped it over Brianna's head, it hung in her hair until he nudged it down to her neck.

"The Shawl of the Fire Maiden," Alan said tentatively. "May it, uh, burn away all doubts. And singe the unholy."

Maya half-rolled her eyes at Alan, who backed up two paces but remained standing.

Carlos approached and eased a plastic shield off Maya's left arm. In both hands he held the silver disc, no larger than a dinner plate. Carlos knelt, extended his arms, and offered the item. After a moment's hesitation, Brianna took it.

"The Shield of *la Profeta*," Carlos said.

Brianna blinked and wiped a sleeve across her eyes.

"With it, you can see *el futuro*. And this future, it is so bright for you, chica—"

"That I'll have to wear Lance's shades," Brianna said as she accepted the gift.

Relieved laughter came quickly from everyone in the room, including Devon.

Carlos stepped back into the half circle forming around Brianna and scuffed her brother's tennis shoes. Lance took his turn and felt his way across Maya's arms. He tugged at the sleeve of her blouse.

"Try again," she said.

From Maya's forearm, Lance lifted a string of small wooden cubes, which clicked as they dangled from his hand. He stage whispered to Maya, "Are these dice?"

"Crappy fake ones."

Lance turned about like a piñata batsman.

"Brianna?"

"Over here."

"Reach out your arm."

Brianna let go of her knees and sat up straight. She extended her left arm toward Lance, and he looped the string of dice around her wrist.

"Without you, we would be lost. Only you can roll to save us all from poison, paralysis, and breath."

Brianna scrunched her nose. "Nothing can save us from your breath."

"So say we all," Alan and Carlos chanted in unison.

As he stepped backward, Lance dug his heel into the top of Carlos' foot.

Maya dumped the remaining trinkets from her arms. With her thumbs and middle fingers, she lifted a plastic tiara with a hand-painted emerald in its center. Dipping her eyes, Maya placed the crown atop Brianna's head.

"Your subjects are beneath you," Maya said, "but our hearts are pure. We would have you bless our kingdom, which brings gifts to the world without asking for thanks. The two noble genres—fantasy and sci fi—come from us, and we sustain them. We brought forth the graphic novel, the adventure movie, even the lowly video game. We spawned the teenage vampires, the steampunks, the Goths. We refresh and sustain the deep legends, the secular myths. Even when the world treats us as untouchables, we stick to our stories. To each other."

Maya giggled, then cleared her throat.

"Each pair of us," she said, "carries the primal bonds of Leia and Luke, Sam and Frodo, Calvin and Hobbes, Kitty Pryde and Wolverine. Together, we rule the kingdom of imagination. We welcome our new members not as peasants but as royalty. From this day forward, you are Brianna no more. Farewell, Brianna. You are hereby reborn as *Princess Brie*. She of the stinky cheese, beloved by those who know bitter rind from sour curd."

Maya nodded to the gathered group, which now included

Devon. The proud father beamed at his young scholar-poet.

"As our princess ripens, she shall repel the unworthy ever more completely. As she ages, she shall grow stronger." Maya spread her arms wide. "All hail Princess Brie!"

"Hail!"

"What is thy command?" Maya said with a bow.

Brie sniffed.

"Next weekend, we play at my house."

"Done," Alan said.

Lifting herself out of the throne-chair, Brie smiled at Maya and surveyed the rest of the group.

"Let's roll some dice, losers."

RANDALL

No professional satisfaction came from editing sloppy lines of security code written by Randall's feckless co-workers. His efficiency at the task entitled him to another break, so he watched once more the "Petco Massacre" on YouTube. This video clip inspired him. It sang to him like a muse. It made Randall believe he'd misjudged the level of mayhem one could sow into the universe—into Alan's clique.

Randall had visited Players to make a modest move in the meta-game he'd invented. Disrupting a joyful gaming session would do a small cruelty to the store's proprietor, who, he deduced, was Dad to one of Alan's new playmates. He now recognized that a greater purpose led him into Players that evening. This new game would test his capacity for patience. Subterfuge must supplant rage. Resentment must give way to reflection.

When he returned to his apartment that evening, Randall had come closer to praying than his parents would have ever dreamed. Knees bent and hands clasped, he asked for the power to recognize those opportunities the Fates would offer in the coming weeks. He asked for the wisdom to seize each as it arrived.

Though he knew grander schemes awaited him, Randall appreciated the power of more subtle pranks. When DVDs began appearing on the shelves of the La Mesa Blockbuster, Randall printed a sheet of stickers that read, "Be Kind, Please Rewind." He affixed one to the inside of many a plastic disc case. He'd loiter at the video rental store in hopes of seeing a befuddled customer plead with a clerk, perplexed about how to accomplish the requested task. He never got to witness such exchanges, but the certainty that they'd happened was satisfaction enough.

In that same spirit, Randall reviewed revenge fantasies suited to the present situation. He pictured himself slipping NyQuil into Lance Langdon's favorite drink, the Caribbean punch Lance put in the company fridge each morning. After gentle tampering, it would smell and taste the same. Lance wouldn't know the difference until Ted found him asleep on his keyboard.

Or, Randall could stay late at work and fiddle with Lance's voice-recognition software. He could set it in training mode, mumble for twenty minutes, then make nonsense corrections until it couldn't tell the difference between English and Mandarin.

Such amusements might bear fruit more readily than Randall's first effort. After entreating Tiffany to strike, he'd heard no news. But taking more direct action had its own hazards. After all, Boldheart's bravery in the Mythos made him easy prey for Alan's trap. Randall would choose caution over courage. A more subtle path to victory would reveal itself.

It was in the spirit of discretion that he'd avoided Lance's cubicle on the floor they shared, the fourth and highest level of the misnamed Mission Valley Technology Tower. As a gesture toward ADA-compliance, Ted Takamura, the eponymous founder and CEO of ProTechTed, had put Lance's seat just six feet from the copier and toner. Thus, Randall had scanned and printed documents at his own desk each of the past fifteen work days to avoid making a Xerox. Theirs was hardly a paperless office, and Randall's plan failed when his laser printer first went gray, then ceased to make any marks at all.

Randall sat still for a time. After much deliberation, he plotted a safe path to the supply shelf that would avoid Lance by going through one door in Ted's glass-walled office then out the other. Eager to begin this minor quest, Randall braced his hands on the arms of his chair and lifted himself quickly. When he tried to stand, he bumped his desk, which shook the walls of adjoining cubicles.

Officemates popped up and stared at him like spooked meerkats. Randall stumbled about his enclosure, and the small mammals around him ducked back into their burrows.

Having lost any pretense of stealth, Randall dashed into the hall and opened the main door to Ted's spacious office.

Ted looked up from his monitor and cocked his head.

Randall hadn't devised his plan with much care, but he'd rehearsed the dialogue.

"Hello, Ted."

"Hello, Randall."

"I am making copies."

"Oh, fine."

"Goodbye, Ted."

"Sure you don't need something?"

With a single query, Ted had thrown Randall off script.

"I, um, need copies."

Ted ran his hand down his tie, straightening it to show interlocking Escher fish. He took off his reading glasses and looked at his employee, who was unsure how to read Ted's expression.

Randall knew Ted admired his sophisticated code scripts and ingenious security countermeasures. Ted had once complimented Randall's aggressive tone in staff meetings by saying he possessed the qualities Crash Davis once attributed to the best baseball players—"an even mix of fear and arrogance." Randall had Googled the reference and found it to his liking. But now, standing before his boss, he sensed Ted toying with him.

"Why would I make copies for you, Randall?"

"I didn't mean—"

Randall looked down. His white dress shirt had pulled free of his pants when he'd banged into his desk. He felt a cool sweat spread across his skin.

Ted made an abrupt nasal snort. Randall had boasted to co-workers that he'd impersonate that signature sound at the company's winter holiday fest. To date, he'd neither delivered on that promise nor attended the party.

Randall felt his stomach boil. Ted was baiting the wrong bear. This grizzly was playing a grander game, and he made a note to find in it an unpleasant cameo role for his employer.

"Just goofing you, Randall. Come over here. I wanna show you something."

Startled by the invitation, Randall hurried around Ted's desk to stand at his side. Randall forgot his reason for entering the office when he saw a zoo of colorful figures running across a 52" horizontal display. The creatures were detailed two-dimensional polygon renderings of the classes and races described in the *Dungeon Lords Adventure Manual*.

"Is this Dungeon Lords Online?" Randall asked.

"What? No." Ted grabbed his mouse and clicked to bring forward a game-credits box with the gothic-script headline, "World of Karnage."

Randall nodded slowly.

"You've never played? The WOK folks were one of our clients a while back. You helped write protocols for them."

"Sure, I remember."

Ted frowned.

"You seem like the kind of guy who'd be into this."

Randall wasn't listening. He pictured the face of the game store owner, the father of Alan's new playmate. That man—Devon was his name—said he'd helped to build this "awful game." Devon seemed ashamed and asked that his association with it remain secret. Randall felt a shudder of excitement. Ideas formed. Possibilities opened.

"Well, let's see what's cookin' today."

Ted slid and tapped and slid and tapped his mouse. He hovered his pointer over a blue-robed man with fiery hair framing his head like an orange triangle.

"That's Theodor the ProTechtor, my Epic level paladin. Cool name, eh?"

Randall watched the other beings walking by Theodor. Bits of text floated up from each character's head.

"Need a priest?"

"Let's PvP."

"FFS, let's go!"

Randall tried to look bored, but he stared straight into Ted's monitor.

"You have to buy the software, then pay a monthly fee, right?"

"That's just the beginning. What costs buckaroos is gathering up all the stuff. Tonight, Theodor's questing with a team of dryads. To get some bling-bling, we're shaking down this huge basilisk." Ted looked up at Randall. "You know, that giant lizard thing in Harry Potter?"

"I know what a basilisk is."

"To get to the Epic levels, or even to the Demis, you either have to play for I don't know how many months or..."

Randall sensed this was a cue to offer an eager, "Or what?" He said nothing.

"Or you pay Third Servants to do the work for you."

Randall was unable to hide his curiosity any longer.

"Third Servants?"

"They're mostly high school and college kids in China, Korea, or wherever. They'll play your character all night for you. They take Theodor on skill-building quests and gather up gold that I can spend on gear, like armor and potions."

"Why would you let someone else have your adventure?"

"Some of the coolest stuff in the WOK requires forming huge raiding parties. Sometimes the treasure, like a magical bastard sword, can't be divided. Players just dice for it. The whole business can be tedious, so I have Third Servants gather up enough loot for me to buy an item outright, then use it on cooler quests whenever I want."

Randall's mind swam with confused excitement. With the same Biblical certainty of his parents, who believed a god had re-animated his zombie son, Randall felt the hand of the Holy

Ghost guiding him. He sensed a higher power working through him in the "strange and mysterious ways" his parents had so often described. Whatever its purpose, he knew the WOK was the next key in his quest.

"Gotta go," Randall said.

"Right." Ted smirked. "To make copies."

Randall hurried out the same door he'd used to enter Ted's office. Back at his desk, he spent the remainder of the afternoon setting up his Karnage account and reading about the game.

On the bus ride home, he could think of nothing but the WOK. Until he discovered his true use for it, he would at least enjoy mocking fellow players through the game's chat interface. Also, he could partake in combat and conquest without the smothering "storytelling" Alan blanketed over everything. Contempt for all things video game had been Alan's childish prejudice, not his own.

Randall pulled a notebook out of his backpack and jotted notes on how to design his new WOK character, including clothes, hair, accessories. His avatar would be a human warrior, and his name would be Boldheart. He tried to remember the teenage Randall who'd created that name. Did it come from watching the Mel Gibson biopic about William Wallace? The handle sounded corny, but this time, Randall chose it as an act of defiance. Boldheart would rise again.

When he got home, Randall pulled down his blackout blinds to cover up the early evening light. Downloading and installing the WOK software took nearly an hour. His home computer wasn't built for demanding graphics, and a basic DSL connection slowed him down.

To pass the time, Randall microwaved three frozen dinners. Macaroni-and-cheese and fried chicken were the appetizers. Salisbury steak was the entrée. A three-serving strawberry shortcake was desert.

When the time came to name his new avatar, Randall cursed

at his misfortune. A latecomer to the WOK, his first preference had been taken by another user. After considering a few options, he tried the plural form. As soon as "Boldhearts" was approved and affixed to him, he realized it sounded like the title of a YA novel.

Through the night and into the morning, Randall ate, drank, and clicked. It was Saturday noon before he took a break. He washed his face in the bathroom sink and gargled water from the faucet. The mirror showed reddening cheeks contrasting against the white dress shirt he wore the day before.

Randall felt dizzy and steadied himself against a towel rack when the cell phone in his pocket rang. He fumbled for it and heard his sister's voice.

"Hey, Randy!"

"What?"

"Didn't you get my text? I totally ditched Brianna yesterday."

Randall held the phone closer to his ear.

"What happened?"

"It was brutal." Tiffany forced a laugh. "I caught her reading some Dungeon Lords thing on her iPad. Then I, like, totally waved it around for everyone to see. She grabbed for it, but when I..."

Randall's heartbeat grew faster and louder than Tiffany's chatter. A jolt of adrenaline shot up his chest and down his arms. Randall felt both exhausted and aglow, as if he'd experienced a "quickening," like in the *Highlander* series. He'd decapitated, albeit vicariously, one of his new foes and had received what little power and knowledge she held. Brianna was a gaming noob, so it wasn't much.

But it was enough to embolden him. Randall decided to spike Lance's drink next Monday. He walked to the bathroom, opened the medicine cabinet behind his mirror, and inventoried the cough syrups in stock. Seeing the bottles made him realize his own throat itched, so he sampled one, then another.

As he got back to his desk, Randall felt his brain lagging behind his movements. Dayquil battled Nyquil for command of his body. Randall suppressed a reflex to vomit the lot of it and go to bed. Staying awake required immediate action.

Randall fished into a desk drawer and found a half-opened pack of energy tablets. He popped two into his mouth and shook them down his throat, a hungry lizard swallowing its prey. To bring adrenaline into the mix, Randall slapped his face. Left cheek, right cheek. Repeat.

That did the trick.

He felt more energy but not enough focus to plan his next assault on Alan. He could always explore the WOK and see if that sparked any inspiration.

A high-pitched squeak came from his phone, which lay forgotten beside his keyboard. He hit the speaker button.

"You there?"

"Sure."

"What were you—never mind. So, you'll go with us to Korea?"

Randall's mind flashed on the conversation in Ted's office from the previous day. What was the significance of Korea again? He remembered the Third Servants. Yes, that was what he needed. He'd hire off-shore labor to keep Boldhearts fighting while he got some rest.

"You will come with us, please?"

"I'll sleep on it."

"Thanks, Big Boy. It really means a lot—"

Randall turned off his phone.

HERMIONE

The nasty incident at the temple of Helios had slowed the journey to the Fairie Realm. Hermione worried that Cynoc's army might arrive first. The greater fear, which she kept to herself, was what would happen when they finally caught up with this malevolent force. If she had been pulled under by the mere wake of this destruction, how could she survive a direct encounter?

On the subject of her brief death, Hermione's companions offered reassurance. Santana insisted it resulted from a tactical error by their party, for which he shared the blame. Angelou commended Hermione's bravery in battle. Lancelot said that her rapid recovery demonstrated stamina.

Those partial truths belied a more ominous one. The sorcerer, barbarian, and priest were all battle-tested, whereas Hermione was a neophyte, unprepared for full-scale battle. She would be no match for the likes of Cynoc.

What Hermione knew was music, a gift that came to her as a child. Befuddled Pale Elven instructors swore she had greater natural talent than any of her kind. After fierce debate on the question, bardic elders broke tradition by bringing in non-elven virtuosos to tutor their prodigy. The gamble paid dividends and her music's power grew. The visiting instructors, however, planted new seeds in their pupil's mind. As these matured into inspiration, Hermione worked in secret to fuse ancient tunes with popular sounds and rhythms forbidden within the Elvenmists.

Hermione debuted her new repertoire in a mountaintop amphitheater, where she performed before an audience of thousands beneath a canopy of redwoods. At the front of the gathering, family, friends, and the weightiest elves in the kingdom sat on stone benches. By the second song, music

Hermione had hoped would delight and amaze met only jeers and curses.

In the fourth row, she met the stare of her first instructor, who had not seen her in more than a year. He jumped from his seat, thrust a finger toward her, and cried, "Heresy!" The outburst was unbecoming an elf, yet the audience cheered in agreement.

Undeterred, Hermione listened to her soft voice reverberating through the amphitheater. She checked her fingering to bend the next chord slightly. When her eyes lifted, she saw two of her brothers rushing through the aisle toward her.

"Burn the lute!"

"Banish the child!"

That ended the concert and started the first riot in the history of the Elvenmists. She barely escaped with her life.

Months later, Hermione's youngest sister tracked her down. The reunion was brief. She begged Hermione to never return, lest she be tried and executed. Hermione agreed, but privately vowed to write music that could open even elven hearts.

Cynoc's massacre made the question moot.

It struck Hermione as poetic that she now sought to avenge her people's deaths with the very music they had scorned. Doing so would mean singing—and possibly fighting—in the heat of battle.

The worries returned. How many more times would her companions have to resurrect her before she could fend for herself? How many chances would she get?

Each day that they followed Devotus' map gave her a chance to learn new combat maneuvers from Lancelot. Less than a week passed, however, before they found the hidden gateway to the Fairie Realm.

The invisible passage required a suspension of doubt. There was no visible entrance. Devotus had given precise guidance that was clear, but baffling. He showed on the map that they had to turn away from the edge of the forest in a precise direction, at a slow pace. This they tried repeatedly, but each time, Hermione or a companion made a remark about the absurdity of the exercise. Devon had warned against doing so. When they repeated the steps one last time, hands clasped over mouths, they entered a broadleaf forest not visible a moment before it appeared.

Luminous dust floated in the shade of beeches and birches that skirted massive oaks. After walking hundreds of meters into the woods, diseased trees with pale brown leaves began to appear. These gave way to gray trunks devoid of foliage, moss, or even bark. What had been a pale blue sky became a blanket of clouds. Gradually, even the forest's sounds disappeared. Hoots, chirps, rustling all ceased. It was as though every living creature had fled whatever they marched toward.

Hermione gasped. "What might this silence mean for the poor little fairies?"

In the forward position, Lancelot led the group into a rapid trot. "Don't break formation!"

In two strides, Angelou took her place beside him, with Hermione trailing and Santana ten meters back, his staff at the ready. Lupita leapt and danced around the sorcerer, her barks urging a faster pace.

Far ahead, a vast clearing could be seen through the trees. An indistinct structure of tremendous size stood in its center, shrouded in smoke. Growing louder as they moved in its direction was the noise of battle.

Lancelot wore a grave expression as he pulled on his helmet. Hermione doubted his leadership acumen, but it was better than Santana's arrogance and Angelou's impulsiveness. Lancelot had devised a tactical scheme whereby they might fight in a coordinated fashion, though Hermione thought his plan untested, at best.

A sharp whistling, and a crossbow bolt found a gap in the hides on Angelou's body. It went clean through her hip, pulling out a stream of blood as it exited. Another glanced off Lancelot's shield and buried itself in an oak.

"Remember protocol," Lancelot said between short breaths. "Angelou leads. Santana trails. No one dies. Armor to the fore." He quickened his stride and moved in front of Angelou. Two more bolts struck his shield.

Crouching low, Angelou lifted the shaft that had pierced her side and inspected it as a connoisseur might do in an armory. Ignoring the blood that trailed from her wound, she said simply, "The bolt is elven."

Hermione plucked a chord on her lute while Santana drew an oval in front of himself with the tip of his staff. Their actions achieved the same effect, as towering translucent shields materialized before both of them. Another whistle presaged a bolt targeting Hermione. Instead of striking its target, it floated harmlessly in the white ether of her magical shield.

"Perhaps the Pale Elves live?" Hermione said.

"More likely," Santana said, "they have been plundered."

From between the trees, five elves jumped out at Lancelot, swords and spears pointing forward. They wore noble garments, but their clothes and skin were as filthy as city urchins.

Angelou stepped forward and swung her trident low. Its razor-sharp tines cut like a scythe through wheat. Four amputated bodies fell to the ground. The fifth elf leapt high, only to find the same fate as his fellows when Lancelot's mace found his gut.

When Lupita and Angelou killed the crippled attackers, Hermione felt remorse. Whatever they were, these were still elves. She fell to her knees.

"Get up, minstrel," growled Santana. "These fiends were not your friends."

"I'm not so sure." Lancelot adjusted the shield strapped to his arm. "They had the same empty eyes as the lot we fought at the temple. If both the worshippers of Helios and these former elves are the same Naughts of which Devotus warned us, what does that mean?

Angelou spat on the ground.

"They shed no tears for us. We shed none for them."

Hermione's face glistened. Her lute hung uselessly at her side.

"I weep not for what they are but what they *were*. Can't you feel it? This Lifeless Knight has taken something from them, if not their lives."

"No time fer mourning, child," said Angelou. "We must find the fairies."

Lancelot pointed his mace forward.

"Just ahead, the sounds of war grow stronger. Hermione— get up at once!"

Angelou extended a hand to Hermione. Instead of taking it, she drew a scimitar from her belt, sprang to her feet, and charged toward the roaring battle up ahead.

"In formation," Lancelot cried.

He and his comrades chased after Hermione, who darted between dead tree trunks and toward the clearing just ahead.

"Remember the plan, Hermione! Oh, by blessed Elahna's bounty."

Lancelot caught up with Hermione just as the forest gave way to bare earth strewn with a thousand or more dead bodies amidst broken shields and weapons. In the center of the clearing stood a battered wooden fortress large enough to contain a town. Its enormous main doors had been staved in, and black smoke billowed up from inside. Well-intact were its walls, made of trees bound together with thick rope. Each trunk stood thirty meters high and ended not in sharp points but with living branches, full with green oak leaves.

At the base of the fortress, Hermione saw perhaps three hundred elven Naughts fighting against—against what, exactly, she could not say. She pointed her scimitar toward the gray sky above the fortress.

"Are those—"

"Fairies?" Lancelot said.

All knew well the fairies, but only by reputation. Fairies were the source of all artefactual magic in the world. Every scepter, staff, charm, crystal, and musical instrument charged with magical power had been created by these beings. Though their crafts were ubiquitous, no one knew the fairies themselves, nor the workings of their society. Since the dawn of recorded history in the Mythos, only a handful of adventurers had ever claimed to see a single fairie.

Hermione shared the common conception of fairies as radiant female adolescents, winged nymphs no larger than the greatest butterfly. That was a far cry from what she now beheld.

Descending into the battle came a V-shaped squadron of silver giants—women whose thirteen-foot height was matched by their wingspan. Their landing shook the ground with the crash of falling boulders. Around their bodies swirled orange-brown swaths of clothing that showed not a ripple when struck directly by swords and spears.

"Can these giants be the fairies of legend?" Santana wondered aloud.

"Either way," Angelou said, "they need our help."

Angelou lowered her trident and charged forward with a battle cry barely audible above the roar of the Naughts. Santana and Lancelot glanced at each other, then followed her lead. Hermione brought up the rear but slowed as she approached the edge of the fray. In spite of their awesome size, many winged women lay among the dead.

"Defend the giants!" Lancelot cried.

At the back ranks of the Naughts, Angelou and Lancelot began thrusting and swinging metal, with Lupita flashing between and behind them to take vicious bites of their enemies.

Hermione shouted at Lancelot, "Turn them!" She snatched his silver unicorn from his belt and jabbed him with it. "Are these not the living dead? Turn them away!"

Lancelot exchanged mace for figurine and thrust it toward the Naughts, many of whom were racing toward him. "Through Elahna's eyes, I shall see your souls flee to the Underworld!"

The silver unicorn in his hand reared back and neighed, releasing a burst of sweet air at the approaching warriors. The Naughts crouched for a moment, then stormed forward.

"Elahna!" Lancelot cried. "Can you not—?"

Wood, metal, and fist pounded Lancelot, and he crumpled beneath his shield. A Naught pulled the helm off Lancelot's head, and Hermione saw fear in her companion's eyes. It was as if some force were draining the priest's deity of her power. Hermione remembered this god of which the Naughts spoke— this Aleh'en.

No matter the origin of this army, she had to act. Hermione slashed at the pile of Naughts atop Lancelot but then hesitated, unsure of whether her blade was flensing friend or foe.

Santana reached down from his toe and up to his head to conjure seamless crimson armor that covered his body. He blew a puff of icy air at his staff, and it became a solid iron rod. After pushing Hermione aside, Santana pummeled Lancelot's attackers with his bespelled weapon until he uncovered his friend's bloodied body.

Hermione pulled her motionless comrade back from the battle, and Santana hurried back to Angelou. Sorcerer and barbarian fought silently, side-by-side, in their different styles. While Angelou jumped and parried to spear the Naughts, Santana met any who dodged his staff with his open palm, which glowed bright red. At his touch, enemies writhed in pain until they felt the snap of Lupita's jaws.

Into the sea of Naughts, Hermione fired a hail of sling bullets, some of which found their targets. She was ill-equipped to stand in the midst of the battle, so it was up to Santana and Angelou to break through the Naughts assaulting the fortress and join forces with the remaining giants who defended it. Slowly, Hermione's companions carved a wedge into the army, which still numbered in the hundreds.

Outside the fortress gates, twenty of the giants stood in a circle that tightened with each loss they suffered. Whether striking or receiving blows, the winged creatures, which Hermione could not conceive as fairies, were as dispassionate as the Naughts. They fought with raw physical force, their stony hands slamming together as iron plates to crush heads and limbs between them. All the while, their wings beat with the speed of a hummingbird's, screeching at an impossible pitch to force many would-be attackers to cover their ears. Naughts who lost their bearings and crawled under the wings were swept up, pureed, and vented out as a red spray.

Though the throng of enemy soldiers thinned, the fairie giants also fell. Through gaps in their flowing vestments, the odd bolt or blade would catch them. After a few such injuries, a fairie's wings would tear and become useless. With her wings silenced and nowhere to hide, the crush of the horde would eventually bear a fairie to the ground.

By the time Santana and Angelou reached them, only six of the giants stood—each wavering under the assault. Santana appeared to have insubstantial wounds, but his combat spells were expiring. His red armor flickered and disappeared. His hands returned to mere flesh. With his staff more useful as a shield than a weapon, he staggered. Angelou looked bruised and bloodied, as she endured a flurry of blows.

Hermione shouted toward Santana and Angelou, but they seemed not to hear. The pair were swept up in the confusion of the battle and had backed into the fortress wall, which left them trapped against it.

When Hermione caught Santana's eyes, she felt an odd sensation—as though a force moved in a loop through her and Lancelot, out to Santana and Angelou, then back again. The feeling urged her to come to their aid, but she could not leave Lancelot unconscious and unguarded.

Thinking through her next move, Hermione fought off two Naughts who came at her from the edge of the battle. She sliced wildly with her scimitar until the pair of attackers dropped. The remaining Naughts—perhaps a hundred—were focused on the giant women, Santana, and Angelou.

Joining in the assault were two of the giants, whose eyes seemed half closed. They moved slowly, their wings battered down to stumps. One of them flailed at Angelou and nearly disarmed her with a vicious blow to the shoulder. If the Naughts had corrupted these giants, as they had with the devotees at Helois' temple, the situation was truly desperate.

Lupita retreated from the battle, almost dragging her belly on the ground. The wolf whimpered and pressed matted fur into Hermione's legs.

A confusing mix of anger and fear made Hermione quiver, then an arc of energy flowed from her helpless companions back into her body. Deep inside her chest, this power cooled into resolve.

Hermione dropped her weapon and unfastened her lute, along with a hairless bow she had whittled on their journey. As she crafted the bow, she had composed and hummed a new song. The tune was an arboreal tribute that seemed more apt than ever, given the devastation of the fairies' forest. She hoped—no, she *knew*—she would sing it well. And strong.

With the wooden bow, she sawed her lute's strings. The instrument moaned, and Hermione layered beneath this a powerful contralto.

On hearing her, one of the Naughts turned around to face Hermione. It hurled a short axe through the air. The steel blade cut through her boot and chipped her shinbone.

Hot pain did not melt Hermione's determination. Grimacing but standing fast, she sang.

Hold my beer and hide your soul
I'm bringing friends who'll swallow you whole
With them in the fight, we've more than a chance
I offer you up to feed the plants!

The air around the fortress grew humid. Hermione's companions, the fairies, and even the frenzied Naughts began to sway as though entangled in seaweed at the bottom of the ocean. Binding ropes that held in place the fortress walls snapped and fell away from the living trunks. Hard bark became supple and mossy, and the tall oaks tilted and bobbed.

The four remaining fairies who fought alongside Santana and Angelou looked out at Hermione, then back at their quivering fortress. With weak wings, they lifted themselves upward and hovered unsteadily above the fray.

Bending over like angry parents swatting their children, the oak walls swung down one trunk after another to crush the columns of Naughts. Each blow seemed to split open the ground, and the shocks alone left none but Hermione standing. By the time the last trunk raised itself back up and stood still, few bodies had been spared. Santana and Angelou, their backs braced against the base of the wall, looked terrified but very much alive.

Hermione rushed at the few Naughts who stirred, and she dispatched them without compassion. When she came upon the final living enemy, she knocked him onto his back and kicked away his sword. She pressed her bloodied boot into his chest.

Before he could speak, a fairie landed hard and crushed the Naught's head with her massive foot.

"There is much you may wish to know," said the fairie, "but you will learn none of it from this wretch's lips."

Hermione wanted to object. They could have interrogated the soldier. But unlike all the others, this fairie had atop her head a filigreed silver circlet that took away nearly all of Hermione's breath.

"Are you—?"

"Yes. I am the Fairie Queen Tinkana."

BRIE

"...and that's all the time I've got today," Alan said. "Sorry, Brie."

That last word caught her off guard. There was no more Brianna in this room. Queen Brie had been a bit much, but once she got everyone to drop the royal title, the new name fit.

Brianna might have accepted Alan's declaration that their evening had come to an end. Brie would have none of it.

"Not so fast," she said.

Alan started to stand.

"Sit—back—down."

The words echoed through the Langdon household. They drew Brie's mother out of the kitchen, through the short hall, and into the den where her two children and their friends sat at a cherry wood table. Brie glanced at her mother, who wore a beige pants suit and a bemused expression.

"Everything okay in there, kids?"

Brie glared at Alan, who reached under the table and gathered his belongings.

Alan said, "We were just finishing up, Mrs. Langdon."

Mary Langdon looked puzzled, but without another word, she stepped back out of the den. Brie wondered what this scene looked like. Her mother had heard stranger outbursts from Lance, who could shout dramatically on any occasion. Hearing one from Brie—her quiet and studious daughter—must have been a shock.

Brie leaned close to Alan and spoke in a slow and serious voice.

"Stop putting away those books."

Alan lifted his new navy blue storage box, then set it back down. Maya and Carlos grinned at each other, as if they knew what would happen next.

"We just cut our way through the nastiest nightmare you've thrown at us," Brie said. "We could have all died in that battle. As it is, you knocked Lancelot out cold."

"Always wear a helmet," Lance said. "Coulda been worse."

"Lots worse," Alan said.

"So now," Brie continued, "you will give us what we came for. We will hear the Fairie Queen's speech."

Alan smirked. "Maybe her speech isn't ready yet."

"Or maybe," Carlos said, "she needs a siesta after watching her sisters get slaughtered."

"Speaking of which," Maya said, "what's up with all the gore?"

"That *was* a little gruesome," Carlos said, "even for you, amigo."

Alan held up his hands in protest.

"There wouldn't have been so much carnage if you hadn't dithered so much. Why didn't you purchase horses for this trip? You could've caught and tamed horses in the time you spent hiking from Devotus' tower to the Fairie Realm. Just because hobbits don't ride horses doesn't mean *you* can't ride horses, or anything else you can saddle up for that matter."

"The hobbits did ride horses," Lance said. "Well, sort of."

"Think past the genre tropes. Close the handbooks and stretch yourselves a little. At Middle Mirth, I want us to show everyone how to play this game right. If we take it seriously, we could maybe even win." Alan ran his thumb and forefinger over his moustache. "I honestly think we could. It would mean a lot—"

Nobody spoke until Maya laughed and said, "Gotta hand it to ya, Alan. Those stone-cold Amazons were a bit disturbing, even for a feminista."

"Disappointed, are we?" Alan batted his eyes and rested his head on his hands. "So it turns out my Mythos fairies aren't singing to the goldfinches and sleeping on nasturtium petals."

"Screw Disney," Maya said with a snort. "Mad props for the

savage pixie chicks."

Alan gestured toward Brie. "On a brighter note, how about our bard's new spell?"

"Yeah, what was that?" Maya said.

Brie's cheeks went as red as the cherry table. She looked for her mother, then remembered that Mom had long since retreated out of the room.

"I wanted to give Brie something special," Alan said. "So her new character carries the Little Lute of Horrors, a relic hidden for centuries in the Elvenmists."

"Cool," Maya said. "But what was the song she played that made the fortress go all Hammertime?"

"It's a musical crafting skill, new for bards," Alan said. "It gives them a little more personality. They can study a high-level spell, druidic in this case, then combine it with physical instrumentation, an original verse, and a unique name for the tune that fits their character conception. That's what Brie did, and it couldn't have been more timely. After our last game, she pitched her idea for this enchantment. She calls it—"

Alan looked to Brie.

"Yes?" Maya said.

Brie's blush deepened. "I call it the Whomping Willow."

"Ah ha ha!" Maya and Lance laughed together. Alan bit his lip but then joined them.

"Oh, no way." Carlos waved his index finger at Brie. "No you didn't."

Maya punched Carlos in the shoulder.

"Yes, I did," Brie said brightly.

"Damn," Carlos said. "I hate that Harry Potter *gabacho*."

"Hermione saved our ass with her Hogwarts topiary," Maya said. "But I gotta go with Carlos on this one."

"I say it was a solid play, sis." Lance held his hand up until Brie leaned over to give him a high five. "And check this out. That wooden bow she used? That was the same cursed cudgel that laid her low at the temple."

"Damn," Maya said in a low voice. "That's pretty badass, sister."

Carlos whispered, "*Música de los muertos.*"

Alan lifted his storage box off the floor and stood.

Brie pounded the table, and the whole group froze in place.

"You're still not going *anywhere*," Brie said. "I'm not letting you out of this house until you give me face time with the Fairie Queen."

"Hermione wants her one-on-one interview," Carlos said. "Give her the goods."

Alan sat back down. He reopened his box and flipped through a pad of yellow paper, as if looking for notes.

Brie heard her mom sniggering in the kitchen. She'd been listening the whole time, maybe while cutting up a turkey for Lance. She pictured her mother stuffing slices into zippered sandwich bags, which Lance took to work for lunch. Mom used a puff-pen to label the bags with an "L" that stood a millimeter high.

Her parental units gave Lance a lot of slack. Would they accept a daughter who became as dorky as her brother? They'd taken her new nickname in stride, but how would they feel about her spending an unchaperoned weekend at Middle Mirth? The question was settled when she heard from the kitchen, "Go get 'em, Hermione!"

"Fine," Alan said with a huff. "You've got fifteen minutes. Brie, what do you want Hermione to do? First, make an ability check for Persuasion."

Maya handed Brie a twenty-sided die.

Brie gave it a roll and said, "Seventeen. What's that mean?"

"With your bardic charisma modifier on top of that," Lance explained, "you've probably won over the Fairie Queen. But only for a few minutes. Alan uses a decay rate for influence rolls, plus you've also got to act the part. Choose your lines carefully.

No do-overs."

Brie felt her heart race. Minutes earlier, when she sang her song and crushed the Naughts, she'd felt a similar pressure. She hadn't choked then, but that only required remembering to use her most powerful spell. This was a different challenge. She tried to summon Hermione's courage. No such luck.

"What words should I use?" Brie said. "Maybe Angelou or Lancelot could talk to her."

"You made the roll," Lance said. "It's all yours, sis."

"Queen Tinkana looks skyward," Alan said. "Flanked by her three remaining companions, she says, 'There is nothing more to be done. Our life here has ended. The Fairie Realm is destroyed. I give thanks that you were here to save us few. We bid farewell.'"

"Come on!" Carlos said. "If we lose the fairies, we're fairly fucked."

Brie looked down. She tried to gather her thoughts.

"Okay," Brie said, "How about, um, Hermione curtsies and says, 'We are humbled to have been of service.'"

"Tinkana extends a thick hand," Alan said. "Her skin shines a brighter silver than you have ever seen. Her hand feels as smooth as tumbled stone."

"Órale," Carlos said. "I have *got* to get Santana some fairie action. Keep going, Brie."

"I beg you not depart. Tell us, how did this happen? There were said to be a multitude of fairies in the Realm. Were those fables, like all else we thought we knew?"

"Tinkana extends her wings to their full span," Alan said. "She stretches her arms and legs, easing the aches in her muscles. The fabric floating about her begins to move more rhythmically, each loop falling into a parallel spiral. Brie, make an Archana check."

A quick roll, a glance down at the die.

"Fourteen?"

"Good enough. You realize that she wears ironcloth, an

enchanted armor only seen before as depictions on elven tapestries. Having witnessed first-hand how these silks brush aside metal weapons, you want to feel it for yourself."

Brie shook her head. "Decorum forces Hermione to keep her hands at her sides."

"Good job," Maya said.

"Santana will let y'all know how it feels," Carlos interjected. "Once he gets to know Tinkana better."

"Eeew," Brie squealed.

Alan cleared his throat. "Tinkana says, 'Our forces would have destroyed this army of scum—those you call the Naughts. According to our sentry, however, they traveled with a dark-plated champion, who flew into the Realm on the wind itself.'"

"The Lifeless Knight," Brie said.

Alan nodded. "As he drifted before our fortress, decaying leaves drew toward him like a train flowing behind a bride. When his feet touched the ground, the earth coursed into his body, and he grew fivefold. At that point, the sentry fled to find me and my sisters."

"So you were not present when the battle began?" Brie said.

"One of the other fairies steps forward. Tinkana bids her to speak, and she explains what she saw. 'The leader of the army raised his visor and spoke. His words had a narcotic logic. He affirmed our fears, nurtured our disappointments. It took all my fortitude to resist his morbid sermon. I could see at once how he claimed the Pale Elves. Like us fairies, they were unprepared for such a confrontation. Keeping to themselves, they lacked immunities to word magic such as this.'"

"Shit balls," Lance said. "Sooner or later, that's the big bad we're gonna have to fight."

Alan continued, "The fairie runs a finger along fresh cracks crossing her face. 'With our wills bent or breaking, the Knight blew a foul wind through our forest. Those who had formed defensive ranks outside the gates ceased beating their wings and seemed lost. He then pried up his breastplate and released a flurry of dirt and rot that swept through us. This was the result.' The fairie points to the body of one of her fallen comrades. The corpse looks withered, gaunt. Even in death, the fairie's eyes seem to look up into the sky, as if searching for something lost in the clouds."

"She died from what—a plague?" Brie said.

"This poison did not simply kill our kind. Our diseased sisters staggered about the battlefield and let the enemy pour into the fortress, whereupon the Naughts slaughtered infants and the frailest among us. The Lifeless Knight wielded a heavy sword that cut through even ironcloth. He delighted in the lives he ended. Slowly, the sickened fairies became our enemies. They turned against us with deadly purpose. When our doom was certain, the Knight cheered his soldiers on, then vanished, as though he had more pressing matters elsewhere."

"I fear we're next on his to do list," Lance said.

Alan asked, "Does Lancelot say that?"

"No, he would—I dunno. I just think we're screwed."

"Tinkana turns toward Lancelot. She says, 'I sense apprehension. That is wise. Only the Knight's arrogant departure saved us from extinction. By the time I joined the fight, it was too late for most. The four of us who did not succumb to the Knight's lingering poison are among the few who traveled abroad in our day, a fact that may have afforded us some resistance. Now, we must again leave the Realm to face this foe."

Brie felt a surge of adrenaline.

"Hermione gestures toward our whole group. 'And you shall face him with *us* at your side.'"

"Tinkana surveys Hermione's companions, then nods toward Lupita. 'With you and the wolf,' she says. 'And the barbarian might help us carry this conflict to a favorable conclusion.' She turns toward Santana. 'This one fought bravely, but not well. That said, he is exceptionally handsome."

Carlos rubbed his hands together.

"Santana winks at her."

"As for the priest, he appears lacking in all respects. Even now, he can barely stand."

Brie felt her cheeks burn hot, as though a passerby had insulted her brother.

"Hermione backs up three paces. She puts her arms around Lancelot and Santana and says, 'We came to the Fairie Realm *together*. Once we finish our business here, we travel back to Mythopolis *together*. If you would deny the company of one of us, you shall have none of us.'"

When Alan grinned and gave a slow nod, Brie sensed admiration coming from the Fairie Queen herself. The feeling was disorienting. Her eyes could see Alan's pasty face and goofy moustache, but her mind conjured a giant stone woman.

"Hermione looks up to meet Queen Tinkana's eyes."

"Nice detail," Maya whispered.

"We have been told that you hold in your vaults a great treasure."

Alan frowned.

"I had hoped you were something more than fortune seekers. As recompense for your mercenary mission, shall I tune your lute? Enchant your boots? What shall it be?"

Brie bristled.

"You misunderstand our intentions. We heard you guard a power that comes not from forge or alchemy, a force that might destroy the Lifeless Knight. We wish to wield it in defense of Mythopolis. Devotus the Wise told us of—"

"You met the gnome?" Alan's expression brightened. "In his tower?"

Brie nodded.

"Tinkana considers this for a second, then says, 'Devotus admits few visitors. I imagine he softened his traps and dismissed a few guardians to make your ascent possible.'"

"His door did open easily," Carlos said. "But—"

"Until today," Alan said, "I had believed him to be the last living being who knew how to find us. Either I was mistaken or one who was dead lives again."

Alan looked up at the ceiling, as if he were Tinkana herself, reviewing a short list of visitors from centuries past. He turned back to face Brie.

"I recognize the power you describe—the Magic Circle. Like Devotus, I know it too well and, therefore, cannot harness it. It is more likely to find you than the reverse. If you feel it, mind well its boundaries. The Circle flickers as a faint flame in the softest breeze. It brings strength and purpose, but only when not apprehended as such."

Lance lowered his head and whispered to Maya, "What's Tinkana getting at?"

"I have a theory," Maya said.

"To defeat this Knight," Alan said, "you will need the Circle, and perhaps more. Our vault holds much that will aid you. Tend to your wounds, and we will take you there directly. Then, we fly to Mythopolis."

"*All* of us," Brie said.

"Of course," Alan said with a wink. "All of you."

Alan exhaled and leaned back in his chair. He looked to Brie. "Satisfied?"

Brie nodded. She felt herself reinhabiting her own body. Hermione receded into some part of her mind where she would await the next summons.

"Then, that's a wrap." Alan turned to Carlos. "Devon dropped Maya off, so she needs a ride."

"Got it," Carlos said.

Brie folded up Alan's cardboard screen and handed it to him. He took it from her and stared at the dragon drawn across its panels.

"Thanks for staying," Brie said.

"Wish I could go longer, but Mom's not doing well right now."

"Is she ill?"

"No. Well, yes," Alan stammered.

Brie remembered what Lance had explained—that gamers sometimes avoided being "disclosive," especially among new friends. Focus on the fantasy and keep real lives at bay. Brie considered whether she and Alan were becoming gaming friends. On the other side of thirty, Alan felt safer than any of the boys at school who might have courted her.

"Mom's just tired," Alan said. "And I'm all she's got."

"That's sad. Your dad is—" Brie hesitated and half-remembered something else Lance had said once. She hadn't paid attention back then, when Alan was just Lance's weird buddy.

"Dead, yeah," Alan said.

Brie felt lost for a second.

"I'm so sorry."

"It's okay. It was years ago. Just resurfaces sometimes for Mom this time of year. I'm going home, I guess, just to be home with her."

"Well thanks for staying a little longer."

Brie slid her character sheet into its plastic sleeve and picked up a set of pink dice with red numbers. When she looked up, Alan had already turned to leave. She was the last one left in the den. She'd spent many evenings curled up there in a big chair by herself, but she suddenly felt alone.

Voices came from the kitchen, so Brie walked there to join her friends. Her mother having slipped away, Lance now presided over the room and was blending frozen mango chunks with coconut milk. He poured the concoction into four skinny glasses.

Maya was in the midst of a passionate lecture. She gestured wildly to Lance and Carlos.

"Outside of this game we're playing, I've never heard of a

magic circle." Maya gave a quick nod to Brie, who pulled up a stool beside her. "Then again, we had a Tolkien reading group at Evergreen, and I remember he wrote something about a circle of light."

Lance looked skeptical. "Is that in The Silmarillion or something?"

"In his scholarly essays, he—"

"Scholarly essays?" Carlos scoffed. "Yeah, those are on my summer reading list."

Carlos and Lance laughed together, and Maya flicked them both on the shoulder.

"Is this about the Fairie Queen?" Brie asked.

Maya turned to face her.

"Kind of. Tolkien wrote critical essays about the genre. Back in his day, he saw themes emerging in proto-fantasy literature. A key idea is that civilizations are fragile social constructions. Evil always threatens to destroy the world—not necessarily the physical world, but the *civilized* world, however we define that. To succeed, evil forces need only extinguish the light."

"So," Brie said, "Lord Cynoc killed the Pale Elves to—"

"I don't think he killed them, exactly," Maya said.

"But they were dead—"

"On the *inside*. He doused their spark."

"Then, what? Hermione and the rest of us, we're the ones 'carrying the fire,' like in The Road?"

"You mean that scene at the end of the book? When the kid asks another survivor, 'Do you carry the fire?'"

"Yeah, and earlier, when the boy asks if the fire is real and how to carry it. His father says it's inside him."

"Okay, so yes, we all carry the light within the circumference of the civilized world. Light symbolizes that which is good—"

"And the darkness represents cannibals?"

"Well, the dark stands for all kinds of evil."

Brie stared at Maya.

"What?" Maya said.

"I don't know." Brie hesitated and looked toward Carlos. "It's just—doesn't that sound a little racist? I mean, dark skin bad, light skin good?"

"Quite so," Maya said. "Unconscious race anxiety plays a powerful role in literature, with no free pass for Tolkien. It's rooted in dualistic thinking, which was all the rage for centuries in Western philosophy. There's us, then there's the *other*. There's good, then bad." Maya pointed at Lance. "There's white." She then pointed to herself. "And there's black."

"And brown," Carlos said.

"Still basically black," Maya laughed. "That's the point of dualisms. All or nothing. If you're not European white, you're the other. Black, Orcish, or whatever, you're evil."

Brie's eyes were open wide. "You don't think Alan's racist, do you?"

Maya folded her arms and pulled back her head to look at Brie directly.

"We're all racist, sweetheart. This game's racist. Why do you think Carlos and I play human characters instead of the other so-called races—elves, dwarves, and such? It's so we can express our ethnicity through our characters. You do realize that Angelou's essentially African and Santana's Hispanic?"

"Santana's *Chicano*," Lance said with a botched accent.

"Really?" Brie said.

"Um, hello?" Carlos said. "You never noticed Santana's spells happen to be in Spanish?"

"Of course I did." Brie bit her lip. "I just figured that meant they were in a magic foreign language or something."

Carlos laughed.

"Spanish isn't a foreign language to me, *chica*. Santana's little Spanish flourishes express a part of me more than him. Speaking of which, what's the deal with Angelou's backstory? A dark-skinned migrant laborer sending remittance home to the clan?

Is your mom Latina?"

"Don't you talk about my mama."

Brie couldn't tell if that was a joke. She found herself the only person at the table unable to laugh. The conversation had to go somewhere more comfortable.

"Didn't Alan make up Angelou's story?" Brie asked. "I know you played the same character at Evergreen, but—"

"Angelou was fully formed beforehand," Lance said. "We talked about it over lunch a while back."

Maya gave Lance a curious look, then turned to Brie.

"I made up her origin for that earlier campaign. But when Alan asked me to lay out Angelou's history, he found gaps. Filled them in on the spot. I didn't protest. Felt like he was weaving her into a bigger story."

Lance nodded.

"Dude, it's almost creepy. It's like he reads our minds."

"Nah," Carlos said, "that's just Alan being Alan. But he's on fire right now. He's obsessed with that Middle Mirth contest. We're building up to something epic."

"That's the right word," Maya said. "Alan's digging deep— maybe into his own psyche."

Brie started to feel lost. She'd heard the word "psyche" but wasn't sure what it meant. Before she could work up the nerve to ask, Maya passed her by.

"Check this out. When you apply evolutionary theory to cultural forms like literature, or the story-game Alan's designing for us, you can see back in time—before the idea of races was concocted. This swords-and-sorcery stuff taps into our prehistoric brain. Picture early humans huddled around a fire, afraid of lurking Neanderthals."

"And wolves," Lance added.

"Don't go ripping on the *lobos*," Carlos said. "They were our companions, not our predators."

"What?"

"*De veras*," Carlos said, "I only stumbled into pre-med by accident. Before that, I wanted to be a vet. At UCSD I took this undergrad class on evolution, and my professor told us that follower-wolves split off from the lupine branch and started a symbiotic partnership with humans. Saved our butts in the ice age. Wolves became domesticated hunting buddies, plus pretty good shepherds and watchdogs. So the magic circle we're in is, so to speak, that same primitive campfire—that same light. When you go deep, it's not about race at all."

"Right," Maya said, "it's about self-preservation. The light keeps us warm and safe. We left cave dwellings to build villages, towns, then cities, like Mythopolis. Those places 'carry the light'. What Alan's done is just remind us of that. Maybe."

Brie spun back and forth on her kitchen stool.

"So do our characters have a special power, or the Magic Circle is...what? A metaphor?"

"I don't know," Maya said. "You'll have to ask Alan."

"He won't tell you anything," Lance said. "Game director's code, remember?"

"Right," Carlos said with a nod. "I doubt Maya's got it right."

Maya smiled and shook her head.

"I'm not even sure Alan knows what it means, or where this is all going. That's exciting to me. This feels more like an adventure in role playing than a role-playing adventure. It's like we're telling a new story together."

"Hope it has a happy ending," Brie said.

Lance laughed. "Not likely, right?"

"No," Carlos agreed. "Not likely at all."

MAYA

After waving goodbyes to the Langdons, Maya scooted out the front door with Carlos to hop into his Civic. Carlos unlocked the passenger door and held it open.

"Señora," he said with a wave of his hand.

"Gracias, señor. And thanks for the ride."

"My pleasure."

Maya slid into a brown bucket seat. Before she finished belting herself in, Carlos ran around the car, hopped into the driver's side, fired up the engine, and flicked on the headlights. The Honda made a geriatric cough, then hummed weakly until Carlos put it into gear.

"Cozy ride," Maya said as the car rumbled down Essex Street.

"It's a piece of *mierda*. But it's smooth."

Maya glanced at the dashboard and jumped a millimeter in her seat. She pointed at Carlos' papier-mâché skull.

"What's that?"

"That's Cecelia Bravo Gaudi Lopez. My totem."

Maya marveled at Cecelia, a smiling white skull about the size of a cat's head with black ink paisleys swirling around its cheeks. Dark eye sockets held flat white rings as pupils that gleamed like metal washers. Cecelia smiled broadly, with perfect teeth. It reminded her of Death grinning in a Diego Rivera mural.

"You are now riding in *El Coche de los Muertos*."

Maya looked at Carlos in mock horror. "Car—of the dying?"

"Of the deceased. Cecelia reminds me of my own mortality every time I drive. If I stay devoted to her, she will steer me clear of danger. I invented her as a more user-friendly version of the Santos fashionable among drug runners. Hopefully she won't ask for a blood sacrifice in exchange for her interventions."

As Carlos navigated around the shoals of dead-end residential streets in the Langdons' neighborhood, Maya detected in the car a hint of mildew, a scent all-too-familiar from her years in the soggy Pacific Northwest. She sniffed harder to confirm it came from the floor pads.

"You inhaling *El Coche's* musk? It's an old car. Can't get rid of it. But trust me, it's better now. Used to stink like a corpse in here."

"A corpse?" Maya said suspiciously. "Am I sitting in a Gothic chick magnet? Do you get gamer girls hot by talking about death? The whole excitement transference thing?"

"Does it work?"

Maya glared at him.

"Just kidding. Cars are Lance's gimmick, not mine."

"Lance doesn't drive."

"Oh, he drives. He drives women wild with his soulful mechanic routine."

The coconut smoothie in Maya's gut rose up to tickle her esophagus. She covered her mouth.

"No, for real. Lance gets innocent lasses to drive him under the freeway then pretends he has sensitive-blind-guy superpowers. 'I can hear the cars talk to me,' he says. 'I know their stories.' Crap like that."

Maya stared at Cecelia. The totem's eyes were as wide open as her own.

Carlos glanced over his shoulder to change lanes as they moved toward an on-ramp. He gently braked and waited for the light to change.

"When the car-whisperer scheme works—and he says it *always* works—he takes it to phase two. He'll say, 'You know, all of my senses are stronger.' He'll reach out his hands and—"

Green light. Carlos punched the gas pedal and roared up and onto the freeway.

"And bang!"

Maya swallowed.

"I think I just had a near-death experience."

Carlos accelerated into the right-hand lane of the freeway. He took his foot off the gas for a second. Keeping one hand on the wheel, Carlos ran the other under his ponytail. His forefingers traced a scar that seemed to run the length of his neck.

"Trust me," Carlos said, "that wasn't even close."

Maya looked away.

"Thank God it was just lunch."

"You're making no sense."

"Young Mr. Langdon tried that ploy with me last weekend."

With shock absorbers long overdue for replacement, the Civic bounced as Carlos rocked forward and back in his seat, laughing and pounding the steering wheel.

"For real?"

"Oh, God. I'm a sucker, aren't I?"

"Did you two, you know, did you—"

"It was lunch."

Carlos giggled. "No dessert, eh?"

Neither spoke for a mile as they traveled amidst the heavy evening traffic.

"Honestly," Carlos said, "I thought his sister was going to make a move on you."

"Oh dear."

"Hey, who can blame her?"

"No, I think Brie just doesn't have a lot of female friends. We're working on a sisterhood thing. Gotta raise her social game."

"Well, you and Brie better get your stories straight. You'll be hot tickets at Middle Mirth in a couple weeks. Usually there aren't *muchas muchachas* there. And nerd-boys can be hornier than Lancelot's holy symbol."

"Trust me, I've noticed. What about you? Got a girlfriend?"

"The polite term for what I have these days is *dalliances*." Carlos sighed. "Had a bona fide girlfriend once. She was big and strong, like Angelou, but with a name from Gone with the

Wind."

"You left poor Scarlett back on the plantation, Rhett?"

"Life went upside down for a while. I just couldn't see her. We fell out of touch."

Carlos signaled and moved into the right-hand lane, then gently decelerated as he exited the freeway.

"Funny thing is, she was a gamer, like you."

"Gamers make good lovers," Maya said with a wink. "They read the instructions on the back of the box before they open it, if you know what I mean."

"Hey, we're experts with costumes and role playing. That's high-level stuff."

"I'm gonna be on the lookout for some cuddle-flesh at Middle Mirth, but strictly of the *female* variety."

Maya checked Carlos for a reaction. He wore a satisfied smile. Unlike Lance, he'd guessed the score before she announced it.

"I thought I'd fly solo this summer," Maya said, "but since I'm going all-in on gamer subculture, I might as well find a fellow traveler. I like working at Dad's store. Maybe I even like this city and the SoCal lifestyle."

"But Devon told us you're going to grad school this fall. In English, right?"

"Comparative lit. Doesn't matter 'cuz I'm not gonna go."

Carlos pulled off road and into a Citgo station. He idled beside a pump and turned off the engine. With unguarded reproach, he said, "Are you *loco*?"

Maya folded her hands in her lap.

"You getting gas here, or what?"

"Life isn't about role playing all night at dining room tables, then exchanging saliva with social outcasts in some convention hotel. My parents both worked at crap jobs day and night so I wouldn't have to take one. They wanted me to have a career. You can choose to work at your dad's toy shop, but your folks didn't put you through college for that."

"Okay, this pep talk is officially a get-outta-the-ghetto lecture."

"It's the truth. Tonight, in the kitchen, you sounded like a scholar. Maybe a bit more pompous than the kind I'm used to, but you're professor material—not some shelf stocker in a board game crack den."

"Here's an idea. Let's stop dissecting my life, and let's turn the tables. If honoring one's parents is so important, how come you haven't said a word about yours until now? Are you performing a lone wolf act? Trying to be a badass *lobo* like Lupita?"

Carlos reached down and flipped a switch to release the gas cap, then got out of the car.

Maya took off her seatbelt, opened her door, and stood to stretch. She looked over the car's low roof and watched Carlos pump gas.

"Wait, is *this* some kind of pity date ploy?"

Carlos avoided eye contact as he swiped his credit card at the gas pump.

"No, I get it. You're as bad as Lance. You're making a play at being the Harry Potter in our group, all tough on the outside and soft on the inside. Is that it? Are you posing as a pitiful orphan?"

Carlos put the nozzle into El Coche's fuel tank and squeezed the handle. The hose hissed as the gas flowed. He looked up at Maya.

"My parents' names were Juan y Esperanza Morales. And yes, orphan is the English word for a child whose parents have died."

RANDALL

Randall reached into his pocket for keys. Just before leaving work, he'd learned that Ted had been robbed. Not Ted's company, nor Ted's home. The site of the crime was World of Karnage, and news of it had shaken Randall. What if this theft had been part of a massive heist involving other accounts, including his own?

He tried his house key upside down and fumbled it. His entire keychain and attached figurine—a tiny, plastic She-Ra, Princess of Power—fell to the floor. As he bent over, Randall noticed his dress shirt had come out of his pants again. His shirts all felt smaller lately, and he didn't even try to squeeze an undershirt beneath them anymore. As he squatted down to get the keys, he noticed on his belly a red cut, or maybe a sore.

Randall stood back up and felt his knees burn from the strain. He jammed his key into the deadbolt. A quick turn, and the lock opened. He pushed the door wide, tossed his backpack on the floor, and rounded his bed to drop into his Office Master chair.

With a click, Randall brought his desktop computer out of its light sleep and reentered the World of Karnage. A quick status check showed that Boldhearts was now an Epic level warrior equipped with +12 Plate Armor, the Helmet of the Neverquest, Baldoor's Gauntlets of Strength, and an oversupply of healing tonics and strength potions.

Randall didn't exhale until he confirmed that his avatar still held in his hand one of the best artifacts to be found—or, in his case, bought—in the WOK. One strike from the Sword of Lies would lull opponents into believing their own overconfident banter. It hid from its victims their plunging hit-point status and magical energy levels until it was too late to remedy either.

He scanned his Guildmates list and found Theodor the ProTechtor. Ted wasn't kidding when he said he'd been robbed. Theodor wore nothing on his bronze, naked body save a shabby pair of black leather boxers, and those remained only because the game required avatars to sport modern underwear, lest a wandering eye glimpse rendered nether parts.

Earlier that afternoon, Ted had called Randall in for a "strategy meeting" to tell him what had happened. Ted had logged in to his account during lunch and discovered that the Third Servants he'd hired to level-up Theodor had betrayed him. After weeks of loyal service as Sherpas on his ascent of the WOK status ladder, they'd liquidated everything he owned. Randall had listened only long enough to grok the situation, then he'd left work two hours early.

After a check to make sure he was the only one logged in to his own account, Randall changed his password. He went to the StirFried blog and typed "robbed" in the search bar. Other players had already posted warnings. In the past week, dozens of Servants had gone rogue. Ted had been hit by what called itself the Levelers' Syndicate, which robbed characters of their possessions then ritually killed and resurrected them, slowly stripping their experience points until they were downgraded to second level, one rung above noobs.

The Levelers claimed to draw inspiration from some Tibetans who had extorted a group of kayakers. After trekking and climbing for days to reach the Yarlung Tsangpo River, the guides threatened to leave their clients for dead unless the adventurers handed over fifty thousand dollars—ten times the price negotiated originally. The guides knew the kayakers had the cash strapped to their bodies, and the hapless travelers had no choice but to pay their own ransom.

Such ruthlessness, whether on the river or in the WOK, struck Randall as more clever than cruel. All the Tibetans and the Levelers had done was tax the carelessness of their charges. Exploiting misplaced trust was often the reason a player won a game, particularly in those like Diplomacy that dispensed with luck.

Randall felt this brush with larceny leading him forward. Through the Levelers, the gaming gods were teaching him to seek out vulnerabilities and exploit them. Divine serendipity would set his course, but both the WOK and the real world swirled with random factors he had to manage on his own. Securing a successful outcome probably required what mortals called "cheating."

A blast from his computer speakers interrupted with a hearty "Hail, Boldhearts!" Theodor the ProTechtor's portrait now sported a modest hemp tunic and robe. Randall watched letters appear one by one as Ted typed, "Questing tonight? I need help."

"Who is this?" Randall typed, though he recognized his boss.

"Ha ha," Ted typed. "No time to waste. Got to get Theodor back on his feet for Stairway to Hell."

Randall didn't recognize the term. Rather than ask Ted and risk a prolonged exchange, he opened a second window on his screen and typed "Stairway" into StirFried. He discovered an international contest synched with local gaming events held across the globe. The prize for the winning team was fifty thousand bucks—the same amount the hippie kayakers had handed over to their captors. Runners-up got garbage—the kind of magical artifacts one could find dumpster diving in any dragon's cave.

Intrigued, Randall read comments that users had posted about Stairway. The WOK had tried small contests before but with mixed results. In their most recent effort, designers had made all characters equal in ability to create a fair fight. With each character perfectly matched, however, every mountain pass and dungeon corridor had become as clogged as a rush hour freeway. That particular contest ended with 647 players tied for first place. Victory came not from superior play but via slightly faster Internet connections.

Seeking redemption, WOK developers were trying something new. In the Stairway challenge, each player's character would temporarily rise to the same high experience level, but they would do so in a haphazard way. Thus, someone who "naturally" built up their character would have the advantage of a more carefully crafted set of traits and tools.

Randall looked back at his WOK screen. Ted had typed, "Well?" Then, a few minutes later, "You there?" And finally, "Randall? I can see you're logged on."

"Not interested," Randall typed.

"You sure?" Ted typed back. "Stairway's same time as Middle Mirth. They'll have a room just for WOK. Or will you be in dumb DL tourney?"

The tournament. He'd forgotten all about it, which was probably for the best.

"It's a stupid storytelling thing," Ted typed.

Randall half-closed his eyes and felt his brain sparking. Synapses forged fresh connections.

"Wait," Ted typed. "You'll be in Korea. Nevermind."

Dark thoughts tumbled through Randall's mind.

"Who am I kidding," Ted typed. "Stairway's outta my reach now."

After a minute of silence, "BRB" appeared above Theodor, who disappeared from Randall's screen.

It all made sense. That's why Alan got those new recruits. No small satisfaction that it took two to make up for Boldheart's absence.

There had to be a way to make their Middle Mirth weekend more miserable than magical. The simplest plan was the most elegant. He would find a way for Boldhearts to win the Stairway challenge single-handedly, while simultaneously ensuring that Alan's group would be humbled in its own quest. He'd wear the king's crown the same day they met defeat.

In the meta-game he'd invented, even those twin accomplishments wouldn't meet the stricter victory conditions he'd set for himself. Greater opportunities lay ahead—something more diabolical than pranks. Something more punishing than humiliations.

Randall coughed hard, then inspected what landed in his palm. As Carlos once told him, green phlegm's never good. There it was.

The violent cough shook loose fresh thoughts. Was he now a stereotypical villain, seeking revenge against a nemesis? Was he becoming what comic book readers recognize as *evil*? That label sounded harsh. Better if modified to evil *genius*. That, he'd always been.

His favorite supervillain, Dr. Impossible, explained it this way. When one's intelligence lies on the farthest end of the bell curve, one has few peers. Society is in no position to judge.

Some villains act out of self-interest, but the more compelling ones take bold actions to move the world forward. When dawn first breaks on this new reality, it might reveal stacks of bodies from the night before. The villain then pays the ultimate price. The most sacred book in the Keller household reached the same conclusion. Even a righteous villain ends up martyred in the end.

The phone in the back of Randall's chinos vibrated. When he reached for it, his chair rolled away from the desk. Steadying himself on his bed, he saw he'd already accepted the call without seeing the caller's ID.

"Randall Keller here."

"Randall?" said a female voice.

"Hello?"

Randall tried to refocus.

"Duh, it's your sister."

"What?"

Randall rolled back to his desk and stared at the monitor. Theodor reappeared.

"We fly to Seoul on Monday. Have you made up your mind?"

Even as Randall switched his cell to speakerphone, he could

hear his sister sniffling.

"It'd be a long two weeks without you, Big Boy."

Randall typed a direct message to Ted: "Am I really off work the next 2 wks?"

"Hello?" Tiffany said.

Ted typed, "You're going to Korea, right?"

"Randy? Did you hang up?"

"I'm here," Randall said to the phone while typing "hang on" to Ted. "I'm not going, sis. Got a gaming convention I can't miss."

Tiffany blew her nose.

"You could play in Korea instead. Bring your laptop."

"No way. I read that the Asian interface is bogus. Some cultural censorship thing. Like, when you kill someone, they fall down and you have to sit through a stupid burial ceremony. Or is that just China?"

"What difference does—?"

"Can u quest now?" appeared above Theodor.

"Look, I'm really busy, sis."

Randall reached out to press the red button on his phone and end the call, but he hit a number instead.

He typed to Ted, "Sorry, flying solo tonight."

"Randy, you promised you'd go!"

Randall jumped up, startled by the phone. He looked at it warily. He stood still for a second. In the same instant, he heard the first curse ever to come from his sister's mouth.

"Gold-dame it, Randy!"

Randall again reached for the "End" button on his cell.

Before his finger touched it, the phone had gone dark.

The Last Full Week in July

LORD CYNOC

As he traveled the Mythos to spread his message, Cynoc found it difficult to convert the fools who dared stand against him.

The kilted halfling sage McQuaid had claimed that questing ennobled her soul and offered countless chances to serve the less fortunate. Cynoc had used his sword to show the upstart that there existed no true magic in the Mythos, only the timeless stream of death that ennobles nothing.

Trost, the nomadic warlord, placed a more practical faith in the sharpness of his steel and the speed of his sword arm. Cynoc had shown him the irrelevance of the former and the inadequacy of the latter.

So many would-be heroes to instruct! The mountain of bodies behind him grew ever larger. As a result, Cynoc's army did not swell as quickly as his reputation. Fewer than six hundred of the Pale Elves he had first corrupted still lived. To replace them, he had brought into his fold a hundred thousand more humanoids, along with many other sentient creatures. Still, he sought an even greater imbalance of forces in his favor.

Toward that end, he made one last stop before embarking on the siege of Mythopolis. He visited the frozen mountain city of Everwinter in hopes that its leaders might see the wisdom of his mission and offer their allegiance. Among all the known settlements, this alpine civilization cared the least for the fables and fortunes of the Mythos. They preferred instead to lead nihilistic lives devoted to nothing more than the slaughter of monsters and the accumulation of wealth, a worldview he found more sensible than most.

Everwinter had brought together three disenchanted human clans, known separately as the Children, the Pardons, and the

Kaliban. They drew up a charter founded on the principle that a soul's innocence and strength must be purchased. For centuries, their city gates opened only for those who could meet the high price of admittance. Those residents who failed to offer regular tribute would be not banished but destroyed utterly—erasing even the faintest, fondest memories of their lives. Those who ascended within their system did so by dint of tireless wealth accumulation and self-aggrandizement.

With his Naught army encamped in a valley, Cynoc rode a thermal draft up Everwinter Mountain to the hinged glacial walls known as the Blizzard Gates. The sentry who met him wore a polished copper helmet that nearly covered her face. Even so, Cynoc could see her gasp when she beheld him, a floating man six-and-a-half feet tall with a massive obsidian sword and dressed in a suit of black armor with the dull texture and red flicker of charcoal embers.

"What business do you have?" the sentry asked. "Do you seek to buy admittance or a fortnight's free passage? Overstay your provisional welcome, and your life will be forfeit."

Cynoc noted a dullness in both the sentry's brown padded armor and her dark blue skin. The high sun's rays cast reluctant shadows across her, as if she existed only within a two-dimensional plane.

"I come to cleanse the world. I have torn down the centuries-old scaffolding of virtue and magic that elves and fairies built to hide the truth of things. I raise an army to complete my mission."

"You are the one called the Lifeless Knight." The sentry raised her halberd, which was tipped with a wedge of sharp ice. "Come no further on pain of death!"

Oh, but he hated that name the people of the Mythos had made for him. He should have commissioned a bard to spread word of his mission while using his preferred title, which spoke more to his motives than his means.

"I am *Cynoc Coldheart*. I could lay waste to your kingdom,

but I visit today as a diplomat, not a warrior. You are a soldier of Everwinter, so your heart already lies all but empty. Release yourself from any delusions of happiness. Spit out any lingering tastes of beauty or honor."

From between his lips, Cynoc blew a stream of air. It carried the sweet smell of a baby's breath mingled with the cook fires of carnivorous grimlocks.

The sentry shuddered, as if sensing the mortality of her own infant daughter. With dwindling conviction, she jabbed her halberd toward Cynoc until she collapsed into the snow. Her body convulsed with sobs, then she sat still. When the sentry looked up, her eyes were dull. Empty.

"Now, you will give me an audience with your King and Queen. I should like to make arrangements with them for the destruction of Mythopolis."

ALAN

Alan waited in the backseat while Carlos walked around the front of his two-door Civic to help Alan's mother out of the passenger seat. Karen's black dress clung to the leather seat cover, then to her own perspiring body. As soon as she stood upright, Alan popped out of the car and shut the door.

Karen hooked a hand around each of their arms, and the three walked out of the parking lot together. Like Carlos, Alan wore a thin gray suit for the occasion. He hadn't tried on the outfit in years, and in the afternoon heat, it felt like a wool coat.

"You okay, Karen?" Carlos said. He examined her face, neck, hands, and ankles with the eye of a physician appraising a reluctant patient.

"That skull on the dash still gives me the willies," Karen said.

"You mean Cecelia Bravo—"

"I know who those names are from, Carlos. That's very dark." She looked past him to the engraved wooden sign that read "Pacific Gateway Memorial Park." She shook her head. "You named your little skull after people who died in automobile accidents, didn't you?"

"One died on his motorcycle."

The trio walked onto a cement footpath that led toward the small green hill at the center of the park.

"Any of those folks from your skull buried here?" Karen said.

"No. They all died in Spain or Mexico."

Alan turned to look back at Carlos' car. He wondered if Carlos was the one who'd painted the Honda midnight black, though Carlos claimed its previous owner had done so.

"I'd always assumed the skull was a Day of the Dead thing," Alan said.

"Sort of. It's more of a daily reminder. Dia de los Muertos is just once a year, like our visit today."

"Really?" Karen asked. "You only come here on the anniversary of—"

Alan knew what she was going to say. The anniversary of "the accident." But it wasn't the anniversary yet. That was still a week away. Alan told himself not to point out his mother's error. He told himself to keep walking.

They shuffled along the path as they passed the first row of gravestones. There were few visitors to the Memorial Park that morning. A pair of older men walked by, both with jeans jackets, one with a purple heart on his chest. The two seniors ascended the same gentle-sloping hill as Alan, Karen, and Carlos, but the men continued on their way after Carlos stopped at the tenth row of graves.

Unable to hold back his nerdly need for accuracy any longer, Alan blurted out, "The anniversary is *next* weekend. Next Saturday evening, second day of Middle Mirth. Ten years exactly."

Carlos sighed and smiled at Alan.

"I prefer to come here the week before the crash. Better memories."

"I'm so glad you came with us this year, Alan." Karen squeezed her son's hand. "It means a lot to me. And to Carlos."

"They're right here, Alan."

Carlos pointed down at the rows of flat stones that ran along the hill in parallel lines every eight feet.

Alan had never seen his father's gravestone. There it was, "John Crandall," plus a pair of dates. Nothing more.

After refusing to come back to the gravesite since the day John was buried, Alan had surprised himself by suggesting that he join Karen and Carlos on this year's visit. It cut a full day out of the gaming weekend, but he knew his company would be helpful to Karen, somehow.

It was less clear what this was supposed to mean for *him*. Alan tried not to think about the accident. Now, looking down at the gravestone, he couldn't focus his eyes. He shifted his gaze toward the stream of cars that roared along Interstate 5, fewer than two hundred meters from where they stood.

The freeway had become louder and more visible as they'd climbed the hill. Its noise wrenched Alan back to images he'd tried to forget. He pictured not afternoon traffic but headlights and tail lights moving up and down it at night. A red car hit the concrete barrier that ran along the center of the freeway. The car swung violently and hit a station wagon. Both cars flew off the freeway, the wagon disappearing from view.

Alan felt dizzy. He wasn't the only one. Karen let go of her escorts and lowered herself onto the grass. Alan breathed in to steady himself, then fell to one knee when he looked back at the freeway and again saw headlights at night. Now a pileup of cars blocked traffic, emergency vehicles on the scene.

Alan turned away and was again bathed in afternoon sunlight. His shadow covered Karen, who sat sideways beside a pair of flat, granite stones that read, "Juan Fidel Morales" and "Esperanza Morales." Carlos knelt and crossed himself. He spoke to himself in Spanish.

"You okay, honey?" Karen said.

"I'm fine," Alan said.

He turned and saw that his mother had been addressing Carlos. She had her arm around Carlos' shoulder.

Alan felt relieved that Carlos was there. He'd accompanied Karen on these visits every year to share in her grief.

Next weekend, when the date of John's death came around, Carlos and Alan would be together at Middle Mirth. But who would be there for Karen? Worse still, why had this problem never occurred to Alan before today?

Carlos turned away from the gravestones and toward the freeway.

"I miss them more each year," he said. "I wish Adelita were here."

Still on her knees, Karen gave Carlos a hug from the side.

"Everyone grieves in their own way, including your sister."

"She was here the day of the funeral, but not once since."

"Just like Alan, until today."

Karen let go of Carlos, wiped away a tear, then reached out to hug Alan. Her body stiffened instead. She tried to stand, but failed. Alan grabbed her arm to prevent a fall. Her skin felt dry, and her limbs twitched. Had she not used her Aspercreme that morning?

Carlos gave Karen the same worried look she often used on Alan.

"I'm not your nurse, but this is very treatable. You need physical therapy. Are you gonna be okay this weekend? I mean..."

"I know, I know. I have an appointment. And I'll be fine this weekend."

Both claims rang false, especially the second. Nobody was *fine*. Not her. Not Carlos. Alan knew he certainly wasn't. Probably never would be. The dizziness returned, and Alan's mind raced back to the freeway, to the grass embankment where he lay belted onto a backboard beside Randall.

Yes, what of the one survivor not here today? After two or three matter-of-fact conversations in the days following the crash, Randall never spoke of the incident again. His parents had dragged him to both funerals, but he was a reluctant mourner. Immersing Carlos into the Mythos, even while still in the hospital, was more than a mercy on Randall's part. It ensured the game went on.

While they studied gravestones, Randall was probably in his apartment. Doing what? Alan had no idea how the best friend he'd ever had now spent his time.

After more than two dozen unreturned phone calls, texts, and emails over the past month, Alan accepted that their friendship would not resuscitate. That loss worried Alan less than what might become of a man who needed their fantasy world more than ever.

The Mythos had released Randall from the rules of his Adventist family and from the disapproval of a social world he navigated no better than Alan himself. Boldheart's righteous fury provided an outlet for all the pain, rage, and menace that surfaced in Randall's outbursts. A few justifiable homicides by Boldheart's sword could vent strong emotions. Hopefully, Randall had found a new game into which that energy might flow.

Alan felt Karen's embrace and realized he'd been crying.

"Come here, honey."

Karen held Alan as tightly as her arms could manage.

Soft tears gave way to the kind of sobbing Brianna had displayed before she became Brie. Alan laughed through the tears at the fear that he, too, would have a new name bestowed on him. When he stopped shaking, Alan regained his bearings. Wrapped in Karen's arms, he watched Carlos shuffle across the grass on his knees, back to his parents' gravestone.

Carlos pulled his Superbarrio figurine from his pocket. In the way pets resemble their owners, the masked man reminded Alan of Carlos. Each was an ordinary person trying to make something special of his life. The world had done Carlos wrong in so many ways, but like a superhero, Carlos seemed to think he owed the world something.

Perhaps Carlos felt a debt to his parents. They'd be proud to know he'd become a nurse. But he was more than that. As Karen once said, he was a "true friend."

Carlos squeezed his figurine and laughed. To the left gravestone, he said, "You always loved the saints, Mamá. Perhaps you could use this one."

He kissed his wrestler and set it where his mother rested.

"You served me well, compañero. Adios."

MAYA

When the cowbell announced Lance's entrance, three young Players patrons moaned a Quasimodo chorus of "Sanctuary! Sanctuary!" Lance smiled and waved his cane in acknowledgement. He walked toward the cash register, a large box under one arm.

Maya gave Lance a nod but stayed in the conversation she'd started with a customer who had her full attention.

In a deep voice with an Italian accent, the customer said, "So we are getting our own group back together. Our chief instigator still lives nearby, in Chula Vista. She's picking up Valerie, who has just flown in from Minneapolis."

"Excuse me," Lance said. "Is Maya here?"

"Just a sec," Maya said to the customer. She took the box from Lance's arm. "Is this the folding chair for Alan?"

"Yup. Dad's waiting outside. Can't stay. Monday night errands."

"I am sorry," said the customer. "Should I leave you two to talk?"

Lance perked up his ears, as if hearing a dog whistle. "Whose enchanting voice am I hearing?"

Maya wanted to say the customer's name, but she'd forgotten it. She slid Lance's box behind the register and pretended she hadn't heard his question.

"I am Patrizia."

"Right," Maya said brightly. "Patrizia will compete in the DL tourney. She and her old friends want to go to Bled Castle instead of us. Can you believe that?"

Lance tapped his cane on the floor.

"If each of your number has such a lovely voice, we shall be challenged, to be sure. Good luck to you all. I must take my leave."

"Wait, I know you. You are the Blind Monk, are you not?"

"That I am."

Lance procured a Sharpie from the pocket of his jeans.

"Would you like an autograph? Where would you have me sign?"

Maya smiled. Through the re-interpretive powers of interactive media, the Petco Massacre had made Lance into a beloved celebrity. The suntanned man he'd beaned had transformed from a victim into the butt of the joke. His taunts and catcalls at the ballpark—from not only that night but many others—had been recorded and assembled. Maya had watched the montage of that boor that now preceded the most popular YouTube version of the Massacre. Thus, Lance had changed from a nincompoop into a nerd ninja who exacted revenge under the handle Patrizia used to address him.

"I do not need an autograph, but I wish you could stay and meet my friends. Is the Padre Princess with you?"

"She'll be with us at Middle Mirth," Maya said.

"Ah, then we will see you on Friday."

"Not if I see you first," Lance said with a grin.

Patrizia reached out and took Lance's hand in hers. As she gave him a firm handshake, he took a bow, ever the apparent gentleman.

When Lance left, Patrizia excused herself and returned to the back of the store, where she was pulling down Dungeon Lords books and arranging them on the back table. Maya watched Patrizia sashay across the room, heels clicking on the polished floor and a diaphanous dress floating around her.

* * *

More than an hour had passed when Alan entered the store and rang the cowbell. He looked surprised that nobody yelled an absurd phrase in reply. The only customers in the store were

Patrizia and the women who sat with her. None seemed to know the drill.

Maya was reviewing a checklist on her clipboard. She gave Alan a nod.

"What're you doing here tonight? We close in a few minutes."

"Who're they?" Alan gestured toward the women huddled at the back table. "They look familiar."

"The tall one in the sundress and heels is Patrizia. She's a dance instructor in New York, if you can believe it."

"I guess I can, and who—"

"I think I'm in love."

Maya studied Patrizia's delicate movements as she stood up from her table. Beside her rose a much larger woman, who gathered up three Dungeon Lords modules. She approached the register with the stride and bearing of a football player, heavy from muscle and flesh alike. A tan t-shirt matched her skin and hugged her broad shoulders.

"You've got quite a selection," the woman said to Maya. "I haven't seen a store this well stocked in years."

"I'm sorry," Maya said. "Patrizia said your names, but I can't remember..."

"I'm Tara. And who's this?"

Alan was able to muster only a soft, "Hello."

"This is Alan. He's the game director in our group."

Tara smirked back toward her friends, who fell in alongside her.

"That makes you my counterpart, Alan. I hope you prove a worthy adversary. This is the rest of our group—Valerie, Patrizia, Quinn."

Maya stared at Patrizia a moment too long.

Patrizia returned the gaze with fiery brown eyes.

Maya quickly shifted her attention to Tara, whose cheeks dimpled as she smiled. Tara was the oldest member, but everyone in this group was early-thirties.

Tara handed three soft-covered books to Maya, who rang them up. Each was an out-of-print module in the *Remembered Realms* series from the late 1970s.

"Been playing a while?" Maya asked.

"Sort of. Off and on."

Tara smiled at the women beside her.

"Mostly off, to be honest. Life kind of sidetracked us. Then a few weeks back, this guy started spamming our private email accounts. He defaced our role-playing blog and started telling everyone we were washed up, afraid to compete in the Middle Mirth tourney. No idea who—"

"It really pissed Tara off," said Valerie, who styled herself as a punk-Goth hybrid, with raccoon eye shadow and silver studs in nose, lobes, and eyelids. Her muscled shoulders were visible through a loose pink tee that read "Bikini Kill."

Valerie snorted.

"So Tara calls us and says we're getting back together. Who cares about retaking our heavyweight title, but a free trip to Europe plus a chance to see these girls again? That made it worth the trouble."

Maya looked at the women as if watching a rare species grazing.

"So, your DL group is all women?"

Tara exchanged a quick glance with her friends.

"If you believe in that gender binary," Tara said, "I suppose we're all chicks."

Alan stood frozen beside Maya, his back to the store's window display. He looked as though he saw the ghost of Ernest Carpenter floating before him. He breathed out the words, "Oh Mighty Isis."

Valerie shot Alan a glance.

"What's the problem with your little buddy here?"

"It's just..." Alan swallowed his words. "You're—you're the Wiccan Convent!"

"Flesh and bone before you," Tara said. "Bad nuns gone back to the forest."

Maya smiled as the women laughed together, though she had no earthly idea what this all meant. She accepted Tara's credit card and swiped it. In four seconds, paper shot out of the card scanner, and Maya tore loose a receipt. She gave it to Tara, who signed with the quill pen beside the register.

"Thanks for shopping at Players." Maya passed the credit card and books back to Tara. "Please come again. Anytime."

"I would like that very much," Patrizia said with one eyebrow raised.

"I mean," Maya stammered, "we'll see you at Middle Mirth."

"Not if we happen to see you first," Patrizia replied with a wink.

Tara and her friends walked out of the store. The cowbell marked their departure. None but Maya and Alan remained. Maya locked the door and flipped the "Open" sign to "Closed." Before she could turn back around, she heard Alan say, "We're dead."

Maya put her hands on her hips.

"What's freaking you out, son? And what's this about a convent?"

"Among the very few people who know about such things, those women are legendary—quite possibly the most famous gaming group in Southern California."

"They sound pretty rusty to me. They were here to dig up story ideas. Isn't their written submission due in—"

"In three days. I FedExed ours this morning."

"See? They've got nothing on us."

"Tara is probably just polishing some new module. She's a genius. Making clever allusions to the classics. The judges will swoon for that group."

"But we've got *you*." Maya punched Alan in the arm. "Besides, we've got two ladies of our own."

Maya slapped Alan's shirt and lowered the register of her voice.

"Not sure about this one, though. Pretty damn butch." Maya laughed at her own joke. "I'm pretty sure Brie and I can take them."

"You wanna get beat up by them?"

"Don't embarrass yourself, Alan. That was just an act. I honed my gaydar in college, and I'm guessing that Tara and Ms. Bikini Kill are both het. Patrizia and the others, can't tell. I have my hopes."

"What?"

"Never mind." Maya noted to herself that she was no longer at Evergreen. "What brings you by at this hour?"

Alan handed Maya a thick manila envelope. It was creased where he'd been clenching it.

"This is for your dad."

Alan walked to the board games section of the store.

"Tell me again why we only played on Saturday last weekend," Maya said. "You barely gave us enough time to inspect Tinkana's treasure room."

"I, um, had to do a thing with Carlos."

Alan pulled from the shelf a large rectangular box with a pastel political map of Africa on the cover. It was a rare Nigerian import—the strategy game "Kleptocracy." Alan turned it over.

"Have you seen this one?" he said. Without waiting for a reply, he read aloud from the back of the box.

"Do you have the cunning and spine to bankrupt a nation? Battle your post-Independence rivals as you gather generals, bury enemies, fill your Swiss bank account, and gas up your plane for the Cayman Islands."

"Yeah, it's a good one. But, Alan, yesterday was our last chance to practice before the tournament."

"I know. It—it was kind of a private thing, okay?"

Maya wanted to press the issue and sensed Alan retreating.

She recalled the strained ride home with Carlos after their awkward exchange at the gas station. Carlos had said nothing more about his parents. He'd changed the subject by explaining, "I heard these Citgo stations get their fuel from Latin America, so I only buy here." He'd raised a fist and joked half-heartedly, "*El pueblo unido!*" Maya had said the Citgo corporation was Venezuelan, and they'd debated the legacy of Hugo Chavez until he dropped her off at Devon's condo.

"Can I ask something about Carlos?"

Alan said nothing.

"What happened to his parents?"

"They died," Alan replied in a flat voice that made Maya shudder. "Ten years ago, as of next weekend."

Maya bit her lower lip. Alan still held the boxed game and stared at it intently, as though reading its description in each of five languages. He'd never looked paler. Maya sensed that his emotional equipment had failed to engage. Instead, it switched him over to conversational autopilot.

As a veteran gamer, Maya had witnessed many such moments. Intimacy impairment seemed almost a prerequisite for a certain kind of role player, and Alan was one of the worst cases she'd seen. Still, there was something about Alan that made her believe she could reach him.

"I'm so sorry. I just—I want to understand. How did they die?"

Alan put the game back on the shelf and turned to face her. He leaned forward and extended his arms to rest on the table edge. Maya settled into the chair across from him.

"My father killed them both."

"Did you just—"

"It was an accident," Alan said without emotion. "Carlos' parents were driving him home from dinner, or something. My dad was driving me and Randall to Middle Mirth. Pathetic, right? Two college kids getting rides from parents. Dad still had my car in his shop, and Randall couldn't mooch one."

Alan sat down at the table, from which he picked up a miniature Jeep. Its metal wheels didn't roll, but he scooted it across the polyurethane surface as if they could.

"We'd heard it was going to be a great year. The big shot DL people were at the convention for a product launch. We missed it."

Maya tried to sift through Alan's words, but his tone was as alarming as the content. The same man who directed their game with the flair of a community theater veteran now spoke in a monotone.

"Carlos' mom and dad were crushed, physically. Our car knocked theirs off the freeway. They landed upside down on a road below the interstate. That's what killed them. My father was already dead. Thrown into traffic. Too careless to bother with a seatbelt. Click it, or bite it."

"Alan, you don't have to…"

Maya raised a hand to stop Alan, but words kept pouring out. A dam had broken.

"So when Mom—she's a nurse, you know—when she assessed the situation, she found the one person who needed saving. Carlos was a mess when she got to him, from what I understand. She administered CPR. Kept him going until the sirens from Scripps Mercy arrived. That's where my mom works."

Alan forced a chuckle.

"Wonder if they paid her overtime."

Maya tried to stay in tune with Alan's feelings, but they came to her as a discordant jumble of sadness, terror, and relief. She wanted to get up and hug him, but he didn't look ready for company. She blinked away water in her eyes.

"Alan, I'm so sorry."

"Mom watched over Carlos for the couple months he stayed in the ward. He was in college back then, but in the hospital, he looked like a busted-up teenager. That's when we met his older sister. She kind of nursed him for a year or so, or tried to, until he could go back to school. She's the one with that dog, the cheese-doodle?"

Maya laughed, then sniffed.

"Cheese doodle, the baby wolf."

"Anyway, Carlos didn't have a lot of visitors at the hospital, and we felt responsible for what had happened. I brought over some DL books for him, and I guided him through one solo adventure, then another. He enjoyed it and caught on fast. Randall and I brought him into our main Mythos campaign. As much as anything, Carlos was spellbound by Randall's performances. It must've stuck. Here we are, still playing ten years later."

Color returned to Alan's cheeks.

Maya discovered she'd been holding her breath. She exhaled slowly.

Alan gave her a curious look, as though surprised to see her sitting there.

CARLOS

Carlos sat on the cement barrier where the sands of La Jolla Shores stopped and the broad city sidewalk began. He'd finished a long shift at Children's and had driven to the beach to sit and think before calling it a night. Watching the waves swell and break beneath the fading sunset calmed his mind, which had not found its rhythm since his visit to the cemetery. He was glad Alan had joined him and Karen, but his being there had stirred up fresh memories.

In case Adelita might be free to get takeout, Carlos called on his cell, but it went to voicemail. His sister was not easily reached.

Seeing the image of his sister on his phone made Carlos think of his parents. Adelita had grown to be the same size their mother had been—five foot seven, broad smile and hips. It was the same with Carlos and his father, whose lean frames and smirking faces were mirror images.

His parents had been so affectionate with each other that Carlos could only picture them arm in arm, his father imitating the deep voice of a Tijuana radio announcer. Gratuitously trilling each 'r', he would bellow "*Vamos al supermercado!*" whenever they went grocery shopping. Carlos' favorite was the Newport cigarettes tag line Juan Fidel used for any happy moment, "*Lleno de gusto!*" Whenever his father affected that sonorous voice, his mother would giggle and press her head into Dad's shoulder.

That was how his parents had looked their last night together. They'd walked from their old station wagon to meet Carlos and his first college girlfriend in front of Miguel's Mexican Cantina. When Carlos had attempted to make an introduction, his mother had backed away, kissed her fingers, and crossed herself. Carlos felt hurt, then noticed Esperanza was looking not at his girlfriend but up toward the forty-foot sign in front of the restaurant. Above the eatery's full name stood a giant rounded "M," painted a deep red and muraled with flowering prickly-pear cacti.

Juan reeled Esperanza back into his arms.

"*Está bien. No preocupas.*"

"*Mamá,*" Carlos pleaded, "*no es McDonald's. Es comida Mexicana.*" He looked back to his girlfriend, saw she was flustered, and reached for reassuring words.

"*Es nada, chica.* She just gets frightened sometimes. I'll explain later."

That evening's awkward dinner conversation, conducted in broken English and nursery school Spanish, passed quickly. Juan paid in cash the moment the bill arrived.

The next and last time Carlos saw that girlfriend was at the funeral. By then, he'd already withdrawn from her, from college, from everything and everyone. Karen, and then Alan, gradually helped him regain his footing. When he reenrolled at UCSD, almost everyone he knew there had graduated.

Carlos picked up his phone to try Adelita one more time. A text awaited him, but not from his sister. With the ringer silenced, he hadn't noticed Maya's note.

"Impromptu meeting 10:15PM @ Wences. Bring Alan but say nada. Iz surpriz."

Maya must have arranged this event, which came after the restaurant's closing time. Carlos' appetite stirred at the prospect of chicken enchiladas.

No, the tingling lay below his abdomen. His body's eager reaction belied unwarranted optimism. Maya had invited him to a late-night rendezvous, but they wouldn't be alone. Even Alan's overactive imagination couldn't write a plausible scenario where the three of them shared a bed.

More encouraging was this. In spite of Carlos' offenses, Maya still entrusted him with bringing Alan, the person he suspected was the real guest of honor.

Carlos rubbed his thighs, hard. The pressure felt good, but he was getting sand on his car seat. He got out and brushed his hands over shoulders, chest, and legs. He shook his whole body and imagined Lupita doing the same. Not the wolf, but his childhood dog.

Memories of little Lupita usually heralded an emotional flood, but not this time. Instead, images of dog and wolf fused together. His heart pumped warm blood into his chest, with a message. Lupita was alive again, at least for the summer.

Carlos hopped back into El Coche and put his phone on the dashboard. His traffic app showed clear freeways. He had just enough time to grab Alan and get to Wences on time. Thirty minutes later, he pulled onto a familiar strip of asphalt, the short driveway that led into the Crandall family garage.

Karen jogged out the front door, her fingers tapping a watch. Even before exiting the car, Carlos recognized the timepiece. A ring of obsidian framed a digital readout that mimicked a sundial. Alan had spied that item at Middle Mirth three years ago. He cajoled Carlos and Randall to pitch in enough cash to buy it as a birthday present. They never told her it referenced a low-level wizard spell, but she'd probably guessed it was something like that.

"You're late, mister."

"I'm here, aren't I?"

Carlos got out of the car and jogged up to give Karen a hug.

She tried to make a scolding face, but her frown looked more like a smile.

"I've kept Alan in the dark, but he knows something's up. Don't spill the beans."

"No problem there. I don't even know what's up."

"Before you drive off, I wanted to ask about something."

"No, I'm not setting up another blind date for the poor guy." This time the frown was real.

"I'm putting no more energy into that, thank you. No, it's

the hospital. We had an odd case, and I wonder what you know about chickenpox."

"It's a bitch, but you knew that already."

"We quarantined a young girl who had it because one of our doctors thought it wasn't a run-of-the-mill variety."

"I haven't heard anything about that at Children's, if that's what you're asking."

"This teenager was being home schooled by her grandparents. I think we overreacted by asking for the whole family to come in for observation."

"If it's a mutation, those are random die rolls."

Karen laughed and pointed an accusing finger.

"You sound like Alan."

Carlos held up a hand to ward off the charge.

"All I'm saying is that a distorted virus usually isn't more virulent—just different."

"When she came in this morning, she was delirious."

"That can happen with the pox."

Karen looked into the distance. Carlos turned around and saw the moon, low and bright in the night sky. No surprise there. Even the Mythos only had one moon.

"You should have seen this girl. So *angry*."

Carlos turned back to face Karen. She looked right at him, but her gaze felt distant.

"Her sister has it, too, but with milder symptoms. We haven't found her little brother yet."

"Can't be careful enough."

The loud clap of a closing screen door announced Alan's arrival. He approached the passenger side of Carlos' car.

"Where are you taking me, Carlos? Mom wouldn't say."

"It's a full moon. I think we're murdering some Londoners tonight."

Karen gave her son a quick kiss.

"Don't be such a bad influence, Alan. Carlos used to be a

good kid."

"Not true," Carlos said as he opened the driver's door. "I used to be more jock than jocular. Now, if you'll excuse us, we have a mystery to solve."

* * *

Carlos pulled the wrought-iron handle on the wooden door to Señor Wences, then followed Alan inside. The restaurant was four times the size of Players, with plaster walls covered in haphazard tin mirrors. The floor held a three-by-three grid of alder tables, each inlaid with a floral mosaic. An employee mopped the floor while another closed the register. At the only occupied table, in the middle of the restaurant, Lance, Brie, Maya, and Devon stood and broke into song, with Brie accompanying on what looked like a ukulele.

"*Ayyy, ay, ay, ay. Canta y no llores...*"

The janitor stood by his mop and joined in. He was the only member of the quintet with a bona fide accent, though he couldn't match Brie's perfect pitch.

"*Porque cantando se alegran, cielito lindo, los corazones.*"

"Please, let's sing none of the verses," Carlos said. "Do you crazy *gringos* even know what that song's about?"

The janitor exclaimed, "*Es una ranchera.* About stealing a daughter away for *amor.*"

"Yes." Carlos laughed. "Yes, actually, something like that."

Carlos and Alan walked to the table, pulled out two of the tall-backed mesquite chairs, and lowered themselves onto stretched leather seats. Six glasses of *horchata* sweated onto the table's tiled surface, which also held a stack of boxes and a large envelope.

"We promise not to keep you past your bedtime," Maya said to Alan, "but we wanted to have a little toast before the convention."

"We realized," Brie said, "that we hadn't spent a minute

together as a group outside the game. Since Middle Mirth gets started on Friday, there's no time like the present."

Lance leaned forward.

"Speaking of which, we have a few—"

"*Regalitos*," Maya said. "Little gifts."

Carlos turned to Alan, who shrugged.

"Your text didn't say anything about presents."

"It was Maya's idea," Devon said. "I'm on good terms with the night manager, so here we are."

"I already opened my present Monday," Brie said. She held aloft the instrument that Carlos had mistaken for a ukulele. "I call it the Spruce Lute."

"On account of it being made out of spruce," Lance said. "And what with it being a lute. Naming things is truly my dear sister's forte."

"This was Mom's idea," Brie said, "but Lance helped choose it. They're getting a guy in Indiana to adapt the sheet music from Cats for lute!"

Lance put a cupped palm to one side of his mouth.

"Don't worry. The music won't be ready for a few weeks yet."

"Very funny," Maya said. "Now, for Lance..."

She reached into the center of the table and handed him a metal box with a plastic handle.

"I didn't have to wrap it, did I?"

All but Lance laughed hard enough to make their chairs shake and squeak on the floor.

"Ouch!" Lance said. "Guess I'm the only one here who's not *mentally* disabled."

Lance ran his fingertips across the lid and over the indentation of a square cross.

"A first aid kit for my cleric?"

"Of course," Brie said. "For when you run out of spells while patching me up."

Maya handed a manila envelope to Devon.

"And this is for you."

"Wait, I thought I was just a chaperone tonight. Why am I getting a present?"

Alan pointed at the envelope. "That one was already coming to you. Not sure it counts."

"Alan brought it for you on Monday, Dad. I kinda forgot it until today."

Devon pulled out a stack of photocopies, but Alan motioned for him to push the papers back inside the envelope.

"It's for your eyes only, Devon. Kind of an insurance policy. I'll explain later."

Carlos waved his fingers in the air.

"Oooh, mysterious."

"Now," Lance said, "Carlos was tough to shop for, so I had his present custom made. What do you get the sorcerer who can conjure anything? Well, I finally figured out what that thing is on your dash."

Maya and Alan glanced at Carlos, who gave a tentative laugh.

"That little object's a skull, right?"

"Correct," Maya said quietly.

"I figured you're kind of into the whole death thing. The skull's probably like one of those candy heads they have in Tijuana for All Saints' Day. Best I can tell, you're not really Catholic—"

"True," Carlos said.

"And you're not really into sugar—"

"True again."

"But, you are a snappy dresser, and I happen to know a thing or two about making an impression with one's outfit."

Lance burst into a staged laugh that became a genuine one. The group backed him up with more hesitant chuckles.

"So, this little item is for your wardrobe."

Lance reached out and felt the table. He touched the two remaining gifts and grasped a flat box, which he pushed in

Carlos' general direction.

Carlos studied Alan and Maya's expressions, or lack thereof, then unwrapped his present. After brushing aside tissue paper, he pulled out a red velvet half-circle cape with darted shoulders. On each point of the collar was embroidered a delicate golden skull.

Lance's eyes lit up and his smile stretched wide with expectation. After a few seconds, Carlos noticed the silence hanging in the air. His arm hair tingled in a way he remembered feeling as a boy when his mother would embrace him.

"It's beautiful," Carlos said at last. He ran his right hand over the embroidery. "Thank you, Lance." He regarded Alan, Maya, Lance, and Brie, in turn. "I like having gaming friends. But you guys? You guys are some classy *gringos*."

Carlos stood up and moved around the table to give Lance a shoulder hug.

"Awesome, right?" Lance said.

"Awesome."

Carlos sat back down and folded the cape in his lap. What he'd do with it, he wasn't sure, but he felt privileged to have received it.

After a pause, Devon motioned to the middle of the table. There sat a wide cardboard box. "The last present of the night goes to Alan."

Alan tore open the package and revealed a folded wooden chair. The canvas support across its back read, "Herr Director."

Maya stood and raised her glass.

"*You* are the gift for me, Alan. For all of us. You create our fantasy world. You're the one who makes our unreality real."

The rest of the group stood with Maya and held aloft their glasses. The sloshing drinks released the sweet smell of cinnamon and almonds, milk and rice.

"Dad has a hundred scenarios on the shelves of his store, but you've made something entirely new — something amazing. We are lost in your world, Herr Director, but we're all hoping to find something there."

"A toast to Alan!" Brie said. "To finding out what's going on in that brain of yours!"

"Wouldn't you like to know," Alan said, and the group laughed.

Carlos smiled at Alan.

"Wouldn't *you*?"

RANDALL

Randall staggered out of his apartment and trekked five long blocks to the Circle K convenience store. Though it hurt his hip and feet to walk, he needed to restock as he pushed through his second full week of nonstop online gaming.

Freed from the ties of work and family, Randall had let himself fall below his modest behavioral benchmarks. He'd spent some of each day using the Internet for erotic self-gratification, but he'd indulged more passionately his principal fetish, consumption.

Circle K was Randall's favorite provider, at least in San Diego. When he was in Phoenix on business once, he'd discovered that the real superstore of pornographic junk food was Quik Stop, a brightly lit palace offering all manner of carbohydrates and the full chemical spectrum of sugars. With thirty-two years of experience, Randall had become a connoisseur of the name-brand delectables nutritionists would only reluctantly categorize as food.

Before he'd moved out of the house and before Tiffany had moved into it, his parents urged him to exercise more self-control. The pressure and heat they applied only hardened his darkest vice into a diamond.

During his senior year of high school, Randall's parents once opened his bedroom door to find him sprawled in bed on his belly. He lifted his nose up toward them, a beached sea lion sniffing trouble in the air. Beneath him lay a dragon's horde of Zagnuts, Chic-O-Stiks, and Boston Baked Beans, scattered like gold coins. Beneath these were empty foil satchels that had once carried Funions but now contained not a wet finger's worth of dust. In his hand, Randall held a hard plastic Bladder Stretcher, a 64-oz plastic cup he'd refilled with an iced "suicide soda" — equal parts Dr. Pepper, orange soda, and root beer.

In tag-team fashion, his parents lit into him that night. They sermonized about their God and His Righteousness, the wages of Sin, and the redemptive power of the Holy Spirit. His slow-growing defiance crystallized as they spoke. They finished with his father saying "Amen" at the close of some homily his mother had recited. Without sitting up, without even blinking, Randall said, "Cleanliness is overrated. Gluttony underrated."

The next night, his parents decided to adopt.

Randall finished his strenuous walk and arrived at the Circle K. Randall congratulated himself on being his own personal trainer. It was good to get some exercise by walking to the store.

His anxious heart slowed as he loaded a hand cart with samplings from each aisle. Appraising the cold beverage case, he snatched three energy drinks. He usually avoided them, but he'd been feeling woozy, perhaps from sitting too long.

Acting as his own doctor, as well, Randall spied a liquid daytime cough syrup and reached for a two-pack. It might soothe some of his aching joints, but it was also a stimulant. "May cause agitation," the label bragged. As he lifted the medicine from its shelf, a teenager in a weathered San Diego Chargers jersey reached for the same bottle.

The boy withdrew his hand and coughed.

"No, you go ahead," he said. "I was just getting some—"

A loud hack erupted from the boy's throat, and two gumdrops of phlegm landed at Randall's feet. The teen wiped his mouth on his sleeve.

"Sorry, dude. I shouldn't even be here. Dad says I have chickenpox."

Randall recognized the red blisters on the boy's neck and stepped back three feet. He had, to date, successfully avoided that particular disease. In a flash of self-awareness, Randall saw some of his own physical symptoms standing before him—the cough that grew more insistent and the spreading rash, already worse than his usual chafes and sores. Randall kept a wary eye on the sickly customer while backing away from him, proffering a credit card to the clerk, then hoisting his plastic bags of treasure.

Heading out of the store, Randall heard the automatic doorbell ring a slow "doo-dung." So many times, he and Alan had gone on food runs and heard that sound welcome them inside, then wish them a happy journey home.

Randall muttered to himself, "God I hate that—that..." Even alone outside the Circle K, Randall hesitated to unleash a bona fide curse. "I hate that *frocking* murderer."

A smile returned to Randall's lips when he realized that, in a sense, Alan and his henchmen had failed to kill Boldheart. Carlos and Lance had left him to die, but the pluralized Boldhearts had been reborn in the WOK, where he was more powerful than ever.

Randall had started the week by testing his alter ego against other players, questing and raiding with the highest-level companions he could find. Thanks largely to the nonstop efforts of his non-thieving Third Servants, Boldhearts already was superior to most WOK characters he encountered.

Few players invited him back, however, after he deigned to adventure with them. As he walked home, he recalled one such outing, when the lead hunter in Randall's group had fled an impending battle. The leader had said into Randall's headset, "Just up the path to the graveyard, there's a gathering of lich elders closing fast. Run!"

Everyone in the group heard him, but some had lingered when Randall convinced the group to stay and fight.

"We'll slay enough," he'd explained, "that once we're resurrected, we can come right back and finish them off."

When an entire lich seminary burst onto the screen, however, Randall did a quick head count and directed Boldhearts to imbibe an olive-shaped bottle of dimensional displacement potion. His swordsman became ethereal and walked away unmolested. The liches, meanwhile, tore through his outnumbered companions, then transformed their fresh corpses into servants.

Randall arrived back at his apartment door feeling warmed by the memory of that brief online encounter. He shifted the plastic grocery bags in his right hand to join those hanging off his left, and dug out of his pocket She-Ra and the keys she guarded. The heft of the bags made for a kind of upper body workout. "That counts as another day of exercise," he'd heard someone say on TV. Not that it mattered.

Stepping inside his apartment, he dropped the bags on his bed and took his beverages to the refrigerator.

The fridge smelled wrong.

When Randall poked his head inside, he saw an aluminum tray holding a family-size lasagna he thought he'd finished the week before. Twice, he'd reheated it in the microwave only to leave it in overnight. It was hard to heed the oven's "ding" in the midst of an online battle. The top layer of noodles appeared green, though he recalled no vegetables listed among its ingredients. A sharp metallic fragrance burned his nostrils. He pushed the dish further back in the refrigerator, shut the door, and put his drinks in the freezer.

Randall turned around to look for his other groceries. They should have been on the laminate countertop by the fridge. They weren't there, though he spied an unopened packet of provolone cheese slices half-buried under piles of empty wrappers, mail, and disposable dishware. He pulled out the cheese and sniffed. No scent meant good to eat, so he reopened the fridge and wedged the package into the meat drawer.

From where he stood, he could scan the entirety of his apartment, minus the bathroom, thankfully. He spotted the groceries atop the king mattress that abutted his desk. Also visible was the overall condition of his dwelling. Even by lax standards, the place was a sty.

A two-week disconnection from work and family caused him to let things slide. The better excuse was how busy he'd been, multitasking. He was working out a scheme to ensure victory in the Stairway to Hell contest. At the same time, he needed a way to spoil Middle Mirth for Alan, Carlos, and the rest of the vermin who gathered there.

To the first challenge, Randall now returned. He logged back into his WOK account. The warrior Boldhearts popped up. Randall looked at the full-screen portrait of his character.

"Mirror, mirror, who is the fiercest of them all?"

Boldhearts was already quick and strong in a fight. Randall had spent hours testing out his character's equipment and abilities—and sharpening his own dull, human reflexes—in the Honor Battle chambers. In setting up these one-on-one contests, the WOK designers gave up entirely on the idea of plot. One character simply fought against another, and the victor earned "honor points," which had roughly the same value as the red paper tickets spit out of Whack-a-Moles at an arcade. When wagering their honor against Boldhearts, few emerged anything but humiliated.

"We are the fiercest and greatest," Randall imagined Boldhearts saying back to him, "but even we cannot prevail as one against many."

Though prideful, Randall was no fool. He'd come to accept that even a ridiculously powerful swordsman could not prevail against entire mixed-class teams. Based on what he'd read from postings at the StirFried blog, this tournament would be less of a footrace and more of a *Death Race 2000*, with each group attacking the others as they clawed their way down the planes of Hell to rescue innocent souls hoarded by Asmodeus, the most powerful arch-devil in the Underworld. One veteran player speculated that victory might come by default, with teams killing each other off until only one remained.

Imagining himself as victorious brought back the rush he'd felt when Tiffany delivered her news about Brianna. That surge of courage had led him to launch Operation NyQuil against Lance. He'd really hit his stride when he goaded one of the most famous DL groups in history to come out of retirement and enter the Middle Mirth tourney. One more obstacle in Alan's path.

For reasons he couldn't yet understand, Randall's thoughts kept drifting back to the game store owner. Though Randall hadn't returned to Players since his Fourth of July visit, he'd researched both daddy and daughter online. He'd put together enough puzzle pieces to guess that Maya's parents had divorced, with Devon heading south to get away from family and work. With Devon gone, her mother had likely become the "bad cop," and Maya idealized her father as a free spirited artist. She'd majored in English literature, so she was clearly susceptible to romanticism. Devon was no different. Only an inveterate dreamer would open a bricks-and-mortar gaming store in the age of the Internet.

A villain often perpetrates his greatest cruelties indirectly, on an enemy's loved ones. He'd seen the Revenge by Proxy trope performed before. The Green Goblin against Spider-Man. Robert De Niro in *Cape Fear*. Devon was clearly a vulnerable target by which Randall could wound Maya, along with Alan and Carlos, who had probably bonded with this surrogate father.

How trusting and generous Devon had seemed when Randall had visited Players. He remembered the words "our little secret." When he first heard that phrase, he'd assumed Devon was ashamed to have built a computer game when he now owned a store devoted exclusively to tabletop gaming. Could there be more to it than that?

Randall fired up his search engine, knowing that online archives are, quite naturally, the most complete for those things conceived and delivered online. The history of the WOK's development had been chronicled in detail by both those who built it and those who played it. Much of the writing was amateur and the sourcing was suspect, but the name Devon Washington was everywhere. He'd been profiled numerous times as a star of early console gaming, and he'd stuck with the industry for decades. When he left the WOK factory two years ago, he'd just turned fifty.

After so many years working on Karnage, how could Devon just walk away? Being tossed out of Alan's group so recently, Randall felt a kinship with the jilted programmer. He resolved to inspect the WOK more carefully to find a crack or crevice where Devon might have hidden a token of his own resentment toward his former colleagues.

In his mind, Randall saw wooden figures move rapidly across a checkered board. He still couldn't see exactly how this meta-game of his worked, but he'd started to glean who the different pieces represented. He sat behind one side of the board, with the mysterious force of the universe at his back. Whoever sat on the other side did not even realize that play was underway. And Randall was winning.

* * *

Through the long night, Randall led his avatar into the most remote regions of the WOK. While running along an alpine pass, Boldhearts came across Saint Magdalene, a demi-level priest Randall had read about in StirFried. This cleric's player bragged online about how her unique healing powers would lead to victory in the Stairway contest.

Swallowing his ego, Randall directed his Boldhearts character to kneel and ask Magdalene, "What rare enchantment endows you with this wondrous gift?"

"No secret," Magdalene said. "I simply honed my abilities to a level none had reached."

"Go on."

Magdalene expounded on the subtleties of her unparalleled prowess. Randall watched her gestures as she reenacted one of her latest miracles. The blathering description made no sense, but his mind was primed to detect the truth. Magdalene's unique combination of talents and item inventory likely exploited a hole in the code, one unseen and misunderstood by players but surely visible to the game's developers.

If this were so, why had the WOK corporation not patched this tear in their fabric and stripped Magdalene of her ability to grant on-the-spot resurrection? The WOK teemed with volunteer spies—players who read the detailed logs that chronicled the minutiae of every encounter in the WOK universe. These self-appointed Boy Scouts had been the first to verify Magdalene's boasts, which they recounted in the developer forum.

But WOK officials took no action. They let Magdalene become something of a mythical figure. Perhaps they treated her as holding what some hackers called a "lottery ticket", an unintended, highly improbable, but essentially benign power. More likely, WOK officials were too embarrassed by the anomaly to acknowledge it as such.

If Saint Magdalene could exist, what else might be out there— perhaps undiscovered? To investigate this lovely possibility, Randall visited the TrollBooth, a site where mischievous WOK players would discuss tricks to play on noobs.

The popular term for such abuse was "griefing". Reading through recent postings, Randall learned where to acquire a cursed quarterstaff that one could resell to gullible young adventurers. Once equipped, it would permanently foreshorten the recipients' arms, unless they could acquire a rare set of gauntlets to reverse the spell. This was the nonsense high school players used to wage virtual snowball fights. Not compelling to the adult mind.

As of yet, no players had uncovered usable "cheat codes" for the WOK. Most other games had fallen victim to the public release of such devices, which granted casual players access to complicated keyboard shortcuts originally built for playtesting. Developers trying out new features allowed themselves the convenience of all-powerful avatars who remained invincible in even the deadliest regions of the WOK.

The discovery and artful use of such cheats might afford Boldhearts the edge he needed, but a greater possibility occurred to Randall. Devon surely had created such codes, and if anyone detected Boldhearts' use thereof, Randall could pin the cheat's release back on Devon, the disgruntled ex-employee. Even as a fallback option, that scenario was more than a step above little Brianna's mortification.

In the search for such codes, Randall had an advantage over every other hunter who preceded him. The WOK's security system was the FunBunker, a shifting array of walls that no one had ever breached, yet Randall knew the system's logic because he'd helped create it at ProTechTed. Better still, if one got deep inside the FunBunker, its last line of defense was nothing more than a username and password set by his boss. Best of all, there was a decent chance that Randall knew those two pieces of information.

Randall wheeled his chair to his bed and opened a Cheesy Blaster. Too deep in contemplation to heat it, he bit through the hot dog wrapped in a pizza slice. Delicious. Brain food. He rolled back to his keyboard and logged in to his work account.

After two hours of careful but furious work, Randall came to the screen he'd hoped to eventually find.

Username?

"Just a minute," Randall said to his monitor. He searched back two years in his work email account and found the message he'd remembered saving. Ted preferred to maintain an active link to clients' security software, should anything go wrong with their deployment. Randall saw the login string, yet he balked at typing it.

It was one thing to break into the WOK for fun. It was something altogether different to do so using Ted's account. Perhaps he could cover his tracks by remotely accessing the servers at ProTechTed and launching his attack from inside the company office. If done carefully, the person who'd be held accountable would be Ted.

"That j-hole has it coming," Randall said with a sniff.

Again, Randall hesitated.

He worked through the cascading effects of his next move. If Ted went down, ProTechTed could collapse. What would become of Randall's job? Then again, he was weary of working under Ted. Finding work elsewhere would be a snap. With the Stairway prize money in hand, Randall could start up his own company.

"Proceed," Randall said with a smile. He glanced at the old email from Ted and typed the project code assigned to the WOK account.

"BunkerWOK041109."

Password?

Randall wasn't the only one who'd noticed how lax Ted was about his own cybersecurity. Ted created memorable passwords that he'd never write down but could recall years later. He'd muttered this particular one to himself while they worked together on the WOK security setup, and Ted had unintentionally reminded Randall of it more than once in the past month.

Password?

"TheodorTheProTechtor."

Invalid username or password.

"Gold-dames. You *never* change your passwords, Ted!"

Even Ted had begun mixing numbers and special characters into his passwords. Now it seemed he'd gone to the trouble of changing his old ones.

Randall opened his mind, and a number came to him. Ted often quoted lines from *Bill and Ted's Excellent Adventure*. One piece of dialogue included a two-digit expression mysterious but sacred to the film's titular characters. Randall's boss was such a freak about that film that every hiring season, Randall expected to meet a new employee named Bill, just for symmetry. Ted had used that number in other codes, so perhaps it was a default.

Password?

"TheodorTheProTechtor69."

Welcome, Theodor.

Free to roam deep within the WOK, Randall clicked through old files and memos and lines of code until long after his side of the Earth had turned its back on the sun.

He got up only when his rumbling gut cried out to him. His joints ached, but he managed to shuffle into the bathroom. He gagged when he approached the toilet. Even the lair of the Cockatrice couldn't produce such odors. After relieving himself in short order, he reached down by the plunger for an aerosol can. After spraying Rainforest Lysol in all directions, it now smelled as though someone had taken ill on a campsite.

Randall felt dizzy and let his head fall into his lap. Was this more than a nasty cold brewing inside him? Maybe the boy at the Circle K was contagious. Did that mean he would have to skip Middle Mirth?

In that moment of doubt, Randall felt Providence touch his shoulder. Alan, Carlos, and everyone else on the DL would be there all weekend. Randall's stomach bug would be in their midst the entire time. They would try to play through Saturday night, nonstop. With a little luck, whatever he had would spread rapidly through the dank basement ballroom the convention rented each year.

From memory, Randall pictured the hotel's layout. He saw dark possibilities. A trip to the hardware store could get him all the griefing supplies he would need.

Randall pulled his mind back to the present. He had much work to do in the WOK, and he wasn't sure how long it would take. Still seated on the toilet, Randall braced one hand on the tub rim, the other on the sink. He didn't manage to get his pants back on, but he reached the bed and changed out his underwear for a pair he hadn't worn in several days.

Once he settled back into his chair, he rolled to his desk and looked at the screen. Like a virtuoso pianist, he raised his hands then plunged them down to pound out a keystroke concerto.

Middle Mirth: Day 1

MAYA

Maya's shoulder muscles trembled from exhaustion. She dropped a cardboard box on the floor, the last of five loads she'd carried from Devon's car. The books inside it jumped when they hit the sealed concrete floor of the basement ballroom in which Middle Mirth would take place.

The enormous room was the underbelly of the hotel known to Mirthers as The Carrion Inn & Suites, which likely charged a rate commensurate with how little they'd developed it. As unadorned as an underground cellar, it had cinder block walls surrounding row after row of folding tables and metal chairs.

Six feet above Maya's head, exposed pipes sloshed with flowing water, but they also provided an opportunity for decoration. Along their full length hung gold, bronze, and silver streamers, artfully arranged like the prom decorations conferees had missed seeing in high school.

As the number of warm bodies in the room passed the four hundred mark, the climate had gone from cold to mild. Many congregated at the three dozen tables set up for DL groups. At the other tables, pre-teens and people old enough to be their grandparents had set up games Maya had only seen in boxes at her dad's store. They dressed in everything from shorts and t-shirts to leather pants and laced corsets—some on women, some on men.

Oblivious to both human and gaming displays, Devon continued stacking books onto the thin metal shelves he'd arranged along the edges of the Players booth. It stood in the middle of the display area, a.k.a. the "game farmer's market", which stretched the length of the eastern ballroom wall.

Local and international companies featured their wares,

with the highlight being the German woodworker who crafted mahogany "fusbol" tables by drilling steel rods through action figures to make lines of soccer players. The table on display pitted the original *Battlestar Galactica* crew against the heroes of *The Hobbit*, whose enormous feet more than compensated for their diminutive stature.

Maya gave her dad a quick peck, then scanned the ballroom for her friends. At one of the rectangular folding tables near the back of the room, she spied a balding man in a short-sleeved guayabera. It looked like Alan, but this man was talking to an unfamiliar young woman whose white summer dress set off an electric-lime hair bun. When the woman turned around, Maya saw Brie's face.

Maya couldn't take her eyes off Brie's giddy expression. She looked so—*elven*. After swimming quickly through the crowd, Maya received a hug and a squeal by way of greeting.

"What do you think?"

Brie turned to show herself in profile.

Maya reached out and touched Brie's left ear, which rose unnaturally high and ended in a point. Braided gold ribbons fell past her lobe.

"Lord, girl. That looks real."

"Not the ears, silly. What do you think of my hair?"

From the opposite side of the table, Lance said, "Mom did it."

"Mom and I did it together," Brie corrected. "It was sort of her idea."

"Does it look as crazy as it feels?" Lance asked.

Maya touched the green bun, which had dozens of silver sequins woven into it.

"There's so much spray in there," Brie said, "it's practically solid."

As advertised, the hair bun was as smooth as a Granny Smith apple.

"That's some mom you've got," Maya said.

"She really does believe in me—in us, I mean. She helped style me into a bona fide minstrel."

"Nobody had green hair in the Middle Ages," Maya said.

"Who knows?" Lance said. "Closer to the Dark Ages, the historical record is pretty thin."

Maya laughed and stroked Brie's hair again. She worried that she'd failed the cause by wearing black shorts and a sleeveless yellow shirt. On the other hand, she was the proxy for a barbarian—not an elven supermodel.

"We got my outfit at Party City, then Mom took me to Mani & Pedi. She had them put this lettuce-colored polish on all ten digits."

Brie raised her foot to show open-toed sandals.

"Then she gave me her salon appointment at Bellagio's. The stylist threatened to make her sign a waiver when she described what we were going for."

Maya recalled her mother's reaction when she'd come home for Thanksgiving sophomore year with two brass studs in her ears. If she'd gotten a hairdo like Brie's at her age, both her parents would've grounded her for a semester.

"No appreciation for the Blind Monk here?"

Lance stood and spun around to show off the brown robe he'd made famous. It appeared to have been tailored, with a fresh rope belt and a bit of cinching in the back to give it more shape. He now had a winged baseball embroidered on the front. The display drew the notice of other gamers. Cries rang out, from "Go padre!" to "Fear the monk!" Lance flexed his chest, the meager girth of which was hidden beneath his robe.

Maya ignored the antics.

"Carlos here yet?"

"Still no sign," Alan said. "Texted him twice."

Alan sat down in his director's chair at the head of the table.

"He okay?" Maya said.

"Probably just running late."

Maya believed Alan's nervous glances toward the main entrance more than his reassurances. She recalled the intimate conversation she and Alan had shared at Players. This convention surely brought up painful memories for him. She wanted to offer some comfort, but she thought it better to dive into their game.

"Why don't we get started?" Maya said. "If we begin now, we'll have momentum by the time the judging begins."

Brie stopped crowd-gazing and took her seat at the table.

"Let me level-up Hermione. I have enough experience to acquire the next bardic song set."

"Okay," Alan said, "but you need to land in Mythopolis first. Let's do that scene first, with everyone. Then maybe Angelou can help Hermione find a bard to train her. Let's do this quickly, okay?"

"Roger that," Lance said. "Bring us in for a landing, Herr Director."

LANCELOT

Held tightly in the arms of Queen Tinkana, Lancelot looked down to see the Mythopolis city guard herald their arrival. Soaring through the cool dawn air, the fairies landed before the northern gate and released their human, elven, and lupine cargo. Though still a prisoner on assignment, Lancelot hoped to be welcomed as a hero. He and Santana's travels had been more fraught than fruitful, but they had completed their assigned tasks.

Guards dressed in splint armor rushed forward, spears and swords at the ready. The lead soldier ran past Lancelot and addressed Tinkana.

"Halt at once! What manner of giants are you? What business do you have at this time of war? You cannot hope to ransom your cargo. You hold captive prisoners, not princes."

Lancelot raised his hands in supplication.

"These are not marauding giants. These are the last of the fairies."

The guards scoffed and steadied their weapons. Lancelot took off his helmet and laid his mace and shield on the ground. He approached the guards.

"They have joined us in the quest entrusted to us by she who governs the Non-Aligned Provinces."

"True enough," said Prime Minister Lesilla as she squeezed between two guards. She wore the same blue-and-white dress and satin sash as when she had first summoned them.

Lesilla looked up at Tinkana, who towered high above her. The prime minister circled an index finger over her head, and Tinkana responded by drawing a hand diagonally across her chest. In common hand, that was crown and sash—an acknowledgement of status.

"I saw you in a vision last night," Lesilla said. "I took you for stone giants, not fairies. Is it true what the priest says—none but you remain?"

"It is so. I am Tinkana, given the title of queen. Without a kingdom, it would now seem an indulgence to call me such."

"I am sorry for your losses."

"As am I."

Hermione bowed before the prime minister.

"As you foretold, the fairies unlocked for us a magical chamber."

"Remarkable!" Lesilla brightened. "Did you find the Magic Circle?"

"We found no such artifact. The vault held nothing the fairies had not made themselves—no ring, circlet, or alien object."

Lesilla sighed and turned to Lancelot.

"There is good news for some, at least. Your first disciples await you at the temple."

"I have followers? But—"

"News of your feats has won your god dozens of new adherents."

Lancelot turned crimson. A rising priest should harbor doubts about neither his god's prowess nor the fate of the capital city. He had both.

"You have honored our agreement and are free to leave, though I beg you stay to defend our city."

Lancelot nodded.

"My disciples would expect nothing less."

"Fear not, fer you shall have my company as well," Angelou said.

Lesilla gave a nod, then she and Angelou touched the backs of their hands together and said in unison, "Swift battle."

Tinkana curtsied with the poise of a Maypole dancer.

"We fairies also stand against the malevolence that destroyed our realm."

Lesilla reached up and touched the fabric encircling Tinkana's thigh.

"Your arrival improves what chance we might possess. We have done much to prepare for this battle. The forest used to reach the edge of Mythopolis, but it is now cleared back two hundred meters. The harvested lumber is stacked, tied, and tarred to form a barrier where our city's walls once stood."

"It is sad," Tinkana said, "to see those walls rise again."

"If only they were made of living trees," Hermione said. "I could make them dance."

Lancelot had not seen for himself the feat she had performed to turn the tide of battle at the fairie fortress. Even so, he smiled for remembering how Santana had described it. This bard of theirs was rising quickly to meet the present challenge. He felt proud of her, not as her combat trainer but because he now counted this elf as a friend.

Lesilla had no idea what Hermione referenced. She let the remark pass without comment.

"Behind those barriers," Lesilla said, "now stands the repentant hermit Devotus, along with many more wizards, warriors, and whole principalities. We have quartered three hundred thousand souls, a full third of which are prepared for combat."

"Then we must prevail," Tinkana said. "If the city falls, so shall the Mythos."

Lesilla raised her right hand and showed its back to Tinkana. The Fairie Queen gently touched it, as she had seen Angelou do.

"Swift battle," Lesilla and Tinkana said together.

The prime minister repeated the gesture with each of the fairies. When she bent over to give Lupita a kiss on the head, she received a paw instead.

Lancelot felt a smile on his face. Past the rolling hills and far down the road toward Everwinter, he noticed a thread of black smoke rising from the enemy encampment. His grin disappeared.

"Swift battle," he said to himself.

HERMIONE

"Give him your lute," Angelou said. "You could not entrust it to better hands."

Hermione tentatively handed her instrument to Almandine, a dwarven bard of rare beauty, even among those in their profession. As he reached for the lute, Almandine's hand brushed her arm. His skin was as smooth as boiled leather, and she felt a shudder of excitement.

Almandine offered a reassuring smile and cocked his head slightly.

"This is a unique artifact you possess. It should serve you well for many years to come."

He tuned the lute's strings, then returned it to Hermione.

"How long has it been since you visited a proper studio?"

Hermione pretended not to hear the question and inspected Almandine's tiny cottage, its roof so low that Angelou crouched unsteadily beneath it. Every manner of drum, woodwind, and stringed instrument hung on the wall. Filling a quarter of the room was a gleaming harpsichord inlaid with jade and turquoise stones. She had never seen anything like it, even at the bardic conservatory in the homeland she had lost to the Lifeless Knight.

"That is Lucille," the dwarf said. "She has trained many an apprentice in her day, including my own dear Yankal."

Hermione stared down at her boots. She tried to brush them with her hand, but their discoloration was not from dirt. It was the dried blood of elven Naughts.

Almandine squeezed Hermione's hand.

"I am sorry for your losses. Know that all things pass in time. What is important is that your friend has brought you to me."

The bard's warmth passed into her. Hermione felt her sorrow settle back into the hidden chambers of her heart. From her pocket, she pulled a jade figurine and studied it.

"When I left the fairies' vault, I had with me so many novel enchantments and items. More powerful strings for my lute, this little jaguar ally. It was bewildering at first, but as I gathered up the treasure, I felt energy rush through me, down my spine, and out to every extremity."

"It just means you are ready."

Angelou nodded.

"You are rising, dear one."

Hermione blushed, having forgotten Angelou was in the room with them.

Almandine walked to Lucille. He climbed two short steps and, still standing, put his hands on the keys. He tipped his head toward a small bench by his side.

"Sit. Play with me."

Hermione moved onto the bench and readied her lute.

"Follow me as I go. Listen to the chords. Play what feels right."

Almandine raised his hands dramatically, then pounded out grave military chords. Hermione tried to keep pace and surprised herself. She filled the room with a stirring counterpoint to the dwarf's surging bass. Every lyric to every song she had ever heard came to her at once, then settled into the back of her mind. When they reached the crescendo, in perfect synchronicity, Hermione felt renewed, perhaps reborn.

ALAN

Lance made a pout.

"How come leveling up is never that interesting with my character?"

"Because you don't play a bard," Brie said. "Maybe next time you advance, Hermione will sing a tribute."

Brie stood up to gyrate, disco style, and sing. "

His...name...is Lance-a-lot, he's not an average sot. He likes to preach a lot, and—"

"Shush!" said voices at the next table over.

Brie blushed and ceased her performance.

Echoing around the acoustically-challenged room came the opening strings and horns of "Foundations of Stone" from *The Two Towers* soundtrack. Over that came a woman's voice.

"Ladies and lords, board gamers and console captains, welcome to the biggest and greatest Middle Mirth ever!"

The crowd clapped as the voice continued.

"Find a seat if you can. Four hundred and seventy registered players, fifteen display booths, plus a LAN den and three special-purpose rooms. So much to do, so little time!"

Whoops and shouts went up from the enthusiastic audience.

"For this record-setting year, we owe thanks to the munificence of a mysterious mensch and his contest. But the mystery ends right now. We open this year's convention with none other than the lead designer of the Second and Third Editions of Dungeon Lords, the still-great and once-humble Jeff Jacobson!"

The music swelled. Out from behind a shoji screen and onto the stage hopped a man in his mid-sixties wearing a tie-dyed dress shirt and dark blue suit. Cheers erupted, and Jacobson waved his arms downward to beg the quieting crowd to calm itself.

"Thank you for having me here today," Jacobson said at the

mic stand. "I've been coming to gaming conventions from the time my long-lost companion Ernest Carpenter first created Dungeon Lords—before some of you were born. Let me tell you, I've seen bigger crowds and stayed in nicer hotels. Who was with me at Comic-Con here in San Diego last week?"

Jacobson raised his own hand, and a few hands went up around the room. Scattered "boos" were also audible.

"Hey now, no hating on the big leagues. Besides, for all the celebrities they had at the Con, they didn't have the two A-listers I see here today. Let's hear it for the Blind Monk and the Padre Princess!"

Lance jumped up and waved on cue. Brie stood more uneasily but acknowledged the applause filling the room. The crowd found its way into a chant.

"Pa-dre prin-cess, pa-dre prin-cess."

Lance grinned at his tablemates and sat back down. With an affected lisp, he whispered, "We are *thuperthars!*"

Jacobson chuckled and tapped the microphone.

"But seriously, this year Middle Mirth has a signature event the big boys don't have. Before the weekend's over, my fellow judges and I will crown the group that best captures the spirit of Dungeon Lords. Decades ago, we began that game with a complex set of rules, a novel set of dice, and a singular mission— to make accounting fun again!"

"Oh—my—god," Alan said to himself, suddenly realizing how he'd fallen into his chosen profession. He doubted he was the only number cruncher in the room, and probably not the only one who enjoyed it. Estimating the life expectancy of a non-insured target class was an entertaining diversion.

Jacobson leaned back into the microphone.

"But seriously, Dungeon Lords was never meant to be about rules, rolls, and numbers. When you peel away the paperwork that mummified its body, you see the flesh of the living game. The true aim is *role playing*, which means more than drawing a stick figure on a character sheet and stealing a name from Tolkien or, God forbid, J. K. Rowling."

The room roared with laughter.

Brie blushed and turned away from her table mates.

"Dungeon Lords isn't about hauling treasure and killing orcs. Trust me, I've killed my share of orcs, half-orcs, even quarter-orcs!"

Along with a few other veteran gamers, Alan cheered the obscure reference to the unpopular *Death Awaits You* supplement to the *Monsters and Mayhem* guidebook.

"If a few orcs must die, it's in the name of a greater purpose, which brings us to this weekend's grand prize. The group whose game becomes a living story this weekend will receive from me, in loving memory of Ernest's legacy, an all-expenses-paid trip to a European gem, the famous Bled Castle!"

Alan was surprised to hear gasps from the crowd. He reminded himself that many were there for other games and likely hadn't heard of their tournament. Nonetheless, the whole crowd soon joined the lusty applause coming from the Dungeon Lords tables.

"Some are here for something else altogether. Who's here for Stairway to Hell?"

Maybe fifty shouts rose from the crowd. Alan found himself being the one surprised.

"What's that about?" he whispered to Lance.

"Online gaming nonsense."

"I see quite a turnout for the Stairway," Jacobson said. "But you guys have to compete with what—the whole world? Wouldn't it be great if the winning team is sitting in this room? If they are, let's hope they're generous of spirit, because whoever wins the Stairway escapes the fires of Hell with fifty thousand dollars!"

Alan gasped, along with those whose games had no higher stakes than bragging rights.

Jacobson tried to wink at the crowd but blinked both eyes instead.

"Of course, that's fifty thousand *before* taxes."

The joke fell flat, except for the lusty laughter coming from the Players booth, where Devon seemed to appreciate the tax-bracket humor. His involuntary snorts caught Jacobson's attention, and the speaker gave him a knowing nod.

"I never forget a face," Jacobson said, "especially when it's on a dude who's four feet high."

Devon waved both hands frantically in front of his chest, as if to discourage Jacobson from going any further.

"Folks, I may be a dying legend, but a living one stands among you."

Jacobson pointed toward the laser-printed Players banner above Devon's booth.

"Standing in front of, um...what is that sign you've got? You opening a dance club?"

The crowd laughed with Jacobson.

"Right over there, you're looking at the greatest codesmith of our time, the humble creator of the World of Karnage game engine, none other than Devon Washington!"

Amidst polite applause, attendees stood on their chairs or craned their necks to find this diminutive wizard they'd overlooked.

"No way," Lance said to Maya. "Your dad created that god-awful video game? That thing pooped on top of everything Dungeon Lords stands for. A real Cleveland steamer."

"The—horror," Alan said softly.

Brie nudged Maya.

"Is your family, like, loaded?"

"Him more than Mom," Maya said. "He doesn't really talk about it."

Alan and Lance stage whispered together, "The—horror."

"So anyway..." Maya looked toward the exit at the back of

the room, then smiled.

"Carlos!"

Into the ballroom he strode, a suitcase in one hand and a crate in the other. He wore a tuxedo shirt with brass cufflinks, pleated slacks with an etched leather belt, black dress socks and loafers. To Alan's delight, he'd draped over his shoulders the velvet half-circle cape.

The golden skulls on Lance's gift had struck Alan as macabre when he first saw them. Since then, it had occurred to him that Lance and Brie—and probably even Maya—had no real conception of what the conference meant to Carlos.

The first year that Alan had suggested he come to Middle Mirth, Carlos had pointed out that a Crandall and Randall car trip to that very event had sealed his parents' fate. Just one year later, Carlos changed his tune. The exact words still made little sense to Alan, though more than they used to. "You can sweep demons out the door," Carlos had said, "but they're more likely to haunt your mind than your home."

With a wave of his hand, Carlos flipped the cape over his chair and sat down beside Lance, who noted his companion's arrival.

"Better late than dead," Lance said cheerfully.

Alan looked at Maya. She grimaced in reply.

Carlos pulled his head back to study Lance for a moment.

"*Sí, amigo. Mucho mejor.*"

SANTANA

From his bedroom window at the Miramar Inn, Santana watched people hurrying about the city. He felt an unfamiliar guilt for resting while others worked into the deepening night, but he needed rest to be of use tomorrow. His body still ached and his ears rang from the beating he had suffered battling alongside the fairies.

Santana saw Lancelot approach the inn, the towering Tinkana beside him. She removed from her circling linens a small amethyst stone, which she clasped in her palms as she made an incantation. The fairie giant shrank until she stood seven feet high, half her normal stature. Lancelot nodded, then shook her hand and departed.

As Tinkana pulled her wings in tight and ducked to enter the inn, Santana readied himself for her arrival. He expected the visit was more than business. She had eyed him curiously ever since their first encounter, when she mocked him in a way that felt more playful than cruel. Though he could not read the body language of a fairie, he had seen enough otherwise sensible female creatures drawn to him, and he hoped for the best. He removed his shirt, washed his face, and tidied his quarters before climbing into bed, as if to nap.

Tinkana's ascent of the stairway sent tremors through both the wood floor and Santana's bones. She and her kind would never become accustomed to indoor life, with or without enchanted quartz. A thunderous pound on the door signaled her arrival. Lupita, who had been lying at the foot of the bed, leapt to her feet. Back legs spread wide and braced on the floor, she let out eight deep barks without taking a breath.

"Lancelot?" Santana yelled from his bed. "Let a poor sorcerer sleep!"

"It is I," said a low female voice.

Santana climbed out of bed and crossed the room with an affected nonchalance. On opening the door, he meant to show a relaxed expression. Instead, he stared wide-eyed at this almost human-sized queen dressed in spiraling fabrics. She likewise seemed to appraise the sorcerer, who wore a ruby amulet and matching silk pants. Healed of all but scars, his bronze chest and arms were smooth and lightly toned. The wiry black hairs on his body glistened.

"Your Highness?"

Tinkana crouched and passed through the doorway. She set herself down on a wooden trunk, gently. Santana cringed at the thought that she might crush the box. It held a precious inventory of items that had cluttered the floor a minute earlier. In a frenzy, he'd tossed into the chest two dozen unlabeled scroll cases and an assortment of enchanted brass rings, which he'd dumped out of a Pouch of Endless Holding.

As if sensing his anxiety, Tinkana shifted herself to lean against an open chifforobe. It tilted far enough for Santana's cloak and staff to spill onto the floor. Tinkana moved herself back onto the chest, hands on either side to distribute her weight. It was hard for a Fairie Queen to maintain a regal bearing in quarters such as these.

Lupita regarded Tinkana warily but decided this giant was no longer a stranger. The wolf leapt onto Santana's bed and buried herself in its coverings. Coiled into a ball, Lupita feigned sleep, a half-opened eye trained on Santana.

"I have business," Tinkana said in a flat voice.

Santana shut the door.

"Then I will be pleased to be your business partner."

"We will make that particular transaction in short order, but first—"

"Who's rushing?"

Adrenaline flooded to Santana's extremities. His heart clenched when he contemplated the sheer mass of Tinkana's body. Seated on an iron-framed trunk, the floorboards beneath her buckled.

"I cannot deny," Santana said, "that I have contemplated the thought of a private meeting with you. Though you were ungrateful to this courageous rescuer on the day we met, even then I took note of your exceptional form."

Tinkana narrowed her eyes.

"I do have some questions," Santana said, "about the logistics of—"

Tinkana waved him off.

"We must address a more difficult matter first."

Santana frowned. He walked to his bed and shooed Lupita, who padded to the door and settled onto a reed mat. Santana ruffled the loose sheets to make his nest appear less unmade, more inviting.

"I come from the Assembly," Tinkana said. "The prime minister related terrible news."

"What happened?"

"The Lifeless Knight has mustered a greater army than she had foreseen. Hoping to spare the capital from a siege, Devotus led a small band of illusionists and two regiments down the road toward Everwinter and met the enemy. There were no survivors, save two mounted scouts."

Santana recalled the gnome in the tower who posed as an incompetent recluse. The illusionist's performance that day now appeared to have been meant to boost Santana's fragile ego. He was sorry to hear of the old man's passing.

"Devotus insisted that the Lifeless Knight was none other than Lord Cynoc reborn," Tinkana said. "He considered himself responsible, indirectly, for the pain Cynoc had inflicted and tried to make amends."

Santana nodded. He and Lancelot agreed Cynoc and the Knight were one, though they had confided only to each other the suspicion that he was the reincarnation of their deceased companion.

"Devotus could work compelling magics," Tinkana said, "but in his day, he was a formidable philosopher. He questioned the received wisdom of elves, fairies, and even the gods of the Mythos. When during his travels Devotus met Cynoc, the gnome's lectures on these subjects darkened the lord's less mature conception of the world to the point of madness."

"Guilt over winning an argument is no reason to get oneself killed."

"Lesilla assured me, this was not suicide. Devotus knew the most he might accomplish was gifting us time to make ready. He and his fellows used their collective power to invoke a false citadel, a compelling forgery floating over the Tar Fields. They hoped to lure the Naught army there. Alas, the Lifeless Knight must possess Cynoc's own talents as conjurer, for he saw through the ruse. He buried Devotus and his allies in their own trap."

"Enough of such horrors. May we turn our attention toward our present situation? You and I are here today."

"Very well."

Tinkana looked out the window. Santana waited for her to gather her thoughts. The fur over Lupita's eyelids twitched. Soothed by the words of their female companion and ignorant of their import, the wolf was asleep, lost in a dream.

"There is little of the Fairie Realm that your world understands. Consider the assumption that we are all female."

"You are all female, indeed," Santana said with a grin.

"That was not true, until now. Every generation, which is to say every century, one male fairie is born. He lives only a few dozen years, but once of age, he mates with those who are ready."

Santana marveled at the career of such a creature. He opened his mouth, then closed it, speechless.

"The last such fairie was locked inside the fortress when the siege began, but he escaped and threw himself into the battle.

That leaves us no choice but to break our pure line."

Santana straightened his back and stroked his pectoral muscles.

"I see where you are heading, too slowly for my taste."

"Conceiving and carrying a child is easy enough. We fairies are even more fertile than we are beautiful."

Seemingly of their own accord, the Queen's wings stretched above her head and flitted tentatively in the cramped room. She noticed their movement and drew them back down.

"But again, that is our second order of business. As the Naughts devour the Mythos, it is not the loss of purity that concerns me. They seem bent on extinguishing the spark of life itself. You and your friends give the Mythos a chance in this conflict, but only a slight one."

Tinkana withdrew a scrap of parchment from her ever-winding garments.

"Fortunately, there is another way out, though not for all of us."

Tinkana handed the scroll to Santana, who recognized its words as Draconic. It was lettered in Hellscript, the calligraphic style most often used to write contracts in the Underworld.

"This was buried deep in the vault," Tinkana said, "waiting to be rediscovered."

Santana shook his head.

"I suspect it a forgery. Even if its author was sincere, it could not contain the power it claims."

"You are wrong on both counts. It is authentic. If used as intended, it will detonate with a ferocity greater than the rocks that fall from the night and split open the ground."

Santana offered the parchment back to Tinkana, but she did not accept it.

"I know its authenticity because I wrote it myself. I did so at the request of a sage who brought to the edge of the Fairie Realm an urn that held the ashes of the fallen druid priest Cuauhtémoc."

Santana's eyes widened.

"Cuauhtémoc? Did you know that I—"

"Indeed. The same bloodline runs through you as did through him. Our spies had heard tales of Cuauhtémoc, who was renowned for his bravery. He died in the Fifth Plane of Hell, immolated in a pit fiend's fiery blast. The sage put his ashes into the urn. We brought the stranger into our realm because we shared his hope that these noble remains could yield a potent magic."

"And this scroll..."

"Contains that very spell," Tinkana said with a nod. "To create a protection that would reconstitute Cuauhtémoc's passion for the natural world, we pulped and pressed his ashes. That is the parchment you hold. When I set to writing, however, I fell into a trance and thought myself a dragon. I awoke to discover I had produced an incantation that would disintegrate one's enemies, but only at one's own expense—and that of any others within countless miles of the spellcaster."

"All the more souls for the Underworld," Santana mused.

"Once I saw what I had written, I tried to destroy it but could not. So I locked it away, deep inside our vault."

"Then we are lucky none before us retrieved it."

"That was not mere fortune. I designed the lowest vault to open only if passed over by—"

"The Magic Circle?"

"Precisely. And you, who can speak the tongue of dragons, must now be prepared to use this morbid scroll against the Lifeless Knight."

"This is the power of the Circle? Unlocking a curse?"

"I cannot say more. You must trust me. When you harness it fully, you will feel the Circle course through you. It will make clear the way forward."

Santana stared at the parchment. On closer inspection, the script was pure. The ink had bonded with the paper. If one held and read it correctly, the spell would execute. Still, it felt hypothetical—more theoretical math than pure magic. Such a destructive force none had ever seen, not even from their present adversary.

Tinkana put her hands on Santana's knees.

"If you see me retreat from tomorrow's battle, it will not be for lack of courage."

Santana put his hands on hers. She felt as smooth as polished river stones.

"I have seen how fearsome you can be."

"If I fly beyond the far hills, I will do so only to secure a future for fairies and the magic we craft for this world. If it comes to that, you must find the strength to use the scroll."

Santana doubted the queen's logic. How could she divine the odds in a battle that would entangle hundreds of thousands of bleeding bodies? She was a creature unlike any he had known. Perhaps her sense of such things was equally remarkable.

"Tell me this," Santana said. "How exactly will the fairies live on if only you survive?"

"I will join with a human male until I feel the stirrings of a child."

"Yes, but how will you choose..."

Tinkana reached out and seized the sorcerer by his waist. She pulled him off the bed and lay him on what felt like a support beam beneath the floorboards. The meeting of their bodies produced a jarring "clang."

Lupita stirred amidst her slumber but did not raise her head.

"Apologies," Santana said as he pulled off his jeweled necklace. "Amulet of Natural Armor."

From inside her clothing, Tinkana removed a vial. She poured its viscous liquid into Santana's mouth. He felt his muscles expand and diagnosed the spell—frost giant strength. He tried to calculate how long it would last, but he lost his focus when Tinkana straddled him. She raised her wings until they touched the ceiling, then reached behind her back and flicked her wrist. The strips of ironcloth circling her body slowed their revolutions, then drifted to the floor until they covered only her bent knees.

CARLOS

Carlos covered his ears to block out the screeching feedback of the PA system.

"Sorry," said a cheerful voice. "Better now?"

Standing on the stage was a young woman in the red suit worn by all Carrion Suites employees.

"I'm Jen, your hotel liaison. I know you're right in the middle of stuff, but I've been asked to tell you a few things about the facilities and make a couple announcements. First off, when leaving the ballroom, please use the main exit toward the back. Go through the double doors, turn right, and you'll head up a stairway. It's the same way you all came in here, unless you grabbed a mop and snuck in through the maintenance elevator."

Jen laughed to no response, coughed lightly, and covered her mouth. "After exiting the ballroom, if you turn left instead of right, you'll head down a narrow hall. The first door of that hallway is the Movie Room."

Jen studied the conference program in her hand.

"Ladyhawke is tonight. Saturday afternoon till Sunday morning, it's The One Ring, the nineteen-hour re-cut edition of the Lord of the Rings trilogy everyone's buzzing about. Your next stop down that corridor is the judges' HQ. All you competitors better stay out of that one. After that is the space designated only for those who identify as female."

A group of women far across the ballroom shouted back at Jen, "Damn right!"

"The Women's Space organizers have all kinds of cool things scheduled — dancing, poetry, and probably some Wiccan rituals, right ladies?"

Women scattered about the ballroom exchanged shrugs, but Maya and Brie nodded at each other affirmatively.

"Last up, it's the Local Area Network room — the LAN."

Jen turned around to point at the wall behind the stage.

"The Middle Mirth folks set up these flat screens, which are wired into a camera in the LAN. They can see and hear us, and we them. That'll keep everyone connected."

Jen waved at the screen and spoke in a flirty voice.

"Hi there, guys."

Looking up in response to her high tone were the faces of assorted boys and men, plus maybe three women.

"That room's usually stupid cold, but with all the PCs humming in there this weekend, it should be warm enough to support life."

Jen leaned forward to whisper into the microphone.

"At least, for a while."

Uneasy faces in the LAN room looked up at the camera mounted on their wall.

"I also need to remind you that the Saturday play-through-the-night is strictly voluntary, but if you stay past midnight, we assume you're here for the duration. It'll be an old-fashioned lock-in, like at a church rec center."

Jen tried to look serious but couldn't help laughing.

"Kidding! Can't do that at a hotel. Fire codes would never allow it."

"It's true," Alan whispered to his tablemates. "As it is, this dungeon down here is marginally code compliant. I'd never insure these guys."

"Final details. There's something veteran attendees know that I probably don't have to remind you..."

"Our phones don't work!" shouted an older man who stood over a large gaming mat shaped like a pirate ship.

"Yup, no cell reception, and that means texting doesn't work either. Even the LAN room is just a snake pit of Ethernet cables, so no wireless there either. We do have two wall-mounted hotel phones here in the ballroom, and you're welcome to use those."

Jen pointed toward the ceiling.

"The other thing to know is that we're fully booked this weekend. Besides you guys, we're hosting a rowdy bunch of regulars, the Cemetery and Mortuary Association of California. They're not yet six feet under, but trust me, they're already three sheets to the wind. We'll have our hands full with them upstairs, so don't make any trouble down here, okay? Now, let the games, um, resume!"

Applause erupted in the ballroom and on the monitors at the back of the stage.

"Luckily," Carlos said, "I already reserved a room on the thirteenth floor."

"Readying for a night of debauchery?" Lance asked.

Carlos put his hands together in prayer.

"That, or at least a sound night's sleep."

"Will the judges be staying up all night Saturday?" Maya asked.

"That's the plan," Alan said. "Either way, I'll try to time it so we peak Sunday morning."

"When do they announce the winners?" Brie asked.

"Not long after play closes at noon," Alan said. "I bet they've already graded the written scenarios we turned in, so all they have to do is add our scores from this weekend."

"I still don't get it," Carlos said. "How do they judge us when we're playing?"

"In the game directors meeting this morning, they explained it this way. Imagine yourself acting in a pilot for a TV series. The floor judges are the studio audience. The producers have already read the script, and they want to see how it looks on stage. Are the heroes compelling? Is the villain believable? Is the director doing excessive exposition? It's a pretty good analogy, since the group that ends up playing in Bled Castle will appear in a Dungeon Lords promotional video."

"Since we're completely out-of-game at this point," Lance said, "I've got to ask, what's with the late arrival, Carlos?"

"Don't sweat it," Maya said to Carlos. "We covered for you."

"We're just glad you're here," Alan said.

"As it happens, I have a reason for being tardy."

Carlos reached down to the covered crate he'd set at his feet when he arrived. Out of it he lifted a tiny brown-and-white dog. Peach fuzz covered its entire body, except for its snout, which poked out like a pink eraser. Its oversized eyes searched the room.

"Gigi, meet the group."

"Yip!"

Brie scratched Gigi's head and cooed at her.

"I just *knew* Cheese Doodle would be this cute!"

Carlos felt Alan's stare before he saw it.

"Relax, I've got it figured out. When she's in her crate, she's quiet as a mouse."

"She certainly *sounds* like a mouse," Lance said.

"If a judge comes by and we have a scene for Lupita, I've got her trained for that."

Carlos squeezed Gigi's shoulders. She let out a falsetto growl. Lance nodded in approval.

"You said you wanted actors, Alan. Sounds like she's a pro."

Carlos set Gigi back down, and she scooted into her crate. He latched the door and pulled a black sheet over her.

"I didn't plan to pack a puppy. Adelita had to go out of town on business and left Gigi with me. The Carrion people are cool with dogs under twenty pounds, and Cheese Doodle's clearly in that weight class. So, here we are."

The lie made Carlos wince. His accounting of the hotel's policy was legit, but he'd probably be hosting Gigi indefinitely. As he was getting ready to go to the convention, Adelita had shown up at his apartment to announce that she couldn't make it through the weekend. She checked herself into Dry Dock, the drug treatment facility Carlos had taken her to twice before. Sober enough to drive herself there, her parting words had been,

"I can't take care of Gigi, and you can't take care of me."

Even after his sister's visit, Carlos would have arrived at Middle Mirth on time, except that he lingered in the parking lot. He'd chosen a spot where he could look out on the San Diego Bay. He wasn't sure if he needed to mark the tenth anniversary of his parents' passing any differently than he had the previous nine, but the roundness of the number spooked him. Carlos laughed to think he might have inherited the numerological neuroses of his Mayan ancestors.

More likely, the apprehension stemmed from remembrance of a more modern form of madness. While still a teenager, he'd followed the story of a Portland man who'd taken a hostage at gunpoint. Local news covered it around-the-clock because years earlier, the gunman had been one of the first responders at the infamous San Ysidro McDonald's massacre. A newly trained paramedic, he'd been unprepared for what his eyes saw that day. Year by year, this guy probably fell apart, but it was the massacre's tenth anniversary that did him in. It took police two days to talk him out of his apartment.

Still ruminating in his car, Carlos had addressed the papier-mâché skull on his dashboard. "Just you and me now," he'd said as he rubbed circles over the crown of its head. "I had to let go of Superbarrio. He's resting with *mamá y papá*. You'll have to watch over me, but also keep an eye on Alan and Karen."

Maya said something about Gigi, and Carlos refocused on her.

"...dog's not gonna be an issue tonight. The judges are done for the day."

"Suits me," Alan said. "I'm getting hungry." He reached under the table and brought forth a large Igloo cooler. "Let's stay here for a wrap-up before we call it a night. Mom and I made some sandwiches. For our Blind Monk, she threw in that Caribbean fruit punch he's always drinking."

"Thanks, but I'm off that." Lance made a sour face. "They

must have switched their formula or something. Stuff's been making me fall asleep at work."

Lance hunched over and spoke like an ancient guru.

"Ah, but food and gaming, partners be. Each of these brings joy to me. Together, they bring ecstasy."

Brie laughed.

"My brother, the poet."

"Good heavens," said a voice Carlos couldn't place. "We've got to introduce you people to better poets."

Carlos turned to see who stood behind him.

"You're the woman from the Wiccan Convent," Maya said.

"*A* woman from the Convent. Not *the* woman."

"Who?" Lance asked.

"Our chief rivals," Alan said playfully. "They're trying to steal our European vacation."

Carlos focused on the woman's round face. She grinned and her cheeks made a pair of disarming dimples. His brain tried to find a pattern match, then discarded the only candidate the search yielded.

"By the looks of it," the woman said, "you've got a pretty ragtag crew. How long you been playing together?"

"Nine years, at least for two of us," Carlos said. "Before that, I knew someone in college who—"

Carlos cut himself off. He closed his mouth and stared at the visitor.

The woman turned to Maya.

"Who's this weirdo in the velvet cape?"

"You mean Carlos?" Maya said.

"Carlos," the woman repeated, but with a strong Spanish accent.

"You know each other?" Brie asked.

"Yes," Carlos said. "This is Tara."

"So it is," Tara said.

Brie smiled at them both.

"Did you meet at last year's convention?"

"Haven't gone to one in years," Tara replied.

"From nursing school?" Maya asked.

"I'm a DEA attorney," Tara said. "We don't fraternize with doctors and nurses. When it comes to narcotics distribution, they're right up there with the cartels."

"From college?" Alan said.

"College it is," Carlos said. "Same old story. Boy meets girl, shit hits fan, girl never calls boy back."

Lance threw up his hands.

"You never call *me* back, either, Carlos. You two sound like lovesick mentals. Did you date or something?"

"Or something," Carlos said.

"I barely knew you," Tara said. "But maybe now…?"

Carlos swallowed.

"Busy tonight?"

"Maybe."

"We're having sandwiches," Lance said.

"Thanks," Carlos said to Lance, "but I think I'm going out to dinner."

"Don't go anywhere," Tara said. "I'll need to make arrangements with my companions."

After one more lingering lock with Carlos' eyes, Tara turned and disappeared into the thinning crowd.

"What just happened?" Lance exhaled with exasperation. "You're not staying for the wrap-up? But in your scene with Tinkana, you were getting to the good part!"

"Yes, we were," Carlos said in a faraway voice.

Alan looked at the sheet covering Gigi's crate.

"What about the pooch?"

Carlos disappeared under the table, then reemerged with a dog crate no bigger than a toolbox.

"Lance, I'd like to owe you and your dear sister a favor."

"Sure, whatever, but we were interrupted right in the middle of—"

Maya reached out and squeezed Lance's hand.

"You'll just have to use your imagination, champ. That's what Herr Director keeps telling us to do."

* * *

It took a few long minutes for Carlos to gather his belongings and quiet his juvenile companions, who all but catcalled when he got up to depart. He felt jealous eyes on his back from every Dungeon Lords group he passed. Perhaps they'd witnessed the power of Alan's direction and felt a sense of relative deprivation. Or maybe it was baser than that. Perhaps they intuited that the handsome sorcerer in the velvet cape was about to get properly laid in this very hotel.

Carlos felt an unfamiliar sensation, perhaps embarrassment? He stretched his jaw open wide to reset his emotional equilibrium. When he got within ten feet of Tara's table, he pulled up a chair and listened while she put her own group's adventure to bed for the night.

"Put down the dice," Tara said. "We're not doing ability checks. Just tell me what you say to Estraven. That'll decide it."

"Shit," Valerie said, "you know I suck at that."

The other women at the table encouraged her, and Valerie gathered herself.

"We beseech you, in the memory of the Maslins, to release our comrade and zir acolytes."

"Why?" Tara said in a low voice. "Why should I do this for zir?"

There was that word again. Tara's group clearly understood the term, but it threw him off long enough to miss a couple of speaking turns.

Valerie stood up abruptly. She twisted her arms together and made a gesture of supplication toward the heavens.

"I summon the virus of Oryx," Valerie all but shouted. "Let the glycoproteins remake my own cells in the image of the creator."

Carlos turned away and covered his mouth, stifling a chuckle. The juxtapositions of medical jargon, borrowed proper nouns, and mysterious pronouns were too much. If he heard another word, he might burst into laughter.

In search of something to occupy his thoughts, he opened his briefcase and read a takeout menu. He and Tara could forego awkward conversation in a restaurant and instead eat a Mexican feast, delivered to his room. No, something lighter—soup and salad? He opened an app to put in an order, then tapped another to choose a Spanish guitar playlist.

"Whatcha doing, stranger?" Tara said.

Carlos answered with what he hoped was an easy smile.

"I made our plans for the evening."

He closed his briefcase, stood, and extended a hand.

"Are you free to join ze?"

Tara laughed.

"Excuse me?"

Only then did Carlos hear what he'd said.

"Me—I mean, are you free to join *me*?"

Tara nodded, took his hand, and led him away. Her fingers wrapped tightly into his own, and her palm felt sweaty. Could be from gaming all day, or perhaps her heart was racing as quickly as his.

Once they exited the ballroom and ascended the stairs toward the main floor, she shoved her shoulder into his own without relaxing her grip.

"Were you listening to our game?"

"Maybe," Carlos said. He opened the heavy door at the top of the stairway and gestured toward the bank of elevators across the lobby.

"We'll dine *en mi casa* tonight."

"You better not be taking me to a staged bachelor pad."

"I'm no bower bird. I can offer only a reasonably clean hotel room."

Tara followed Carlos to the elevators. They watched together as the floor indicator moved down from nine to eight to seven. It felt like a countdown. Tara tapped her foot in time with the changing light.

A bell dinged, doors opened, and they stepped inside. Carlos pressed the button for the thirteenth floor, and the doors closed before anyone else joined them.

"If you were listening in," Tara said, "what do you think? Our gaming style is a bit different—more theater, less math."

Carlos felt the elevator car rising but tried to keep his blood pressure low. The effort this required left him little energy for subterfuge, and a snicker snuck out before he could stop it.

"I'm sorry, I only eavesdropped enough to catch bits and pieces."

He squeezed his eyes closed and gritted his teeth, but hard laugher followed.

"Honestly, I couldn't even pick up a single thread in there. You might as well have been speaking Dutch."

Carlos braced himself for slaps, punches, kicks. Instead, Tara gave a light laugh of her own. Their elevator stopped, doors opened. She released her grip on Carlos' hand and stepped onto the floor, muttering "fuck" a dozen times or more. Her body was still heading in the right direction, but her mood wasn't. He refused to let the fantasy outdo reality. This evening had to end at least as well as Santana's had.

"Hey, I was being a dick just then. Look, every group is different. Alan taught me to play the game one way. You guys play it another."

"Valerie would correct you for calling us guys."

"No, I get it. I work with women who call each other guys, but I remember feminist stuff from college. I may be a bit out of date on all that, but—"

"Estraven insists on ungendered pronouns."

"What?"

"The *ze* you heard—that's non-gender specific. That's what the quing—the unity of king and queen—requires. I baked that stuff into my version of the Mythos at Valerie's request."

"Shit, I'm not even sure I understand what I think is an explanation."

"That's *precisely* our problem," Tara said with a sigh. "Which room's yours?"

Carlos pointed to his left.

Tara led the way down the corridor. She seemed to almost race walk, with quick glances back at Carlos to make sure she hadn't passed his room. Maybe she had to go to the bathroom. He hoped that wasn't the reason for the rush.

"I know one of the judges is grooving on our group," Tara said, "but Jacobson clearly doesn't get half the references. We built our Mythos almost in exile. We rebelled against Middle Earth tropes by infusing Butler, LeGuin, Atwood—hell, even McCaffrey. The higher-order magic and mischief in our world involves genetic engineering, parthenogenesis, and yes, linguistic warfare between competing matriarchies."

"Holy shit."

Another involuntary laugh had Carlos covering his mouth.

"Alan has bent the universe a bit, but—"

Carlos spied his room number approaching and reached out for Tara's shoulder. He missed and grabbed her waist. Tara returned a playful smile. Carlos fumbled his plastic key card, which fell to the floor.

"I guarantee you," Tara said, "our group has built a world more original and daring than anything else in that basement. But the judges weren't present to see me build it, year by year. They don't understand it, let alone how it came to be."

Carlos couldn't believe himself. He picked up his key and

held it at the ready, but he didn't use it. At least for the moment, he was more interested in the Mythos than in the Earthly quest that brought them to this door.

"When you say that, I think maybe I can see what Alan's doing. We're not just trying to finish off this Cynoc dude. We're fighting with him over the world itself. He's forcing us to defend it."

"Defend it, or transform it?"

"Both, maybe? Either way, it feels like our world's about to explode."

"No, that's *me*. If you don't open that door, I'm gonna pull down my pants and pee. Right here. On the carpet."

Carlos pushed in his key and the door beeped. Tara turned the handle and rushed inside.

RANDALL

Randall squirmed in his hard plastic chair. The seat wasn't generous enough, and its metal arms pinched him when he sat up straight. He had to teeter on its edge and pitch his torso forward to sit with any comfort. He wanted to scratch his sorest spot, but he retained just enough self-consciousness to refrain from reaching inside the crease where his belly folded over his waistline.

Fifty-four boys and men, plus three women, sat with Randall in neat rows of tables that held up their custom gaming PCs. Randall's wireless connection established itself, and he prepared to log in to the WOK.

"Five minutes to launch!" said a convention staffer.

By design, Randall was among the final contestants to sign in. He'd waited until the last minute to arrive, both in person and online, to avoid detection by Alan, Carlos, and their lackeys. As far as he could tell, they had no idea he was there. He'd seated himself outside the LAN room camera's field of view, but on the wall-mounted monitor, he could see everyone in the main ballroom as effortlessly as a hawk circling above its prey.

Username?

"Boldhearts."

Password?

"Frock^Alan."

Against a cloudy backdrop, a demon flew onto Randall's screen. The red-eyed beast dove out of the sky and into a dormant volcano. Behind it trailed a banner: "Welcome, Boldhearts, to the World of Karnage 2011 Stairway to Hell!"

Randall sat back in his chair, even when a staffer shouted, "We're live!" All around him were clucking keyboards and shuffling mice, plus the gulping of soda and rustling of snack bags. As advertised, the buzz of human and electronic activity was warming the room. The online action was also heating up.

Boldhearts stood on the lip of a volcano into which hundreds of figures descended every minute. When the waves of arrivals slowed, a mixed group of adventurers circled cautiously behind Boldhearts, and Randall turned his avatar to face two female monks, two warlocks, a male paladin, and a female shaman.

Boldhearts lifted his massive sword. Runes along its edges pulsed from yellow to red. Every other second, the weapon seemed to breathe air in to cool itself, then exhale a flicker of flame. Boldhearts stood tall in a solid suit of black armor with the image of a screaming goat head etched into its breastplate.

Randall put on his headset but chose to use text.

"Hello," Randall typed. "Care to die?"

On Randall's screen, the paladin made a signal with his hands, and the warlocks unleashed a wave of fiery missiles, each of which struck Boldhearts' armor to modest effect. Boldhearts swung his sword and hit the two approaching monks with a glancing blow. Before launching their own attacks, the monks hesitated.

As was always true in the WOK, Randall could hear audio chatter from players whose characters were within range.

One of the monk players said, "Things are fuzzy, but—there he is!"

"I got him," said the other.

The monks turned away from Boldhearts and attacked their startled companions.

"What? No!" shouted the paladin.

Chaos ensued. One of the warlocks doubled over. The shaman at the back of the group reached down with her hands to heal him, but when she did so, she also became disoriented and assaulted the paladin. As Randall's enemies fought one another, their images became sepia-toned ghosts of their former selves.

Randall chuckled.

"What's the matter?"

"Crap," said the paladin. "Did you cast a spell?"

"Why don't you go spread some good cheer where the real action is?"

Boldhearts put his sword back in its scabbard and nudged into the volcano each of his erstwhile attackers. The five gray figures quickly mixed among the masses hoping to rescue innocent souls held captive in the Underworld.

Unsatisfied with his first villainous taunt, Randall added another.

"Sorry you couldn't stay and chat."

Randall lifted himself from the edge of his chair and cracked his neck. The important part of his labors was long-since completed. His work in the WOK was likely done for the day, fewer than ten minutes into the tournament. With just the wave of his sword, he'd brought to completion the project he'd launched during his two weeks home from work.

After remotely breaking the seal on the WOK's security from ProTechTed's office servers, it had taken Randall several hours to find what he wanted. Alternately pounding on his keyboard, reading up on new hacks, and befouling his bathroom, Randall had devised his plan within the inner sanctum of the WOK, the fabled developer "Sandbox."

For his own projects at work, he used a comparable workspace, a closed environment in which he could test out different security protocols without anyone learning his tricks, pointing out errors, or interrupting his creative process. The Sandbox consisted of three windows. One represented a microscopic parallel WOK and the others showed file lists and lines of code.

Scrolling through the main file structure, Randall opened a folder called "Stairway2Hell." He gleaned nothing about the competition that hadn't already leaked into the player community, with one exception. Developers discussed giving Asmodeus a spell that could alter the behavior of other characters.

The demon's "charm" would disorient adventurers and cause them to attack anyone other than the demon himself. The genius was that players would assault their teammates deliberately, having mistaken friend for foe. For the players deceived by this spell, the images on their screens would remain false, so long as no counter-spell disrupted the charm.

One variation made Asmodeus' charm permanent for the duration of the Stairway challenge, which would have drawn the ire of players who would have victory stolen from them with a single touch. The second tweak made the spell's effects brief but highly infectious, such that charmed characters would spread their affliction through combat. One developer had posted a Sandbox comment that dismissed this variant as drawing on "one of the many stupid mods Devon had built and failed to discard."

One of *many*?

Randall donned his noise-cancelling headphones and queued up Metallica.

"Make it so," he said to himself and started dissecting the Asmodeus code, pulling out loops and commands to reproduce the strongest version of the demon's spell for his own personal use. Ever the careful coder, Randall made sure to render Boldhearts immune.

As he worked on this problem, Randall had a dark inspiration. If Magdalene the healer had found a way to cheapen resurrection, perhaps Devon had experimented with the opposite—a genuine form of death from which a character could never recover.

Randall scanned a few thousand lines of discarded experimental code before undertaking a more careful search. Coding notes related to "immortal" yielded nothing. "Murder" offered only false leads to strings of dialogue, one of which ("murder the king and the crown shall be yours") he recognized from a ridiculous quest that rewrote Macbeth into a pointless battle royale.

A search for "death," however, yielded hundreds of results, one of which caught his eye.

"Devon – True Death."

Two years ago, it seemed, Devon had written code that could pull a character out by its roots from the WOK server farm.

Randall tried out Devon's method on a gnomish archer that the Sandbox offered as a crash test dummy. The code's execution was just that—a dramatic death followed by the permanent deletion of the test subject. Randall tried to respawn the gnome, but it was gone.

In a world of extra lives and saved games, committing digital murder was exhilarating. Randall found his lungs had no breath. He pounded his chest to recharge them.

The speed metal album had stopped playing. Randall reset it to the first track, adjusted his headphones, and began another typing binge.

Sooner than he would have let himself hope, he'd tipped Boldhearts' sword with a new spell, cloaked in the form of Asmodeus' charm but poisoned with forbidden magic. His version of the WOK's Sword of Lies now shimmered with a deadly subroutine.

A sense of sporting fun made Randall give the sword a one-in-five chance of failing each time it struck an enemy. Though not as generous as Anton Chigurh's coin flips in *No Country for Old Men*, it was a kind gesture, nonetheless.

To test his new ability, Randall dispatched a pair of noobs who'd wandered far from the Level One training areas and into a cavern. Boldhearts greeted them with a gentle thwack from his sword, which set off a chain reaction. In two minutes, his victims had killed one another, plus another unfortunate who had followed them into the cave.

As best Randall could tell, all three characters were erased. Only one of these players had the good sense to seek advice in the user forums, which Randall monitored for that very reason.

"My character can't resurrect."

"Hey, rookie. Go to the base camp or the nearest graveyard and wait for it to respawn. When you die you lose some experience points, but it's not a huge deal."

"No, I did that. My character is gone."

"Stop whining. Reset your browser. Reboot your computer if it crashed. It'll work."

But it didn't work.

Randall had ended the existence of this character, who lived not a single full day in the WOK, and he had done so leaving no forensic evidence of his crime. Boldhearts barely appeared in that sector's play logs, which also hid his charm, just as it would have done for Asmodeus.

Such reflections on the past week and the weekend underway gave Randall focus, even while the LAN room continued to buzz with activity. For the first time in years, Randall's heart and gut felt equally full. The restlessness that had plagued him the past two months was gone.

In its place came the peaceful contemplation of his coming victories. He would win the Stairway competition, of that he was certain. Boldhearts would stand alone, enthroned not by war, birthright, or acclaim. He would be the first king seated by default.

Even if a mindful WOK official caught on to his scheme, the scandal's electronic trail would trace back to Devon's developer files and to Ted's user account. Both would have their reputations damaged, and that would score Randall substantial consolation points.

More importantly, Boldhearts' efficient conquest of the WOK left Randall ample time to carry out his most serendipitous plans for Middle Mirth. Cashing in on the admiration his Boldhearts character earned, he'd gather up a sycophantic army of online gamers and bring genuine grief to his former friends, while tipping over as many of the human cattle at the convention as he wished.

The scales of justice would be set right. Randall had been banished from his starring role in Alan's weekly game only to resurface as the master of a larger and more important one. He was now the true game director, the builder and destroyer of all known worlds.

Middle Mirth: Day 2

ANGELOU AND LANCELOT

Even for early dawn, the air outside the main gates to Mythopolis felt unusually cold. Angelou squatted to pull her body in tight. She lowered her head to the same height as the wide ranks of gnomes and dwarves who stood alongside her.

Together, they formed the first line of defense, a hundred meters outside the improvised city walls. Each soldier held an iron-tipped spear, its back end braced in a two-inch hole and pointed forward at an angle as sharp as its tip. From one end to the other, the spear bearers formed a wide arc that shielded the northern side of the city.

A divination spell had told the prime minister that the battle would come to them here, and her guess was better than any other. If raised spears could hold the enemy at bay for a minute or more, the archers and wizards behind them could do considerable damage. Their army could hold the city indefinitely, so long as the healers inside it kept sending reinforcements back to the front lines.

Beside Angelou stood Santana, resplendent in a scarlet robe over his loose white tunic. Was it an enchantment that kept him warm in such light clothing, or something else? Santana had been staring at the fairies flying above the city. The presence of those giants gave him heart, but a memory of Tinkana also offered a more physical comfort.

Angelou had no such luck. A stronger breeze hit her, and she couldn't shake its chill. She turned to Lupita, who sat on her haunches between Angelou and Santana. The wolf glistened with frost, something Angelou had never seen during a mid-summer dawn. Angelou reached down and stroked Lupita's back. The animal looked upward in appreciation.

"If we destroy this Lifeless Knight, I swear that I will discard these hides of mine and begin wearing furs."

Lupita eyed Angelou warily as she ran her hand through the wolf's thick coat.

* * *

Lancelot stood beside Hermione on the same stone dais where they had first met. His chain-mail armor felt like a coat of ice, and he paced to keep himself from shivering. Hermione stayed warm in a forest-green dress, which she had insulated with cloth padding and belted down with leather straps in a style fashioned after Angelou's patchwork hides. Behind them the elder bard Almandine sat on a stool, accompanied by a massive kettle drum and an apprentice arranging an assortment of horns.

The ground shook as another column of Mythopolis soldiers marched out of the city. Their improvised armor and shields rattled as they moved. These volunteers lacked the discipline of a standing army, but they stepped with conviction.

"If we prevail in this battle," Lancelot said to Hermione, "we will have proven our mettle not only to ourselves but to the entire Mythos, including those who may someday follow us to its farthest reaches."

Hermione nodded politely.

"We wish for different things. What comfort I might feel today comes not from grandiose thoughts but from the songs I rehearse for war."

Lancelot clapped Hermione on the shoulder.

"You are more than a wandering minstrel now. You are the music to which these soldiers shall dance."

"I should rather they do so in a ballroom than in battle. If we slay this demon, I wish to settle into a peace in which I might become more entertainer than warrior."

A guard atop the gates clasped both hands on his sword and

waved it in a high circle: enemy approaching.

"The Lifeless Knight!" the guard shouted. "He comes alone!"

Lancelot drew out his mace, and Hermione shouldered her lute. They stepped off the dais together and jogged out of the city. Striding behind them in a suit of purple leather armor came Prime Minister Lesilla, amidst a phalanx of parliamentary guards.

When Santana and Angelou pulled up alongside Lancelot, he pulled his helmet down tight to mask his eager expression. He did not wish to confess a genuine curiosity about their enemy and the power that propelled him.

Tinkana flew above the group as it stepped onto the road leading out of Mythopolis. Lesilla moved quickly through the assembled troops, slapping the back of her hand against one after another soldier's own and saying solemnly each time, "Swift battle." A wave of motion went through the front line, which raised and reset spears more firmly in the ground.

The dawn had brightened slightly, but it retreated back to dusk as a black figure rose over the hill nearest the city. The enemy flew toward them faster than an eagle and landed thirty meters in front of the spearmen, just as Tinkana landed beside Lancelot.

"Hold your weapons," Santana said. "This is nothing more than a projection."

Real or not, Lancelot recognized the man before him, and Santana's nod of recognition showed that they both knew this face, with its piercing auburn eyes. This simulacrum of their lost friend stood tall, muscled, and massive. Solid plate armor covered every section of his body, with finely crafted splints protecting the joints at his elbows, shoulders, waist, and knees. He held no shield, but rested both hands on an enormous double-edged obsidian sword. Were his neck not coarse and lightly scarred, he would have looked as invincible as a deity among mortals.

Santana nodded at the floating image.

"So, we meet again, Boldheart."

The image smirked.

"Am I wrong?"

Santana rapped his staff on the hard paving stones that led back toward the city gates.

"This body is merely a new weapon, albeit an exquisitely sharp one. To honor both what I was and what I have become, you may address me as Cynoc Coldheart."

"What is the purpose of your visit?" Lancelot asked. "We wish this battle to commence at once so we may dispatch you all the more quickly."

"Your quarrel is not with me. I am but an errand boy for Aleh'en, the Supreme God above all others."

"Heresy!"

Lancelot hissed with forced conviction.

"None but you bear responsibility for your cruelties."

"The Creator is neither good nor evil. He sets the stage, then guides us as it pleases Him. I bring the revelation of our powerlessness."

Lancelot's elbows and wrists tingled, as if he could feel just such a god pulling the strings of his own life.

"As much as your fallen swordsman's body has become my own, so have I become an instrument of the one who would remake your world."

"Remake us?"

Tinkana pushed Lancelot and Hermione aside. She towered over Cynoc's image.

"You were entombed because you ravaged the Mythos. You emptied cities and souls alike. Had you not been stopped, you would have burned the Mythos down to coal."

Cynoc waved his hands in a dismissive gesture.

"I came to refresh what had gone stale. It is from your resistance that such vast destruction ensued. Those who mew like kittens to lesser gods and magics must be silenced, lest they obscure our true condition."

Lancelot spied Santana surreptitiously wiggling the fingers of his right hand behind his back to sign the word "*mentiras*." He had seen this casting trick before and knew it would heighten momentarily the emotional acuity of Santana's hearing. He read the sorcerer's frown to mean that he detected only sincerity in their enemy's voice.

How could such conviction about a false god have carried Cynoc so far? For her part, Elahna seemed powerless to stop him. She had not been able to heal the dying worshippers of Helios, nor turn back the Naughts in the Fairie Realm. Would she be of no help now?

"You are right to doubt your god," Cynoc said to a startled Lancelot. "She speaks falsely when she tells you of the purpose of your flickering life. There is none."

"This is a hollow theology you preach," Tinkana said. "These four souls standing beside me have gathered a power far greater than yours, or even mine."

Tinkana pulled her fingers into a clenched fist, which she waved before Cynoc's image.

"They shall stand against you from inside the Magic Circle!"

"There exists no such thing. You have bewitched these sots, who naïvely imbibe the misplaced courage you serve them."

Cynoc narrowed his eyes and regarded the group, which exchanged shrugs and doubtful glances. Only Santana wore a confident smirk, not unlike that of a bluffing card player.

The image of Cynoc grew to ten, twenty, then thirty feet high, ever more indistinct as it rose. Thick clouds formed high above, and a voice like thunder burst from the sky.

"Hear me, people of Mythopolis. None of you shall live as heroes after this day. No legends shall be born. Lay down your cares, your causes, your hopes—but not your weapons. Carry them with you into battle against those who pretend to stand with you. They are neither friends nor kin. As it has ever been, you are alone."

Cynoc gripped his sword in both hands and raised it high. Even as his image wavered and dissipated into the clouds, his voice remained.

"Empty your hearts of poison and lies, and you may fill them again here, this day, with fresh blood."

Angelou relaxed the grip on her trident as the image of Cynoc turned to mist. She stepped back into the front lines of spearmen. The gray sky seemed to drain the trees and grass of their color. It was mesmerizing, as if the horizon of the world were disappearing.

A penetrating chill swept through the barbarian. She set down her trident to rub the rough hides wrapping her body. Her three companions moved to different positions among the troops stationed inside and outside the city.

She had grown to trust these comrades-in-arms. Not for the greatest warrior in the Ring Bone clan would she trade any of them—not even the wolf. It brought warmth back to her chest to know that the greatest friends she had ever known would stand with her as she faced her greatest foes.

No sooner had Angelou let herself relax than the first wave of attackers arrived. Out of the fog came a swarm of flying blue lizards, each with leather wings that beat across a twenty foot span. Saddled to these creatures were armored knights brandishing lances as long as their mounts were wide. More disquieting still, the jagged edges of both riders and beasts flickered, an unnatural quality for what seemed to be living things.

As the knights and their mounts crashed into the spearmen, Angelou could see their features had a disquieting flatness, as if each were a copy of the same drawing on thin sheets of parchment. Each rider had a sharp nose, the same triangular clump of hair, and a mouth that opened and closed in only rough approximation to their battle cries.

Angelou pulled tight the laces on her yellow fleece boots—a pair of magmasins she retrieved from the fairie vault. Once tied securely, her feet almost burned with energy. Only constant motion could cool her soles and ankles, so she hoisted her trident and burst into a run.

The velocity was incredible.

Her body moved so fast her dreadlocks cracked the air like whips. Angelou leapt ten feet off the ground and swung her trident wildly as she darted from one great lizard to another. One lurched and screamed. Another spun around and fell. A third dodged her razored tines, only to see its rider impaled. Amidst the mass of spears, lances, swords, and arrows, Angelou became a blur of yellow and black, out of which sheets of blood flew in all directions.

Cutting through a swath of enemies, Angelou heard a call to battle from the prime minister, who had climbed a spiral staircase to stand atop the gates. Lesilla thrust one arm forward, her hand bent upward. Her signal triggered a roar from inside the city. Seconds later, out through the gates rode a full cavalry of shimmering metal and flowing robes—the Mythos nobles who led the city's charge.

One inauspicious moment later, a boulder launched by an Everwinter ice giant found its target. A rider and her horse were crushed. Out of the city rushed the head cleric, the Very Reverend Colbert. He dragged the noble's limp body back to where Lancelot and priests of all faiths tended to the wounded, or bestowed blessings on the dead.

Lest morale flag too soon, thundering music inside the city reached the ears of the Mythopolis army. Hermione had begged to stand alongside Angelou but agreed to send forth songs atop the city's dais where they first met. From that platform, she strummed her lute in sync with Almandine's drumming and the haunting bugle counterpoint of his homely human apprentice.

Bards scattered across the battlefield used amplificatory magics and common hand signs to relay a song all the soldiers knew.

We're all of us connected
We're in the home we've always known
Evil company's expected
Stand together, we're protected

Even amidst the blossoming horror of the battle, Angelou felt a potent purpose well up inside her. Hope and heroism rode together on the sound waves emanating from Hermione, who roared out a couplet.

Foul fiends beset
Our capital today
We'll ne'er forget
We sent them all away

Santana darted past Angelou. He signaled for his fellow sorcerers to channel their combined power toward the filthy trolls and elves who led the next wave of the Naught army over the hills and toward the city. The team of conjurers pulled balls of lightning down from the sky, and as each hit the ground, electricity leapt from one flailing body to the next. The combined effect was devastating.

Angelou smiled in satisfaction at the result until, above the crackling and smoking carnage, Cynoc himself came into view just beyond the fray, floating inches above the ground. Behind his body dragged a moving carpet of dirt, slime, and blackened air. When he stopped meters short of a buckling line of spearmen, the trailing muck merged into his person. Cynoc stabbed his sword into the ground and pulled up his breastplate with both hands. Out of him exploded a hot and pungent wave of filth that splattered every soldier within sight.

* * *

At his improvised healing station inside the city gates, Lancelot heard what sounded like a boastful roar from the Naught army. Into the city blew putrid air that had the unholy reek of moist organs pulled from a day-old corpse. Lancelot convulsed and vomited his undigested breakfast. He sank to his knees, dizzied and sick.

By the time he regained his balance, Lancelot's field hospital had dissolved into chaos. His fellow priests had worked together to send refreshed soldiers back into battle, but now his colleagues stumbled like drunkards.

Most of the clerics shook off Cynoc's bewitching plea to join his army, but one rogue priest picked up a flail and brought it down on the unguarded skull of Reverend Colbert, who collapsed in agony. The mad priest screamed in rage, and the color drained from her face. When Lancelot deduced she had become a Naught, he ended her life without hesitation.

Perhaps one in twenty of the city's army had likewise joined the enemy. Lancelot had expected a worse result, and he took heart at the resistance to Cynoc's siren call. The Pale Elves, monks, and fairies who had succumbed more readily were no less brave than those who fought today. Perhaps they lacked something else.

Tinkana had said each of her sisters who stood to the last against the Naughts had ventured outside the Fairie Realm. None in the Mythos, Lancelot realized, traveled farther or wider than those who lived in and around the commercial metropolis they now defended.

LANCE

Someone leaned against the back of Lance's metal folding chair. He'd convinced his friends to stay in costume all the way through Middle Mirth. This might have been another fan paying respects to the Blind Monk, but alas, the visitor had a familiar voice.

"Am I dead yet?" Devon said.

"Da-ad," Maya whined, "you're interrupting our game."

"Shoot, who died?" Brie said. "I got distracted reading up on bard songs."

"Nobody died," Carlos said.

"Actually, he *did* die," Lance said. "Well, Devotus died. Alan told us a while ago."

"Wait," said a male voice Lance didn't recognize, maybe a teenager. "Who died?"

"Yeah, who?" said another boy, a bit higher and squeakier than the first.

"Excuse me?" Lance said politely. "Do we know you?"

"I'm Peter, and this is Simon. We're, um—"

The boys laughed.

"Wait, do I know you guys from somewhere?" Alan asked. "Maybe from Balboa, ah—"

Peter giggled before brushing away the question.

"Not likely, mister. We're here for the games and stuff. Anyway, who died?"

"Second day of the con," Simon said, "and one of you already bit it? Crap!"

"Not to worry," Devon said. "'Twas only my cameo character who passed away."

"Who are you? You the dad?"

"There's only one?" Devon said.

Simon and Peter whispered something about "later tonight." Their footsteps signaled a hurried exit through the double doors.

Lance shook his head.

"What in Hades—"

"Probably just nervous fans of yours," Maya said. "Or maybe they were here for the Padre Princess but too shy to look her in the eye."

"Celebrity stalkers?" Lance said.

"Not likely," Brie said.

"Or deadly Night Stalkers?" Maya laughed. "Anyway, bummer about Devotus. Did you know your gnome was gonna die, Dad?"

"I am not at liberty to say."

Alan bumped his cardboard screen, which meant he probably hovered over the table. Lance leaned forward and heard him whisper, "No more distractions. Look who's coming."

Clicking footsteps approached, either heels or expensive dress shoes.

Lance poked Carlos.

"Is it your new old girlfriend, lover boy? We still have no details. We want details."

"Shush," Alan hissed and slapped Lance's arm. "Jeff Jacobson's coming. Stay in character."

"For real?"

"Yes, sir," Carlos said, "and the head judge just gave Maya's dad a hug."

"Devon, it's so good to see you," Jacobson said. "I heard you spent all your WOK earnings on a store that sells tabletop games and RPGs. Remarkable."

"Guilty as charged," Devon said. "Perhaps you might—"

"I'd love to bounce some ideas off you regarding Dungeon Lords."

"Then it is Alan with whom you will want to speak. After the tournament, of course."

"Of course. Been hearing good things about your little group, Mr. Crandall."

Jacobson's clipboard snapped, and he shuffled the papers on it.

"I'm not supposed to say such things, but Isabel has given you high marks on interplay. When you're alternating between different characters' points of view, she says you have a seamless 'table dynamic,' as we call it."

Lance bit his lip.

"Don't worry. I'm not judging right now. It's the official dinner hour—you guys included. I came here to ask whether you had a bona fide name. Entry sheet just says Crandall Group."

"I..." Alan hesitated. "I didn't know we had to—"

"The module you submitted was very clever. I like where you're going with this old story. Do you conceive of this as a stand-alone sequel, or is it part of a larger project?"

"I, um—"

"Since we are mid-game," Lance said in a solemn voice, "Alan would rather not say."

"Of course. Protocol. Well, I'm keeping my eye on you folks."

Lance again heard the clicking heels of Jacobson's shoes as he walked away.

"You heard the man," Devon said. "Time for dinner. You have two hours to—"

"That—was—awesome!" Lance said. "Right? It was, wasn't it?"

"Definitely," Brie and Maya said together.

Carlos whistled.

"You think we could really win this?"

"Why not?" Alan said. "Unless he's feeding the same line to everyone, just to be polite."

"That visit was a compliment," Devon said.

He coughed and cleared his throat.

"I guarantee you that Jeff Jacobson is not chatting up many game directors. Now, I've already obtained a meal for myself, of which I shall now partake. I take my leave."

Lance pictured Devon bowing before footsteps signaled his departure

"Okay," Carlos said, "let's eat, but we're not following Devon's lead and eating at Alamo Taco. What gringo names their franchise that?"

"That's not the worst part." Maya laughed. "One of their slogans is, 'Because life is better covered in cheese'."

Brie made a retching sound.

"Learn to Type 2 diabetes with Mavis Bacon and Queso."

An increasingly familiar voice came from behind Lance.

"Don't be picky," Tara said. "The dining options here are few."

"You coming to whisk our Carlos away again?" Lance asked.

"*Hombre*, please," Carlos said.

Tara must have leaned over, because as she whispered, Lance felt the tip of her tongue catch the lobe of his ear. A shock went through his neck.

"Maybe I just wanted to remind you who's gonna steal that trip to Bled Castle."

An embarrassed smile on his face, Lance regained his composure.

"I remember it the other way around."

Lance turned about and accidentally touched Tara's forearm. He felt cool beads of perspiration on her skin.

"How was your evening with our sorcerer?"

"Good lord," Brie said. "Show some class, Lance."

The direction of Brie's voice shifted toward Carlos.

"But seriously, Gigi had to sleep in Lance's bedroom last night. I'm sure she'd tell you herself if she could, but that boy's den is stanky."

Alan's chair slid back, perhaps so he could stand.

"Let's stretch our legs, go get some food. If we eat with Tara and her Coven—"

"Convent," Tara said.

"If we eat together, then nobody gets an edge. We'll leave and return at the same time."

Tara laughed.

"Truth is, I was picking up Carlos for a second date, but I won't object to chaperones."

"Works for me," Maya said. "Will Patrizia be coming?"

"Ye-es," Tara said in a lilting voice. "Why do you ask?"

"Great. I'll leave Gigi with Dad and catch up in a minute. If I get stuck, I'll meet you at...Where are we going? Alamo Taco?"

"No," Tara said, "the ladies have already settled on McDonald's."

MAYA

Maya picked up Gigi's crate and glimpsed Carlos interlacing his fingers with Tara's before withdrawing his hand, as if fearing detection. Maya smiled at the hint of shyness in a man who presented himself as more suave than sweet. Given all he'd been through, Carlos deserved a little love vacation with a long-lost girlfriend.

Maya's own appetites stirred as eight college-age women in frilly dresses danced through the main doors, holding each other's hands and spinning in a circle. Into their midst ran Patrizia, who spun through a complicated vertical movement that looked like a blooming lily.

The scene reminded Maya of the modern dance she'd seen during her visit to Yale as a prospective student. Just when she'd rejected the idea of going to graduate school, the comparative literature professor hosting her took Maya to an improvisational ballet workshop. It was Maya's first glimpse of the institution's vitality.

As gracefully as she had entered the dance circle, Patrizia leapt out to catch up with Tara and Carlos, who left the ballroom together. Maya followed Patrizia's steps until she heard a "Yip!" and felt the weight of Gigi in her crate.

Turning back toward the Players booth, Maya considered whether she should give up and take a summer celibacy pledge. Besides that, someone like Patrizia would already have a girlfriend.

The convention buzz had died down. Dozens of people had left for the dinner break, though some groups were still playing Dungeon Lords. Most seemed absorbed in their games, but a few looked tired, bored, or both.

At one of the oval tables featuring experimental games, Maya studied the colorful *Alternate Histories* board, which twisted six feet down the length of a table like a python. Curious to see it in action, Maya sidled up to an unoccupied chair and leaned against it. She set down Gigi's crate and watched for a few minutes. Each player held a set of cards and took turns using them to bend the timeline and produce one or another eventuality.

To the pre-teen girl seated nearest her, Maya said, "Whatcha trying to make happen?"

The girl looked up with vacant eyes, an unwanted orphan meeting a prospective mother for the hundredth time.

"Doesn't really matter. Always ends the same."

"I'm sorry?"

"The game ends. We count up our points."

The girl coughed onto the cards in her hand and wiped her mouth.

"A guy came by a while ago and pointed out how dumb the game is."

"Looks fun to me."

"Yeah, whatever."

Maya picked up Gigi's crate. She found herself scanning the ballroom, though she wasn't sure why. Something seemed amiss. A few of the people seated at the board game tables had the plastic WOK badges hanging around their necks, which surprised her. She had the impression that hard-core online gamers had no interest in tabletop fare. Besides, wasn't their worldwide challenge thing still underway?

Bumping into her came a scrawny man with wire-framed glasses who might have been Alan's age. In a white Padres jersey and Navy baseball cap, he looked like a homesick sailor adrift in a sea of unfamiliar games.

"Excuse me," Maya said, "I didn't see you standing there."

She spied a WOK lanyard hanging from his neck.

"You in the online gaming tourney?"

The man looked toward the front of the room, where the flat-screen monitors showed a half-empty LAN room.

"I was down in the volcano for, uh, maybe an hour, tops. Got hit with some nasty charm. Died on the First Plane of Hell."

"You didn't jump right back in?"

The man scratched the back of his head.

"Can't. My character's dead. Beyond resurrection spells, healing charms, even graveyard digs, far as I can tell."

"But, I thought—"

Devon had explained the game to her years ago, before he refused to discuss it ever again. This didn't sound right, but maybe the rules were different for the contest.

"Doesn't matter. It's like the big guy back in the LAN room says. WOK's a waste of time for the likes of me. My character never would have amounted to anything. Don't think I'll bother coming back tomorrow."

The sailor-man turned away and shuffled toward the main exit with the vigor of a zombie past its bedtime.

Maya headed straight to the Players booth, set down Gigi's crate, and approached Devon, who was eating his dinner at a card table.

Devon wiped green tomatillo sauce off his chin.

"Having fun, dear daughter?"

"There's a strange vibe here today."

"It does seem quieter."

Devon set down his fork beside what looked like enchiladas drowning in an American cheese sauce.

"Perhaps the conferees have settled in a bit."

"I don't think that's it."

Maya looked at the monitors above the stage at the front of the ballroom.

"Did you notice the LAN room is almost empty?"

"I wondered about that myself, and—"

Devon took a quick bite of enchilada, chewed deliberately, then swallowed.

"You know I don't care about that nonsense, Maya."

Maya stared at her father.

"Can characters ever die in that game?"

"What game?"

Maya recalled their code name for the WOK.

"You know—the Scottish Game."

DEVON

Devon closed his eyes. He hated it when Maya brought up the WOK, but he realized it was inevitable. At Middle Mirth, he was surrounded by reminders of the project that led him to end a lucrative career. Maya was an adult, and he felt like a father who could no longer avoid telling his daughter a dark family secret.

He considered instead using the chance to inform her she was adopted. She wasn't, but it would serve to deflect. Devon chuckled to himself.

"What's so funny?" Maya said. "I know you don't like to talk about it, but someone just told me lots of WOK players saw their characters die. I don't mean they ran out of Hit Points. I mean they really couldn't bring them back to life."

Maya knew little of that accursed game and was undoubtedly mistaken. Unlike Alan's Mythos, one couldn't experience meaningful death in the WOK.

Years ago, Devon had helped develop what he hoped would become a compelling multiplayer universe, but commercial decisions robbed it of any gravity. The point of contention had been players falling in love with their WOK characters.

Unlike arcade-style games, WOK players didn't want to burn through lives in rapid succession. Instead, they built up characters slowly, over weeks and months of gaming. Bonding with a specific character became vital to enjoyment of the game, and players spent in-game money, or even real-world money, changing their avatars' clothes and hairstyles. Marketing department surveys revealed that players thought of their WOK characters as friends, lovers, alter egos, or children. Letting characters truly die would offend paying customers, who would abandon the WOK and lead its owners into bankruptcy.

Devon tried to prove that theory wrong. He ran a "limited-lives" version of the WOK on a parallel server for months, until he exhausted his division's play-testing budget. He collected encouraging consumer satisfaction data, but his report's arrival had poor timing. That same week, someone showed the company's CEO an episode of *South Park* that featured an online gamer killing off everyone else's characters and dooming the industry. Spooked by the satire, Devon's project got the axe. Issue closed.

"You can't die in the Scottish Game," Devon said. "It's impossible."

"Under any circumstances?"

The flat screens at the front of the ballroom showed only two occupied tables in the LAN room. It had looked empty all afternoon. Perhaps his clever daughter was onto something. Looking more closely at the monitors, Devon noticed that most of the absent players had removed their PCs altogether. That was strange, indeed.

"I suppose WOK death is a theoretical possibility."

Devon immediately regretted his words. The day before he'd quit that job, he'd surreptitiously reinserted into the developer Sandbox the essential code from his unauthorized version of the game on the hope that it might tempt a future colleague who came across it.

The next day, he felt like a guilty Poe protagonist and attempted to undo his handiwork. Alas, the company had terminated Devon's primary account before he could undo what he'd done the previous day. There might be other ways in, but Devon took this deterrent as a sign to leave well enough alone.

Even after departing from the company, considerable licensing royalties still flowed into Devon's account each quarter as compensation for having built the WOK's engine. If his rogue code ever resurfaced in the game and traced back to him, he'd soon meet a stranger who'd hand him an envelope and announce, "You've been served."

Devon didn't like the prospect of losing those checks. He recommitted himself to never saying another word about the WOK to Maya or anyone else. If what she said was true, he would need to do more than keep quiet. Visiting the LAN room would draw attention, but he could go up to the lobby, get online, and go into the WOK as just another player.

When Devon returned his attention to his daughter, he sensed that she was as lost in her own thoughts as he'd been in his.

"Are you not late for dinner with your friends?" he asked.

"Right."

Maya lifted a dog crate from the floor.

"Um, can you watch Gigi?"

"I would, dear, but I have other business I must attend to this evening."

"What? No, please. I can't take her into a restaurant."

Devon sighed and reached out a hand. A crated Chidoodle would make him a conspicuous presence upstairs. For the first time in years, he craved retreating into the immersive fantasy world of the WOK. On the Internet, nobody knows you're carrying a dog.

LANCE

Lance picked up his telescoped cane and—with a "snap!"—extended it to full length. Before he could tap it on the ground, someone snatched it from his hand.

"You won't need that," Tara said. "I'd like you to meet my friend. Valerie's wearing sixteen ounces of metal on her face and a cut-off tee from some hardcore band."

"It's Le Tigre."

"So it is."

Lance recognized Tara's tone as faux-patronizing. It was the kind of insult-meant-to-show-friendship he enjoyed exchanging with Carlos. Hearing these two women use it with each other excited him beyond reason.

"Valerie, meet Lance. Quite the tiger, this one. He's more handsy than a teenage boy, but he doesn't mean anything by it. He's straight-up blind and would appreciate an escort to McDonald's. Now, Lance, Valerie's been playing DL since high school, so you can probably learn a thing or two from her."

Valerie hooked her left hand around Lance's right elbow. The quick tactile connection reminded Lance of his final year at what he called "blind camp". Prospective mates all but groped one another in plain view of the few sighted counselors, none of whom had the nerve to intervene.

"Hope you're not allergic to me," Lance said.

"Only allergic to assholes," Valerie said. "You're more of a dork, right?"

Lance sensed a trick question but bit at the bait.

"Full-on dork."

"Cool. So, who do you play in DL?"

"A cleric named Lancelot."

The hair on Valerie's arm felt soft, but her skin felt hard—almost rough. Did Tara mention she worked out? He imagined tracing his hand up to her broad shoulders and felt a guilty rush. He reminded himself that she was a chivalrous chaperone, not a date.

Valerie steered Lance to follow the others.

"Shouldn't a character named Lancelot be a knight?"

Lance smelled on her something between cough syrup and sport stick. When they ascended the stairs out of the ballroom, though, a sour odor from the basement hallway assaulted him. Mildew in the carpet?

"Hey, sorry. Lancelot's a cool in-your-face name."

"Like *Hermione*? That's what my sister named her bard."

Valerie snorted.

"No, that's different."

Lance bit his lip at the chance that Brie might be just nearby. His worry increased when Valerie whispered, "*Hermione*? That's just dumb."

Lance shared in a conspiratorial laugh, but he also felt defensive. This stranger had made an uninvited dig on his baby sister, yet it was more than that. Lance felt protective not just of a sibling but of a comrade. Brie the butterfly had emerged from the Brianna chrysalis.

Warm sunshine hit Lance's face when Valerie guided him out of the hotel lobby and onto the sidewalk. Lance lowered his shades and looked for the sun. He loved that Bruce Springsteen's maternal admonition did not apply to him. If the sun was where the fun was, he was happy to gaze at it. That glowing orb was one of the only things he could reliably see, even in a clear sky.

A "Don't Walk" signal chirped, and Lance let Valerie bring him to a stop. He felt her arm turn slightly and got the sense that she was regarding him, possibly checking him out.

Lance straightened his posture, held his jaw firm, and nodded knowingly. He could look quite handsome on a bright day, when the sun lit up his blond mane and made his midnight-black Ray-Bans seem a more natural accessory.

"Based on what little I know," Lance said with a smirk, "I sense that you're a bit mean. Let's take a hypothetical. If you went to Vegas, would you book a room at the Excalibur Hotel or just visit the hotel to mock the tailoring errors in the staff's Renaissance costumes?"

"I would mock, but how would you know the costumes at Excalibur look wrong? I mean—"

"Because I'm blind, right?"

"Right."

"And you're sighted—at least for now?"

"Yes. What?"

"Hey, anyone who doesn't already have a disability is only temporarily able-bodied. TABs, we call 'em."

"Fine, I'm a TAB, but you're dodging my question."

The "Walk" sign beeped, and Lance entered the intersection with Valerie. When he felt her leg elevating slightly for the curb, he stepped up to the sidewalk in stride.

"Okay, here's how I know about what they wear at the Excalibur. When I graduated college, my parents took me and Brie out to the Dark Ages Banquet in Del Mar—you know, the medieval theme restaurant?"

"You actually went to that freak show?"

"So we get there, and they put us next to the royal box seats. It's pretty cool, but when dinner comes, the whole place starts to stink, like the company picnic at a rendering plant. The food tastes as bad as it smells."

"What does this have to do with the outfits at the—"

"Patience."

Lance pushed his elbow into Valerie's side.

"Just before the jousting gets underway, I reenact my dinner."

"Sweet."

"The barmaids and squires, and even the King and Queen, start fussing over me. I mean, this is bad PR. The blind college kid hurls up the mutton. So I become dehydrated and have to get fluids at the ER and everything. My sister and mom sit there with me through the night, and we discuss every stitch and seam they'd seen and that I'd felt on the restaurant's staff."

"Sounds like a cool mom."

"The coolest."

Lance's mouth felt dry from his monologue. He licked his lips.

"When I finally fall asleep, Brie gets on the Internet and pokes around. Turns out they don't wear period-appropriate outfits, and—here comes the kicker—they buy their clothes from the same overseas costume supplier as Excalibur. Better than Halloween-grade rags, but still."

Valerie's pace slowed, and she swung in front of him to open a squeaky door.

"We've arrived at Mickey-D's. Thanks to your story, I'm craving mutton and mead."

"We shall try to accommodate you, milady."

Lance heard voices—Alan, Brie, and Carlos, plus Tara and the rest of the Wiccan Convent. He cleared his throat.

"Please notify Alan and the others that their healer has arrived. You may now safely order whatsoever you wish, and to indigestions I shall minister forthwith."

ALAN

Alan heard Lance's announcement but didn't respond. Lance had none of his attention. Neither did the burger variations on the giant McMenu, nor the impatient cashier who stood behind the register. Alan's point of focus was the back of the restaurant, where Randall Keller held court at a rectangular dining table. Seated on either side of him were eight young men and teenage boys, each with laminated WOK nametags dangling from their necks.

"Just ignore him," Carlos said.

"Ignore who?" Valerie and Lance said at once.

"I think he means Randall," Brie whispered. "He's eating here too."

"Randall's at the conference?" Lance asked.

"Who's Randall?" Valerie said.

"He's, um…" Lance sighed. "He was in our group before Brie and Maya joined up. Works the same place I do, but he's been avoiding me for weeks."

Carlos and Tara ordered first, followed in quick succession by Alan and the rest. While waiting for their food, Tara and her friends seated themselves at the pressed wood table adjoining Randall's. Alan and Carlos sat at the next table back in the two seats farthest from their former companion, with Lance and Brie beside them.

Lance leaned forward and whispered to his sister.

"I wanted to sit next to Valerie."

"I don't think she's your type."

"I thought every woman was my type?"

"Well, I think women are also *her* type."

"You sure?"

"No, I just—"

Randall raised his voice loud enough for all to hear.

"Boldhearts will be the last one standing. It's as simple as that. He doesn't have to kill Asmodeus or save any souls. He just has to steer clear of the chaos. He's already killed the stragglers who refused to enter the volcano."

Randall coughed and wiped his mouth with the cheeseburger wrapper in his hand. A broad smear of ketchup outlined his lips. Before him lay the remnants of his order—spiced jumbo fries, an oversized Coke, and two empty granary-shaped boxes that had carried McBarnyards, the three-layered sandwiches that floated ham over chicken over Angus beef.

Eyeing the women sitting with Alan, Randall snorted.

"Of course, serious gaming isn't for everyone. Little girls and the wussies who take tea with them would rather tell each other children's stories and play with their dollies."

Alan's danger sense tingled. Valerie leaned across her table and toward Randall.

"Can you keep it down over there? Nobody cares about your massively-multi-boring video game."

Randall studied Valerie like a wily predator estimating its prey. Alan had seen Randall eye many prospective victims over the years, but he'd never seen that gaze returned the way Valerie did.

"I don't mean any offense," Randall said. "It's just sad that people still play make believe with pencil swords when there's real gaming to be had."

"No," Valerie said, "what's sad is you guys. You're like those Neanderthals sitting by the campfire in Plato's cave. You stare at flickering images on screens that are as crudely rendered as your characters."

Tara jumped into the fray.

"That's not it at all. These WOK-ers are junkies, strung-out over there in the LAN. They're all curled up in their crack den, ready to turn tricks on each other for just one more minute online."

The Wiccans burst into what sounded like cackling, and a stirring of sympathy in Alan's stomach caught him off guard. Only then did he recognize Peter and Simon, the members of Randall's court seated closest to him. Those were the same two boys who'd quizzed him about the death of Devotus. Alan recognized Simon as the tall and skinny one, whereas Peter's head couldn't have reached Randall's shoulder even without the boy's twenty degree slouch. Despite their different statures, the teenagers shared the same bloodshot eyes and angry cheek zits that resembled stripes of war paint.

"We're power gamers," Simon said. "The WOK is where the action happens. Bash in the doors, get into battle."

Brie nudged Carlos.

"Sounds like you."

"Kinda does," Lance said.

Carlos tried to look aghast.

"I should hope not."

"Boldhearts could kick your ass!" Simon shouted to no one in particular.

Peter snapped his fingers.

"In five seconds flat, Randall's character would put you on the DL for good."

Alan shifted uncomfortably on his hard plastic seat and considered the unintended truth of that statement. The reinvigorated Cynoc Coldheart he'd created might, indeed, be more than Santana, Lancelot, and the rest could handle. Though he'd created the scenario they now played, Alan remained as unsure as his players how it would end. The uncertainty felt— liberating.

Tara laughed at Peter.

"Listen to yourself. You sound like a third-grader. 'My big brother could beat up your big brother.'"

"It's sad," Valerie said. "Sad like an oil-painting of a clown."

Randall squeezed himself out from between bench and table

and stepped back. A long-sleeved Mötley Crüe shirt hung over his unsteady body, which swayed as if dizzied by the movement.

"I just—"

Randall tried to swallow, but grimaced at the effort it took.

Alan girded himself. He expected to hear a diatribe about how he and Carlos had mistreated Randall, or some such delusion of persecution. But Randall looked fatigued, and Alan hoped he might escape unscathed.

In a raspy voice, Randall said, "I don't know how you can still play that—that kindergarten bull-ship."

Peter, Simon, and others beside Randall offered encouraging laughter. Randall took a sip of his soft drink and caught his stride.

"You're like ice skaters in the frocking Olympics. You have stupid judges saying who's the prettiest, who does the cutest spins and twirls. Meanwhile, I'm making real frocking money— fifty K—in a real contest. *I'm* the Olympian, speed skating circles around you j-holes."

Randall rubbed his wrist across his lips.

"You, your game, and your lives are all pathetic."

Alan cringed when Valerie displayed her middle finger.

"No," Tara said, "don't dignify that speech with a response."

Tara stood and motioned for the Convent to follow.

"Our order's up, and we'll eat it elsewhere."

"That's right," Randall said. "Walk away with your pussycat tails between your furry little legs."

Carlos raised himself to full height. Alan's pulse quickened.

"Are you sure you want to do this, Randall?"

Carlos took a step back from his table and closed half the distance between him and Randall.

"Are you *completely sure* you're ready to settle up?"

Simon and Peter glanced at each other uneasily. Alan shared their apprehension about what might happen next.

"Down boy."

Tara gave Carlos a withering look and clucked.

"They can play their game, and we can play ours."

"You don't even know what the real game is," Randall said with a chuckle. "You infants—you have no idea what we're playing now."

Tara shook her head and led the Convent up to the counter, where they picked up their food. As her friends walked out the door, Tara turned back, walked past Carlos, and stood two feet from Randall. She poked him in the chest.

"You are a sad beast of a man, whoever you are. I hope you know your mother does not love you."

Randall's jaw hung open as Tara turned and walked out of the restaurant.

Carlos unclenched his fists and exhaled.

"Let's just grab our crappy food and leave."

Lance and Brie rose but Alan remained frozen in his chair. Sweat from his armpits dripped down his sides. He wanted to get up, fill his drink cup, pick up his burger, and go back into the sun, but he couldn't take his eyes off Randall, who looked as immobilized as Alan felt.

Unlike his posse, Randall hadn't flinched when Tara had approached, but she had caught him off guard. Now that Tara and her friends had departed, he seemed to regather his energy.

Randall picked up his half-eaten cheeseburger and pulled it open. After clearing his throat, he spit the viscous contents of his mouth between his burger's sesame seed buns. With surprising swiftness, he flung the sandwich across the restaurant, and a ground beef patty hit Alan in the face with a splat. Its cheese half-congealed, the burger hung on Alan's nose for a beat before falling into his lap.

From every direction came gasps and whispers. For five long seconds, the hiss of the fryer was the loudest noise Alan could hear. Those seconds felt like a minute.

Carlos stepped slowly toward Randall. He reached forward

with both hands, pushed Randall's chest lightly, and spoke in a quiet voice.

"How do you think you're gonna get away with this? We put up with your *chingada* crap for all these years. We listened to you whine like a baby and give Alan shit about every last thing he did. What do you want now, Randall? What are you asking for?"

By way of reply, Randall released a loud, carbonated burp.

Carlos stepped back and punched a table. He looked to Alan for what felt like permission. Alan shook his head. Carlos turned away from Randall and brushed Brie on the shoulder as he passed. She, in turn, nudged her brother to leave.

"Come on," Brie said to Alan. "We'll get you cleaned up outside."

"Go on," Randall said with a chuckle. "Run back to your dungeon. See how much fun you have splashing in your kiddie pool tonight with—with your little kiddies."

Alan ignored Randall's taunts and blocked out of his mind the swiveling heads and chatter around him. Still seated at his table, he dipped a napkin into a cup of water Brie had left behind, then wiped his face. His pupils dilated, and he saw a giant octopus squirm to make itself comfortable on a small molded bench at Randall's table. As it slipped to the floor, the disoriented beast shot out a jet of ink.

Before he could add more nautical detail, Alan tried something new. He quieted his thoughts. His mind resisted, eager to tug him out of the present and into a fantastic land of never-was.

Alan closed his eyes slowly and reopened them to see reality restored. He could see and hear Randall's defiant laughter. Instead of anger or despair, Alan felt regret. Pity. This cruel giant, who accepted the back-pats of an adoring entourage, was the sum of his own choices. Whoever he was becoming, for whatever unknowable reasons, Randall was no longer Alan's responsibility. After so many years held in thrall to Randall, Alan felt *free*.

Alan gave his companions a beatific smile, only to see Lance frowning with worry. Brie was on the edge of tears. Maya had just entered the restaurant but Carlos blocked her entrance with one arm, while motioning with the other for Alan to retreat.

Carlos was right. Randall no longer had a claim on Alan's time and attention, but this physical attack signaled something more sinister. The Randall who stormed out of Alan's house those many weeks ago left in an impotent rage. This display was something else altogether. Alan looked into Randall's red eyes and saw a malevolent potency worthy of the Mythos villain Alan had created.

Alan stood and picked up his order from the counter. Before tossing his wet napkin in the trash, he spied brown mucus on it. He glanced again at Randall, who convulsed with self-congratulatory laughter. Alan visually inspected Randall's face and body. He was as red as a tomato and stood hunched over, like the sycophantic Peter beside him. Alan discarded the napkin and followed Carlos, Brie, Lance, and Maya through a gauntlet of gawkers at the restaurant's entrance.

Once outside, Alan tugged Carlos' sleeve.

"Does Randall look all right to you?"

"Who gives a frock?" Carlos said with a sneer. "That guy doesn't need healing. He needs a punch in the nose. If I'd been wearing surgical gloves, I would've socked him."

Alan handed a small paper bag to Maya.

"You're welcome to my cheeseburger. I don't want it. Carlos is right, McDonald's is cursed."

RANDALL

Once outside the McDonald's, Randall saw no sign of Alan. That was disappointing. The line about the kiddie pool was not Randall's finest work. He'd hoped to deliver a better burn before Alan retreated into Middle Mirth.

Truth was, Carlos' physical threat had caught him off guard. Rage had always been Randall's forte, but if Carlos had escalated the conflict today, Randall would have spent the rest of the weekend in the Emergency Room.

"What ya lookin' for?" Simon asked.

He and Peter had pulled up beside Randall. They shaded their eyes, squinted, and tried to see what distant object held their leader's attention.

"I'm absorbing natural light. I'm breathing fresh air. We've been cooped up a long time already. Tonight will be even longer. We need to gather our strength."

Peter nodded. He was pale, with eyes watering from more than sunshine. The symptoms looked familiar, since Randall had endured them a few days earlier. That was stage two of whatever had entered its next phase inside Randall's body. Meanwhile, the onset of the illness was well represented by Simon's intermittent mania and lethargy.

Why it moved through them so quickly, Randall couldn't guess, but there was no doubting it was increasing in both infectiousness and virulence. It had bided its time inside its giant host, but someone had cast an acceleration spell on the virus, with a massive splash effect on everyone near him.

Simon hopped from one foot to the other.

"I can't just stand here. Let's at least go over the plan again. Make sure everything's set."

"Not here. Run along. I'll find you back in the LAN. If you want something to do, re-check all the access points."

"Roger that."

Simon nudged Peter, and the two boys headed back toward the hotel.

Randall turned away from them and scanned the parking lot outside the conference. There was no sign of King Turd, but a leisurely walk through the rows of cars would clear his lungs, even if he didn't find Alan or his vehicle.

He recognized nearly all the Dungeon Lords bumper stickers he encountered. "Keep honking, I'm reloading my crossbow" was a classic. "Replace this text with your own, or delete it" was a joke that excluded non-players, which was all for the good. "My other car is a Charger" had a jarring double-meaning in San Diego. Sure enough—Arizona plates.

"Gamers don't die, they just level up" was one he'd bought for Alan. The gift had been appreciated, but it was meant as a not-so-subtle hint to be less stingy with experience points.

A strip of text he hadn't seen before struck him as petty: "WOK = DL minus Imagination."

What nonsense. In a few short weeks, Randall had unleashed more creative destruction on the WOK than he'd ever managed within the narrow confines of Dungeon Lords.

Randall pointed out that particular bumper sticker to a woman passing by.

"The sentiment *itself* lacks imagination," he said with a smirk.

The woman clutched her Middle Mirth bag closer to her side and quickened her steps toward the main entrance.

A reflective back window on the stickered car showed Randall that she probably reacted not to his words but to his visage. His eyes had been watering longer than Peter's, and a crescent crust lay under them like a footballer's eye black. As usual, red blotches ran down his cheeks and neck, but today's had an angrier, scarlet hue.

Randall sighed and looked back at the car's bumper. On its opposite end lay a blue sticker featuring two twenty-sided dice and the words, "Jesus Saves! (and takes half damage)."

"Truer words," Randall muttered.

If he owned a car, he'd stick that shopworn joke on it just to rile up the parents. Then again, at this point it was hard to imagine any way he could deepen their disappointment.

Randall sighed.

His family would never appreciate what he was about to accomplish. Faith in the divine anchored their world, but they couldn't understand that a holy spirit guided every move he'd made leading up to this weekend. A petty snubbing had set him in motion, and that affront still boiled the supercharged blood that ran through him. Yet a higher purpose inspired the trap he lay for Alan's group and the rest of those attending what the hotel liaison had aptly compared to the Adventist lock-ins Randall had endured as a pre-teen.

Of course, the greater glory went to his own intellect, which had engineered this elaborate plan. The endgame remained dodgy, but one way or another, he'd reemerge Sunday morning as a liberator. He would bring up from the dungeons hundreds of weary registrants, all released from the bonds of fantasy. Free at last, young and old alike would return to a world that could make use of them in paying jobs, or at least internships.

All these good works would come to fruition for him to behold, unless he failed his own saving throw against poison.

DEVON

Devon adjusted his laptop and fidgeted in the oversized chair that served as his improvised office in the hotel lobby. He'd put a "Gone Fishin'" sign on the Players booth and had another vendor keep an eye on his wares, though he knew he could trust the innocents at Middle Mirth.

He had queried a few refugees from the LAN room about their experience in the Stairway tournament, but after a few unsuccessful interviews, he'd confirmed the necessity of seeing for himself what was happening in the WOK.

That led him to the WiFi-accessible lobby and its shaggy orange furniture. The chair he sat in was so deep and high that even if he put his butt on its edge, only his toes could touch the ground. Had he not been so absorbed with his online detective work, he would have felt self-conscious as a little man in a dark suit sitting like a child in a big chair. He was particularly conspicuous since, by his estimation, the Cemetery and Mortuary Association attendees all had horse faces and beanpole physiques reminiscent of the undertakers in low-budget Westerns.

In addition, Devon was the only hotel guest with a dog crate at his feet. The sheet covering Gigi had slid off to allow her to monitor passersby. When Peter and Simon strode into the lobby, she let out a string of high-pitched "yips" that sounded enough like a cell phone alarm to draw scant notice.

"Are you—Peter?" Devon said to the boy with the hunched posture.

Peter squinted, then smiled warily.

"You're the one who died in DL."

"I am that and more, I hope. Would you be kind enough to answer a few questions? I see your WOK badge, and—"

"Don't talk to him," Simon hissed.

Simon nodded for Peter to follow as he walked away. When

Peter remained still, Simon made an exaggerated sigh and trudged toward the basement stairwell.

Peter blinked at Devon with eyelids so puffy Devon could feel his own eyes itch.

"Is it true that you're one of the original WOK developers?"

"It is."

Peter's eyes opened as wide as they could.

"That's so cool."

Gigi kept barking and threw herself twice against her walls. Devon slid forward in his chair and tapped the crate with his foot.

"Why are you not off playing in the WOK? Is your character dead?"

"Yeah, but I took down almost three dozen before I croaked. It was a bloodbath in the volcano. We all became what we're calling 'daisy pushers.' If somebody with the daisy charm touches you, your character becomes mortal and can die for real. But you also gain the ability to spread the charm, so why not make others suffer before you go?"

"And now your character is dead forever?"

"Yup."

"You realize that is *not* how the game was designed."

"Well, we figure it's a surprise feature of the challenge, kind of a hellish plague to keep us away from Asmodeus. And man, it's working. Nobody's gotten past the First Plane of Hell, and the devil's probably doin' a lot of paperwork down on the Ninth. There were tens of thousands playing when the tourney started, but Randall's character—Boldhearts—is gonna be the only one who survives."

Devon thought he recognized both the names he heard.

"The dude never even goes into the main battle areas. He picks off the few late arrivals as they appear. Done a lot of old-fashioned killing that way, but mostly he shoves 'em into the volcano, where they succumb to the daisy charm and slaughter each other. At this point, just about everybody who registered is dead."

"Are the players not upset about losing their characters?"

"Sure, some are, but not me and Simon."

Peter smiled.

"We've been listening to Randall dissect the WOK, and when you think about it, it's a pretty dumb game. It's a bunch of j-holes sitting around and jerking each other off."

Devon cleared his throat. He was surprised to hear a criticism of the WOK that made even him bristle.

"The WOK website now says that after Stairway, our characters will all resurrect, but Randall, who knows this game inside and out, says don't count on it."

"And where is this Randall now?"

"We're all just getting back from dinner. He's restocking supplies or something."

"What about his WOK character?"

"He's fine. Everyone can power down for up to three hours each day. I'm keeping track for him on my stopwatch."

Peter looked at his wrist.

"Gold-dame! Time's almost up."

Peter bolted out of the lobby. Gigi's agitation subsided.

One of the funerary conventioneers still in the lounge regarded Devon. She leaned forward.

"I'm sorry to be listening in, but it sounds as though there've been a terrible number of deaths in your community."

"It's about time," Devon said without thinking.

The woman raised her eyebrows and recoiled. She gathered her bags and left.

Devon scooted back in his chair and resumed typing, more furiously than before. He was dismayed at how easily he'd been able to reenter the Sandbox. He had a few access codes stashed in his long-term memory, and the incompetents who built the WOK's security system had not purged unused identities or required password updates since he'd left.

Clouds gathered in the twilight and reflected off a building across the street. By the time the streetlights turned on, Devon had worked around the Stairway registration deadline and dropped a powerful new character onto the lip of the volcano. Trying to keep his persona innocuous, he gave his night orc an unremarkable name and equipped Orcus with little more than a guisarme, a nasty pole weapon with a hook and blade at its end.

Orcus approached the only other figure visible on the volcano's edge, a massive knight who leaned on an obsidian two-handed sword. Devon rolled his mouse over the warrior's helm, and "Boldhearts" appeared. Beneath the name was a readout counting down from 0:29.

It appeared that Randall had expected no remaining adversaries. He'd left his character unattended long enough that in thirty seconds, Orcus could attack without resistance.

A clutch of hotel guests passed by, and a hulking figure slunk behind them, as if casing the lobby. Devon thought he recognized Randall from when they met on the Fourth of July, but before he could confirm his identity, the figure moved out of his line of sight and toward the stairway. No matter. For the moment, the man was less important than his avatar.

"Hang in there, Cheese Doodle. This might be over in a quick minute, then I can take you on a pee walk to celebrate."

The timer on Devon's screen disappeared and the word "Ready!" replaced it. Devon slid and tapped his index finger on his touchpad to give Orcus the command to poke at the knight, who did not move. Orcus reached into his pack and downed a three-pak of strength, speed, and dexterity potions. Glowing with power, the night orc's stabs became forceful and rapid. On one vicious thrust, a hip plate fell to the ground. The knight started to bleed, and the green health bar beside him dropped below half full.

"Down you go!"

On Orcus' next thrust, Boldhearts seized his attacker's weapon and tossed it down the volcano. He raised his own sword, and words appeared above his head.

"Who sent you? How did you get in here?"

Devon gave no response. He wished he'd made a godly character of his own to murder Boldhearts, but he wouldn't have been able to cover up his tracks, not without a day or more of deft coding. As it was, Peter's careless chatter had given him an opening, and conventional combat would have laid Boldhearts low if only his owner tarried a few more seconds.

In a last-ditch effort, Devon hurled every explosive item he had at Boldhearts, who took bursts of damage but healed himself more quickly than Orcus could inflict harm. When Orcus ran out of ammunition, he let the knight approach.

Boldhearts raised his sword. In a flurry of swings, he slashed left and right across Orcus' breastplate.

"Whoever you are, you are not invited to join in the fun."

One more flash of the oversized sword and Orcus ceased to be.

As Devon had expected, he saw no resurrection instructions appear on the screen. There was no trace of his hastily built orc in the shadow user account Devon had set up an hour earlier. He laughed at the satisfaction of finally seeing mortality come to the WOK.

Triumph gave way to dread. Death had come, but not on his terms. As for his own fate, and that of his royalties, there was nothing more he could do to stop whatever sequence of events was in motion.

A clap of thunder sounded outside. Gigi whimpered and rattled her crate. Devon shut his computer, climbed out of his chair, and bent down to pull the dog into his arms. Seated on the floor, she let him stroke her quivering back. Devon wasn't sure how long he'd been comforting the frightened dog in his lap when he heard Maya approach.

"Dad? We've been looking all over for you."

"Well, here I am."

"We need you, Pops. Alan had to leave all of a sudden. He said you'd be able to step in."

Devon put Gigi back in her crate.

"Is Alan okay?"

"Yeah, it was something with his mom. Sounded like she had a fall. He said you could be our substitute game director. Said he'd already cleared it with the judges."

Devon brightened.

"I am sure he did. The boy is a bit of a seer, is he not?"

"He does work in insurance."

"Good thing my policies are up-to-date. Let us go forth and discover what he has in store for *you*."

ALAN

King Turd slid into a space in the short-term parking lot. From there, Alan ran through what was becoming a hard summer rain before entering the emergency wing of Mercy Hospital. At the reception desk, he explained who he was and who he hoped to see. A friendly volunteer escorted him down a fluorescent hallway.

Most rooms had shut doors, but a few stood open. From one bed, a badly abraded face gave him a nod. Painful road-rash, no doubt. Another room featured two parents hovering over a teenage girl. The mother wiped the child's forehead with a damp cloth. A third showed a bearded man about his own age, sleeping under a damp sheet. Alan's mind played a trick on him. He thought he saw a WOK lanyard hanging from the bedpost.

Alan arrived at his mother's room to find her abed, with a lightweight cast on her right foot.

"Already got you plastered up, I see."

"It's a walking boot," she said, "not a cast."

With both hands, Karen held a mug that read, "World's Worst Nurse." It was a legendary gag gift, which she'd received for working there twenty-five years.

Alan offered a gentle hug and felt the heat from her drink, which smelled of Irish coffee. He sat down on a rolling stool beside her bed.

"You didn't have to come. One of the candy stripers made me dictate a message to you, but I told her not to send it. Clearly, she disobeyed a direct order."

Alan had received the text while washing himself in the hotel bathroom, using a bar of Lava soap he'd been carrying in his briefcase for weeks. It had read, "Had a nasty fall. Still at Mercy. Please visit before 11. Need ride."

"What happened, Mom?"

"Remember that time, a few weeks ago, when I had the flare-up and spilled all those pills? It was like that. This time, I was carrying a knapsack for a boy who'd been rushed into ER. He'd left his belongings in the waiting room. I retrieved them for him and was jogging back down the hall when I tried to sidestep a puddle. My ankle seized. I fell down, hard."

"Did you break anything?"

"Just a hairline fracture. I'll be off my feet for a while."

Karen frowned.

"I probably ruined the poor child's books, which went right into the water on the floor. Worse, it wasn't water."

Alan grimaced.

"And wouldn't you know it, they were *your* books. I mean, they were Dungeon Lords manuals and the like."

"Really? That's pretty random."

"Not really. The boy was from your convention. That's why he came to Mercy—because we're so close. He was dehydrated and disoriented, but nobody's sure what he's got. Looked like chickenpox to me. One of the doctors said it was only *like* chickenpox. The nurse who got the kid set up in his bed started showing similar symptoms, so they moved both off the main floor to isolate them."

"Sounds nasty."

"Are you playing all night? I worry you and your friends aren't getting enough sleep. Wait—"

Karen opened her mouth in shock.

"You had to stop your game to visit me, didn't you?"

"No, I—"

"Oh, dear. You didn't win your tournament?"

"No, Mom. It's okay. They're fine. We're doing fine."

Alan placed his hand on Karen's shoulder.

"They'll probably play straight through till tomorrow. Devon's filling in for me."

"The man from the game store?"

"I'd made arrangements for him to pinch-hit in case I had to step away. I didn't tell the group at first because I didn't want them to worry. I'm sure Devon's up-to-speed. He's got the whole module I wrote, plus a copy of my notes."

Karen set her mug on a tray table and sniffed at Alan.

"What's that scent? Some kind of soap?"

"Yeah. Got in kind of a mess. I tried to wash it out, but..."

Karen clucked when Alan showed her the two dark stains on his shirt.

"That smell reminds me of your father. Do you remember how close the two of you used to be?"

"I remember Dad was kind of crazy."

Alan felt uncomfortable talking about his father in any setting, but sitting in the hospital it was harder still. He got up and shut the curtain, then returned to his stool and rolled to the edge of Karen's bed.

"Your father ended up very bitter. He withdrew from me— from us both. You knew he drank some, but that was just part of it. He'd slide into these blue funks. He'd quarrel with himself, if not with me. Promise you won't end up like that. Don't disappear on me."

"I won't."

Alan squeezed Karen's elbow, and she beamed at him.

"I'm here now, aren't I? I've been paying attention, or trying. The arthritis, the anniversary this weekend. I got worried. That's why I made contingency plans."

Karen raised her foot from its pillow. She wiggled her toes, which poked out of the boot holding her ankle in place.

"I'm supposed to keep it elevated, but it's getting sore."

Alan rolled his chair to the foot of Karen's bed and reached out with his hands. He gently massaged her toes, one at a time.

"Am I doing this right? You're the nurse."

"That's great, honey."

Karen picked up her coffee mug and took a drink.

"As for nursing, your mom's retiring from that profession."

Alan continued rubbing her toes and didn't look up when he spoke.

"I kind of figured that out on my own. I've put in a request for a bump up to full time."

Karen frowned.

"You hate that job, honey."

"Hate's a strong word. I've come to realize it's a natural extension of my skill set. Even with your pension coming, we'll need the money. In any case, I think I want a more regular work week."

"What about your game? Don't you need the extra time for it?"

"Like you've always said, Mom, that's not a job. It doesn't pay. In fact, it costs money."

"If you win the tournament this weekend, you get a vacation. That's worth something."

Alan's thoughts returned to his friends, who were playing into the night in their hotel basement. He pictured Devon directing the game beneath the tall cardboard screen.

"I hope they'll be okay without me in that cinderblock crypt. Last year, I remember it got pretty cold in there at night."

"I don't want to pull you away from them, but I'm sure you've prepared them well for whatever's coming their way."

Karen drained the last drop from her mug.

"They'll be fine."

Alan gave Karen's toes one last squeeze, then released them. He met her gaze and tried to read her eyes. She seemed happy — maybe happy for him. Maybe proud.

"Alan, do you remember that Leo Lionni book you had as a child?"

"Who?"

"Frederick — that was the book's title. About a field mouse."

Karen raised herself up higher and swung her body to let her legs dangle over the bed. She might have been getting up to look for the book, but then remembered where she was.

"I maybe recall the pictures. Watercolors? No, cut-paper collages. I can see a fat little mouse on a stone wall."

"That's Frederick."

"Did you read it to me?"

"John would read it to you, until you were old enough to read it to him. You know, you're like him in some ways."

"Like the mouse?"

"Yes, but also your father. He wanted to make the world more fun, more joyful. He tried to do that for us, honey. He just never found a way."

Karen smiled broadly and locked eyes with Alan.

"I can still see the two of you on your bed, reading together. He loved that book even more than you did."

"The mouse, Frederick, didn't ever do any work. Is that right?"

"All summer and autumn, the mice gathered grains and supplies, while Frederick took in the beauty around him. It frustrated his cousins. But they were family, so when the snow came and they retreated into their burrow, they shared their food with him."

Falling into her stride, Karen gestured dramatically as she talked. Alan remembered that his father used to do the same when he read aloud.

"The winter went on and on, and soon the mice had to ration the last bits of wheat. When they grew weary and worried, Frederick told them to close their eyes. He recounted the heat of the sun in July, how its rays would reach under their fur to caress their skin. The mice almost sweated from the warmth of his words. When they became sad at the darkness of the cave, Frederick painted pictures in their minds of blooming spring flowers, or fiery autumn leaves. He offered his cousins the one gift he had—his imagination."

"You can't eat imagination. Did the mice make it through the winter?"

"Of course they did, honey."

Karen laughed and kicked Alan playfully with her good foot.

"It was a children's book—not one of your horror stories where everyone dies."

HERMIONE

A cold drizzle replaced the fog that had come with the first wave of Cynoc's army. Hermione wiped moisture from her eyes, and in that moment, a golden dagger slashed her chin. She stepped back to the edge of the dais, blood trickling down her neck.

"A slice!" screeched the dagger. Though held in the hand of a staggering elven Naught, the weapon danced of its own accord. "A nice clean slice to entice my master!"

Before Hermione could reach for her scimitar, the dagger yanked forward the arm of its bearer—this time low and toward Hermione's side. She barely had time to deflect the stab with her lute. The eager dagger shattered the instrument but snagged on its glowing strings. Hermione jerked her arms back and pulled the weapon free from its owner's hand.

"Noooo!" the dagger cried.

The gut strings holding it had been spun out a century before, crafted from the intestines of a harpy. Despite a vigorous effort, the dagger couldn't saw itself loose.

"Releeease me!"

Hermione dropped the yelping dagger, then stamped her boot down hard to snap it in half. With a merciful impulse, she swung her scimitar to finish the dagger's former owner.

A soft drumbeat behind her suggested that Almandine played on. When Hermione turned around, she discovered only heavy raindrops striking the kettle drum. Almandine lay weeping and wounded, holding close his dead apprentice. A few stray bards shouted songs above the din, but Hermione felt her comrades' morale waning.

Just outside the city gates, Angelou and Lesilla sloshed through thickening mud. While fighting off a throng of Everwinter mercenaries, they backed their way toward Hermione.

Their adversaries thrust ice-tipped halberds forward with a strange symmetry, which made dodging them easy enough. Even so, there were too many of these clones. One blade after another caught a scrap of armor or patch of flesh. Death would come soon, if only by a thousand pokes.

Angelou moved in light hops, favoring her right leg. Lesilla also looked weary. She held up a towering shield, which she braced with both arms. It deflected the fiercest blows but left her no means to counter the onslaught.

Hermione reached into her belt pouch for anything she might have held in reserve. She pulled out a small jade cat from the fairie vault. When she brushed it against the edge of her scimitar, it released green sparks and a feline cry. She threw the totem toward Angelou. It grew into a full-size leopard, legs outstretched mid-leap. The cat landed gracefully and leapt between Angelou and Lesilla. Razored claws flashed left and right. The startled attackers scattered. In that moment of opportunity, Angelou and Lesilla scrambled back into the city and raced up the short stairs of the dais.

Lancelot climbed up to join them. He spread his hands wide.

"Restore us, Elahna, in the name of all that grows for your glory."

Allies standing nearby began to glow. Hermione felt her neck wound closing. Angelou's torn leg muscles bulged anew, stretching her slack troll hides into place, tight against her skin. Many others, however, including two of the larger fairies, remained prone on the ground.

"Where's Santana?" Lancelot said. "That was my last major healing prayer."

"Somewhere back outside," Angelou said.

"We're holding," Lesilla said, "but another wave comes over the hills."

Lesilla surveyed the scene inside the gates and saw worried

faces looking up at her. She tried to spread her arms wide and raise them high, the common hand symbol for defiance. The gesture might have infused in her soldiers a burst of courage, but Lesilla could not lift either arm above her waist.

Lesilla patted Hermione on the shoulder and descended the dais stairs.

"One of their high priests cursed me. I shall tend to it at the temple, then regroup at the Roundhouse."

In the distance, far beyond Hermione's retreating comrade, an enormous ogre climbed through a gap in the rebuilt city walls and pushed aside the clutch of spears that greeted it. Before the beast could enter the city, Tinkana swooped down and carried the creature aloft. The Fairie Queen ascended quickly, then hurled the ogre down to crush a clutch of Naughts. Hermione saw the beast's head rise once more over the city walls, though it appeared dazed. Tinkana descended feet-forward onto it, and a definitive crunch meant it had cushioned her landing.

Hermione turned to Lancelot.

"Tinkana has joined Santana in the heart of the battle."

"She may be the last one of her kind alive," he replied. "They chose the strongest as their queen."

From Tinkana's vicinity came a high-pitched buzz, then a sickening grinding sound. A delicate pink spray shot up over the walls. Another foe had been obliterated by razor-sharp fairie wings.

Hermione refocused on her own responsibilities. She reached down to retrieve lute strings entangled with the broken dagger. Gathering eight usable strings, Hermione stretched them wide.

"Today is *not* the day the music dies."

With those words spoken, the flickering frame of a yellow harp appeared before Hermione. A quick harmonic strumming reassured her that she had conjured an instrument tuned in G.

The rain became a downpour. Hermione shook off sheets of water and chose a barbarian ballad in the hope that it might afford Angelou an extra measure of spirit. When Hermione began to sing, Angelou joined to create a surprising harmony.

We shout loudly, voices strong
Sing together, all as one
Ground is bloody with our foe
Fight together, watch them go

All around Hermione, Mythopolis soldiers raised fists and shields and shouts. They re-gripped their weapons, cracked their necks, and charged behind Angelou, Lancelot, and Hermione out of the city gates and into the thick of the fray.

DEVON

"This," Devon said, "is the point at which Alan would likely say something clever."

"You're doing fine," Maya said.

"I don't know," Lance said. "What was the deal with that rhyming dagger? 'A slice to entice' wouldn't come out of Alan's mouth."

Carlos laughed, then mimicked the squeaky voice Devon used for the weapon.

"Releeeeaase me!"

"That dang thing wrecked my lute!" Brie growled.

Devon coughed softly, then louder to clear his throat.

"I confess that I have no prior experience with bringing voice to inanimate objects."

"It's not that," Brie said. "The dagger was funny. Almost cute, if it hadn't kept stabbing me. It's just that we're getting to the scary part."

"She's right," Carlos said. "Even Santana's done being a smart ass. This shit's serious now. Cynoc will kick our ass if we don't stay focused."

"Do you want notes, Devon?" Lance said. "If so, I might ask that you avoid jargon from outside the DL lexicon. I heard a judge standing behind me seethe when you said a healer offered 'milk of the poppy.' And the raven watching the battle from atop the city gates? A bit too on the nose."

"I caught those," Maya said. "Just follow Alan's notes, Dad. You'll be fine."

Devon looked at the pages spread out before him. He'd read through them twice, but the detail was staggering. Scripted sections were easy to follow, but he hadn't used the tables on Alan's screen. He kept that cardboard barrier in place for now, but only to sustain the illusion that he was making proper technical calculations.

"Can I trigger my spell yet?" Carlos said from the opposite end of the table.

To see Carlos' face, Devon stood and peered over the cardboard divider, as he'd done all evening.

"Just lower the screen," Carlos said. "I don't think Alan's coming back anytime soon."

As a parent himself, Devon appreciated the sacrifice Alan was making to check on his mother. He still didn't understand the particulars, but Alan had warned him well in advance that he might need to excuse himself. When Devon asked his daughter about it, Maya would only say that it was a difficult time of year for Alan's family. She said the same went for Carlos, but the man had played all through the evening with as much gusto as anyone at the table.

"And when I cast my spell," Carlos said, "you really need to roll for its effect this time."

Devon blinked but maintained a blank expression.

"I wondered about that myself," Lance said. "Three times I heard nothing when die rolls were required."

"I might have missed one in there," Devon said. "My apologies."

It was a false confession. Leave it to his daughter to catch the lie.

"Look," Maya said, "we all know you gave Angelou a break. She and Lesilla never should have made it back inside the gates. There's no way those trained ice mercenaries could have missed us both, especially with Angelou limping."

"I did give her that limp," Devon protested.

He could read the faces around him. Nobody was buying it.

"Lesilla and I both should have taken more damage. I was distracted, trying to save so many soldiers. I forgot to mind the flank attacks. Alan would have punished Angelou for that oversight. You and Alan are on the same page when it comes to mortality in fantasy. Gotta play it straight and let the bodies fall where they may."

"If a doting father cannot spare his own daughter's barbarian, so be it. But let's dispense with the pretense of this screen. Its charts mock me."

Devon reached for Alan's cardboard wall, but Maya steadied it with her own hand.

"Don't," Maya whispered. "Jeff Jacobson's coming. It'll look unprofessional if we can see your notes."

Devon checked his watch. 12:12 AM.

"Didn't they announce they were calling it a night?"

Lance tapped the table.

"They said they'd take a break for six hours, starting at midnight. What time is it?"

"We're past that already," Carlos said.

"Well, he's here now," Maya said. "Look busy."

Two seconds later, Jacobson approached. He wore a purple judge's sash across his collared shirt. The Middle Mirth staffer accompanying him wore a WOK badge and a stern expression.

On seeing the badge, Devon suspected they might want a private word with him. Back at corporate headquarters, they had probably figured out what caused the massive die-off online. Sleuths would have found the mortality code he'd left in the Sandbox and recognized his signature style.

Devon laughed to himself. He loved hyperbole, but for once, he would be able to use the word "catastrophe" without exaggeration.

"Greetings," Devon said. "Shall we step away to—"

"Sorry to be a bother," Jacobson interrupted. "I'm afraid we've got ourselves a sick child."

The Middle Mirth staffer brought forward a boy Devon recognized as Peter.

Jacobson gestured toward the Wiccan Convent's table.

"Someone over there said there's a doctor in the house."

CARLOS

"Sí," Carlos said, "that's me. I'm your doctor."

As he stood, Carlos bumped a table leg. From inside her crate, Gigi gave a tinny "woof!"

"Is that a dog?" Jacobson asked.

Gigi barked in earnest, and Carlos smiled.

"Long story."

"Another time," Jacobson said.

He nudged forward a Middle Mirth staffer, who had her arm around Peter's slumped shoulders.

"Now, if you'll excuse me, I'm going to take a quick nap in the Judges Room, though I should probably just go upstairs and call it a night. We're supposedly taking shifts. We're all feeling a bit loopy."

"Good night," Devon said cheerfully.

When Jacobson left the ballroom, the staffer coughed to get the table's attention.

"This boy, Peter, says he's feeling queasy. You have something you can give him?"

Peter itched his chest and moaned.

"My gold-dame skin itches *bad*."

The boy lifted his shirt to reveal three red stripes across his belly, as if a leopard had raked its claws there. The raising of Peter's arm revealed an unrelated symptom, the familiar musk of a body unaccustomed to deodorant.

Carlos recoiled at the smell, which reminded him of how Randall's scent used to build like a gathering storm if they played through the night. For Peter's benefit, he tried to mask his disgust with professional sympathy.

"It's probably just an allergy."

Carlos dug into a bag beside Gigi's crate. He accidentally knocked her door open, and she hopped out. Gigi hopped about and barked at Peter until Carlos scooped her up.

"My sister's dog has a skin condition. I had some aloe gel in here, but I used it all up."

Lance reached under his chair and produced his new first aid kit. He opened its lid and turned it so that Carlos could see its contents.

"Healing professional to the rescue! Is one of these an allergesic cream?"

"I think you mean *analgesic*, medicine man."

Carlos plucked one of the tubes from Lance and handed it to Peter.

"This should work. Rub in as much as you need, then get some rest."

Peter scratched himself, but Carlos brushed his hand away.

"Don't do that. It'll only get worse."

Carlos pointed toward the stage, where a few other people had already camped out.

"Go get some rest. It's warmer in here than in that cave of yours."

Peter offered a sheepish "Thanks." He took a few tentative steps, then turned back to Carlos.

"Hey, about the phones and all that. We were just griefing you guys, okay?"

Most of what Peter said sounded like gibberish. As for the phones, Carlos *loved* that the basement ballroom was a cell dead zone. It made Middle Mirth an oasis in an over-connected world. Down here, he'd get no anxious texts from Alan, no emergency calls from work. It was like going back to a time when nobody carried a phone in their pocket.

"Trust me," Peter said. "I know that dude's a badass. He practically broke my hand earlier this summer at a LARP, but he's cool. I mean—"

Peter's voice trailed off. He turned away and shuffled toward the stage.

Devon yawned and reached high to stretch his arms.

"We have seen many weary souls since midnight, have we not? And how about us? Are we pushing through till dawn?"

"You know we are," said Maya. "I couldn't sleep if I wanted to."

"Ditto that," Brie said.

Carlos held up his dog.

"Gigi says, 'Enough talk, let's play.'"

"Agreed," Lance said. "Let's show 'em how this game works."

DEVON

With Jacobson out of sight and no WOK staff lurking about, Devon let his attention return to Alan's notes. He'd made scant progress when Carlos, still cradling Gigi, interrupted his reading.

"Can I use my potion now?" Carlos said.

"But of course."

Devon opened the *Spellcraft Compendium* and held up a finger.

"The scarlet sorcerer tips his head back and gulps liquid from a slim decanter. He, um, begins to glow? Let us see now. He—"

"I've got it," Carlos said. "Santana whispers *transfiguración* to Lupita, and—"

"No, no," Devon said, "please allow me. I can render our game's details well enough. Behold..."

Lupita returned an anxious look at her master, who grew in size so rapidly that he soon towered over Angelou. In seconds, his broad shoulders came even with the Fairie Queen herself. Across his back, his signature cape swung like a heavy curtain.

Santana whacked his staff on the ground, and it assumed the form of a thorny branch. Whirling his body about, Santana harvested the crowd of Naught elves, orcs, and goblins like so much wheat. With Lupita fighting more cautiously underfoot, he sliced his way toward Tinkana, who slapped and crushed her adversaries.

The sense of power coursing through Santana did not wane when he saw a necromancer approach flanked by a dozen ghouls in his charge and many more behind those. Before the beasts' gruesome faces became distinct, a stench announced their presence.

"Oh, that's just nasty."

Brie waved her hands in front of her face.

"It already smells bad enough in here without that image in my head."

"Pretty righteous," Lance said. "I think we've got ourselves some actual undead. About time."

"Turn them away!" Brie said to her brother.

Devon looked around his screen at Lance.

"Is that what you would like to do?"

Lance rubbed his hands together.

"You bet it is."

"Roll an undead turning check."

Lance cupped his rounded die in both hands, shook it above his head, and slid it across the table. The die spun toward the outside of Devon's screen and knocked against it. Once settled, the die said in a silky voice, "Fourteen."

Devon dragged his finger across a chart.

"With that roll, plus your charisma modifier, you can turn away plenty of these beasties."

Lance picked up a handful of six-sided dice and tossed them onto the table. They clattered in front of Brie.

Brie read out the numbers and did some quick math.

"Pretty average, I guess."

"Even so," Lance said with a snap of his fingers, "that's a pretty hefty number of ghouls turned away, I'd say."

Lancelot held his totem high. Out of it emerged a glowing unicorn that charged toward the onrushing ghouls. It raised its forelegs and made a shrill whinny as it whipped its hooves through the air. Eleven of the unearthed corpses turned in panic to claw through their kin and flee toward the far hills.

"That was decent undead zapping," Lance said, "but my holy symbol can't turn away the rank-and-file Naught soldiers, right?"

Devon nonchalantly lowered his eyes to scan Alan's notes.

"Correct. Naughts are not undead, per se."

"Omigod!" Brie said with a shriek. "That scene with Lancelot's unicorn was just like Harry Potter's Patronus stag."

"Um, maybe?"

Devon ducked behind his screen. He had, indeed, appropriated the image from a Potter movie, albeit unconsciously. The faux pas could be toxic to their reputation among tournament officials, but a quick scan of the ballroom showed no judges nearby.

Maya nudged Brie.

"Ix-nay on the Arry-hay Otter-pay."

Brie clamped her lips together and put her hands in her lap.

"What's Hermione's got left?" Carlos said.

"Sadness," Lance said. "I think her conjured instrument is about to go poof. Haven't six rounds passed since it appeared?"

Devon made a mark with his pencil.

"Indeed, they have."

Hermione's golden harp disappeared suddenly, leaving a tangle of strings in her hands. She stepped back to gather her wits and ducked under the clawed hand of a hissing ghoul. Scores of the creatures pressed forward, some stopping to tug and gnaw on the limbs of fallen warriors for necrotic nourishment.

Maya reached toward the center of the table, and Devon stood to watch her. She lifted her metal Angelou figurine to move it across the cream-colored oilcloth grid on which Alan had mapped the terrain in front of the city gates.

"I'm running in a wide arc around the fray to take a stab at the necromancer who brought these ghouls to the party. My boots give me automatic initiative. Plus, I've got a blind-side attack because of my target orientation."

Devon realized he'd never had the chance to watch his daughter closely during a role-playing game. On hearing the intensity in her voice, he sat back down and smiled from behind his screen. She was engrossed in the story and experiencing the kind of "deep immersion" he'd tried explaining to software engineers for so many years. He considered the unthinkable— that he should let her stay on at the store. Ease up on the parental pressure.

He'd joked with her about that subject the week before. "If you win the DL tournament and go to Europe," he'd said, "I will have to fire you. You have insufficient vacation hours set aside." She'd accepted that as fair.

In truth, whether Maya and her friends won or not, he had to "fire" her. If he let her stay at Players past the summer, her mother would drive down the length of I-5, find Devon, and murder him. Then there wouldn't be a Players at which his daughter might work. The alternative scenario not only spared his life but also left his daughter in graduate school at Yale. A rather golden parachute, that was.

"Dad?" Maya said patiently. "Can I go yet?"

"Of course."

Maya rolled her twenty-sided die.

"With the attack angle and modifiers, that comes to eighteen." Devon nodded.

"With a swiftness and force that surprises even her, Angelou's trident pierces the necromancer's back."

"Ooh!" Maya shouted. "If he's skewered, I get a chance to throw him."

Devon nodded, and Maya re-rolled her twenty-sided die.

"Boom goes the dynamite!"

"Awesome!" Lance said. "You roll a natural twenty?"

"Indeed," Devon said. "With ironic intent, Angelou throws the necromancer's body into his undead entourage. Remorselessly, they rip apart their master's corpse."

"Eww!" Brie said. "I would've rather cast an ice storm or something. Coulda zapped them all at once, nice and neat."

"You will get that chance, for it is your turn."

"I'm keeping my last spell in reserve."

Brie pointed at a cluster of ghoulish figurines Devon had arranged on the map.

"I'll toss holy water on those guys instead."

"Roll for missile weapon."

Brie tossed her twenty-sided.

"Three."

Devon glanced at Alan's charts.

"Hermione pulls from her belt a corked flask and hurls it into the fray. It flies wide to hit the ground with no effect."

Lance leaned toward Devon's end of the table.

"Unexploded ordnance?"

"Precisely."

"Bummer, sis. Shoulda let the Blind Monk throw it."

Carlos glanced at his character sheet.

"I've only got a couple spell slots left. Brie, what are you saving your last one for?"

"For our inevitable battle against you-know-who. I was thinking—"

Brie jumped out of her chair suddenly.

"Ooh, I know this is bad timing, but I've gotta run to the bathroom."

Maya laughed.

"Use the one in the foyer of that movie room where they're watching The One Ring. Might want to take off your elf ears, girlfriend, or they'll think you're one of them."

"Well, I am one of them, aren't I?"

Brie harrumphed and ran her fingers over her ears, one of which was drooping. She pressed the wayward accessory back into place before dashing out of the ballroom.

Hoping her absence would give him a minute to catch up with the players, Devon settled back into his seat and flipped through Alan's pages. He had to make sure he was ready for what was coming.

"Why don't you lower that screen?" Carlos said. "I can barely see you. The judges are gone. We won't peek at Alan's notes."

"Honestly," Lance said, "you can trust me not to look."

"I suppose I could—"

Devon laughed a beat late at Lance's joke, then folded up the cardboard over Maya's frowning objection.

"If we are being frank with one another, I confess my inability to grok all the charts on that screen. Do you have any idea how hard Alan's job is? All the plusses and minuses and situational modifiers that go into every roll? Remarkable."

"You get used to it," Maya said. "Angelou's usually plus six, but, I guess, not always. Like just now."

"Exactly my point. The rules only make sense when you see how they interconnect. I can see why Alan's a good actuary. He can remember and apply conditional probabilities in each unique instance. One cannot simply do all the math on the fly."

"Consider my vantage point," Lance said. "Braille reference tables are brutal. I've given this some serious thought. There are ways we could use iPads to—"

Devon waved his hands at Lance.

"No, no, no! Do *not* grind all this beauty down into the bones of a video game."

He crossed his forefingers over one another.

"I am making a holy symbol, Lance. Back demon! Back I say!"

"Easy." Maya laughed. "Hear him out. I don't think he meant—"

"No," Lance said. "I don't want to twist it into WOK 2.0, or some such abomination. I'm just saying, I have ideas for how to take the headache out of game directing, and—"

Devon jumped in his seat when Brie slammed the doors shut on reentering the ballroom. She looked pale and shaken.

"Omigod, omigod, omigod!"

Brie pressed both hands over her mouth, and her head jerked forward.

"Gonna upchuck on us, princess?" Maya said.

Brie nodded vigorously.

"Almost, for real."

She stood still for a few seconds before stepping gingerly to her metal folding chair. When she reached it, she seemed wary of sitting down.

"It's super gross in the women's bathroom. It's like somebody—"

She covered her mouth and nose again.

"You okay?" Carlos said.

Brie released her hands to rest them on the back of her chair. She breathed in and out.

"Sorry, I just freaked out for a minute there. You think the battlefield in front of Mythopolis is disgusting? Try the ladies' room."

Devon told himself not to worry. After all, Brie was the most squeamish of the group. Even imaginary ghouls caused her skin to turn a shade lighter than her green hair.

"Somebody threw up on the toilets," Brie said. "Not in them—*on* them. Even the sinks were filthy, like that nasty scene in Bridesmaids."

She shook her torso like a wet dog, as if that might clear images from her mind.

"On the plus side, I now have neither the physical need nor the desire to use the bathroom. Ever."

"Sounds nasty," Maya said. "Is the film still running?"

"Yeah, but nobody's watching it. The couple dozen peeps in there were asleep. They didn't look very comfortable all sprawled out on the floor, some writhing around."

"Oh, you sweet innocent," Lance chuckled. "They were probably making out."

"I doubt anyone could get very cozy with the odors in there. The carpet—oh, God! It smelled like a sick child's bed sheets."

"That's got to be an exaggeration," Carlos said. "I know that smell well. I've inhaled sick-sheets many times at Children's. *Mierda*. Now you've got it in my head. I can't—"

Carlos made a sour face, then lifted Gigi and inhaled Chidoodle scent.

Devon smiled and wished the little dog was under his nose. He reached for his room-temperature cup of coffee and took a drink.

"Ladies and lords, shall we return to the game?"

"If the city gates are clear," Lance said, "I'd like to lead Brie and Angelou on a charge to rejoin Santana, Lupita, and Tinkana. We've gotta regroup, and that's where the action is."

"I don't see why not. Do you follow him?"

Brie and Maya nodded their assent.

Devon walked around his screen to the oilskin map on the table. He moved three figurines, along with a pair of city guards, then returned to his chair.

"Inspired by your heroic rush into battle, two soldiers fall in behind you."

"Can Santana see Cynoc?"

Devon quickly looked left, then right.

"Santana whips his head about for a moment, as if trying to remember something he had lost. Alas, he cannot hold the thought in his mind and resumes his enraged slaughter of the Naught army."

"Oh, right, my giant berserker spell. Guess I'm attacking again?"

"Roll."

Santana's sharp staff ripped through two Naught warriors, then caught on the hide of the most fearsome ogre on the battlefield. The beast hefted a glowing hammer with a head the size of an anvil. He brought it down on Santana's left shoulder. In his agitated state, Santana felt no pain, but he heard an ominous snapping sound, as if his clavicle had split in two. He lost his footing in the mud, but before the ogre could land another blow, the Fairie Queen spun around and brought her wings down onto its head. The acrobatic maneuver pureed the ogre down to mid-torso, ending his villainous career.

"That was no rank-and-file thug."

Devon ran his finger along Alan's handwriting.

"He was Gross Austin, battle champion of the ogre clan. He would not have gone down but for the lucky roll I made on Tinkana's behalf."

Devon paused again to read his pages.

"Oh, but cruel irony. Austin wielded the Hammer of the Scots, an unbreakable artifact forged—"

"—in the Fairie Realm," Brie said.

"Correct."

Devon read Alan's note aloud.

"Fairie wings can break only when beat against magic weapons."

But what did "break" mean, in terms of hard numbers? The first sheet of paper in the manila envelope Alan gave to Devon was blank, except for these words: "Rule #1. When in doubt, make it up. Quickly!"

Behind his screen, Devon rolled a ten-sided die three times. He frowned.

"Oh, crud," Brie said. "Tinkana's wings."

"What's she gonna do?" Maya said.

Devon considered his options.

"Want to hear it from her perspective?"

Carlos nodded.

The violent hum of her wings ceased, and the Fairie Queen inhaled the scent of burning leather. Numbness in her back turned into a sting, then crippling pain. She reached behind herself and felt two badly tattered wings. She tried to show Santana what had transpired, but he lurched forward to attack again, oblivious to the injuries that rendered his left side as useless as an untended marionette.

Soon, Tinkana feared, Mythopolis would be overrun. The battle's outcome was no longer in doubt. Hundreds of Naught soldiers, who had once been elves, goblins, even gnomes, climbed up the city's rubble walls. The slick ground impeded their progress more than the thin reinforcements defending their capital.

To test her wings, Tinkana propelled herself toward the top of the city gates. She could barely rise above the snapping jaws and gnarled hands of the Naught horde. She landed awkwardly in the mud. Through driving rain, she ran toward Hermione, Lancelot, and Angelou, who fought beside one another.

"You have felled enough enemies," Devon said, "to afford you a few seconds of conversation with Tinkana before engaging the next wave of attackers."

Devon looked at Brie with plaintive eyes.

"Tinkana says, 'You must aid me!'"

Brie returned a worried expression.

"How? We can barely hold our ground."

Maya leaned forward.

"We have to find Cynoc. If we can defeat him, the tide will turn fer us."

"Tinkana says, 'I believe he entered the city minutes ago.'"

"Drat," Lance said. "How could we have missed that creep? I mean, 'How did we miss his entrance?'"

"He used a spell to blink past us all. Now I must ask a cowardly favor. I must flee at once. My wings are too torn to heal, and I haven't the strength to fight my way out. If I perish, the fairies die forever. Our magic is the lifeblood of the Mythos."

Brie raised her hand.

"How may I be of aid?"

"Can you fashion me wings?"

Devon pointed his pencil at Carlos.

"Santana is coming out of his transformation spell, so he can hear this."

"Great," Carlos said, "so the gist is that we're in deep trouble. Tinkana's probably toast, and this reanimated Cynoc can fight like a knight *and* cast spells."

"Remember that your foe is an elder lich."

Devon saw blank faces around the table.

"Oh, dear. You did not previously know that little detail, did you?"

"No sweat," Lance said. "We won't tell Alan you spilled the beans. We'd kinda guessed he was something like that. Anyhoo, can I do another round of turning? It's the best Lancelot can manage at this point."

"The good news is you are next in the queue. Go ahead."

"Who's got the initiative after Lancelot?" Maya said.

"I am afraid that is the bad news. I will permit you but one guess who goes next."

A brilliant unicorn sprang from Lancelot's hand and kicked away the last of the nightmarish ghouls. Though the searing light of Elahna had found its mark, Lancelot sensed a terrible force approaching, one more powerful than even his god.

The wet earth parted wide, and a tall figure blinked into view in front of Lancelot and his companions. For an instant, the falling raindrops came to a stop. There stood Cynoc Coldheart, his dark armor as slick as glass in the heavy rain. In one hand, Cynoc held Boldheart's obsidian sword. In the other, he held a bloodied purple sash, which hung like a sling bearing a heavy object.

Cynoc lifted his visor. His sparkling eyes and wide smile made Lancelot shudder. He returned Lancelot's gaze and acknowledged Santana's presence with a nod.

"You and your friend, whose body I now enjoy, have given me so much. I feel obliged to offer something in return."

Cynoc swung the purple sash forward. It released the head of Prime Minister Lesilla, which fell to the ground and rolled to a stop, face-down in the mud.

"I have all but finished my work. The champions of Mythopolis lie dead. Now, it is your turn."

Tinkana tried in vain to beat her wings. The effort caused her right radial bone to snap. The loud crack drew Cynoc's gaze.

"Ah, the last of the fairies."

Cynoc raised his sword.

"I shall start with you."

Devon set down the Cynoc Coldheart character sheet and glanced at his watch. He pretended to cover a yawn but closed his eyes and coughed. He felt something leave his mouth and found a lump of brown mucous in his hand. With a cloth napkin plucked from his jacket, he wiped up the offending phlegm.

He'd noticed the group was getting restless, probably awaiting Cynoc's return. On another sheet of paper, Alan had written the edict, "If you sense a lull, pick up the pace."

Devon tried to ignore that advice as long as he could to delay what he feared was inevitable. Cynoc's combat statistics and spell casting abilities were formidable. He remembered playing in a Dungeon Lords campaign decades earlier in which he and six friends had fought unsuccessfully against the original Lord Cynoc. That was an even contest, but this reincarnation Alan had created was something else. The battered adventurers were doomed. Perhaps Alan thought judges would prefer seeing a tragedy over a more conventional triumph.

"If I may be so bold," Devon said, "I suggest we take a five-hour cat nap. We can play out this ending when the judging resumes at eight in the morning."

"Is it really that bad, Dad? I mean, for our characters?"

"I did not say that. I simply think we could use a rest. Even so, this is your evening."

Gigi had curled up in Carlos' lap. She shifted about to get comfortable.

"Cheese Doodle may feel differently," Carlos said, "but I'm amped. If Alan were here, he'd say, 'Play on, judges or not!'"

"Truth," Maya said.

"Yay," Brie squealed. "My first all-nighter!"

"Besides," Lance said, "who knows how long this Mythopolis battle will take? There's so many moving parts. It might turn out that if we picked it back up in the morning, the last round of judging would be wasted on a jumble of die rolls and table checks."

"Let's forge ahead, but play it straight, Dad. Don't keep Cynoc alive just so the judges get to see us finish him off."

"That eventuality should not worry you." Devon bit his lip. "But again, I say too much."

"Game on," Maya said. "Angelou's at full health, thanks to Lancelot's potions. She's still dancing and stabbing at warp speed. Cynoc said he'd come for us next. Let's see him try."

"Okay," Brie said, "but first, I've got a question. That long-winded speech of his—didn't that squander Cynoc's combat initiative?"

Devon had no idea whether such a rule existed. He hesitated—but only for a moment.

"That it did."

Brie pulled open the bright green bun on her head and flipped her hair, which settled softly on her shoulders.

"Then I know a certain elf who's got a turn coming to her."

Hermione moved away from Cynoc and extended her arms toward Tinkana.

"Let me hold you. I will carry us away, if I can manage it."

The Fairie Queen retrieved her amethyst crystal, squeezed

it tightly, and shrank to the bard's height. As they embraced, Hermione's arms slid between the fairie's ironcloths and touched Tinkana's stony skin. Hermione sang so softly that only Tinkana could hear.

Love lifts pain that holds you down
Take my hand and leave the ground
Only wind is all you'll feel
As you let your body heal
This world for us, no longer real

In a rush of air, bard and fairie lifted into the sky. Cynoc craned his neck to watch them fly hundreds of meters up and away. Even as her companions disappeared from view, Hermione felt their strength inside her, raising her higher and faster than she could have imagined.

"Cool," Maya said. "That takes care of Tinkana, but it leaves only three of us to battle Cynoc. Who's go next?"

Devon remembered one of Alan's admonitions about a game director's intuition.

"With your indulgence, I would like us to shift gears at this juncture. I sense that our story requires a more singular point of view. Carlos, are you up for it?"

"Sí, Santana *está* listo porque *es* listo."

"Um, I will take that as a yes. Maya and Lance, have your dice at the ready. Pick up your cues when they come. Let us proceed."

SANTANA

"It has come to pass," Santana said to himself. The throbbing in his left shoulder made it hard to focus, but he gathered his thoughts and set a plan in motion.

With his good hand, he pulled from his belt a wool pouch. He had almost no feeling in his left hand, but he willed it to lift a scrap of parchment from his breast pocket.

Cynoc laughed.

"What petty magics have you in store for us today?"

Santana sensed apprehension behind the boast. He looked to Angelou and Lancelot with widened eyes and mouth agape. With what little movement his body could still offer it was the closest he could come to the common tongue hand signal for help.

His companions took the cue. They went on the offensive.

Angelou jabbed her trident into a thin gap between Cynoc's breastplate and his hip armor. The perfectly aimed attack pierced flesh, but its principal consequence was rage. With armored hands, Cynoc grabbed the tines of Angelou's weapon, spun it around, and speared her thigh with such force that it struck bone.

Lancelot attacked more wildly. The blows from his mace sounded like a harried blacksmith pounding out a horse's shoe. His efforts earned nothing more than a counterattack. Cynoc's mailed fist knocked the wind from Lancelot and left him staggering.

Lupita lunged. Smooth canine teeth pierced Cynoc's gloves and tore open his palm. In reply, the flat of his sword caught the wolf's haunches. Cynoc launched Lupita into the gathering Naught army, which converged on her.

Delayed but undeterred, Cynoc pushed through his would-be attackers and raised his sword to strike Santana. When Cynoc closed within three feet, the sorcerer held out his pouch and squeezed.

"*No entrar,*" Santana whispered. A crystalline dust burst from his hand, then expanded to form a rosy half-sphere ten feet high that enclosed Santana and Cynoc.

"No!" Lancelot shouted. He pounded on the magical half-sphere with his mace. Each soundless strike recoiled, as if pushing against a powerful spring.

Angelou wrenched her trident out of her own leg and tried to stab Cynoc. The magic shell deflected each attempt.

"What can we do?" she pleaded to Lancelot.

"Nothing," he replied with resignation. "We can do nothing."

The Naughts withdrew, in awe of whatever magic might hold within it their powerful leader. Lupita escaped their grasp and ran to Lancelot's side. As the priest pressed a gloved hand against the familiar half-sphere, Lupita did likewise with her paw. Both withdrew quickly when the surface singed them.

Cynoc tried to raise his sword, but his backswing hit the inside wall of the translucent enclosure. He chuckled to himself, then slammed the hilt of his sword onto Santana's broken shoulder to shatter it entirely.

Santana screamed in agony and collapsed from the force of the blow. His left hand, now useless, dropped the scrap of parchment it had held. He searched frantically with his other hand until he found the paper lying in the mud. Santana raised it to his eyes, but before he could focus enough to read aloud its spell, Cynoc stomped an armored foot down on the sorcerer's breastbone. The blow pierced Santana's lungs and robbed him of breath. A wave of blinding pain held him fast.

"This?" Cynoc roared. "This is your plan? You would hold me inside a cage of ground up fire beetles? Your powder and incantations cannot hold for long one such as I. Happily, you have trapped me at your peril. And for what purpose? So your friends might attempt a futile retreat? Bah! You sacrifice yourself for nothing."

Cynoc grabbed Santana's neck and lifted the limp sorcerer's face toward Lancelot and Angelou. Both stood helplessly outside the sphere.

"Take one last look at your friend," Cynoc said. "This fool you took for a hero had nothing in his robes but parlor tricks. You know nothing of where true power lies."

Santana's sight returned in time to see Angelou's eyes fill with tears. Power surged through him. The sensation was akin to something he felt momentarily when pinned against the fairie fortress. This energy had been building inside him all day. He suspected it ran between and among each of his companions. All at once, he felt the might of Angelou, the heart of Hermione, Lancelot's ambition, even the fierce loyalty of Lupita.

After taking a painful breath, Santana spoke in a weak voice.

"There is a strength we possess. It stands in opposition to your own power. We do not understand its operation, but we wield it just the same."

Santana tasted blood and drew another breath.

"This is why, in spite of all your might and your army, we still stand together on this battlefield."

"There *is* no Magic Circle!" Cynoc roared.

As if to prove his point, he swung his armored foot into Santana's side. The snapping of ribs echoed in the shell.

"Your death will be proof enough of that."

Lying limp on the ground, Santana's vision was all but gone. His ears rang like cymbals. On the edge of unconsciousness, he moved his focus away from the pain coursing through his body.

His mind replayed a scene from the previous night, when Tinkana came to his chamber. He recalled an exquisite pressure as she straddled him. Her hands, which felt like polished marble, slid over his chest. A tear below her eye grew full and wide, then dropped onto his cheek. She cajoled him to keep at the ready the same scrap of a scroll he now clutched but could not see.

That evening, he experienced an exceptional slumber while the Fairie Queen whispered into his ear, over and over, the scroll's enchanted words. In his mind's eye, Santana could see the calligraphic letters written on the parchment. He began to say them aloud.

"What is this? Your last words are Draconic gibberish? Do you really believe the thinned blood of dragons flows through you?"

Santana continued the incantation.

Cynoc Coldheart raised the point of his sword over Santana's heart.

"I will not pity you, nor even pay the courtesy of despising you. I will only fulfill my promise to extinguish you."

Before the blade impaled him, Santana mouthed a final word, puckered his lips, and blew a kiss into the air.

An explosion of pure hellfire shook the world like an earthquake. For the instant that it lasted, the magic shell turned opaque. As white as a pearl.

DEVON

"And then?" Maya said. "What happened next?"

Devon was confident of his description but uncertain of its consequences. Would Santana's magical fire beetle shell be able to contain the entire physical force of the Cuauhtémoc scroll? Even if it did, would there still be a destructive sonic blast? A blinding flash? Devon turned away from the table and coughed into his elbow.

The main doors of the conference hall flew open and banged against the walls. A woman about Devon's height and age staggered toward their table. Her name tag, "Isabel Candela, Rules Committee Chair," swung across a peasant blouse, which draped over a billowing skirt.

"*Dios mío, me duele tanto,*" Isabel whimpered.

Her vacant stare was returned by all but Lance, who turned slightly to his side. When Isabel got within three feet of him, she held her hands over her face and convulsed.

Acting with reflexive speed he didn't know he had, Devon grabbed Lance and pulled him out of his chair. As he did so, Devon stepped on Lance's robe. Lance spun around, and Devon fell until he grabbed the edge of the table to steady himself. It was in that slumped over position that a stream of warm vomitus struck him, followed by Isabel's collapsing body.

Gigi yipped in alarm. She tried to squirm out of Carlos' lap, but he picked up the tiny dog and raised her high, a firefighter lifting a child above the flood.

Devon gasped and choked at the foul smell of Isabel's sickness, but he managed to extricate himself. He got Isabel into a sitting position on the floor. Their table was a mess. Gone was the tableaux of carefully arranged figurines. Alan's map would clean up easily enough, but many of their papers, excepting plastic-sleeved character sheets, would have permanent yellow stains.

"This lady appears ill," Devon said.

"*De veras?*" Carlos said.

With his foot, he slid Gigi's crate far away from dripping ooze coming off the table. He bent over and slipped the dog back into her mobile home.

"Safer for you inside," he whispered.

Lance found Devon's empty seat and took it for himself. Devon picked up Lance's overturned chair and did likewise.

Isabel writhed and moaned.

"Quite frankly," Devon said, "I am not feeling so well, either."

"What's going on?" Lance said.

"More sick people," Brie said. "I swear to you, the kids watching that movie looked just like this. We've got a situation here."

Devon surveyed the ballroom and reckoned perhaps half of the forty Dungeon Lords teams were still present. Almost every player had their heads on their tables, slumbering in their chairs. It was as if a powerful wizard had cast a sleep spell. Devon didn't see the Wiccan Convent, then he remembered that the group had left when the judges quit for the night.

Maya approached with the paper towels they'd been using to wipe at their oilskin wherever the makeshift walls of Mythopolis had crumbled. On one edge of the map, a pencil lay atop a brown pool of ink. A splash of water had absorbed a few of the dry erase marks Devon had made to render city gates.

"Dad, you need to go home," Maya said. "Get yourself cleaned up. Go to sleep. Alan will be here in the morning. I can get someone to cover the booth tomorrow. Maybe we can get you a cab?"

"Agreed," Devon said weakly. "Are you staying here?"

Brie squatted beside Maya.

"Tara said they were spending the night in the Women's Space. She and Patrizia invited us to join them."

"That's the plan."

Maya's expression brightened. She picked up her overnight bag.

"Before we call it a night," Brie said, "we should pick up this mess."

Lance scanned the table with his hands and retrieved one of his braille Dungeon Lords books. He scooped up dice, including his talking twenty-sided, and put them in his robe's wide pockets. Feeling about for his mechanical pencil, he flinched when he reached the pool where a water bottle had spilled.

Lance wiped a moist hand on his pants and shook his head.

"Yours truly is not volunteering for cleanup duty. I'm not touching that table until we get a night janitor down here."

"That's a good idea."

Carlos sized up Isabel.

"Let's get a custodian and some hotel staff. These people who've gotten sick, they need to go home. Or straight to a doctor."

Isabel tried to stand but failed. She clutched her side.

"Earlier this evening," she said, "we had parents pick up a pair of *niños* who were running fevers. I saw more like them tonight and went to call an *ambuláncia*, but I couldn't. The hotel *teléfonos* have no dial tone. *La puerta* at the top of the stairs is jammed. I banged, but nobody came."

Devon expected to see a skeptical expression on Carlos' face. A frown and furrowed brow suggested otherwise.

"We'll double check the doors and phones," Carlos said. "If she's right, we may be stuck here until we can summon help, or until Jen and the other hotel staff discover the problem. Meanwhile, we're not splitting up. Agreed?"

RANDALL

"Here we go!" Simon shouted to the fourteen people gathered in a corner of the frigid LAN room. He poked his head over Randall's right shoulder and looked at his screen.

"I wish Peter were here to see this. Where'd he go?"

An angry voice on the other side of Randall said, "He wimped out like he always does. He's sleeping in the ballroom with the others."

"Well, screw him," Simon said. "How many j-holes are left in the tourney, Randall?"

"Only one, besides Boldhearts. I'm going down right now to finish him off."

Randall clicked his mouse. For the first time since first logging on, Boldhearts leapt into the throat of the volcano and landed on the First Plane of Hell.

Simon pushed back against the throng of onlookers and made a sound between a cluck and a cough.

"Give him some frocking room. Boldhearts is unstoppable, man. He's a killing machine."

Killing. The word gave Randall a warm sense of satisfaction. Overnight, his swordsman had become renowned in the WOK. There probably wasn't a registered player in the Stairway tournament who didn't know his name.

On Randall's screen, Boldhearts traversed the First Plane and quickly found the only other living soul in the Stairway tournament, a badly wounded spellweaver dressed in a red robe. The words "Who's that?" appeared above the stranger's head.

"Boldhearts," Randall typed.

"You look like a fire-nymph."

"I'm not a fire-nymph. That's an illusion. You're still charmed."

"No doubt. How come you're alive?"

"By the will of the Gods."

"Why?"

"In a moment, you can ask them yourself."

Boldhearts thrust his sword through the robed figure, who collapsed and faded from the screen.

Simon led a cheer from the thin crowd in the LAN room.

"Awesome! You hear that? 'Ask them yourself!'"

Everyone in the LAN room joined Simon in congratulating Randall, who gave them glory-by-association. One of their own had just won the Stairway tourney.

Randall basked in the adoration of his fans, who had a greater role to play that they understood only dimly. They were now shock troops in his meta-game. Their principal deployment was drawing near.

The victory conditions Randall had set for himself were threefold, and he'd met the first two. The WOK's worldwide devotees were now humiliated, hopefully in a way that would ultimately ruin Devon Washington's reputation, or bankrupt him via lawsuits. Check.

Randall also had disrupted Middle Mirth and its puerile games. If all went well, the convention would be cancelled before dawn broke on its third and final day. Check.

All that remained on the agenda was a more personal matter. To ensure the defeat of Alan's group in their Dungeon Lords contest, Randall had badgered a handful of competent rivals into joining the competition. That was going well enough, but Randall was an honorable sportsman. As his plans had taken shape, he'd given himself a challenge more worthy of his strategic prowess.

Success required not merely defeat but the literal—and possibly permanent—enfeeblement of Alan, Carlos, and those who stood with them. In all likelihood, his enemies were only now realizing that whatever evil they'd been battling in the Mythos was trivial compared to the real danger they faced here, tonight.

Randall whispered to Simon, "Did you check the phones?"

"Don't worry, they're dead. Before he bailed, Peter and I did just like you said. The jacks snapped right off."

"And they're still in the ballroom playing Dungeon Lords?"

"Last I checked."

"Then the time has come to tell the others about our little prank."

"We'll give them a good scare, won't we?"

"Epic horror."

"Righteous!"

In his excitement, Simon jumped an inch off the ground, then hurried about the LAN room, coughing all the while.

Randall got up from his chair slowly. Though he felt exhilarated, his body was sluggish and sore. He was glad he'd already carried out his part of the scheme—the details of which he'd shared with not even his lieutenants.

While Peter and Simon had disabled the land lines, Randall had carried four sticks of epoxy to the top of the basement stairs. After mixing together the green and white Magic Bond, he'd jammed a long putty-snake into the gap between the stairway door and its frame. The putty had hardened by now and would only yield if slammed with a battering ram from the other side. With equal ease, he'd done the same to the ballroom's emergency exit, which none had used or noticed all weekend.

Even if Peter, Simon, or one of the others discovered the exit doors were sealed, they'd assume it was part of the griefing. As Simon put it, Randall's scheme would "turn out the lights and give everyone a scare." They were giving this year's Middle Mirth a memorable bit of mischief, an elaborate practical joke.

But Randall was no jokester. He wasn't doing this for laughs. By placing his faith in the gentle hands of fate, Randall had discovered and pursued a far more compelling endgame strategy.

The design was pure evil.
Its name was Toxic Warfare.

ALAN

Alan's father sat on the edge of his son's bed. He held open the *Dungeon Lords Scenario Builder* and read it as a bedtime story.

"This is the part you never let me get to, Alan—the part where you join the action and save the day."

"That's not how I wrote it, Dad. Let me tell the story."

"Trust me, you're in here."

"They'll have more fun if I hang back. Let me have it."

John turned the book away from Alan's outstretched hand and flipped ahead several chapters.

"They need you to do more tonight, one of them especially."

"Where does it say that? Show me!"

As John handed the book to Alan, a thunderclap shook the window.

Dizzy and disoriented, Alan was surprised to find himself in bed. He sat up straight. To shake himself loose from the dream, he tried to recall the evening's events.

He drove his mother home from the hospital in a heavy rain. The air was humid, and his clothes were soaked with sweat by the time they got home. He tried to look after his mother, but she worried that he had a fever and urged him to sleep before returning to the convention.

Alan looked to the clock radio beside his bed. It wasn't even 3 AM. He checked his phone for texts. None.

The urge to pee became paramount. Alan pulled himself out of bed and dashed into the hall bathroom. After relieving himself, he washed his hands. In the mirrored door of the medicine cabinet, he stared at the mottled red rash on his face. He opened the cabinet and retrieved hydrocortisone ointment.

"You are a sick puppy," Alan said as he worked the salve into his skin.

It occurred to him that his cheeks looked like Randall's did at the McDonald's. Was it a contagious condition? The thought of that beast lumbering about, touching everything and everyone at Middle Mirth, made Alan shudder.

He recalled Randall's menacing expression when he threw the burger bomb. It was eerie the way he laughed so easily, even when Carlos challenged him. Though in terrible physical condition and in a perilous situation, Randall seemed at ease— even joyful, as though everything was going his way.

By relaxing his mind, Alan tried to get inside Randall's. Weighing potential explanations for Randall's disturbing behavior, he found himself thinking about Cynoc Coldheart. The connection wasn't purely theoretical. After all, Alan suspected he'd unconsciously created the villain as a kind of Mythos tribute.

Alan took a deep breath.

"What would Cynoc Coldheart do?"

In a flash, he got an answer.

His next thought, *crap*.

CARLOS

Carlos carried Isabel to the stage and laid her down. She had tied her purple sash around her head. When Carlos touched it, she moaned.

"My skin is on fire," she said. "*No me toque, por favor.*"

Carlos pulled back his hand. Isabel's neck was blistered and shedding dry, almond slices of skin. Her eyes were bloodshot.

"How long have you had this rash?"

"Only today. It itched this morning. Now it stings."

Carlos looked at the other prone bodies on the stage. There was Peter from the LAN room, trying to sleep. Beside him lay Devon, who announced he would "rest his eyes for a spell." A dozen others in similar condition on makeshift beds of towels and blankets. Though fatigued, every one of them had enough energy to moan and twist about, likely finding it impossible to get comfortable with the bright red sores on their skin.

"What's the status report, doc?"

Lance's voice was cheerful, but Carlos sensed anxiety beneath it. His face looked no less worried than that of Maya or Brie, and he expanded and collapsed his cane every few seconds.

"I don't know," Carlos said, "but that woman—Isabel? I'd swear she has chickenpox, or something like it. Whatever it is, it's ridiculously contagious."

"More so if you didn't have it as a kid?" Brie asked.

Carlos nodded and considered his own medical history.

"I know 'cuz I've had it already," Brie added. "Lance gave it to me when I was little."

"I've had it," Maya said.

"But not *me*," said a distorted electronic voice. "Not until now, it seems."

Carlos turned toward the flat-screen monitors on the wall, which seemed to have been pointed into a dark corner of the

LAN room. The screens now showed a close-up image of Randall, who stood amidst a clutch of swaying men and boys, each with a WOK lanyard hanging about his neck.

Randall's skin appeared almost sky blue, with red splotches running down his cheeks and neck. A Mötley Crüe shirt rode high enough to expose his belly, which looked as though it had been run over by a tractor tire.

"*Jesucristo*," Carlos said as he crossed himself. "Can you hear me, Randall?"

"We turned the mics back on. I'm not deaf."

"You really do have chickenpox, my friend. Catching the virus at your age is very dangerous. We've got to get you out of here."

Randall shook his head.

"Alan hid this frocking disease from me when he had it. Now that I've got it, I can't wait to give it back."

"You won't get that chance tonight, *hombre*. The lucky bastard went home hours ago."

"What? How did he get out of—I mean, when did he—"

Randall rolled his tongue over swollen lips.

"No matter, I will take a special pleasure in tormenting you, Carlos the Betrayer. Carlos the Usurper. I'll enjoy poisoning you and each of those little leeches clinging to you."

"Whatever it is you're ranting about, you need to calm down, *cabrón*. Don't go anywhere until we get someone to you. You need medical attention, but something's jammed up the basement door. And the phones are out of service."

Randall chortled. His entourage laughed with him until they became a chorus of coughs.

"Oh, you needn't worry on my account. I'm not the helpless swordsman you left to die. You are the one in peril this time. This is your tomb, not mine."

Randall pointed back toward his PC.

"I've already finished one killing spree. Not a frocking soul stirs within the WOK, thanks to me. Alan kicked Boldheart into the grave, then you and Lance buried him alive. But he is risen! Now he's coming for you!"

"You're delirious," Carlos said. "This isn't Dungeon Lords or World of Karnage. Don't make this into a game. What you have—what is spreading down here—could really hurt people, including you. You've got computers in there. We can Skype the hotel's 800 number."

Randall raised his middle finger at the webcam. The back of Randall's hand was beet red.

"Look at yourself, *pendejo*. You might be coughing up blood."

Devon wiped his mouth, and a red streak ran down his face. His voice rose weakly from the stage.

"I fear I share that same symptom, and I already had the pox as a child."

"I'm at a loss," Carlos confessed. "I've seen some spooky viruses north and south of the border. Maybe this is something nastier than Grade A chickenpox. I can't think of a more hospitable setting for a mutation to spread than this *chingada* petri dish of a basement."

"Bottom line?" Maya said with a snort. "This ain't good."

"No," Randall said, "that's where you're wrong. Providence offered me this infection. I brought it here as a gift. I'm so generous that I'm giving it to all you j-holes."

The small crowd behind Randall looked nervous and confused, but they didn't miss their cue to laugh—and cough—behind their leader.

Lifting himself unsteadily, Devon pointed at the wall monitors.

"Look at that. See the metal door at the back of their room?"

"Damn if that doesn't look like a service elevator," Maya said. "Didn't Jen say something about it during orientation?"

"Might require a key," Brie said.

"Perhaps, or perhaps not," Devon said as he stepped off the

stage. "I shall go find out."

Carlos reached for him.

"No, you're weak. You've got to rest."

"I'm already infected. We've got to do something."

Devon broke into a wobbling run. As he crossed the ballroom, he stumbled over Gigi's crate, jarring open its door. He picked himself up and headed out the exit, while Gigi ran wild in the ballroom.

"Does chickenpox make people crazy?" Maya said.

"Not usually, but like I said, we're witnesses to something new."

"Dad was already a mutant, but now? He's gone rogue."

RANDALL

From the look of things, Randall's defenses would get an early test from the mad game store owner.

"To arms!" Randall cried. "The assault on LAN castle begins."

The twenty or more remaining LAN loyalists let up a cheer, but it lacked the oomph that Randall had imagined when he'd designed this scenario. These were his orcs more in body than spirit. They had the requisite disfigurement in the form of blemishes, which had opened into sores on those who couldn't quiet their itchy fingers. Yet they looked listless, more tired than hungry for battle.

But ready or not, war was coming to them, or at least their first taste of it.

"Assume the V-wing formation," Randall said.

The LAN army obliged and spread into two lines that opened wide at the doorway, then joined at the back of the room. When Devon entered, he ran directly into the jaws of the enemy. He showed the spirit Randall's legion lacked. Though outnumbered twenty-to-one, he slipped through their grasping hands and ducked their swinging broomsticks to slide all the way to the elevator door. He reached up and punched at the control panel.

The effort was futile. Only a maintenance key would open that door. Unlike every fantasy landscape Devon had ever programmed and Randall had ever traversed, the Carrion Suites dungeon lacked a hidden key for looters to find. There was no wandering janitor at this late hour, no hidden compartment that held an artifact the adventurers required.

"Put him in the pen," Randall instructed.

Grunts acknowledged the command. Soon, Devon was prone in the back corner of the LAN room, exhausted and caged by a precarious box fashioned from folding tables.

Randall clasped his hands behind his back like a confident

field marshal and approached Devon. What he found was not a quivering captive, but what looked like a dying man. Devon rolled over and, face down on the concrete floor, dry heaved with five sickening convulsions.

The LAN lackeys standing nearby had to turn away. Even Randall felt queasy at the display.

"Thanks for volunteering to be my first captive," Randall said.

Devon grunted. Banter with the captive felt obligatory, but perhaps it would not be possible.

"I may be your enemy tonight," Randall said, "but I'm not really the villain here, am I?"

The idle comment drew a confused stare from Simon, who'd assumed the role of chief lieutenant after Peter's desertion. Even Simon was not privy to the full scope of Randall's plan, but unquestioned genius in the WOK had earned an unconditional trust on this battlefield.

If all went as scripted, this wouldn't be a battle so much as a slaughter. Randall could see the checkmate approaching in the game that only he was playing consciously at the convention. The demoralized souls who remained sealed in the Middle Mirth dungeon were now absorbing a more physical blow from Randall's virulent illness.

On the verge of destroying the gaming world where he'd once lived, Randall saw for the first time that the exit from Alan's group was only the most recent expulsion he'd suffered. He'd endured his parents' theology long enough to learn its arcane rules, yet in the end, their pastor had forbidden his attendance at church and had advised that his parents push him out of their own home. This they had done.

Despite such indignities, he couldn't make a clean break from his family, God, or games. His curses still came out distorted, lest he offend some supernatural authority. Even now, as he took a torch to the unprotected nest of the San Diego gaming community, he did so in the spirit of—what else?—a game.

"Don't make this into a game," an oblivious Carlos had warned him. Failure to grasp their situation made them easy prey, but for the same reason, Randall worried about Alan's absence. That was the one move Randall hadn't anticipated. Alan's uncanny intuition might have prompted his escape, even if he hadn't conceptualized it as such. Randall couldn't account for why the most passionate player in this whole stink of gamers was missing.

Whether served hot or cold, revenge was unsatisfying if the dinner table held an empty seat.

Maybe Alan would return for the battle's epilogue. He'd cry over the disfigured friends he'd left behind. Maybe the scabs on Lance, Carlos, and their wenches would never heal, and Alan would never forgive himself for abandoning them. Their scars would remind him how Randall had trapped and branded the entire herd, for life.

But what if this virus was something worse? Carlos said it could be a mutation. That was just a clever countermove—a plea to call off the biological attack. It almost worked. When Carlos said the word "dangerous," it caused gasps in the LAN room. Randall had to allay his minions' fears. He reminded them that what they spread through the underworld of the Carrion Inn and Suites was just a flu. It was a mean trick, nothing more.

Surveying the room, Randall worried that his illness might have caused excessive collateral damage. His soldiers sat slumped over in their chairs, foreheads resting on the cool surface of folding tables. The LAN room looked like nap time at nursery school more than an operational barracks.

Still, he dared not wake them. They had to conserve what strength remained. Sooner than not, they would march on the enemy. Randall's ensuing victory would become, throughout the gaming world, legendary.

CARLOS

The screens behind the stage told Carlos all he needed to know. Devon had run into the LAN and straight for the elevator. He'd punched its control panel to no visible result. Moments later, Randall's horde had enveloped the poor soul and pulled him out of view.

Maya hopped down to the floor.

"That's does it. Let's go."

A "crack" echoed across the ballroom when Lance whacked his cane on the stage. If he did so out of frustration, his voice didn't let it show.

"Listen up. Job one, we've got to keep Randall where he is. Job two, if he is truly bent on spreading whatever he has, we've got to keep everyone else away from him."

Brie nodded.

"We can stack up the sicklies by the stage, then direct the others to the opposite end of the ballroom."

Randall's voice crackled again on the monitor.

"You can't stop me if you can't find me." He turned to look off-camera. "Simon, hit the circuit breaker."

Every screen went dark, then the ballroom became midnight black. Two seconds later, a faint chain of fluorescent lights became visible along the top edges of the walls. It was only enough to show the crudest outlines of shapes—bodies, tables, little else.

"Emergency lights," Brie said. "They've got them at Grossmont for when the power goes out."

Maya reached into her pocket.

"Get your cell phones out."

"They don't work down here," Lance said.

"No, for the light."

Maya's phone gave off a soft glow that lit her face like a camp counselor telling a ghost story.

"Right!" Brie said. "Call me a dork, but I've got a resinous wood torch app on mine. No kidding."

In a few clicks, Brie held in her hand the dancing image of a flame.

"Cute," Maya said, "but seriously, use a flashlight app if you've got one—whatever's brightest. We've got to get to Dad and anyone else Randall's infected. Remember what Carlos said. This isn't Dungeon Lords anymore."

"I don't know," Brie said. "This could be another monastery or wizard's tower full of traps and villains. We know this story. We can do this."

Carlos put a hand on Brie's shoulder.

"Whatever works for you works for me, Hermione."

Under her dim phone light, Maya put one tentative foot in front of the other and stepped off the stage.

"Follow me."

The clicking of Lance's cane on the cement floor signaled his rapid movement across the ballroom, well ahead of his comrades and nearly out of sight.

"Lights or not, some of us already know the way out. The blind shall lead."

Maya, Carlos, and Brie, fell in behind Lance and headed into the hallway. The first door they came to bore a sign that read, "Movie Room."

Brie stepped forward.

"Brace yourselves. The stink's gonna be unbelievable in there."

Even before Brie pulled the door open, Carlos recognized the odor she'd described earlier—an olfactory signal of unventilated sickness. He recalled a global health professor who, on the first day of class, explained that human brains were hardwired for repulsion against that smell. Evolution had taught us to retreat from the places where doctors most need to go.

"Let me take a look," Carlos said.

He entered the room and saw firsthand what Brie had described. Slouched over chairs or prone on the floor lay twenty or more bodies. Young and old, they were dressed like elves and hobbits for a Tolkien styled *Rocky Horror Picture Show.*

Carlos knelt beside one prone teenager and weighed the risks of direct contact. His own wrists had reddened, and his breaths were short and shaky. When Carlos tried to stand back up, he lost his equilibrium. The music in the room swelled while the movie projected on the wall showed Frodo and Sam grappling with Gollum inside Mount Doom.

"Hang in there, little buddies," Carlos said to the image. "You've still got to make it through about four more endings in that story."

Refocusing on the task at hand, Carlos roused a pair of boys dressed like Pippin and Merry. They had what looked like dog hair glued to the tops of their bare feet. The boys rose wearily.

"Up we go."

Carlos took Pippin by the hand, and Merry followed.

"Back to the Shire with the lot of you."

* * *

Maya and Brie received the first wave of bodies from the Movie Room. They took turns escorting their patients back to what Lance now called—with unparalleled tact—the "mass grave" at the foot of the stage.

As the Movie Room emptied out, Carlos joined Lance, who had his back pressed against the wall as he inched down the corridor and listened for the approach of Randall or his lackeys. When he reached the next door, his hand swam across a large poster-board sign.

Lance turned around and asked, "What's the door say?"

"Judges – Keep Out," Carlos replied.

Lance tried and failed to turn the door's knob.

"There might be people in there still. Are Brie and Maya done evacuating the film fans?"

As if on cue, their two companions approached.

"Judges still in there?" Maya said. "They're probably as sick as anyone. Remember what Isabel looked like."

"Let's get them to the, uh…" Brie paused. "Let's get them to sick bay."

Lance quivered as though cockroaches ran up his legs.

"There will be no genre-mixing in this quest of ours, dear sister. Besides, the term is misleading. It's not as if we're providing the poor bastards any medical treatment."

"Or even the companionship of a holographic doctor," Maya added with a grin.

"Lance is right," Carlos said. "We're running a mortuary down here, not a field hospital."

Brie gasped.

"Just a metaphor," Carlos said. "People aren't dying. They're just ill. Today is *Dia de los Enfermos*."

"Am I catching whatever this is?" Brie said.

"Look at her neck," Maya said. "That stripe is as crimson as your cape."

"Looks dry," Carlos said, "like eczema."

Lance reached out to touch his sister's neck. Caution seemed to trump compassion, as he withdrew his hand.

"Earlier," Brie said, "when we were on the stage talking with Randall through the monitors, you never said whether *you* had chickenpox as a kid."

"Maybe. I don't remember. Either way, looks like anyone can catch it."

"Yeah, but Randall looks ten times worse than anyone else. You said it was probably more dangerous for—"

"What would you do with me at this point? Take me to sick bay?"

Maya cleared her throat and inspected the door to the Judges

Room.

"Let's see how they're doing in there. It's a simple knob-lock. Who's got something thinner than a credit card?"

Carlos handed Maya a UCSD Library ID from his wallet. She slid it into the crack between door and frame, gave it a quick downward flick, and the door drifted open an inch.

"Never question the power of libraries," Maya said.

Even with the door open a crack, foul air rushed out of the room.

Maya pinched her nose and stepped inside, the others trailing behind her. Both the room and its occupants were in disarray. Seven sweaty men and women walked about aimlessly, sometimes tripping over each other and knocking books and plastic cups to the floor.

Maya raised her cell phone and said, "Hello?"

A female judge snapped her head around to look at her. Through teeth thick with saliva, the judge hissed, "Get out! All players must get out!"

The other judges and convention staff in the room converged on Maya.

One spat out, "We will penalize you. What's your group name?"

Lance waved his cane in front of himself like a weapon.

"Hold!" he shouted, while pulling Maya back. "You're sick. We're trying to help."

A deathly pale Jeff Jacobson swatted at Maya and moaned, "We don't need your help."

Before Jacobson could manage another swing, the clicks of little dog claws announced the arrival of Gigi, who leapt through the air like a supercharged purse puppy. She twisted her torso mid-flight, possibly aiming for Jacobson's outstretched arm. That target being too high, she settled for a pant leg. Jacobson shook himself but couldn't escape the jaws of Cheese Doodle. She growled at the lowest frequency her vocal tract could muster, and the judges backed away, frightened beyond reason.

Somewhere behind him, Carlos heard Brie cry out.

"Let go of me!"

A tall Middle Mirth staffer, bent forward like a praying mantis, ran his fingers through Brie's loose green hair.

"Pretty green straw," he said. "Give it to us."

Lance wheeled about and shouted.

"Get your damn dirty hands off my sister's head!"

Turning his torso slightly to the right, Lance swung his cane over his head and down on the hands clasping Brie. The crack of the cane's impact caused the cowering judges to press themselves against the back wall.

Lance raised his cane like a musketeer.

"None shall pester the Padre Princess but me!"

Brie gave Lance a quick squeeze.

"Nice cane work, brother. Time to retreat."

With Gigi bringing up the rear, the group scooted back out of the Judges Room.

"This is bad," Carlos said. "This virus going around is making people flat-out nuts. That's symptomatic of encephalitis or meningitis. Those normally take longer to set in."

"What's the cure?" Lance asked.

"This thing's spreading so fast, there's no guarantee it'll be treatable if we don't get people out of here quickly. We can leave the judges where they are. Those back in the ballroom are already resting, and—"

"Oh, no!" Brie cried. "The Women's Space! We've got to rescue the Wiccans!"

Brie held out her cell phone to illuminate the hallway. With Lance by her side, they led the way to the next door. Beside it hung a poster featuring a life-size image of the warrior princess Xena, sword extended forward. Inside the room, shouts and moans could be heard over up-tempo Celtic fiddle music.

"Let Maya and me go in first," Brie said. "Stay close."

Maya nodded and pushed on the door. As it swung open, a flying hairbrush hit her shoulder.

Women dressed in billowing print dresses hopped and spun madly. Some wore fabric butterfly wings, most of which were torn and hanging loosely off their backs. Interspersed among the dancers were staggering men, WOK badges dangling from blistered necks.

Brie motioned for the others to follow her into the room. While she and Maya tried to calm the women, Lance and Carlos split up and traced the walls, each whispering, "Tara? Valerie?"

The plan fell apart quickly as the LAN zombies made it impossible to pull the women away without getting grabbed — or nearly bitten, in one instance. After a minute of parrying the intruders, Brie backed herself up against an oak bookcase on the far wall of the Women's Space, away from the chaos.

"I found them!" Carlos shouted over the din. "They're over — Gigi, no!"

The little dog had found her way inside. She made a string of friendly, excited barks in sync with the beat of the Celtic rhythm. When a LAN dancer picked her up, Gigi's barks turned to yelps.

Carlos felt the situation spinning out of control but couldn't think clearly. He didn't want to leave Tara's side.

"Somebody, please, do something!"

Brie grabbed ahold of the bookcase beside her. She jerked it forward, and it crashed to the ground with a thunderclap.

"Stop!"

Nobody moved.

"Look at yourselves," Brie said. "You're sick — maybe every one of you. We're going to get you out of here, but you need to calm down."

A man from the LAN room stood up, but Brie pointed at him and yelled.

"Sit down! You need to rest."

He complied. The room remained quiet while Brie and her

companions extracted Tara, Valerie, and Patrizia. Once they were back in the hallway, Carlos pulled Brie aside.

"Was that the Whomping Willow spell?"

Brie laughed.

"I suppose it was."

* * *

"You okay?" Carlos asked Tara.

Tara dusted herself off.

"We lost Quinn. She went to watch the movie hours ago, before things got crazy."

"I think Brie found her earlier," Carlos said. "Put her back in the graveyard."

Tara covered her mouth. Before she could speak, Brie interjected.

"It's not really a graveyard. Not really a sick bay either. It's just—she'll be okay."

"We've secured all the rooms but one," Lance said. "Now it's time to find a way into that elevator at the back of the LAN room."

"Which means," Carlos said, "we'll have to get past Randall and his lackeys."

"Randall's the freak from McDonald's?" Valerie said. "He came in the Women's Space a few hours ago. Looked like a demon. Scared the crap out of us. He scratched at himself and touched everyone like he was spreading cooties at recess."

"Last we saw," Carlos said, "he was back in the LAN. That's where we're headed. If you're up for it, we could use some help."

Tara, Valerie, and Patrizia huddled, then agreed to join the cause.

Walking close together, the group turned down the hallway toward the LAN room. They had advanced only a few feet when Carlos stopped and held his phone close to a door. Its metal sign read, "Custodial Closet."

Carlos shook the door knob

"Locked."

Maya swiped his library card once again, but it could only push back the latch part way.

"It's loose, but it's catching on the strike plate. I don't think I can jimmy it."

"Allow me," Tara said impatiently.

She slid the card and rattled the knob until the door opened, then stepped into the tiny closet. Looking the room over, she pulled out anything that appeared useful. She handed a push broom to Maya, paint buckets to Brie, Valerie, and Patrizia. Lance received a metal trash can lid, which he hefted in his hand before fashioning it into a shield.

She then motioned for Carlos. When he squeezed beside her in the cramped space, she made a show of giving him a large halogen light. Tara held onto one last item, a thin box of pilot-light matches.

"What are those for?" Carlos asked.

Tara pointed to the hall.

"There are smoke detectors and sprinklers all along the ceiling. Unlike everything else down here, they probably work. If we could reach high enough, we could use these matches to set them off—"

Carlos shook his head.

"No, I don't think—"

"Listen to me."

Tara held Carlos' face in her hands.

"Let's activate the sprinklers right now. That'll trigger the fire alarms and get us out of here."

Carlos snatched the matches from Tara and jammed them into the back pocket of his pants.

"The water would be like ice. Plus the shriek of those alarms? Someone—hell, nearly everyone down here could go into shock."

Tara frowned.

"You really think so? This can't be that serious."

"Actually, it might be, especially for those who've never had chickenpox."

"I don't think so," Tara said. "I never got it, and I'm—"

Tara turned away and coughed. She wiped her mouth on her sleeve, which bore a red smear.

"I'm basically fine."

Carlos pulled his hands away from Tara and backed out of the closet.

"We've got to get you out of here. We've got to get everyone out of here—alive."

"Then let's use the matches."

Tara reached for Carlos again.

He stepped back.

"Can't you see what's happening? This virus is blooming not only on our skin but in our heads. Everyone's going loopy, myself included. You're right to want to do something. Maybe, if someone could get to the elevator..."

In that moment, Carlos knew what he had to do. He ran two fingers down the scar on the back of his neck. He felt some responsibility for their predicament, having failed over the past decade to inspire any appreciable maturation in Randall. By way of atonement, he would lead the charge against his former friend and accept the greatest risk of further exposure.

"Quiet," Lance said. "I hear something. Down the hall, coming toward us."

Shuffling and hacking could be heard around a bend in the corridor.

"It's Randall's army of diseased goons," Carlos said. "We don't have time for them."

Carlos turned toward Brie.

"Try to distract them, then get Tara out of here. She's never had the pox."

ALAN

"But I tried the basement door," Alan said to the petite desk clerk. "It's locked. So's the auxiliary exit."

The clerk, who wore the same red suit as the rest of the hotel's front-line employees, crossed her arms.

"Neither of those doors lock, sir."

"Well, then they're jammed, apparently. Try calling the extension in the downstairs ballroom."

"I don't know the extension."

"What?"

"The basement doesn't get much use. It's not very attractive."

Alan felt the clerk's eyes on him and sensed her negative assessment of his utility and appeal. The first clean clothes he'd found in his dresser—a white undershirt, cut-off shorts, and white canvas sneakers—were soaked from running across the hotel parking lot in pouring rain. Thin hair stuck to his head as though penciled onto his scalp.

"Can you call Jen, then? She's the convention's hotel liaison."

"In the middle of the night? I'm the only reception clerk here. Plus, I heard Jen's sick and might not come back this morning."

Alan leaned closer and read the clerk's nameplate.

"Kimberly, I would like you to find that basement extension number and let me call down to it. I can wait."

With a dramatic sigh, Kimberly reached under the counter and lifted a black binder. She idly flipped through its pages, then lifted her phone and pressed four numbers. Handing it to Alan, she said a curt, "Here."

Alan held the receiver tight against his ear. The phone rang once, twice, three times.

"They're not answering."

"Maybe because nobody's down there. Everyone's asleep."

"This isn't an early-to-bed crowd. Most don't even have

rooms booked. Trust me, they're down there."

"Well, why don't you just go open the door and—"

Kimberly put a finger to her lips.

"Oh, right."

Alan handed Kimberly the phone, then pulled it back.

"You might want to disinfect this thing before using it again. I think I've caught something."

"Thanks for the heads-up."

From an empty cookie plate on the counter, Kimberly retrieved a napkin. She squirted hand gel onto it then took the receiver and wiped it down. Her expression softened.

"Tell you what. Let me get the night janitor."

She walked a few feet to the next reception station.

"On this other phone."

While Kimberly dialed and spoke into the phone, Alan considered the new evidence at hand. When he asked himself what could account for the dysfunctional doors and phones, none of the scenarios his mind offered were attractive.

Kimberly hung up and returned to her station.

"J. R. said he'll be down in a few minutes."

"In the meantime," Alan said, "you should call an ambulance. Or the police."

"Wait, why? Which one?"

"Both."

Alan wiped rainwater off his brow.

"And for good measure, throw in the fire department. Whoever can get here first."

CARLOS

When it flashed "Power Saver Mode" and shut down, Carlos pocketed his phone and turned on his flashlight. Pointing it forward, he could see nine or ten diseased WOK players blocking the last section of hallway before the LAN room. To draw their attention, Brie and the Wiccan Convent began singing and banging on their buckets.

The racket had its intended effect, and Carlos shouted, "Forward!"

Cane and push broom raised high, Lance and Maya followed Carlos as he charged down the hall. The trio raced between bewildered columns of WOK players, but one caught hold of Lance's leg, while another pair grasped the long handle of Maya's push broom.

Carlos made it through the open doorway. When he entered the LAN room, however, two sets of hands shoved him from behind. He lost his grip on the flashlight. It skidded to the far wall, where it shot a bright beam up to the ceiling.

"Lance?" Carlos called. "Maya?"

The reply—"On our way!"—came from a distance.

"Your friends," said a guttural voice at the back of the room, "might be delayed."

The halogen's beam was back-lighting Randall, who held a cell phone close to his chest to give his chin a pink glow. Randall laughed, and his cheeks danced like flames in the ghostly light. The rest of the room was so dark that Carlos couldn't make out what lay between him and Randall. When he tried to step forward, he tripped over an upturned chair and had to catch himself.

"After all you've taken from me, it's generous of me to offer you this disease."

"I don't want any trouble, Randall. I never wanted to fight

419

with you."

"Bullship! You waltzed into our lives and stole Alan's friendship. Like a sorcerer, you possessed him. Then turned him against me."

Carlos' steps felt unsteady. For a moment, he found it hard to breathe. He leaned against the edge of a table for support. Maybe ten feet from Randall, he felt his heart slowing.

"I didn't ask to become part of your world. I never meant to push Alan, Lance, or anyone away from you. You did that."

"Alan was too naïve. I should have protected him from you."

"We should have saved you from yourself. Now all I can do is get you out of here. Get you to a hospital."

Randall's palm appeared to hold something that glistened, as wet and scaly as a fish head. Carlos remembered that evening's incident at McDonald's and guessed it was a snowball of accumulated mucus mixed with loose skin. Randall moved slowly toward Carlos' table. He cupped his hand and reached forward, then turned off his phone's light.

"You're the one going back to the hospital," Randall said. "Let's see how quickly I can turn your world upside down."

Before Randall could launch his attack, Lance burst through the doorway, cane held high. The LAN guards swung at him but clanged their fists on Lance's metal trash can lid. Lifting his Ray-Bans like a visor, Lance scanned the room for any contrasts sharp enough for his eyes to detect. Randall stood, poised to strike, in front of the bright light on the far wall. With his free hand, Lance dug into the side pocket of his robes and pulled out a handful of dice. Taking quick but careful aim, he hurled the many-sided shrapnel at his back-lit target.

Direct hit.

The shock of the tiny blows threw Randall into a rage. He let out a frustrated scream and pawed at his chest and waist, madly fending off a swarm of bees lest they sting him again. His panicked gestures threw him off balance, and he fell sideways to the floor.

"Sixteen," said a soft female voice.

Randall looked left and right.

"Who is that?"

"Nine."

"What the halberd?"

Carlos heard footsteps down the corridor and squinted to see Maya run wildly into the doorway. She hit her knee against a table leg and spun until she landed on her knees.

"What's happening?" she said. "What can I do?"

"Just buy me a second," Carlos replied. "Take a swing at the talking die!"

Randall rose to his knees and tried to get his bearings. From his pants came that same voice again.

"Ten."

"Ten's good enough with my kick-ass modifiers," Maya said.

She rushed forward and jabbed the flat end of her push broom against Randall, who fell back over. Tumbling forward after her thrust, Maya fell out of view. Carlos heard a loud thump, like a skull on concrete, and was relieved to at least hear Maya groan.

A rapid clickety-clack signaled Gigi's arrival. The Cheese Doodle moved too quickly to see, but the signature sound of her tiny claws headed straight toward Randall. Growls and snaps suggested vicious needle-teeth rending Randall's pants or socks, until a loud smack sent the dog away, yelping in pain.

Carlos felt the sting of that blow as sharply as if it had struck him instead. He could feel his body shutting down, but determination propelled him into action. He recalled Tara's advice and considered it. There were risks to be calculated, but he didn't have time for the math.

Prone on the ground, Randall pulled out from under his hip the talking object he must have recognized. Half drowned in sputum, the white die sang triumphantly, "Twenty!"

Hearing that high, holy number emboldened Carlos. He

crouched low, then jumped high enough to land squarely on the table in front of him. After a quick swipe of one long pilot match against its box, Carlos raised his thin torch until the smoke alarm screamed.

Sprinklers on the ceiling dribbled cold water, then burst open like thunderclouds. As he'd hoped, the control panel by the maintenance elevator lit up instantly. Carlos leaped off the table and planted his feet on the ground. He swung his cape off his shoulders and wrapped it around Randall's squirming upper body. Mustering what strength he had left, Carlos dragged Randall to the elevator.

Carlos reached up and pressed the button on the panel that read "L." The up arrow didn't light. The doors didn't open.

Carlos felt his knees buckle. He struggled to stay upright, then collapsed on top of Randall. Craning his neck, Carlos could see that the indicator above the elevator showed the car remained one floor up from "B." He prayed to his papier-mâché skull, asking Cecelia Bravo Gaudi Lopez for a miracle. For the indicator light to change. For the metal doors to open.

His eyelids felt heavy. Carlos tried to stay alert. He felt the cool rain on his face, the twitching of Randall's body, the ringing of the alarms. Gradually, even these stimuli faded.

A soft fog settled over Carlos' mind. He felt himself slipping away.

ALAN

On the short ride down from the lobby, Alan lost his composure. He tried to release anxiety by punching the elevator car's metal wall. It did him little good, and he snapped rudely at the night janitor, a white-haired old man with a beak nose and initials sewn into his brown jumpsuit.

"How slow is this stupid thing?"

J. R. said nothing. Three seconds later, the doors opened onto the LAN room. It still had the spot-illumination of the halogen pointed at the ceiling. The light revealed little more than the soft rainfall of the sprinklers.

No volume of water, however, could wash the stench from the air. Sealing the doors had kept more than bodies from escaping the hotel basement. A warm cloud of sweat and sickness rushed the open elevator car.

"Lord above," said J.R.

"If only," Alan said.

The janitor switched on his flashlight. It cast a long shadow away from two bodies collapsed four feet in front of the elevator.

"Carlos! Randall?"

Alan knelt down and pulled his two friends apart. He felt Carlos' chest. It rose and fell, but too slowly.

"They okay?" the janitor said.

Alan nodded.

"We'll need help. Fast."

J. R. waved a flashlight beam across the room and out into the hallway. Writhing convention guests littered the floor. Outstretched arms reached toward the light. Pleading moans echoed in every direction.

"It's like a nightmare in here," J. R. said.

He pulled out a ring of keys and unlocked the elevator's control panel.

"You manage this lot. I gotta make sure there's no fire before I reset the sprinklers. Can't touch the circuit breaker till then."

"Fuck that. Just get those EMTs. Now!"

J. R. half-nodded and whispered, "Can do." He backed his way into the elevator and punched its keypad. Metal doors shut with a loud thunk.

Randall twisted around to free his head from Carlos' cape. In a raspy but lyrical voice, he said, "Who is this before me?"

"What in the hell did you..."

"Prince Crandall?"

"We're gonna get everyone out of here, starting with—"

Randall reached up and grabbed Alan's hands in his own.

"All these years, I followed your commands. I fought alongside you."

He tried to draw Alan closer but hadn't the strength.

"Do you not recall?"

"Of course I do. We had many a victory, you and I."

Alan tightened his own grip on Randall's slippery hands. He dragged Randall toward the elevator, set him down, then punched the call button.

Randall grabbed Alan's left hand.

"Was I not loyal? Was I not true?"

"You're delirious."

Alan shook himself free from Randall and stepped toward Carlos' limp body. The elevator door re-opened, and Alan quickly pulled Carlos inside. With a yip, Gigi bounded in after him. The small dog licked Carlos' face.

Keeping one foot in the open door, Alan reached back for Randall and tugged at his shoulders until he lay beside Carlos. Alan punched the "L" button. The elevator rose.

Randall locked eyes with Alan.

"You betrayed me. You left me to die."

"For that, I am sorry."

Alan's heart slowed to a steady beat. He exhaled a lifetime of tension. A ghost flew up from his stomach, through his throat, and out his pursed lips.

He regarded Randall and Carlos, lying beside one another.

"Sometimes, a character has to die to move the story forward."

Epilogue: Two Years Later

ALAN

"Boom!" Lance said. "Did you hear that roll? Critical hit, baby."

Alan sighed with satisfaction to see Maya, Brie, and Lance sitting at his table for the first time in a year. Each looked small, almost like children, sitting in the tall wooden chairs he'd bought from Señor Wences when the restaurant went out of business. The deep brown of the alder-and-leather dining set clashed with his condo's white walls and olive carpet, but he didn't care. Besides, it was his home, so he'd only follow his rules.

"Lancelot recalls the technique Angelou taught him," Alan said. "Drawing strength up from his hips and through his trunk, the priest swings his mace with tremendous force into his adversary's body. The fatal blow hurls the last living Naught into a boulder, whereupon it completes its long-delayed journey to the Underworld."

"Oh yeah!" Lance said.

"Cheers explode from all around him," Alan continued. "Each of the forty acolytes leap upward in unison, billowing their clean white robes and causing the golden skulls on their collars to dance. None wears a smudge of mud or a smear of blood, for they have done nothing on this final purge other than standing at a safe distance and raining hailstorms of stone bullets from enchanted slings."

"I get it," Lance said, "we're overmatched."

"When they found the last known regiment of Naughts," Alan said, "they discovered only twelve crazed hermits, who lived off beetles and bat dung in a remote cave outside Everwinter."

"Gross," Brie said.

"Hold on," Lance said, "I've got something for this. Lancelot leaps onto his chestnut stallion to circle his priests. He holds his mace high and says, 'We have done what the people of Mythopolis sent us to do!' I then do that thing Hermione taught me, where I turn my horse in a full circle to make eye contact with every one of them."

Alan smiled and said, "Their faces glow from the warmth of their leader's approval."

"As they should," Lance said. "Lancelot holsters his mace and points a mailed finger skyward. 'Fighting together, we have rid the Mythos of this dread plague. With these good works, we honor the true Giver of all Life. All hail Aleh'en!'"

Maya poked at Alan.

"Isn't that a bit much? Lancelot worships your namesake?"

"Omigod," Brie said. "My brother is such a suck up."

"Just going for irony," Lance said. "My priest has become as devout as I am irreligious."

"But isn't Aleh'en evil?" Brie said.

"The malevolence was Cynoc," Alan said, "not the god he channeled. Didn't you read my first published DL module, The Return of Cynoc?"

Brie blushed.

"Maybe not all of it."

"It shows a few different ways the story can go, depending on how players respond to their circumstances. In the end, that's what the story's really about—choices."

"And my character's choice," Lance said, "was strictly pragmatic, as is his nature. I'd forgotten how much fun it was to play that dude."

"Enough about my brother's fickle priest," Brie said. "What about Angelou?"

"Alright," Alan said. "New scene, inside Angelou's yurt. Tattered troll hides hang on the wall in this modest room, which serves as the dean's office of the barbaric academy. Angelou adjusts the centaur coat on her shoulders. A young barbarian enters, head hung low."

"I got this," Maya said. "This is the one you told me about. So, Angelou's writing in a ledger. She doesn't look up at the girl but says, 'Do you know why you were called here, lass?'"

Alan gave a childish pout and said, "I failed to defeat Smug."

"I need more setup," Lance said.

"We're getting there," Alan said. "The child's hideous orc visage would have startled many, but Angelou had seen worse since opening the Ring Bone Academy to all comers. Conine was the most physically gifted of her class but was also the homeliest. She—"

Maya broke in with a growl.

"You were not called here fer failing to kill a silver hydra. Your error was fighting alone."

"Conine hops about the dirt floor like a boxer," Alan said. "She whines, 'None of the others can keep up. I move as fast as you did at the Gates of Mythopolis, when you slayed Lord Cynoc!'"

"A tall tale, that is. Even I could never have defeated that monster. I only wish—but never you mind. Remember the answer to the heroic question, 'Death, where is thy sting?' It is here, in my heart and memories."

"Conine scratches her head and asks what that means."

"It means death is no trifle. But I can see that you yearn fer battle. There is no greater agony than bearing an untold tale inside you."

"The young Conine harrumphs and storms outside your yurt. Do you follow her?"

"I shouldn't, but yeah, I'll see where the little brat went."

"You step out just in time to see the last orange and red hues of the sunset."

"Don't you mean *suns*-set?" Brie suggested with a giggle.

"Actually, no," Alan said. "Angelou remarks to herself that even before news arrived of Lancelot's triumph over the Naughts, one of the suns began to fade. This evening, the second orb is barely visible as it nears the horizon."

"Cool," Maya said. "Is there enough light to track down that little scamp?"

"Conine stands just a few feet away. She sees you and says, 'Defeating Smug was going to be *my* story!'"

"Angelou reminds her that she is lucky it was not her *last* story. Strength comes not in the arc of your sword, little orc. It comes from the circle you step into when you take common cause with comrades. To achieve greatness, we must then suspend disbelief in both ourselves and one another."

"I do not want my legend mixed up with priests, wizards, rogues, and—bards."

Maya groaned dramatically.

"Angelou stands and feels the pain of the unhealable wounds in her knees. She says to Conine, 'If you are ever fortunate enough to travel with a bard, pray to Aleh'en fer an elf. Those buggers are well-nigh immortal. Like it or not, they will keep telling your tale long after you have left this world.'"

"Omigosh," Brie said, "that's so sweet, Maya."

Maya leaned out of her chair and gave Brie a kiss on the cheek.

"Angelou was sweet on that bard, you know."

"What?" Brie said. "For real? Hermione might have been into that."

"Total rip off," Lance said. "Now all I want is to hear Alan narrate that scene."

Blows from both Brie and Maya struck Lance's shoulders.

"Don't be gross," Brie said.

"Actually," Alan said, "Hermione's up next. Though we'll find her in a corner of the Mythos a thousand miles from Angelou. After this last scene, we can retire these characters and drop some fresh ones into my newest module."

Maya beamed back at Alan.

"I can't believe you're working for Jeff Jacobson."

"Just a part-time gig. No big deal."

"What's the new module called?" Brie said.

"In English, it's called The Unforeseen Eclipse. It's the second title in the Mitología series simul-published in Spanish and English. Next year, we're holding the first Central American Mythos convention in Guatemala City."

"That's awesome," Maya said.

"I'm carving out a niche for what we're calling narrative modules. The plotting's more open ended, so the game director can let things unfold organically."

Maya left the main room and entered the adjoining kitchenette to open a cupboard.

"What's with all this healthy food in here, Alan? Lost a little weight, have you?"

"And shaved his moustache," Brie added.

Alan touched his lip.

"It turned white, and that was that."

Maya narrowed her eyes.

"You've got a girlfriend, don't you?"

"Well, I—" Alan steadied himself. "I'm seeing Jacobson's niece. We met at a DL event in Anaheim."

"Ooh," Brie said. "Tell, tell, tell!"

"Sounds like a catch," Lance said. "If you need a dating coach—"

"Please, fool," Maya said. "Alan's the catch. He's practically an empath. Girls dig that."

Maya opened the refrigerator and withdrew a red bottle, which she arranged on a tray with six glasses.

"For our toast, sparkling gooseberry juice."

Brie licked her lips.

"Yummy."

Lance fingered the lacquered frame of his chair.

"You guys remember when we got together at Señor Wences the week before Middle Mirth?"

"Of course," Brie said. "Carlos loved the cape you gave him."

"Sad they had to burn it," Maya said. "Shouldn't there be insurance for something like that? Alan—you know about that, or did you quit that job?"

"It wasn't a recoverable loss," Alan said. "I kept the job, but I'll phase out if the DL gig goes permanent."

Brie stood up and stretched.

"How 'bout you, Maya? How long does it take to get a Ph.D.?"

"Not quite halfway there. It's a five-year slog, or worse."

"You're still playing DL though," Lance said. "More than anyone else here, right?"

"It's what I'm writing about, so—"

Maya froze when a maniacal laugh echoed all around the condo's walls.

"That's the doorbell," Alan said. "Probably Mom and Devon."

Karen opened the door and said a cheerful "Hellooo."

"Who's hungry for Thanksgiving leftovers?" said Devon, who came in behind her with two grocery bags.

Maya gave her father a peck as he put the food on the kitchenette counter. She helped him unload plastic containers of green beans, sweet potatoes, chicken, and macaroni and cheese.

Karen pulled a pint of gelato from a freezer bag. She popped the tub open easily, without strain. She caught Alan's gaze and cleared her throat.

"The arthritis is under control, but thanks for the concern. I'm doing my physical therapy. You eat dairy, Maya?"

"My daughter will eat dairy, fish, cow, orc...but do *not* tell her vegan girlfriend."

Brie gave Maya a nudge.

"Nobody told me you had a special someone."

"You know her—Patrizia, from the Coven."

"Makes total sense," Brie gushed. "She's gorgeous. A dancer, right?"

"Dance instructor. In New York."

"She taught Morris dancing to Valerie and me," Lance said.

Brie sniggered.

"I'm just relieved that my brother's dating a folk dancer, not a pole dancer."

"Though in the latter case," Alan said, "she might land a job at Players, the worst-named store in history."

"But still open for business!"

Devon raised a fist in triumph.

"With Lance as my collaborator, we will revolutionize the very concept of a game shop through new software that augments traditional tabletop gaming."

Lance shook his head.

"Devon keeps talking about animated holographic figures moving on the table, and I just want to get our map projection working."

"Each player," Devon explained, "has a personal touch screen on the table, while the game director uses a WidePad that shows modified probabilities for every character and monster in play. No more tedious tables and charts. Better still, one can still use physical dice. The director tells the computer what the roll is for, then the tabletop screen sees the bottom die face, interpolates its top, and announces the result."

Maya smirked.

"I can't believe you're back in software."

"One must accept the gifts one receives. Speaking of which, did you tell them about your dissertation topic?"

Devon beamed with pride and ignored his daughter's pleading eyes.

"Her advisor said that if she could not explain her thesis to her own mother, it probably made no sense. And I am here to testify, she succeeded at precisely that task last week."

"Fine," Maya said, "but no making fun."

Lance raised two fingers in a Boy Scout pledge.

"Solemn vows all around."

"When Tolkien wrote The Hobbit," Maya said, "he was trying

to resuscitate northern European mythology. He tapped into deep cultural norms, like loyalty, bravery, and friendship. In a similar way, DL celebrates the values that youth culture—and modern society—devalues."

"What was the title of the conference paper you sent me?" Devon asked.

"Post-Medievalism and the Transgressive Cultural Resurgence of Mythic Narrative: A Re-Problematization of the Fantasy Tradition from Tolkien to Dungeon Lords."

Lance gave a hearty laugh.

"A well-attended talk, I'm sure."

"Actually," Devon said, "that paper has exploded on LitNet. My little girl is a regular Che Guevara in her chosen field."

Maya looked at Alan.

"Watching Herr Director at work, I realized we all need the freedom to invent new narratives, while drawing on the most evocative ideas embedded in our cultures. In return for playing within the narrow DL rule system, we get to see what traditions merit saving and which we should reject."

"By that logic," Lance said, "wouldn't crappy video games do the same thing?"

"They could, but only games like DL require narrative co-creation, which connects us with the oral tradition of communal storytelling. They pull us into a make-believe world circumscribed by the suspension of disbelief. If we can stay 'in game' long enough with others, we learn about ourselves, how to rebuild society, how to widen the Magic Circle. Right, Alan?"

Alan nodded. He felt the presence of a kindred spirit.

Devon dug into a container of stuffing. His chewing was the only sound in the room until he said, with a full mouth, "I am so hopelessly proud of her."

"I'll bet you are," Karen said, her eyes on Alan.

"It's official," Lance said. "Maya's the singular egghead in this group of nerds."

Brie pointed at her brother.

"No, you are the nerdliest nerd. Maya doesn't know about the deal you inked this week, does she?"

Brie pulled a Droid out of her purse and tapped until it made the sound of a diesel engine. Soon it was playing the sound of a gentle stream of cars and trucks.

"Don't think I'm a total jerk," Lance said to Maya.

"Honey, I already think you're one of those."

Maya walked up to Lance and gave him a shoulder hug.

"But you're *my* jerk."

Lance adjusted his Ray-Bans.

"People make all this money off new age music and relaxation soundscapes, like crickets and ocean waves, right? Well, I sent an auto demo last summer to Sacred Noise, and they sent me a contract."

"I know that label," Karen said. "We listen to their CDs at my yoga studio."

"There's a huge archive of public domain traffic recordings made by the US Department of Transportation, from freeways and highways all over the country. Dates back fifty years. Brie and I mixed them into 90-minute tracks. She thought up the name for the series."

"Highway Z," Brie said. "But the real kicker? They would sign us only if we went by the production name Blind Monk and Padre Princess."

"Can you believe it?" Lance said. "It's still a thing."

"Where did you find the time to do that while working for me?" Devon said.

"You don't own me. Besides, my sister's career is stranger than my hobby."

"All Alan told me," Karen said, "was that you played music with your friend Tiffany."

"I can't believe you ever forgave her," Maya said. "Very big of you, Princess."

"I wasn't *that* gracious," Brie said. "She's the one who reconciled. When she got back from Korea, I could see Tiff was genuinely sorry. And when she explained that her brother had put her up to it...Anyway, I told her about the lute Lance and Mom got me, and we started joking about modern tunes we could cover using Renaissance instruments."

"So, I'm watching TV," Lance said, "when some dumb stay-in-school public service ad comes on. One of those The More You Know spots."

"And right then and there," Brie said, "we had the idea for my band, The PSAs. We have a cult following in L.A. and Chicago. Our YouTube channel created enough buzz overseas for us to tour Seoul and Kyoto. We're in the studio next month to record our first album, Duck and Cover."

"There's another 'Satyrical rock' band in Auckland," Lance interjected. "They're gonna tour together."

"What we lack in groupies," Brie said, "we make up for in theatrics. My Hermione costume, essentially a grass bodysuit, is subdued compared to the rest of the band. Tiff's chainmail bikini scandalized her mother when she drove up to see one of our L.A. shows."

"Again," Devon said, "I marvel at the extent of your hobbies."

Lance sighed.

"Alas, something had to go. For me, it was Dungeon Lords."

"Ditto," Brie said. "I tried turning Tiff onto it, but it reminded her of Randall."

An awkward silence moved the group into action. Alan went into his kitchenette and brought out plates, while Lance and Brie cleared the table of paper, pencils, and dice. Karen slipped away to the restroom. Even after she returned, the conversational lull continued.

"Good heavens," Karen said, "it's not like Randall died or anything."

"I don't even talk about him anymore."

Maya looked at the jar of blood-red sun-dried tomatoes she'd opened for the salads.

"I'm still not sure what happened that weekend."

"I know it's hard to feel sorry for Randall," Karen said, "but when he checked into Mercy, he was sicker than anyone knew. One of the cheeky nurses dubbed the virus Dungeonnaires Disease, then everybody started calling it that. Randall's doctor figured it incubated in him for at least a couple weeks before the convention. That awful basement was the perfect place for it to spread when his lesions blossomed and became contagious. It triggered rashes, nausea, pneumonia—"

Maya put the lid back on her jar of tomatoes.

"Now I remember why I never asked about those details. Living through it was enough."

"Well," Karen said, "Randall almost *didn't* live through it. He got severe encephalitis."

"The way Mom explains it," Alan said, "the brain panics and wreaks havoc. Photophobia, manic behavior, disorienting joint pain. Took a long time for him to recover. Lost his job."

"His firing was for industrial espionage," Lance said. "He broke into company files to trash the WOK. That game had to revert to a backup server that had been offline for months. It reset the whole WOK world back half a year, and the company refunded the poor bastards who lost that chunk of their online lives. Civil lawsuits got Randall's wages garnished for life."

"Tell me this," Alan said, "if Randall specialized in writing security protocols, how did he design the gaming code that caused so much chaos?"

"He was an accomplished programmer," Lance said, "but he claimed he didn't act alone. Said he just moved things around that others had already written for—"

"Of course, nobody believed him," Devon interjected.

"And yet," Brie said, "he got back in his parents' good graces."

"Oh, yes," Karen said. "Alan showed me his video channel."

Brie laughed.

"You've gotta see it, Maya. He's a youth pastor now somewhere out in Texas."

"Abeline," Alan said.

"He rails against the sins of gaming," Brie said. "Tiff thought it was a put-on, but last Christmas, their whole family got together and she snuck a peek at his laptop. He'd removed every pre-installed game—even Minesweeper."

"For real," Alan said. "He reached out to me last February, on my birthday. Invited me to visit. First time he'd called since— well, since everything went sour. I was curious enough to make the trip. Met him at his office, a little glass enclosure in a mega- church the likes of which you wouldn't believe. Brie's got it right—there was even a little etched sign by the door that said, 'Youth Pastor'."

"I'm telling you," Brie said, "he's *huge* online."

"But not as huge in person anymore," Karen said. "Randall looks ten years younger in the picture Alan showed me."

"Church paid for the staple thing," Alan said. "He's got a personal trainer, a gym, and—"

"I've heard that place is like a city," Brie said. "Office building, social services, amusement park, cathedral—all smushed into one. Tiff said their parents were appalled."

"Yeah," Alan said, "when Randall gave me a tour, he said the same thing. I'd say they're being picky. Their heretic son comes back into the fold only to be shunned for being the wrong kind of Christian."

"I just can't see it," Lance said.

Maya snickered, then winced at the faux pas.

Unperturbed, Lance said, "Brie and I listened to a podcast of one of his sermons. It was about playing only the Game of Christ. Rejecting luck. Some shit like that."

"I got to see him give that talk live to a bunch of teenagers," Alan said. "He talked about trusting the providence of the

Prophet, though I couldn't follow the theological thread."

"Was he as creepy as ever?" Lance said.

Alan paused. That wasn't the right word for Randall, but maybe there wasn't one.

"Did you talk about what he did?" Maya said. "Did you get an apology?"

"Not as such. We both had things to confess, or at least explain. I didn't bring it up until the day was winding down. I waited till I saw my cab arrive, and he shrugged it off. Said he didn't mean for things to get out of hand. Said he wasn't in his right mind."

"Never was," Lance said. "I won't ever trust that guy. Those happy clappers in his mega-chapel are a gullible lot. I'll bet he's up to something in that new castle of his."

Alan laughed to himself. Randall had found his castle after all.

"Trauma can change people," Karen said. "You just never know how."

She glanced at Alan, then at the rest of the group.

"We should be thankful Randall's still alive. I was there at the hospital when they first lifted his panis—"

"Excuse me?" Maya said.

"The flap of skin that hung over his stomach. When they raised it—"

Karen bit her lip and shook her head.

"Oh, the gore under there, more green than red. The infection was so bad. He's lucky he didn't have the seizures that tormented poor Carlos..."

Alan's mind went back to that awful weekend. He remembered how eerie it felt, returning to the same hospital he and Randall had shared with Carlos so many years ago. This time, it was Randall's life that required saving. As Randall improved, Carlos' condition worsened. Doctors induced a coma to help his body recover. Didn't release him for a month. Even then, he wasn't healthy enough to resume his studies.

From his pile of papers, Alan withdrew an air-mail envelope.

"As it happens, I have a hand-written letter from Carlos sent for this very occasion."

"Give me that."

Brie snatched the letter from Alan's hand.

"Maybe Tara wrote it—"

"Or Adelita," Lance suggested.

"No, it's his handwriting," Alan said. "Read it."

Brie cleared her throat.

What a crazy year it's been since I last saw you guys. It was great to have Alan and Karen at our wedding, but I miss having us all together.

I'm teaching DL to some of the kids here in Merida. We're using the Spanish-language translations I've been writing for Alan's modules. (Thanks for the dinero, buddy! Can't wait to see the next one.)

Tara and I have set up a one-stop-shop medical-legal free clinic. She's working on a civil case against global agribusiness to hold them accountable for local environmental problems. While she tries to patch up Mexican law, I'm patching up Mexican bodies. Mostly pediatric infections and broken bones. And yes, you morbid little monsters, I have treated a case of chickenpox.

Gigi's a happy pooch. When Adelita came out to live with us, the Cheese Doodle had a surprise—strange looking brindled puppies. We have no idea who the father is. I think they're Aztec Truffle Hunters.

That's better than the name the school kids gave me. They call me El Brujo, the Witch Doctor. I like to think it's because of the cool stories I tell about our adventures in the Mythos. But I'm afraid it's from my stomach scars, which are more visible than that old snake on my neck. Remember that one, Karen? Tara says that in a swimsuit, I'm still a handsome devil, but I think I look like an actual devil. Or maybe a reanimated corpse.

So...we have big news, or little news, I guess. On November 1, Tara gave birth to Juan Morales, a baby to kick off this year's Day of the Dead. Juan de los Muertos. Those of you who knew a baby was on the way, gracias for not suggesting Elizabethan names. And Karen, I'll thank you for not reminding me of the odds that I'd been sterilized by the pox. Juan has my eyes, I swear.

As you can see from my writing, I'm doing much better physically. When I come back to finish my degree, maybe Tara and I can host the next reunion.

No, I won't see you at Middle Mirth. Ever.

Good luck with your crazy projects, within and beyond the Magic Circle.

Love,

Carlos

Maya went to the counter and poured sparkling juice into glasses, which she handed around the table.

"Now that Carlos has paid us a visit, it's time for our toast. This is, after all, the official second annual reunion of the Bled Sextet."

Brie said, "I still think Jacobson gave us the prize because we saved the convention."

"But we didn't save the hotel," Lance said. "They got sued like crazy."

"Rightly so," Alan said. "I told you guys that place was a deathtrap."

"Did you?" Lance said.

"Well, if I didn't say it, I thought it. They were smart to settle up."

"I remain honored," Devon said, "that you count me as a full-fledged member. All I did at Middle Mirth was get sick like everyone else."

Karen leaned in close to Alan.

"How about I raise my glass as Carlos' proxy?"

"Fair enough, Mom. To the Bled Sextet!"

"To us!" Lance said.

"To the best circle of friends I'll ever stand among," Maya said.

Everyone raised a glass and drank.

Brie wiped gooseberry juice off her lips, which glowed the same color as her cheeks.

"Let's visit Hermione at the Miramar Inn before we call it a night."

"Agreed," Alan said. "There's probably a certain narrative symmetry to that."

Lance offered his white die to his sister.

"If you need to make a charisma roll or something, use my twenty-sided."

Brie recoiled.

"After where it's been, I don't know how you can touch that thing."

HERMIONE

The younger faces in the crowd drew tight with fear. Little sleeves wiped teardrops away from tiny eyes. To calm the children seated before her, Hermione waved her hands and brought gentle snowflakes down from the ceiling.

"All within the shell went pure white," Hermione said.

In the front row sat a boy with a familiar face, though his name did not come to mind. She scooped a handful of snow off his head.

"As white as the snow on this sweet lad."

Hermione turned to face the wider audience.

"A distinct sound emanated from that spot, one not heard before nor since. It was the cry of the world being reborn, of nothing exploding into everything. It had no more physical force than the breeze of a sparrow's wings, but it knocked to the ground every living creature."

"How did you survive?" the little boy asked. The snow on his head melted into his eyes.

"No one remained standing, but none outside the shell died, either. Not then. When we regained our footing, we looked back to where Santana and Cynoc had fought. The shell remained impenetrable. Within it was only ash, finer than pixie dust, and Santana's ironwood staff, an indestructible artifact carved centuries ago by the Fairie Queen herself."

Hermione heard the soft thump of a hand-held drum, struck like a dirge by her new apprentice, Singring. The wiry gnome wore a lime frock that made her look like a cucumber. It clashed against Hermione's deep-green dress, which was woven from blades of prairie grass and embroidered with glitterfish scales.

"Without their leader stirring the poison inside them," Hermione said, "the Naughts fled—unrepentant, but disorganized. We slew every enemy we could find, but some escaped."

"To that, I bring good news," said a deep female voice at the back of the room.

Hermione shielded her eyes from the colored light pots she had conjured onto the ceiling for her performance. She could not locate the speaker until she heard the voice again.

"I have word," the woman continued, "that the High Priest Lancelot and his disciples have tracked and slain the last hold-outs this very week."

Hermione placed the voice and raised her hands high.

"Let me end my story there and propose a toast."

She snapped her fingers to make a full glass of wine appear before each member of her audience, with giggleberry juice filling the children's cups.

"To the end of Cynocism!"

The audience stood and cheered, "Huzzah!"

Singring welcomed embraces and back slaps, while Hermione slipped away to visit with her old friend. She found Tinkana sitting on a stone bench beside the hearth, scarred wings folded against her back. She had assumed a form no greater than eight feet tall, thanks to the same amethyst stone that had enabled Hermione to carry her away.

"Good to see you," Tinkana said, "and even better to hear you."

"And you."

Hermione hugged Tinkana and offered her a vacant stool. It was a seat beneath Tinkana's station, had she still been a queen. That life was gone, and with it, protocol.

A ten-pound wolf pup with light-brown curls lay by the fire. Hermione reached out to stroke it, and the wolf pushed its nose under her hand.

"Let her be, Lobito."

Tinkana grinned at Hermione.

"Yes, Lupita's had new pups."

"Awfully small and a bit curious looking for a dire wolf's brood."

"I believe the father was some sort of domesticated canine. This one's the smartest of the litter. He insisted on joining us tonight."

Hermione tipped her head to the side.

"Us?"

Tinkana laughed at the bard.

"I haven't taken a new lover, if that's what you mean. Not yet. No, I came here with this little devil."

The boy Hermione had comforted with snowflakes ran toward them and jumped into Tinkana's arms. The queen's clothing collapsed against her skin where the boy nuzzled her.

"This is Santino."

Tinkana stroked the child's wet hair. His eyes closed and his breathing slowed. Tips of small, folded wings poked up behind his shoulders. He had the fine cheekbones of a sorcerer Hermione had once known.

"Yes, he is Santana's son. The potency of dragons and the magic of the fairies, together. He is a marvel."

"This changes the story, doesn't it? Santana didn't really die."

"Only in the mundane sense of the word."

Hermione nodded and looked into the fire.

"This helps me understand the choice he made. When I lifted you from the battle, I sensed that our future depended on saving you, but I feared it meant losing him. Even then, I felt as though our fates hinged on the roll of a die. What remarkable odds we must have overcome."

Tinkana laughed lustily and shifted Santino in her arms.

"Surely you don't disbelieve in the power of Aleh'en to shape the course of things in the Mythos simply because you had a hand in bringing them about yourself? You don't really imagine that all your adventures and escapes were managed by mere luck? You are a very fine person, and I am very fond of you. But you are only quite a little bard in a wide world after all."

"Perhaps. But don't forget that the world's made up of nothing more than its very smallest parts."

Hermione clapped her thighs. Lobito responded by rolling onto his feet and leaping into her lap.

"Whatever the gods might have in store, at the end of the day, the balance of things still hangs on our own decisions and the fleeting visits of good fortune upon us."

"Thank goodness you can still believe that," Tinkana said.

Santino appeared to have fallen asleep in Tinkana's arms. She stood and lifted her child.

"We are far past this one's bedtime, so let us call it an evening."

"Agreed," Hermione said with a wink. "This is as good a place as any to end it."

Acknowledgments

For reckless encouragement and far from feckless feedback, thanks go first to Andy, Brian, Carlotta, Cate, Gretchen, Joel, John, Jon, Justin, Les, Max, Ralph, Ruth, Todd, and my big sister. For medical guidance, I am indebted to Nurse Dan. Perry provided genre insights, as did Michael Drout, via his writings. Ideas about games and gaming culture were inspired by the writings of Gary Fine, Katie Salen, and Eric Zimmerman. TSR and Hero Games get a wag of the finger for introducing me to the time-consuming pleasures of role playing. Café Fenix in Santa Fe provided a venue for reading portions of this text aloud. Babs, Danni, Imad, and Sarah provided editorial guidance. Greatest appreciation of all goes to Cindy, who made—and makes— everything better. Any mistakes that remain can be blamed on my human avatar.

About the Author

John Gastil is a writer and professor living in State College, Pennsylvania. His other novel is *Gray Matters*, a political science-fiction story about how digital technology could shape our lives as the world's population and its democratic systems grow frail. Gastil's nonfiction includes *The Group in Society*, *Democracy in Small Groups*, *Hope for Democracy*, and other titles on group behavior, political communication, and public opinion. In writing *Dungeon Party*, Gastil drew on his experience growing up in San Diego, California playing fantasy role playing games. When not giving lectures, conducting research, or writing fiction, Gastil spends his time playing all manner of tabletop, console, and mobile games and relaxing with family, friends, and an energetic standard poodle named Lucretia.

COSMIC EGG
BOOKS

FANTASY, SCI-FI, HORROR & PARANORMAL

If you prefer to spend your nights with Vampires and Werewolves rather than the mundane then we publish the books for you. If your preference is for Dragons and Faeries or Angels and Demons – we should be your first stop. Perhaps your perfect partner has artificial skin or comes from another planet – step right this way. If your passion is Fantasy (including magical realism and spiritual fantasy), Metaphysical Cosmology, Horror or Science Fiction (including Steampunk), Cosmic Egg books will feed your hunger. Our curiosity shop contains treasures you will enjoy unearthing. If you have enjoyed this book, why not tell other readers by posting a review on your preferred book site.

Recent bestsellers from Cosmic Egg Books are:

The Zombie Rule Book
A Zombie Apocalypse Survival Guide
Tony Newton
The book the living-dead don't want you to have!
Paperback: 978-1-78279-334-2 ebook: 978-1-78279-333-5

Cryptogram
Because the Past is Never Past
Michael Tobert
Welcome to the dystopian world of 2050, where three lovers are
haunted by echoes from eight-hundred years ago.
Paperback: 978-1-78279-681-7 ebook: 978-1-78279-680-0

Purefinder
Ben Gwalchmai
London, 1858. A child is dead; a man is blamed and dragged
through hell in this Dantean tale of loss, mystery and fraternity.
Paperback: 978-1-78279-098-3 ebook: 978-1-78279-097-6

600ppm
A Novel of Climate Change
Clarke W. Owens
Nature is collapsing. The government doesn't want you to know
why. Welcome to 2051 and 600ppm.
Paperback: 978-1-78279-992-4 ebook: 978-1-78279-993-1

Creations
William Mitchell
Earth 2040 is on the brink of disaster. Can Max Lowrie stop the
self-replicating machines before it's too late?
Paperback: 978-1-78279-186-7 ebook: 978-1-78279-161-4

The Gawain Legacy
Jon Mackley
If you try to control every secret, secrets may end up controlling
you.
Paperback: 978-1-78279-485-1 ebook: 978-1-78279-484-4

Readers of ebooks can buy or view any of these bestsellers by
clicking on the live link in the title. Most titles are published
in paperback and as an ebook. Paperbacks are available in
traditional bookshops. Both print and ebook formats are
available online.
Find more titles and sign up to our readers' newsletter at
http://www.johnhuntpublishing.com/fiction
Follow us on Facebook at https://www.facebook.com/JHPfiction
and Twitter at https://twitter.com/JHPFiction